THE MAD SCIENTIST'S
DAUGHTER

THE
MAD
SCIENTIST'S
DAUGHTER

CASSANDRA ROSE CLARKE

SAGA  PRESS

SAGA PRESS

AN IMPRINT OF SIMON & SCHUSTER, INC.

1230 AVENUE OF THE AMERICAS, NEW YORK, NEW YORK 10020

FOR ROSS,
WHO IS NOT THE ROBOT

PART ONE

ONE

Many years later Cat still remembered the damp twilight on her skin and the way the dewy grass prickled and snapped beneath her bare feet as she ran up to the edge of the forest that surrounded her childhood home. Her mother had let her stay out late that night so she could catch fireflies in a jar, and she lay among the tumbling honeysuckle and ropes of wild grapevines with the jar held aloft, holding still and waiting for the fireflies to buzz through the opening so she could trap them inside.

As the night fell soft and sparkling all around her, Cat watched the fireflies climb up the sides of the glass, the glow of their abdomens transforming them into intermittent stars. Somewhere around the front of the house a car door slammed, once and then twice, but she ignored it, knowing her father to come home late from his meetings in the city. But then the light came on in the screened-in back porch. Immediately, Cat slunk down into the shadows. She was at an age where she liked to spy, where she liked to note undetected the goings-on of adults. The round, familiar silhouette of her father stepped onto the porch, followed by another figure, tall and thin and angular, a figure Cat didn't recognize. She clutched the fireflies to her chest and crept around the perimeter of the yard to get a closer look. Those fireflies she hadn't caught blinked on and off in the darkness, and Cat's jar glimmered faintly from between her hands. On the porch, behind the gauzy screen, the unfamiliar silhouette sat down. Her father leaned over it, their shadows blurring together. Cat slid across the grass. She crept up to the porch, near the steps, to the place where the screen had been ripped away from the frame a few weeks ago by the old raccoon that came around the yard sometimes. She tucked the jar under her arm and stood on her tiptoes and peered through the screen's gap, and she saw her father's broad, expansive back, a narrow sweat stain tracing along his spine. Of the stranger she saw nothing but a pale, slender arm, hanging motionless off the side of the plastic chair, and a foot covered in a dirty old sneaker.

Her father straightened up and took a step back. He put his hands on his hips. He said something, too soft for Cat to discern over the sounds of cicadas whining in the trees and the ceiling fan clicking rhythmically inches from her father's head. He sighed. Then he walked across the porch to the wicker table in the corner and set down a thin metal tool that gleamed in the porch's yellow light. There was a person sitting in the plastic chair, only he didn't seem like a person at all. His eyes focused on Cat, and she yelped and ducked into the crawl space beneath the stairs.

"Do we have a visitor?" said Cat's father, his voice booming out into the night. Cat huddled in the cool, moist dirt beneath the house, her jar pressed between her chest and her knees. It smelled of cut grass and old rainwater. The screen door slammed. Footsteps rattled Cat's hiding place. Then her father's face appeared, as white and round as the moon. "What have you got there, Kitty-Cat?" He pointed at her jar of fireflies.

"It's my light-jar."

"I see," said her father. "And a lovely light-jar it is." He reached under the stairs and plucked her out, swinging her through the cool night air and bringing her to rest on his hip. "I have someone I want you to meet."

Cat buried her face in his soft shoulder.

He carried her into the screened-in porch. The light inside was weak and old-looking and buzzed like the cicadas outside. The man sitting in the plastic chair looked at Cat's father, then at Cat. His eyes moved before his head did. They were very dark, like two holes set into his face.

"Cat, this is Finn. He's come to stay with us."

Cat didn't say anything, just pulled the firefly jar to her chest and wiggled out of her father's grasp so she slid down the side of his leg. Finn nodded and then smiled at her.

"A child?" he said. Cat wanted to run back out into the darkness.

"Yes, Finn," said Cat's father. "That's right. My child. My daughter." His enormous hand ruffled Cat's hair. He knelt down beside her, and she looked at him. "Why don't you show Finn your light-jar?"

Cat didn't want to show Finn anything. He unnerved her. In certain ways Finn resembled the few adults Cat had seen in her short life—his height, his long torso and limbs, the solidity of the features of his face—but otherwise he was completely different from the boisterous scientists who came over some evenings for dinner parties. His eyes loomed steadily in the buzzing light of the porch. His skin was much too fair, sallow beneath the swath of black hair that flopped across his forehead.

She decided he must be a ghost. He was an adult who died. Her father brought him here to study him. This was the only logical explanation.

Cat hugged the jar tight against her chest. Finn didn't move, didn't even twitch the muscles in his face.

"Don't be rude," her father said gently. "We need to welcome Finn into our home." He straightened up, and Cat took a deep, shaking breath and stepped forward, feet rasping across the porch's painted wooden floor. She held the firefly jar out at arm's length and looked over her shoulder at the porch screen dark with nighttime. When the weight of the jar lifted out of her hands, she scurried back behind her father.

"*Photuris pennsylvanicus,*" said Finn. "The woods firefly."

Cat's father laughed. "Latin names," he said. "Good to know that scholarly upgrade is working nicely."

Finn held the jar up to eye level, but in the light, Cat noticed, the fireflies looked like ugly brown beetles.

Cat tugged on her father's sleeve. "It's only outside," she whispered when he glanced down at her. "It's only a light-jar outside." She wondered what would happen if Finn stepped beyond the boundaries of the porch, if the yellow light made him visible, if his true nature would cause him to melt back into the shadows.

Finn ignored them, turning the jar over in his hands, gazing at it with his peculiar, dispassionate expression.

"Oh, of course!" said her father. "Finn—" Finn's head jerked up. "Let's go outside. Come along."

Finn stood, his narrow body unhinging at the waist. He handed the jar to Cat and smiled, but Cat grabbed the jar and pushed through the door, out into the cool, dampening night. The fireflies glowed again. She could hear them knocking against the glass.

"How lovely," said Cat's father.

"Lovely," repeated Finn, as though the meaning of the word eluded him. For a moment Cat stood in the darkness, her back to Finn and her father. She wasn't ready yet to see what Finn had become in the darkness. The surrounding forest rustled and shimmered against the starry sky. The glass from the jar was warm beneath her hands. She wondered if fireflies could protect you from ghosts. Probably not if they were trapped in a jar. Cat bit down on her lower lip, and then she unscrewed the lid and the fireflies streamed out, leaving streaks of light in their wake. Cat dropped the jar to her side. She took a deep breath. She turned around and gasped.

Finn had blended into the darkness, just as she predicted, but his eyes, gazing levelly out at the forest, shone as silver as starlight.

* * * *

That night, Cat couldn't sleep. Whenever she closed her eyes, she saw two flat disks of silver, and her heart pounded violently up near her throat. She pulled her reading tablet out of its drawer and turned it on. She tapped the little ghost icon to bring up all the ghost stories contained in the database of the house's main computer, and she began to read, looking for clues as to how to protect herself from Finn.

She was beginning to grow drowsy in spite of her need to feel afraid when she heard her parents' voices seeping through the walls of the house. She slipped the reading tablet under her pillow and climbed out of bed and padded softly into the hallway. A sliver of light arced out from beneath her parents' door.

"A perfect tutor," her father was saying. "You said you didn't want to send her to that school in town—"

"This is *not* what I meant, Daniel. He . . . It . . . It's unsettling."

"He's not an it, darling."

Cat curled herself up beneath the empty telephone alcove and set her chin on her knees. She wondered if Finn could hear them arguing, too. She wanted to knock on the door and tell them to keep their voices down, since it was potentially dangerous for a ghost to hear any discussion of itself. And she knew Finn wasn't far away, either: earlier her mother had set him up in the attic bedroom, where the walls slanted down at an awkward angle and the air was always warm no matter the outside temperature. Cat had helped, carrying the heavy metal fan up the creaking stairs, its cord snaking down behind her, while her mother opened the windows, stirring up clouds of golden dust.

"It's hot up here," Cat said, rubbing the sticky, itchy dust out of her eyes.

"Won't matter." Her mother sighed. "Your father insisted we bring the fan." She turned toward Cat. "Come along, it's past your bedtime."

So it was entirely possible that Finn had his phantom ear pressed to the attic room's wooden walls, listening in on everything her parents said. Assuming he hadn't slipped out already, in the form of cold damp mist, or possibly a cockroach. Cat gnawed on the hem of her nightgown. Surely her father, who was a brilliant scientist, knew how to contain him.

Inside the bedroom, Cat's father said, "Let's talk about this in the morning."

The rim of light disappeared. Cat's eyes widened. It would be dangerous if Finn caught her unaware in the dark. She crawled out of the alcove and crept back along the hallway, making sure always to step at the place where the floor met the wall so the boards wouldn't squeak. When she came to her bedroom she stopped and peered down the hall, at the door leading to the attic stairs. The air-conditioning kicked on and that familiar roar gave her a sudden burst of courage. Cat skittered up to the attic door. She pressed her ear against the smooth cool wood, holding her breath in tight: but there was nothing, no sound, no movement. No light under the door.

Cat went back to bed. Exhausted, she fell asleep.

* * * *

Over the next few weeks, it became apparent that her mother had lost the fight Cat overheard that first night: Finn stayed. In the mornings he came down from the attic bedroom and sat with the family as they ate breakfast, although he ate nothing, only kept his hands folded on top of the table. Cat always watched him with caution, hoping she could find some clue as to his nighttime activities. One morning he returned her gaze with a weird smile, and she yelped and kicked her heels against the legs of the table so the whole thing wobbled.

"Cat, stop it," said her mother, reading the news on her comm slate.

Cat paused for a few seconds. Finn had turned away from her. *He knows I know!* she thought, and immediately kicked the table leg again.

"Caterina Novak! What did I tell you!"

Cat drank the last of her orange juice and then slid off the chair so that she pooled on the floor underneath the table. She considered the three pairs of feet: her father's, in his woolly slippers, her mother's, bare, with chipped pink polish on the toes, and Finn's, in heavy black boots. She crawled beside her father's chair.

"I'm going outside," she told him.

"Oh?" He smiled down at her. "Why don't you take Finn with you? And show him the garden?"

Cat's heart began to race. She didn't look over at Finn. She willed herself to stay calm. "Do I have to?"

"Don't be rude," her mother said without looking up.

"I would like to see the garden," said Finn.

"See?" said Cat's father. "I think that settles it. Show him your citrus tree."

Cat stood up and so did Finn, pushing his chair back neatly. He smiled at her again. He seemed exceptionally polite for a ghost, although it was possible that was how ghosts tricked their victims. She clomped over to the door and stepped outside. The light was pale and hazy. "It's this way," she said, leading him around the side of the house. She heard his feet rustling the overgrown grass.

When the garden came into view, small and neat and boxed in by its black fence, Cat broke into a run, stopping only to unlatch the gate. The garden hadn't yet completely unfurled itself, and most of the blossoms were only tiny fists pushing out of their stalks. The climbing roses had been pruned back a few weeks ago; the hyacinth poked unscented out of a stretch of black soil. Cat ran over to her citrus tree and leaned against it, watching as Finn stepped through the gate and stopped and looked around the garden as though he'd never been outside.

"This is remarkable." Finn pointed at the Texas wisteria. "*Wisteria frutescens.* I have never seen it before."

"It grows all over the place," Cat said. "It grows in the woods."

Finn turned toward her citrus tree. "*Citrus limon,*" he said. "Lemon tree."

"Yeah, I guess," said Cat. "It's mine." Her citrus tree was the same height as her and covered with flat waxy leaves, although no lemons yet. She had planted it with her mother last year, digging up the soil with a plastic shovel, watering it dutifully during the summer drought.

"I understand." Finn walked over to the tree and reached up to rub one of the leaves between his thumb and forefinger. He was close enough to Cat that she could see the fibers in the fabric of his T-shirt, thin and faintly worn. It looked like the T-shirts her mother kept folded up in a drawer to wear when she worked in the garden. It didn't look like the T-shirt of a ghost.

Cat had a sudden idea. "Hey, do you want to see the cemetery?"

Finn dropped his hand and turned toward her. "The cemetery?" His voice sounded different, higher pitched, like a child's, like a girl's. When he spoke again, it had returned to normal. "I've never seen a cemetery."

Cat nearly clapped her hands together in her excitement. Her hypothesis was correct. (Her father had taught her about the importance of hypotheses.) Finn had forgotten that he was dead. He had forgotten the place where he was buried. Maybe he wasn't the bad kind of ghost at all, just the lost kind. Cat ran out of the garden, back toward the house. "Come on!" she shouted. Inside, she plopped down on the kitchen's cold tile and put on her shoes. Finn walked in, looked down at her, then back up at her parents, still sitting at the kitchen table.

"We are going to the cemetery," he said.

Cat's father took a long drink from his mug of coffee. "Well, that's wonderful," he said. "I knew you two would get along if you had the chance."

Cat's mother didn't say anything.

Cat jumped to her feet and went into the living room to grab her sketch pad. Then she ran back outside, letting the screen door slam behind her. Finn followed. She led him down to the woods, still dark and fragrant with the last vestiges of night.

"You can take the road," said Cat. "It's quicker. But the cars go really fast. Which I guess wouldn't be a problem for you but it would be for me."

"I prefer the woods."

They walked along without saying anything. Broken branches and empty pecan shells snapped beneath their feet. At one point Cat glanced up at Finn and the sunlight filtering through the tree leaves had covered him with dark, shadowy spots, like a leopard. He even had a leopard's bright, fluorescent eyes.

Eventually, the woods opened up into the clearing that housed the cemetery. Cat climbed over the sagging, rusted metal fence. The lemony sunlight made her eyes water. It was the right time of year and the cemetery was covered with a thick blanket of wildflowers: bluebonnets and coreopsis, black-eyed Susans and phlox. She knew most of the names from picking bouquets here with her mother. That year the wildflowers were so numerous Cat could only make out the very tops of the gravestones, most of which didn't even have names on them, only initials and dates from two centuries ago.

Cat turned around, half expecting Finn to be disappearing in a cloud of light or steam. But instead he stood at the edge of the cemetery, wildflowers rustling around his ankles.

"It is lovely," he said.

"That's what my mom always says." Cat frowned. This must not be the right cemetery. Finn took a few steps away from the fence, toward the center of the cemetery where the old oak tree twisted up against the cloudless blue sky. Cat trailed behind him. The sun reflected off his dark hair. He stopped, tilted his head toward the swaying, rippling flowers. Cat froze. Maybe he had found his grave.

But Finn just scooped something up off the ground. He turned toward Cat. He smiled. Cat decided he had a kind smile, even if he was a ghost. She took a few hesitant steps forward, and Finn uncapped his hands. There, bright against his curved palms, was an enormous black and orange butterfly. It fluttered its wings once. Cat leaned in close and saw the tiny fibers on its black antennae.

"*Danaus plexippus*," said Finn. "Monarch butterfly."

"No way," said Cat. "My computer told me those were extinct."

"They were only thought to be extinct," said Finn. "However, with the stabilization of the North American ecosystem, the species has been able to recover." The butterfly folded up its wings and then, as though it had been waiting for a lull in the conversation, shot back up into the indolent air and disappeared into the branches of the oak tree.

Cat didn't understand. Finn turned away from her and continued exploring the overgrown paths of the cemetery. Cat decided she was glad he had not disappeared back into the afterlife: any ghost who could revive an extinct species of butterfly, extracting it from the blossoms of graveyard flowers, was the sort of ghost it might be handy to have around.

* * * *

The spring turned into summer turned into fall, the heat heavy and dry as kindling. All the plants died. The grass turned brown. The sunlight caramelized. In the afternoons Cat's world—the woods, the yard, the exterior of the house—looked like some ancient, crumbling, amber-tinted photograph.

After the day at the graveyard, Cat adjusted quickly to the presence of Finn, especially when it became apparent that he spent most of his time in the basement laboratory with her father. Being a ghost, he never got angry or condescending with her the way her parents' friends did, and sometimes he even watched cartoons.

Cat carried on about her business.

On one of those gilded, sweltering afternoons, Cat's parents called her down to the dining room table. She had been up in her room playing on her computer, because in September, in the middle of the day, it was still too hot to go outside.

Her parents and Finn all sat at the table. Her parents looked more serious than usual. Finn stared straight ahead. "We need to talk about your education," her mother said before Cat had even had a chance to climb into the tall wooden chair. Cat frowned. *Education?*

"We've put off sending you to school," her father said. "Just figured we'd let you run around the woods, figure things out for yourself." He leaned back in his chair and smiled. "But you're getting to the age where you need something a little more formalized." He glanced over at Finn and nodded. "Your mother and I have decided . . ."

Cat's mother clenched her jaw but said nothing.

"We've decided that Finn should act as your tutor."

Cat looked from her father to Finn. Finn blinked and then smiled. As much as she liked his smile, she didn't want him to be her tutor. She didn't want to have a tutor at all. "Why can't I go to school?" Not that she wanted that, either.

"The school in town isn't very good," her mother said. "Your father and I were going to teach you ourselves, but now that Finn is here, well . . ." She rubbed her temple.

"He'll be able to devote more time to your studies," said Cat's father. "Won't you, Finn?"

"Yes, Dr. Novak."

"Finn knows a great deal, Cat. He can tell you more about the plants in the woods than I or your mother ever could. He'll be able to teach you arithmetic. You'll like that, won't you?"

Cat shook her head. She didn't trust numbers. They never stayed still for her. Her mother sighed again. But her father just leaned conspiratorially over the table and said, "Plus, he has a huge store of stories at his disposal."

Cat pushed forward. "Really?" Neither of her parents was fond of stories.

Finn nodded. She wondered why he'd been holding back on her. She thought he only knew the Latin names for plants.

"What kinds of stories? Could you tell me one now?"

Cat's father laughed and leaned over to her mother. "See? They'll be fine," he said, as though neither Finn nor Cat were in the room.

And so, just as the heat finally, mercifully broke, Cat's routine changed completely. She had to get out of bed every morning at six thirty whether she wanted to or not. She could no longer watch cartoons on the viewing screen her parents had installed in her room. And although Finn still let her run more or less wild through the woods, she could do so only during the time allotted—in the mornings—and all of her adventures were accompanied by not only Finn but his incessant lessons. *"Allium stellatum,"* he said when she showed him the wild onions she had braided together to make a wreath. "Pink wild onion." He paused. "It once grew wild across the Northern Hemisphere, although various ecological changes in the last two hundred years have caused it to die out completely in the American Midwest and parts of Canada."

"You're boring," she told him.

"I'm sorry," he said. "I don't wish to be."

But Cat only set the wreath of wild onions on her head and ran off to find the secret fairy trails threading through the under-brush of the forest. She hadn't seen a fairy yet, but she still wasn't convinced they weren't real, and she wanted to draw one in her sketch pad.

In the afternoons, Cat slumped listlessly at a desk in the spare bed-room that had been set up as her classroom. Here Finn taught her the incomprehensible patterns of arithmetic (which she hated), the systemic complexities of the study of science (which she tolerated), and literature (which she adored). He recited to her the *Odyssey* and

Metamorphoses and the violent versions of the fairy tales she had heretofore experienced only as sanitized cartoons, and she followed along on her electronic reading tablet, the words lighting up as he spoke them. *Of bodies changed to various forms, I sing.* She'd never encountered any stories as intricate or compelling as the stories he gave her, nor anything that made her sigh when she read it. She liked best the stories about people becoming other things. Stories where women became swans or echoes. In the evenings, when Finn disappeared into the mysterious recesses of the laboratory, Cat went out to the garden or down to the river and wondered what it would be like to be a stream of water, a cypress tree, a star burning a million miles away. Occasionally, Finn told her stories that were also true.

"I find history fascinating," he said. "Do you?"

"I guess," she said. History was certainly more interesting than math, but there were no sea monsters or witches in real life, only wars and diseases and ecological disasters, humanity nearly dying off in places with names that sounded made up. Australia. New York. Tajikistan. Paris. Resuscitated by something Finn called "ay-eye"— computers, he said, built to replace all those lost people. Cat didn't like hearing about it because it made her depressed, because history never had anything to say about the old brick house in the middle of the forest, with a laboratory in its basement and a garden in its backyard.

But despite the stretches of languid boredom in the afternoons, Cat grew accustomed to her lessons with Finn, to his stories and the sound of his voice, steady and patient as he explained multiplication and division or the taxonomies of the plants growing in the woods. Sometimes she stopped listening and watched him, in the sleepy room where he taught her lessons, the sunlight shining across the left side of his body. He never snapped at her or asked why she didn't understand fractions yet, the way her mother sometimes did. He always answered her questions with long and elaborate explanations that she sometimes didn't understand—but at least he answered them, unlike her father. She wondered if all kids were lucky enough to have their own personal ghost-tutors. She suspected they were not.

*   *   *   *

Cat's mother was throwing a Christmas party. She had planned it for weeks, fussing over the lights Dr. Novak and Finn installed on the outside of the house, disappearing on day trips into the city and returning with bags of new dishes Cat was not allowed to look at, much less touch. She hung garlands around the banister of the stairs. She coordinated the ornaments on the Christmas tree in the living room with the decorations in the hallway so everything in the house sparkled red, white, and silver, like a frozen candy cane.

Cat hid from all this madness by sneaking down to the laboratory to watch Finn and her father work. Her daily lessons had been canceled for the time being, as her mother needed to have the spare bedroom set up to receive guests, or possibly to store empty boxes. She wasn't clear, and Cat wasn't sure. "You can stay down here," her father said. "But don't get in the way."

"I'll just sit under the table."

Her father laughed, and Finn smiled at her. Cat curled up like a snail and peeked at them through the tangled knot of her hair.

Cat didn't really understand what her father did. He talked about it at dinner sometimes, with her mother, who Cat had come to understand used to do the same sort of thing but didn't anymore, and with Finn, who despite being dead also seemed well versed in the subject. They used unfamiliar words and elaborate abbreviations that weren't listed in Cat's reading tablet. Whenever she asked her father about it, he said, "I work with cybernetics, honey," but Cat didn't know what that meant. Finn's explanation had sounded too much like the dinnertime conversations.

From her vantage point under the table, Cat could see only their feet moving back and forth, shuffling over the cold gray cement. They spoke softly to each other in comfortable and assured tones, and Cat heard the sound of typing, the occasional whir of a machine. At one point something clattered and then began beeping urgently. When she stuck her head out to investigate, her father shooed her back under the table.

"Don't make me send you upstairs," he said.

Cat leaned back against a nest of wires. They felt like hands buoying her up off the chilly floor. It was cold that day, colder than normal.

Finn rattled off a string of numbers. "Interpret," said Cat's father.

"All systems functioning," said Finn.

Cat's father shuffled closer to the table under which Cat was hiding. "Very good, very good," he muttered, too softly to be directed at Finn. "Glad to know that's working." Under the table, Cat frowned.

"Daniel! Have you seen Cat?"

Cat's mother's feet clicked into the laboratory. They stopped directly in front of the table, and then Cat's mother leaned down and held out her hand. "There you are," she said. "We need to go into town."

"Why?"

Her mother smiled warmly. "To buy you a dress, sweetheart. For the party."

"Can I pick it out? Anything I want?" Cat had recently learned that she loved dresses.

"Within reason. Come on, let's get your coat."

Cat crawled out from under the table. The lights on the computers on the counter blinked amber and blue. Cat took her mother's hand and waved good-bye to her father and Finn. Then she clomped up the stairs two at a time in her excitement.

Cat's mother drove into town with the heater turned on high. The air hit Cat straight in the face and dried out her eyes but her mother wouldn't turn it down. Cat breathed against the window, traced her initials in the fog of her breath. She drew a face frowning from the cold. She waited for her mother to chide her for smearing the glass but she never said anything.

Outside, everything was gray: the sky, the road into the town, the bark on the trees.

Cat's mother went straight to the children's boutique near the town square, the one across the street from the pie-and-coffee shop and the old post office, the one she always said was too expensive. Multicolored lights blinked in the window, illuminating the mannequins wrapped in taffeta and silk. Cat bounced up and down in her seat. She could hardly believe this bizarre expression of kindness. She wondered briefly if there would be a trade-off, like in the stories Finn read to her.

"Yes, I'm sure you're thrilled," her mother said. "Think of it as an early Christmas present."

"Oh, thank you, thank you!" Cat hopped out of the car and ran into the shop. The dresses looked like rows of ice cream.

"Looking for a party dress?" said the woman behind the counter. Cat's mother sighed and nodded her head, wiping away a few loose strands of hair.

"Darlin', the whole town's talking about that party."

"Don't remind me. Cat!" Her mother took hold of Cat's arm, directed her toward the back of the store. "Why don't you look at the ones that are on sale?" she said. "You might find something you like there."

Cat didn't know what it meant for something to be on sale. She went to the back of the store. "Can it be any color I want?" she asked.

"Yes." Her mother walked back up to the front counter. "I don't know where she gets it from," she said to the cashier, loudly enough that Cat could hear her. "I could have cared less about dresses at her age."

Cat looked through the sales rack, rubbing the fabric of each dress between the palms of her hands. She examined the way the dresses looked in the shop's bright overhead lights and considered the placement of lace and bows. Her favorite color now was seafoam green, and because the sales dresses were all out of season, seafoam green was plentiful. But nothing struck her.

She moved back up to the front of the store and started looking through the stiff Christmas dresses on display there.

"And I told him, you married a *cyberneticist*. I didn't sign up to plan this kind of thing. Honestly, sometimes I think we just went in the wrong direction. Never thought housewifery would come back in style." Cat's mother sighed and glanced at her watch. "Have you found anything yet, Cat?"

Cat shook her head and burrowed into the dress rack.

Everything smelled of starch and potpourri.

"Some important people are gonna be there, that's what I heard," said the woman at the counter. "There to see that . . . project of his." The woman dropped her voice low. "Everything is going all right, I hope? I saw on the news—another attack down in the city. Totally dismantled the thing. Fundies, naturally."

"Oh, don't even get me started," said Cat's mother. "I've already had to chase off the preacher from that damned Pentecostal church twice this month."

"Hope the party won't get 'em all riled up again. I heard from Angeline that Daniel's been the focus of a couple of sermons."

At that moment, Cat found the dress she wanted: dark blue satin, princess cut, with a froth of tulle pushing out the skirt. A pair of tiny white gloves lay draped around the hanger. When she saw that dress, her heart swelled up the way it did when she read Finn's stories, the way it did whenever the flowers in the garden bloomed.

"It's beautiful," she sighed to herself. And then, louder: "Mommy! I found it! The perfect dress!"

* * * *

The day of the party the air in the house was ionized, as though an electrical storm was brewing over the horizon. Cat put her dress on early and ran up and down the stairs, sliding in her socks across the living room's wooden floors. Her mother was too harried to tell her to stop, and just told her to stay out of the way and out of the kitchen. Cat went to find Finn. The laboratory was empty, so she walked up to his room and knocked on the door. "Come in," he said, and she did.

He sat at the desk in front of the tiny octagonal window that looked down over the house's driveway. There was a suit laid out on his bed, a blue tie beside it. Cat picked up the tie and draped it around her neck like a scarf.

"Are you excited about the party?" Cat asked.

"It's going to snow." Finn turned around in his chair so that he faced her. Behind him, the computer monitor spun through row after row of plain gray text.

"I've never seen snow." Cat sat down on his bed and kicked the wooden frame. "Daddy told me it doesn't snow here."

"I have never seen it, either."

"Really?"

He shook his head. Then he turned back to the computer. He touched the screen, and the text stopped moving. There was a low, electronic beep.

Cat frowned, wondered briefly if something was the matter with him, and then went back downstairs.

As the sun set and the decorations outside twinkled on, and the house began to smell of all the food cooking in the kitchen, Cat's mother scooped her up and carted her into the bathroom, where Cat's wild hair was smoothed out and curled. Her mother wore a long silvery dress and makeup, and she smelled of rich, syrupy perfume.

"Hold still," she said. "I'll never get these knots out."

Cat watched in the mirror as this beautiful version of her mother curled Cat's hair into little mahogany-colored ringlets with a curling iron that felt uncomfortably hot next to Cat's scalp. It took a long time. When she had finished, she told Cat to shut her eyes and then she sprayed a great cloud of something that smelled like the inside of the hair salon in town and left a sticky residue on Cat's cheeks. Cat shook her head like a dog. Afterward, her mother took her downstairs, set her down on the couch, and strapped Cat's feet into a pair of synthetic leather Mary Janes.

"Now," said her mother, "the guests will be arriving soon. I want you to stand in the foyer with Finn and your father and take their coats, all right?" She smiled then, and Cat smiled back. In the light of the Christmas tree and the candles, her mother looked like a movie star. "Show off your pretty new dress."

The doorbell chimed.

"Oh shit, they're early. Daniel! Get down here!"

Cat was ushered into the foyer, where she stood next to Finn, who looked strange in his black suit. The guests trickled in: old men with pretty young wives, old women with old husbands. The pretty young wives were especially inclined to coo over Cat, to twirl her around so the skirt of her dress flared out. The old people just handed her their coats and then turned their attentions to Finn. "Remarkable," said one, an old man, his back stooped.

"Remarkable. Astonishing."

Another reached out with a shaking hand and pressed his palm against Finn's cheek. "Look at that skin. Thought they only came in metal."

Finn just looked at them. Sometimes, when Cat was staggering beneath the weight of too many coats, he excused himself and helped her carry them into the master bedroom, where they threw them in a pile on the bed.

"This party sucks," said Cat.

"It's not how I would prefer to spend my time, either," said Finn.

The adults filled up the living room, laughing and drinking from frosted glass tumblers. The scent of all their different perfumes and colognes and powders stirred together in the dry, overheated air and made Cat's head hurt. She tried to crawl under the coffee table, but her father caught her and swept her up in his arms. He seemed more cheerful than usual.

"Almost dinnertime," he said.

Cat's mother stepped into the living room and clapped her hands together twice. All the heads in the room turned toward her. "If you all want to come into the dining room," she said, her voice trailing off, like she had planned only the first part of what she wanted to say. Cat's father deposited Cat back on her feet and held her hand as they walked to the dining room table, which had been laid out with a red and silver tablecloth and pots of fresh poinsettias, in addition to those expensive new dishes her mother had bought in the city. On each of the plates was a square of folded paper with the name of a guest written on it. Cat was positioned between her father and her mother, with Finn on the other side of the table.

"Why can't I sit next to Finn?" Cat asked, tugging on her father's sleeve.

"Because we need to give our guests a chance to talk with him."

"She seems awfully attached," said one of the older ladies. "How intriguing."

Cat glowered at her. She didn't like all this interest in Finn. She had no idea scientists were so interested in ghosts. "Finn tutors her during the day," her father said, sounding faintly embarrassed.

Dinner was a strange, multicourse affair, with Cat's mother bringing in little pieces of toast covered in shrimp and cream cheese, and then a spinach salad, and then a pair of roasted turkeys. After each course she leaned against the doorway and sighed as everyone else filled up their plates. Cat poked at her food. She noticed how everyone snuck glances at Finn while they ate, as he sat watching, his hands in his lap, his place setting empty.

"Does it normally join you for dinner?" asked one of the pretty young wives.

"Finn joins us for all of our meals," Cat's mother answered primly. Cat could feel her looking at Cat's father over the top of Cat's head. She slunk down low in her chair.

"So tell me about your memory processors," said one of the old men. He was talking to Finn, his fork poised above his plate, leaning a little over the table.

Finn recited a string of numbers and abbreviations Cat didn't understand.

"Goddamn." The old man turned to Cat's father. "You responsible for that, Novak?"

Cat's father glanced down at his lap. "Partially," he said. "Finn's creator had designed some incredibly elaborate personality programs—beautiful work, really—but I did some upgrades when he got here. He wasn't designed to be a laboratory assistant, for example. I hooked him up to the lab systems so he'd have the necessary programming to help me out."

"And you added a tutoring program, I'd presume?" It was the older woman from before. She smiled indulgently at Cat, who scowled down at her plate.

"Oh, of course. It was pretty neat. I was actually able to upload a bunch of educational software, using the connection I'd already established in the lab—"

Cat didn't understand why they were talking about Finn as though he were a computer. It must be a scientist thing. She slid farther and farther down in her seat, until her mother grabbed her by the arm and jerked her back up.

"Sit up straight," she said, smiling strangely, her teeth showing. Cat ate another bite of turkey. It was too dry. Then she realized she was hearing something strange, a sort of musical plinking against the glass of the dining room windows. She twisted around in her chair and pulled aside the gauzy cream-colored curtains. She saw the reflection of the table in the glass: the poinsettias, the half-eaten turkeys, the guests, her own pale face. But over all of that was a flurry of white powder that struck the window and melted on contact.

"It's snowing!" she shrieked.

Everyone stopped talking and looked at her, at the windows. Cat turned to her father. "Can I go outside?"

"Honey, we're in the middle of dinner," said her mother.

"So? I'm finished. And Finn can take me. Can't you, Finn? He's never seen snow, either."

"It is true, I have not," he said when everyone looked at him.

"Will you take me outside, Finn?"

"Certainly."

Cat dropped off the edge of her chair and ran over to where Finn sat. Some of the guests tittered uncomfortably. Cat slipped her hand in Finn's, and then her father said, "Be sure to put on your coat, Kitty-Cat."

"I'll make sure she is appropriately dressed," said Finn.

"That's amazing," one of the guests said. "I'd never have thought *they* could be so—"

Cat dragged Finn out of the dining room into the foyer. He helped her put on her coat and then he wound one of her father's old scarves around her neck. Finn didn't put on a coat. Ghosts don't feel the cold.

Cat ran out the front door. The air was filled with swirls of white, and some of the snow had already stuck to the dark ground in patches, like sugar dusted across the top of a chocolate cake. The cars parked along the drive were fringed with ice, and whenever Cat breathed out she could see her breath like a miniature cloud.

She tilted her head back and felt a cold stinging thrill as the snow-flakes melted on her tongue.

Finn walked into the middle of the yard, his hands held out in front of him. The snow piled up along the ridge of his fingers. Cat scooped up a tiny handful of snow and mud. The fabric of her neat little white gloves stuck uncomfortably to her skin, but she shaped the snow into a ball and threw it at Finn. He jumped when it disintegrated across his back, then turned around.

When Cat laughed, he smiled.

"Do you think any of those old people are going to come out here?" she asked. "I hope not. I don't like them."

"I believe they wished to finish their meal."

"They just wanted to keep on talking about you when you weren't there." Cat formed another snowball, not caring that her embroidered gloves were getting wet and dirty. She threw this one at a red car parked in the yard. "They're weird."

"Do you know how snow is formed?"

"No, but I bet you do."

And of course he did. He began to explain the necessary conditions for the existence of snow: the amount of moisture needed in the air, the highest possible temperature. Cat didn't listen to him, just ran through the yard pretending she had transformed into a snowflake that refused to hit the ground and melt. She jumped and pirouetted and flapped her arms until she was out of breath. She ran back up to Finn.

"Why were they talking about you like you were a computer?" she asked.

"Because I am a computer," said Finn. "I'm a machine." Cat stared at him. She was cold, too cold to enjoy the snow, which had completely enveloped the yard and the spindly gray trees and the frozen, empty garden. The forest was silent and still. She and Finn were the only movable things in the entire world.

"You don't look like a computer," she said.

"I know," he said.

Cat considered this. A computer and a ghost had similar characteristics. Neither required food or air or scarves to keep them warm in the snow. And if he was a computer, it would explain why he didn't disappear that day in the cemetery, why animals were not afraid of him.

"You're not like the other computers in the house, though," she said. "Or the ones you told me about, that helped build the cities. You look like a person."

"I believe I'm one of a kind," he said.

Cat shivered then, from the cold and nothing else. Snow dusted across Finn's black hair, turning it gray. It clung to the fabric of his suit.

"I thought you were a ghost."

"Ghosts are not real."

Cat frowned. She didn't believe that, but she did decide she liked knowing her favorite person in the world wasn't dead.

"I don't mind that you're a computer." She ran up to him and wrapped her arms around his legs, leaning her head against his hip. He put his hand on her shoulder, and the weight of it seemed to sink straight through her.

"I'm glad," he said.

They stayed out for a little longer, as the snow fell thicker and thicker around their feet. Finn helped Cat build a tiny, two-foot snowman. Cat didn't want to go back inside, even though she was shaking and shivering in the cold, even though the light in the windows was golden and warm. She found two thin black sticks and stuck them in the snowman's side and drew a crooked smile on his face. The hem of her dress was soaked. The cold seeped through the bottom of her shoes and burned her feet. But she still didn't want to go in. She didn't trust the grown-ups waiting in the house, the people who knew Finn for what he was the minute they laid eyes on him, the people who called him *it*.

TWO

One Saturday, Cat's parents woke her up early. The sun hadn't even risen yet and they appeared in her bedroom, turning on the lights and yanking down the blankets of her bed.

Cat slid her head under her pillow.

"Wake up, Kitty-Cat," said her father. "We've got a surprise for you."

No surprise could be worth waking up in the dark empty time before dawn.

"We're taking you into the city."

Cat pulled her head cautiously out of its hiding place, opening one eye and then the other. The city? She was nearly twelve years old, and they'd never taken her into the city before. The drive was too long, they claimed. She'd get bored. So whenever they went they left her with Mrs. Fensworth down on the Farm-to-Market road, whose house always smelled of pralines and mothballs.

"Why?"

"I have to run up there for some errands," her father said. "We thought we'd make a family trip of it."

"Is Finn coming?"

Her mother and her father looked at each other, a look that had been passing between them more and more frequently in the last few months, an arc of electric current Cat didn't quite know how to define.

"No," her father said. "He needs to stay behind and do some things for me."

Cat slid out of bed and blearily dressed. She skipped breakfast—it was too early, and the sight of her mother eating a cereal bar turned her stomach—and they set out as the sun peeked pink and violet over the edge of the horizon. Cat fell asleep in the car after they passed through town, at the place where the road was lined with scrubby rows of cotton.

When Cat woke up, the car was stopped. She rubbed at an ache in her neck. Her parents laughed in the front seat. Cat pulled herself up and looked out the window, blinking. The sun was high and bright, and they were surrounded on all sides by cars, glinting glass and metal and shimmering waves of exhaust, and then a ring of decaying skyscrapers, their innards wrapped in the steel cast of construction.

"Why aren't we moving?" Cat said.

"Traffic jam," her father answered. "We'll be out of it soon."

Cat craned her neck to look out the window. A pair of impossibly tall cranes swung in tandem across the bleached sky. Everything glittered. Cat rubbed her eyes.

"Where are we going?" she said. "How far is it?"

"Not far," her mother said, peering over her shoulder into the backseat. "There are some shops in downtown your father needs to go to. We can stop and get Vietnamese food, too."

Cat had never eaten Vietnamese food. She sighed and leaned back against her seat. She wished Finn were here. Her parents never talked to her.

Thirty minutes later, the traffic suddenly cleared away, and Cat's father drove the car into the center of the city. Cat stared out the window, watching as the skyscrapers grew taller and more elaborate. All the signs of construction disappeared—the cranes, the scaffolding—leaving just the city, brand-new and shining like the inside of a diamond.

"It's amazing what they've done," her mother said. "Every time I come back here they've rebuilt more and more." Her father nodded in agreement.

They parked in an underground garage that seemed to spiral down toward the molten core of the earth, and then rode a narrow, fast-moving elevator back up to the surface. Cat's head spun. When they stepped out onto the street, Cat immediately shrank back against her father. She had never seen so many people in one place. There were forgettable people in gray business suits and beautiful women in bright-colored miniskirts. Teenagers stood in clumps at the light-rail stops, gazing vacantly into space, tiny lights blinking at their pupils. Cars slid along the wide road, reflected in the glass of the skyscrapers, which up close looked like the walls of a mirrored maze. And threading through the stomping, rushing feet of all the pedestrians were city-stamped worker-bots, sleek as beetles, that sucked up dirty slips of paper and cardboard cups and trails of broken glass.

Her parents went first to a used electronics shop, the walls festooned with wires and circuit boards, the shelves crammed with ancient, dusty computer shells. ANTIQUE AND CURRENT blinked an LED light hanging above the door. When they stepped inside, Cat's father strode up to the man at the counter, called out a name in greeting—Cat didn't catch it, but from the sound of their friendly, familiar laughter her father and the man knew each other. Cat slunk down the aisles, bored. The old fluorescent lights flickered overhead. Cat made her way to the back of the store. Another LED sign: ROBOTICS. A doorway closed off with a black curtain.

Cat stopped in front of the doorway. She listened to her father's laughter drifting up from the front of the store. Then she wrapped her fingers around the curtain. Tugged it aside. She poked her head in.

It didn't look that much different from the rest of the store. More old computer parts. The light back here was dim. Cat eased her way past the curtain. Her interest, piqued by the blinking sign, was starting to fade.

Something tugged at the corner of her vision. She swung her head around: she wasn't alone in the room. A tall, wide figure leaned against the wall opposite, unmoving, gazing at her. Cat stood still while her eyes adjusted to the dimness. It wasn't a person, only a mannequin. Metal. An old robot, like the kind Cat saw occasionally on old Internet shows, the ones made before Cat was born. It didn't even look that much like a person. She didn't know how she could have been fooled.

Cat took a deep breath, her heart still beating rapidly in her chest. She thought she heard her mother say her name out in the store—*Daniel? Did you see Cat?* Then the curtain's rings scraped against the wooden rod in the doorframe. Light flooded the little room. The robot looked like a toy.

"I should have known you'd be back here." Cat's mother leaned against the doorway, resting one hand on her hip. "Come on, back outside. There's a lot of expensive stuff in here."

"I didn't touch anything," Cat said. "I was just looking." Her mother murmured in the back of her throat, acknowledging that Cat's claim had been heard, and ushered her out into the flickering light of the main room.

"That robot didn't look like Finn," Cat said.

"What? Oh, you mean the automata shell. No, I imagine it didn't." Her mother didn't glance down at her, just walked quickly toward the storefront, away from the back room.

"Automata," said Cat. She liked the feel of the word on her tongue. It was like a foreign language.

"Yes," said her mother. "That's what we called them when I was a little girl. They were all over the place. More automata than humans back then."

Finn had told Cat about that period in history. They brought in robots to help rebuild the cities—*infrastructure* was the word he used. Just until the world had repopulated itself.

"They don't make them anymore," Cat's mother said. Cat and her mother emerged from the maze of the store aisles. Cat's father was still laughing with the man at the counter, his face red.

"That's not true," said Cat. "Daddy made Finn."

"Daddy did not make Finn," her mother said sharply. "And Finn's different. The automata were just—factory equipment, really. Finn is . . ." She stopped, bit her lower lip. Her brow crinkled. "Daniel, are you finished?" She pulled away from Cat, walking in long, purposeful strides.

Finn is what? thought Cat, but her mother was already tugging on her father's arm, was already corralling Cat out in the bright, busy street.

They took the light-rail to a Hong Kong department store, where all the glass windows sparkled in the sun and the clothes looked like ice cream sundaes. Cat's father needed to be measured for a new suit, and so her mother pointed her in the direction of the girls' clothing section but Cat didn't see anything she liked. She rode the escalators for a while until she found the Japanese grocer in the basement, with its bakery and confectionary shop. She spent the next half hour looking at the mochi lined up in their neat, rainbow-colored rows, at the elaborate, fancy cakes glistening in the art gallery lights, until her disposable phone rang. Her mother, calling her back up to the men's department.

"Is there anything you want to look at, Kitty-Cat?" her father asked as they walked out onto the noisy, sunny street. "Just tell us if you see a store you want to go into." Cat didn't see anything that interested her at all until they went down a cool, shady side street. She spotted an enormous fiberglass statue of a *Tyrannosaurus rex* guarding the door to a shop with the words FIVE AND DIME painted across the window. Then, below that: PRE-DISASTER COLLECTIBLES!

"Can we go in there?"

"It's just a bunch of old crap," said her mother.

"Pretty much the only thing the Disasters didn't destroy," said her father. "People's crap."

The door chimed when Cat walked in. The air was cool and slightly stale and smelled of cardboard and old fabric. It was an antiques store, Cat realized, but not the sort that opened up along the main street in her hometown and sold only musty, ugly old furniture. Here there were swaths of homemade lace and piles of rotting quilts, little glass salt and pepper shakers in the shapes of animals, an entire shelf of honest-to-God books with yellowed crumbling pages, piles of tarnished old-fashioned silverware, rusted street signs dotted with starry holes. Then Cat found the looms.

The looms were lined up in a row on a rickety foldout table, three or four small ones, with strips of striped fabric rippling over the table's edge, blowing back and forth in the breeze from the air conditioner. Cat followed the fabric to the center of the loom, where it split out into several rows of yarn.

"What'd you find here?" Her father walked up to her, crossed his arms in front of his chest. "Ah, looms. One of humanity's first complex machines; did you know that?"

Cat twisted around to look at him. "How do they work?"

He shrugged.

The shop girl walked up to them, her hands tucked away in the pockets of her skirt. "I can show you." Her hair was the color of maraschino cherries and curled around her shoulders. Her eyes were lined in black kohl. Cat wondered if she would look like that when she was older. She hoped so.

"That'd be great." Cat's father squeezed Cat's shoulder. "She's our little artist."

The shop girl smiled. "I'm an artist, too," she said. "This is my day job." She dragged one of the looms around in front of her and sat down in a metal chair next to the table. She picked up a spool of yarn and threaded it through the yarn already pulled taut on the loom, then lifted up the wooden middle section and pushed it down to the place where the fabric began.

"It's easy," the shopgirl said. "Here, you try."

And Cat did, weaving the yarn through carefully, then combing it down.

"There, leave it hanging," said the shopgirl. "Now thread it back the other way. Good."

As Cat worked, all her agitation from the day, all her residual boredom from the computer repair shop and the department store, melted away. She watched the fabric appear, a blur of green and white like river water. She got lost in the rhythm of lifting and combing.

"She's a natural," said the shopgirl. She leaned in close to Cat and smiled brightly. "You'll be showing down in the Stella in no time."

Cat turned to her father and made her eyes big and shining. "Can we buy one?"

* * * *

The first thing Cat made on her loom was a scarf for Finn. She set the loom up on the coffee table in the living room and ran upstairs to ask him which colors of yarn he wanted her to use.

"I don't need a scarf," he said. "It would be unnecessary."

"Aw, come on!" Cat was used to this sort of thing by now. "Just tell me what colors you want."

Finn looked at the basket of yarn scraps Cat had convinced her parents to buy, along with the loom and a yellowing book of instructions, from the antiques store.

"What colors do you like?" he asked.

Cat rolled her eyes. "How about brown and blue? It's more manly."

"That would be acceptable."

So Cat wove a brown and blue woolen scarf, working on it that evening after dinner while Finn was in the laboratory with her father and her mother watched old movies in the living room. She felt her mother staring at her.

"What are you making?" she asked.

"A scarf for Finn."

There was a long and uncomfortable pause. Then her mother said, "I don't think he needs a scarf, sweetie."

"I don't care. It's a present."

Her mother sighed and turned up the volume on the speakers.

Cat finished the scarf the next evening. She stretched it out along the couch. It was a little wobbly at the end, where she had first started, but for the most part the stitches were neat and even, and the sides didn't waver back and forth. Cat folded the scarf into a neat pile and walked down to the laboratory, taking the stairs two at a time. The door was shut. She knocked. No one answered. She knocked again, and then she tried the doorknob, and the door clicked open. She peeked her head in. Nothing but rows of blinking lights.

"Finn? Daddy?"

"Cat!" Her father's voice boomed out from somewhere in the back. "Stay where you are."

Cat froze, clutching the scarf to her chest. Her father came out through one of the dark doors at the back of the room. Even after the door had clicked shut, he kept his back pressed against it for a second longer before walking toward Cat.

"Where's Finn?"

"He's busy right now. Why don't you run back upstairs and watch a movie?"

"I wanted to give him this." She thrust out the scarf.

The weight of it made her palms sweat.

Her father stared at the scarf with a strange, indiscernible expression. "Oh, Cat," he said slowly.

Cat pulled the scarf back up to her chest.

Her father rubbed his forehead. "Finn is kind to you, isn't he?"

"He's my friend."

Her father frowned. He glanced over his shoulder at the dark door. Cat had never seen the room beyond that door—it was part of the lab where she wasn't allowed. Her father turned back to her. "Cat, Finn's kindness, his, ah, *friendship*—it's a program. Like the games on your computer." He wiped his forehead. "He was programmed to respond to certain actions and requests in a certain way. He was programmed to be polite. He doesn't . . . He doesn't form attachments the way you or I do."

Cat stared at her father. "I know," she said. "He told me."

"Did he?"

Cat shrugged. Finn had never said anything of the sort to her, but she knew her father was lying about Finn's inability to form attachments. She could tell by the way her father didn't meet her eyes as he spoke. He always did that when he didn't want to tell her the real reason she couldn't do something.

"Tell him to come find me when he's done."

Her father's shoulders sagged.

"Promise!"

"I promise."

Cat stayed up late that night, reading under the covers. She kept the scarf on her bedside table. She listened for the sound of someone— of Finn—knocking on her door, but it never came, and eventually Cat crawled out of bed and picked up the scarf and slipped out into the dark hallway. She could hear her father snoring in his bed- room. She padded down the hallway and up the narrow attic stairs, keeping one hand pressed against the dusty wall to steady herself. A light burned in Finn's room. She rapped lightly against the door, pressing her ear to the wood.

"Finn," she said. "It's me."

"Come in."

Cat pushed the door open. Finn looked up from his computer.

"What are you doing?" she asked.

"Running diagnostics."

"I finished your scarf."

"Oh?" Finn folded down the computer and stood up.

"Did Daddy tell you? I went down to the lab but he said you were busy."

"Dr. Novak told me nothing," he said. "May I see it?"

Cat frowned. She held out the scarf, and Finn picked it up and let it drop to the floor. It was almost as tall as he was. He examined a section of it, running his fingers over the yarn. "Fascinating." He looked up at her. "I looked at the history of weaving when you told me you planned to weave me a scarf. Would you like to hear it?"

"Not really." Cat sat down on his bed. "Do you like it?"

"The scarf?"

Finn looked down at the scarf and then back up at Cat. "Yes," he said. "Thank you." He wrapped it around his neck and smiled at her. Cat laughed. It looked silly on him.

"It's very late," he said. "You should be asleep."

"I know." Cat sighed and stood up. She wanted to hug Finn the way she did when she was a little kid. But out of nowhere, she was overwhelmed by a wave of shyness, and she hung back toward the door, her heart hammering.

"I'll see you in the morning," she said, and crept back down to her bedroom.

* * * *

It was a few months after Cat's thirteenth birthday. She had spent the morning down at the river painting dragonflies with the watercolor set she had saved for and purchased from the tiny art co-op on the outskirts of town. She wasted a lot of time down by the river these days, in her plastic sandals and yellow two-piece bathing suit, painting and drawing and daydreaming. She was interested in light at the moment: light and the way it reflected off the surface of the water, how it glared against the bone-white stones along the shore. When it grew too hot to stay outside any longer, Cat trotted back to the house to drink a glass of limeade in the air-conditioned kitchen.

"Algebra!" Cat's mother exclaimed just as Cat walked through the door. "She barely knows algebra! What good is a programmable tutor if he can't even teach her *algebra*?"

Cat's father didn't say anything, only looked at Cat standing in the doorway. Her mother glanced over at her. "I knew algebra when I was ten years old," she said.

Cat bit on her lower lip to keep from talking back. She carried her still-damp paintings into the living room. Her mother's voice drifted out of the kitchen: "Put on some real clothes before you go up for your lessons!"

Cat rolled her eyes but didn't respond. She laid her paintings across the coffee table to dry. She kicked off her shoes and collapsed across the couch and tried to ignore the fervent hum of her mother's voice, rising and falling like a radio. She had no intention of changing out of her bathing suit. The weather was too hot, and she liked wearing it. Cat stood up and stretched, felt each notch of her spine snap into place. Then she trotted up the stairs to the spare bedroom. To learn math. Algebra. She even hated the sound of the word.

Cat sat down at the table set up in the center of the room. Finn looked up from his laptop and smiled at her. "Would you like to change out of your bathing suit?" he asked. Cat shook her head no, drawing her bare stomach tight against her spine.

The algebra lesson that day was like all the math lessons that had preceded it. Finn presented Cat with a simple equation, an unnatural mixture of letters and numbers. Cat stared at it. She tapped her fingernails, currently covered in peeling green polish, against the table. Her head seemed full of cotton candy. Finn waited for her to respond: he didn't cajole or plead or mock, but sat silently beside her, his hands folded in his lap. The air conditioner kicked on. Eventually Cat began to write out her calculations, her simple, neat rows of arithmetic, but then the equation started to shift and muddle, and the letters transposed themselves over the numbers and vice versa—the 5s became Ss, the Ss became 5s. Cat threw her digital pen across the room and slouched in her seat.

"I can't do it," she said. "I'm too stupid."

"You're not stupid."

"Mom thinks I am."

"You are not stupid."

Cat pushed her hair, damp and sticky with river water, away from her face and looked at Finn. He pulled out a spare pen and leaned over her writing tablet. He was close to her. Cat felt light-headed, and she knew it had nothing to do with her inability to understand math. She was on the precipice of something. It coiled inside her like a snake and made her fidgety and distracted, especially around Finn and his constant stream of algebraic equations. But the algebraic equations were not the problem.

Finn wiped away all of her work on the learning tablet. "Watch," he said. Then he wrote out the solution to the equation, slowly and neatly, stopping after each line to look over at her. Her cheeks warmed. She tried to memorize the way the solution looked when it was correct. She tried to forget all her frantic scribbling in the margins. She tried to ignore the distraction of his closeness to her.

Finn wiped the learning tablet clean again. "Now you try."

Cat took the pen from him and worked through the equation, glancing over at him occasionally for assurance. When she had finished, he said, in his even way, "That's correct. Very good." He smiled. "You're not stupid."

"Thanks." Cat meant it. She knew that he never said anything ironically. And so it went for the rest of the afternoon, working through one equation after another, Cat struggling to find the common concepts between each individual problem. But they were all fragments of glass, glued back together to make a vase that had shattered a long time ago.

It was difficult for her to concentrate on algebra for more than an hour. Eventually, she noticed only Finn's fingers, tapering down into points. Or his hair, which tended to fall into his eyes. She made note of the mechanical way he moved. The shape of his spine, his shoulders, his waist. He wasn't an adult, not really, so it was okay for her to see all these things.

Some nights under the covers of her bed Cat drew pictures of him. She used to use the electronic drawing tablet her father had given her for her birthday, but recently she had switched over to paper from the art co-op, expensive and rough against her skin, her fingers smudging the charcoal as she worked. Her bedsheets were coated in a fine layer of black dust. She sprayed the drawings with hair spray and kept them in a folder in the back of her closet, away from the paintings of flowers and dragonflies she knew to be more innocuous, even though she could not quite give a reason as to why—she suspected it was related to the panicked feeling bubbling up inside her, the appearance of feathery golden hairs along the incline of her thighs, the reason her mother hated her yellow swimsuit.

"Very good," said Finn. Cat blinked. Finn switched off the learning tablet and all the math blinked out of existence. Cat laid her head on the table. The sunlight streaming through the windows was bright and hot.

"You are improving," said Finn. But Cat only sighed.

*　*　*　*

Time passed. Cat learned enough algebra to prompt her mother to ask about trigonometry. There was a fight at the dinner table, and Cat stormed up to her room and slammed her door shut so hard the walls of the house shook. Then, only a few weeks later, Cat's parents announced she would be attending the consolidated high school in town the following autumn.

"What?" she shrieked. They were sitting at the table in the

kitchen—her parents and Cat. No Finn. A storm churned up the soil outside. It had rained constantly that summer.

"I don't want to go to school," Cat said. "I thought you said it wasn't very good. Why are you suddenly changing your minds?"

Her mother sighed and pressed her hand to her forehead. Her father leaned forward over the table.

"We think it would be a good idea for you to make some friends," he said. "Friends your own . . . age."

Cat slouched down in her chair, arms crossed over her chest. *School.* She associated the word with things she had seen on shows or read in stories: a place where you had to sit in the same room for eight hours a day, where you couldn't run through the woods in the sparkling mornings, where kids would torment you because you didn't have the right haircut. Cat touched her own reddish brown hair reflexively.

"I won't go."

"You have to," her mother said.

"Why? Because you said so?"

"Basically."

Cat wanted to scream. Instead she pushed away from the table and put on her rain boots and raincoat and went outside. The trees thrashed and shimmered from the rain. Through the foggy kitchen window she could see her parents sitting at the kitchen table, leaning forward, faces intent. Talking about her. She kicked at a patch of loose grass, and it splattered out across the yard, mud mixing in with the rainwater. Cat trudged toward the woods. *School. They can't make me go.* But she knew they could. Her parents' acts of injustice had been increasing lately, to the point where Cat could barely stand to look at them. They ignored her all through her childhood and now suddenly they wanted to take an interest in her development.

Cat walked all the way down to the river, slipping a little over the wet grass, grabbing on to the tree branches to make sure she didn't fall. The leaves came off in her hands and pasted themselves to her skin.

The river had risen since the last time she'd been out here, a few days ago. Then it had been calm, but now it twisted and churned and swirled with clouds of silt and mud, rushing up against the cypress trees. Cat stood right at the water's edge and watched as it carried along smooth round stones and broken sticks and clumps of drowned grass.

The rain dripped off the hood of her raincoat and into her eyes. She grabbed hold of one of the trees and leaned out over the water, and that's when she saw Finn, standing several meters away from her, looking out over the river, not moving, not wearing a raincoat or boots. His hair curled with the weight of water.

"Finn!" Cat shouted. He turned, and she waved. Then she began to make her careful way along the river's edge toward him. She had done this many times before, clinging to the cypress trees' low-hanging branches to propel herself along. But today she was upset by her parents, by the threat of school, and the rain kept falling into her eyes. She lost her handhold on the trees and fell. Time slowed until it became immeasurable. She hung suspended above the water rushing toward the sea, the rain dropping in perpendicular lines across her bare face.

She was in Finn's arms.

He'd caught her, nearly instantly, even from the place where he'd been standing. He pulled her away from the edge of the water until they were on more solid ground, away from the loose soil eroding into the river. His body beneath his wet clothes was warm, the way a computer is warm when it overheats. His arms wrapped around her stiffly. When he removed them, the places where his skin had touched hers tingled.

"Are you hurt?"

She shook her head and tried to draw herself up, but she was embarrassed at having almost fallen into the river, embarrassed that she had to be saved. Her whole body was flushed and hot. She pushed her hood away and fell down into the mud and closed her eyes against the rain.

"What are you doing out here?" Drops of water, steely and cold, landed on her tongue.

"I was thinking."

What do you possibly think about? Everything in the universe?

"I have to go to high school next fall." She rolled over onto her side. Finn sat down at the base of a twisting old oak tree. Leaves and twigs were caught in his hair. His pale skin shimmered from the rain. He looked like a fairy.

"Yes, Dr. Novak told me."

Cat sighed. "I don't want to go."

Finn didn't say anything. Cat rolled over onto her back. The rain fell harder, weaving through the net of leaves overhead, smelling faintly of metal.

They stayed there for a long time, unspeaking.

*   *   *   *

Cat started at the high school in town. Her parents could still tell her what to do. That first day, everyone stared at her when she walked into the courtyard with a bag slung across her chest. She wore a dress she had made from looking at videos on fashion sites on the Internet, but she could tell instantly it was all wrong, she was all wrong.

The other students whispered about her all day, and then all week, and no one spoke to her except her teachers. Between classes, when she had to walk through the crowded, noisy, humid hallways, Cat's heart pounded and her breath came out short and gaspy. People stared at her and the weight of their eyes was so heavy Cat thought she might burn up. She was constantly dizzy. She walked close to the rows of lockers to keep herself upright, one hand running over the line of padlocks.

She had spent too much time alone in the woods, in front of a loom, with Finn.

During lunches those first few days, Cat walked off campus to the neighborhood across the street. The houses made her nervous, but during the heat of the day nothing stirred and no one looked out their windows. She ate the lunches she packed at home in the shade of an enormous hibiscus bush, then walked back to school for her afternoon classes.

On Friday one of the security officers caught her. She was sent to the office, her heart panicking. They searched her bag for drugs. When they didn't find anything, the assistant principal came and sat down in the chair beside her and said, "You're not in trouble, but I'm going to call your parents to let them know what happened." She paused, twisting her mouth in concern. "You can't just go traipsing off campus during lunch."

On the ride home after school Cat dug her nails into the palms of her hands and tried not to cry. Her mother just leaned her head against the window and looked tired.

The weeks went by. Cat didn't make any friends. She was behind in her math and engineering classes even though her teachers all acted like she should be ahead. She was bored by the business and marketing classes. She thought she'd like her English class but everything they read was simple and boring. There was only one art class, an elective for seniors.

When she complained about this to her parents, her mother said, "We let Finn coddle you, sweetheart. The math is good for you. You'll be better prepared for the job market."

Cat was full of hate. It was the only way to describe it. She walked around campus during the day thinking *I hate I hate I hate*. She hated her parents, she hated the kids at school, she hated her teachers. She even hated Finn, because he hadn't stopped this from happening.

A month went by. Then, on a day so hot and bright it felt like August, a boy came up to Cat as she sat beneath the magnolia tree in front of the school. She had finished her lunch and was sketching on her electronic drawing pad. The boy walked right up to her and stared at her until she glanced up. She knew he was popular. He exuded an air of being adored.

"You're Novak's daughter, right?" He tilted his head to the side and squinted.

Cat nodded and looked back down at her drawing. It was a woman's face. It didn't look like anyone in particular.

"What's your name?" the boy asked.

Cat tilted her head up at him. He was smiling. She didn't trust him, but she told him her name, and he nodded thoughtfully. "So Novak finally let you out." He crouched beside her and looked her in the eye. "I'd always heard he had a daughter but no one told me she looked like you." He grinned. "Wish they had."

Cat gazed at him with a sense of mild alarm. She didn't know what to say.

"I had a tutor at home," she said. "That's why I didn't go to school."

"A tutor! Shit." The boy ran his hand over the top of his hair. His name flashed into her mind: *Erik Martin*. "You know everyone talks about your dad." He laughed. "The mad scientist. That's what my uncles all call him."

Why would you tell me that? But she only tightened her fingers around the edge of the sketch pad.

"Yeah, I dunno. I met him once. He seemed cool." Erik leaned back on his heels, wobbling. He put one hand out for balance. "There was some crazy robot thing with him, though. Almost looked real. He said it was his *assistant*."

"That's Finn."

"Wait, it has a name?" Erik threw back his head and laughed. "Oh fuck, man. Wait'll Andrew hears about that—"

"He's not an it." Cat clenched her drawing pen in her fingers. Sweat dripped down her spine.

"He?" Erik stood up and frowned at her. "Nah. You don't understand. They can't be *hes*. They're just machines. You wouldn't call your oven a he, would you?"

"No," said Cat. "Because an oven is just an oven."

She stopped. Erik looked down at her, his features darkened by the shadow of the magnolia tree.

"Just like Daddy, huh?" he said. "My uncle says that's the problem with letting damn scientists come live around here. Brings in money, I guess. Brings in a lot of creepyass robots, too. Like, that one time I saw it, it kept staring at me, and—"

"He's not an *it*," Cat said. "He's a person." All the hate she carried around inside was building up like a second skeleton. It tingled in the tips of her fingers. She slid the drawing pad off her lap.

"A person?" Erik's eyes narrowed. "No, it's just a machine made to look like a person." He rocked back on his heels and tilted his face up toward the sky. "So they can steal jobs from us easier. It plain ain't right. That's what my preacher says." His face dropped down. He looked Cat straight on. Her entire body shook. "I mean, your dad made it, right? A human being? Way I see it, any robot that close to a person is an abomination."

He spoke so casually, as though it were a fact, as though he had no idea how it hurt her.

And for a second the entire world fell away, and Cat felt only a white-hot anger burning at the core of her heart, radiating out through her limbs. Then in one clean motion she slid to her feet and fell upon Erik Martin, her hands curled up tight into fists. They hit the ground, Cat on top, Erik squirming and shrieking beneath her. She heard feet pounding against the sidewalk. People jeering and yelling. Cat slammed her fist into Erik's nose and heard a crack and cried out at the burning pain in her own knuckles. He scratched at her face, and she scratched back. Her hair was flying everywhere, and the sun illuminated all the red in it like she'd caught on fire.

Hands grabbed her by the shoulders and pulled her away from Erik. He crawled backward over the grass. A column of blood was smeared across the lower half of his face, from his nose to his chin. Cat tried to catch her breath, her chest heaving.

"The hell did you do to her, Martin?" shouted the security guard. He tossed Cat aside and stalked over to Erik. The hand Cat had used to punch him was covered in blood, her knuckles jutting out at unnerving angles.

"Nothing, man! We were talking. She fucking went crazy." Erik stood up and wiped at the blood on his face. The security guard whirled around.

"We have a zero-tolerance policy toward fighting at this school," he said to Cat. "Now, if he touched you—"

"He didn't touch me." Cat glanced at the dissipating crowd of students. No one would meet her eyes but she felt the lingering ghosts of their stares. And for once it didn't bother her. She felt strong, powerful. Amazonian. "He said something about . . . about my father."

The guard rolled his eyes. "Okay, I've heard enough. I'm taking both of you to the office. Come on."

He took Erik's upper arm in one hand and Cat's in another and led them up the front steps, into the cold, dark school building. Cat heard the sound of blood dripping across the tile floor, and she rubbed her hand against the edge of her shirt.

Erik leaned around behind the security guard. "Bitch," he hissed.

"Martin! Don't you say another word to her."

The assistant principal kept Cat and Erik separate while they waited for their parents. She sent Cat to the nurse's office first, and the nurse poured hydrogen peroxide over the cuts on Cat's knuckles. Cat clenched her teeth but didn't scream. Her hand was swollen and red and wouldn't straighten out. The nurse wrapped it in a bandage.

Both Cat's mother and father came to the school. When Cat walked out to meet them they regarded her silently, her mother's eyes narrowed into two angry slits. Her father looked disappointed. This was worse.

"A fight, Caterina?" her mother said. "A *goddamn fistfight*? What were you thinking?" Cat didn't say anything. She looked from her mother to her father and back again. The adrenaline from the fight had disappeared, and now she was exhausted.

"They've suspended you for the rest of the day," her mother said. "I hope you're happy."

Her father frowned.

When they arrived back at the house, Cat threw her bag on the couch and headed toward her room. But her mother slapped her hand on Cat's arm and made her sit down. "Tell me what happened," she said. Cat's father came into the living room and sat down in his reclining chair.

"You won't like it." This was the first thing Cat had said to either of them since they picked her up.

"No, I don't expect we will." Her mother glanced over at her father.

"He said—" Cat stopped. She looked up at the ceiling. She already knew what their reaction would be. Her hand ached. "He said Finn was an abomination."

"For Chrissakes," said her mother, just as her father said, "Oh, Cat."

"Are you happy?" her mother said to Cat's father. Cat wanted to curl up into a ball and disappear. "I told you you shouldn't have brought that thing here—" She looked at Cat and held up a finger. "Don't start with me, either."

Cat buried her head in the arm of the couch.

"Sweetie, I don't think it's that big a deal—"

"Daniel! She punched a boy *in the face*."

"Oh, please, Helen. That was Frank Martin's kid. You're going to tell me he didn't deserve it? The little shit's got date rapist written all over him."

"I can't believe we're arguing about this." Her mother stood up and pulled at the ends of her hair. "You're grounded," she said to Cat. "No. Scratch that. I'm not letting you stay in this house anymore than I can help it. I'll . . . sign you up for community service. Something." She stomped out of the living room.

"Daddy," said Cat. "Daddy, I'm sorry, I just—"

"I know," said her father. "Give her time to cool off."

"You're not going to send Finn away, are you?"

Her father sighed and stared out the window. The sunlight reflected off his glasses. He looked immeasurably sad. Finally, he said, "There's no place else he can go."

*　　*　　*　　*

That evening, Cat walked out to the garden. Everything was dead from the autumn heat. She sat underneath her citrus tree and turned on her music player and closed her eyes. She was able to move her hand now, though only barely. In her mind she watched the fight with Erik Martin over and over again. She remembered how she felt afterward, her hair loose and wild, her hand dripping blood. She wondered what she looked like to all those spectators. She wondered what they would say about her when she went back to school tomorrow.

When Cat opened her eyes Finn stood over her, watching her in the violet twilight. Cat took off her headphones.

"You shouldn't have done that," he said.

"Oh God, you, too?" Cat sighed and kicked out her feet. "Did he tell you why I did it?" Cat knew her mother never talked to Finn if she could help it.

Finn shook his head.

"I was defending you," she said. *Abomination.* Her face flushed with anger.

"Why would you do that?"

"Because you're my friend! Jesus!" Cat threw up her good hand. "Why is that so hard for everybody to understand?"

Finn sat down in the grass next to Cat. The hot, dry wind blew his hair across his face, covering up his eyes' faint silver gleam. "You're my friend, too," he said after one of his long, mechanical pauses. "But I don't think violence is ever acceptable—"

"Yeah, yeah, I know." Cat paused, looked up at the stars. "Remember when you taught me all the constellation myths?"

"I don't see what that has to do with—"

"I loved those stories," said Cat. "I loved all the stories you read me. They don't really encourage us to read in school. It blows. All calculus problems and computer programs. Finn . . ." She looked over at him, the tips of her hair tickling her bare back. "Finn, do you think I'm pretty?"

Finn stared at her. "Pretty?"

"You know, beautiful. Hot. Whatever."

"I do not—" Finn stopped. His eyes vibrated, and his brow furrowed. "May I think about this?"

Cat immediately regretted asking him. She laughed to make herself think it didn't matter. "It's not really a thinking-about sort of question," she said. "Forget it. It's okay if you don't."

"I believe it is for me." His eyes continued to vibrate. "A thinking-about sort of question." Cat heard the inflections of her own voice, as though she were listening to herself on a recording. She stretched out on the grass, lying on her back, her hands over her head. She didn't know why it mattered if he thought she was pretty. Cat had never considered her own prettiness before that moment. So why now? *No one told me she looked like you.* But Erik Martin was an asshole.

"I bet everyone at school hates me now." She looked at Finn sideways through the grass. "At least you don't hate me."

"I cannot hate," he said. "The programming inside me won't allow it."

But Cat had turned her face back toward the night sky. The cicadas were buzzing and the night air was warm and sweet on her skin and she didn't comprehend at all what Finn had just said to her.

THREE

Because Cat had, apparently, broken the nose of the most popular boy in school, two girls in eyeliner and knee-high boots came up to her in the courtyard the morning after and told her the fight was the most badass thing they'd ever seen.

"Holy shit," said the first girl, whose name Cat later learned was Miranda. "Holy *shit*, you don't know how many times I've wanted to smack that smug little bitchass face of his."

Miranda and the other girl, Ashley, took Cat over to the place where their friends slouched in the branches of the courtyard trees, looking like clothes hung out to dry. The air there smelled of cigarette smoke. Cat had noticed them before, these people, this clump of trees, but they had always looked through her as though she were invisible.

"Okay, assholes," said Miranda. "This is Cat. Be nice to her."

And so Cat suddenly found herself with friends her own age, friends who were not Finn. The travails of school became instantly more sufferable, though Cat never quite felt as though she belonged. Her clothes weren't really right, no matter how many times Miranda and Ashley went shopping with her online—she didn't inhabit them properly. She disliked the taste of cigarettes and the burn of them against the back of her throat. She didn't recognize the names of the augment games Miranda uploaded onto her comm slate, and she hated the raucous, screeching music they listened to in Ashley's bedroom after school. But none of them asked her leading questions about her father or about Finn, and none of them wanted to be engineers, even if they also didn't like to read. Although Miranda did like photography.

"Let me steal your soul," she always said, stalking around smoky parties with her camera. It was an old analog camera, one that used up rolls of ancient film she bought from a vendor through the Internet. Miranda knew how to develop the film and the prints herself. She had a lab set up in the spare bathroom in her parents' house, the lone window taped over with aluminum foil and moth-eaten black fabric, a red light installed above the mirror.

"I told them it was, you know, chemistry," she explained to Cat while swirling a sheet of photography paper in a tub of oily chemicals. Cat watched the images appear, the darkest parts first: the pupils of the eyes, the muddy shadows. The photograph showed one of the bands that played the VFW hall on Friday nights, the lead singer screaming into his microphone as he leaned over the edge of the stage.

In an ostentatious display of trust, Miranda lent Cat one of her old cameras, a Nikon FM10. "Break it and die," she said.

Cat kept the camera in the top drawer of her desk for a few days before she used it. She didn't know what to take pictures of—Miranda already had the VFW shows covered—and she didn't want to waste film, even though Miranda had told her that was the point.

"You want to burn through miles of film," Miranda said when she told Cat she'd let her borrow a camera. They stood in her bedroom, Miranda holding the camera out in the space between them. "You have to. Just to find that one perfect shot."

"That's so wasteful."

"That's the beauty of it," said Miranda. "The beauty of waste. We don't see it much anymore. Everything becomes something else." She dragged on her cigarette and made quotation marks with her fingers. *"Progress."*

Eventually, Cat took a few pictures of the garden. She took a picture of the river. They were both such dull subjects. So she decided to go after her family: her father hunched over a soldering iron and circuit board in the laboratory, her mother frying steaks in the kitchen. She smiled indulgently as Cat peered through the viewfinder.

"From your friends at school?" she said. Cat nodded and went to find Finn.

He was up in the stuffy attic bedroom, tapping patiently on his computer. The minute Cat walked in the humidity curled her hair into ringlets. "Let me steal your soul," she said, cocking her shoulders back like she'd seen Miranda do. The words were marbles in her mouth.

"I don't understand," said Finn.

Cat snapped his picture, and then stood on his bed and took another. Finn turned back to his computer. Cat laughed. "I just want to take your picture." She jumped back down to his dusty floor. The sunlight streaming through the windows made his hair glisten. She took a picture of him typing. He glanced over at her and smiled faintly, in that way he did whenever she used an idiom he didn't understand. Suddenly and inexplicably emboldened—by his confusion, by the lemony sunlight—she reached over and put two fingers along his jawline and turned his face so that he was looking right at her with his black eyes. The skin of his face was soft. She did not expect softness.

For a moment, she didn't move, just kept her fingers pressed against his jaw. They stared at each other. They were so close their noses almost touched. Then Cat dropped her hand to her side, stepped back, lifted the camera up to her right eye, and pressed the button that seared his image into film.

A few days later, Miranda showed her how to shake up the film in plastic canisters, how to stretch it out in the darkroom, how to line it up under the glass of the photo processor. Cat made a contact sheet with all the pictures she had taken, and then carried it into Miranda's bedroom to look it over. She half expected Finn to be missing from the tiny thumbnail-size pictures, like a vampire.

"That's a good one." Miranda leaned over Cat's shoulder and pointed at one of the portraits of Finn, the one where he stared straight into the camera—straight at her. "It's intense. Who is that?"

"My father's assistant," said Cat softly.

Miranda made an odd noise in the back of her throat. She fell back down on the bed and lit a cigarette but didn't say anything. Warmth stung Cat's cheeks.

She ended up making prints from only three of the pictures on the contact sheet: one of her father, one of a spray of water from the sprinklers, and one of Finn, his eyes unfathomably black.

* * * *

Cat went to a party on a balmy spring night. She was nearly seventeen. Her parents let her go, no questions asked, because they were heartened by the fact that she had friends and went out most Friday nights. She even brought home a boyfriend named Oscar, who despite his long hair and ratty coat met with her parents' approval because he was, as they put it, *her own age.*

Oscar picked her up the night of the party in his noisy old Chevy, the one his redneck father sold to him for five dollars. Cat had been waiting for him on the porch, and the headlights nearly blinded her. She threw her hand up, caught in the spotlight, and then ran through the dewy grass and climbed in. Oscar nodded at her and turned up his music, and they roared down the road into town. The truck still smelled faintly of the emu his father raised. Cat sat primly in the seat beside him, aware of the stiffness of her hair, the itchiness of her spangled, low-cut top. She had painted her fingernails dark blue earlier that afternoon in Finn's room, leaning against his bed while he worked at his desk, holding her hands up to the light. Now the polish felt heavy and thick against her nails. Her eyelashes were weighed down by mascara.

The party had already begun to spill out into the hazy night when Oscar and Cat arrived. Oscar threw his arm around Cat's shoulders and indolently dragged her through the garage to the backyard. Someone had strung blinking LED lights from the trees. An old refrigerator filled with cheap beer lounged next to the fence. Oscar got one for himself and one for Cat. When she drank it, she repressed the urge to make a face—she'd never gotten accustomed to the taste of beer.

Miranda showed up a little later, her arm slung around the waist of the drummer from some local band. He had graduated a year ago but he still hung around the high school, flirting with the same three or four girls. Cat knew Miranda had been trying to get this drummer to date her—or maybe just sleep with her, Cat could never tell which—for the last few months.

Somebody dragged a sound system outside and put on music. Miranda and the drummer disappeared to one of the bedrooms inside. Cat stuck close to Oscar while he told stupid jokes with his friends, because all the people she knew at the party were either inside or stoned, and impossible to talk to either way. She watched Oscar swig from his beer bottle. Whenever he laughed, he bared his teeth. She realized she didn't like Oscar that much. But she did like that he liked her.

After a while, Oscar took Cat by the hand and led her to the edge of the yard, to a spot where dewberries grew wild against the fence. His face glistened with sweat. He smiled down at her.

"Oh, Cat," he said. "Meow. You're so hot."

"Thanks." This was what Cat always said.

He leaned in and kissed her. *Finally*, Cat thought. There was something slick on his tongue. A piece of waxy paper. He pulled away.

"Now," he said. "We wait."

"Wait for what?" Cat could still taste that flat waxiness. It filled up her mouth, sticking to her teeth. Dread pooled in her stomach. "Fuck, Oscar, what'd you give me? Shit. *Shit*." She scraped at her tongue with her painted-on fingernails. She knew it wouldn't do any good. Oscar laughed.

"Calm down—it'll be fine." He wrapped his arm around her, put his mouth close to her ear. "You said you'd be willing to try it with me."

And she had said that, maybe a week and a half ago. She hadn't meant it. They'd just had sex on the couch in his living room.

Oscar guided her back over to the lights of the party, sat her down in one of the foldout lawn chairs. Cat picked at a loose thread dangling from the hem of her skirt. Her heart pounded. She didn't know what was going to happen to her—she wondered if she would be able to trick herself out of it, if she could stay within her own head. Once Miranda had slipped into the bathroom at the beginning of lunch and then went to Business Communications with wide, strange eyes and wrote out a marketing presentation, her fingers banging violently against the keyboard. She always bragged how she made an A on that assignment.

The wait seemed to last for hours. Cat ran her clammy hands up and down the sides of her legs. The feedback from the sound system made her head hurt. The party was shrouded in humidity and smoke, and a girl on the other side of the yard laughed, and that laugh echoed over and over again in Cat's head, that laugh like a bird crying out, and Cat was suddenly drifting apart, breaking down into molecules and then atoms, and she knew she was not a girl anymore but a ghost, a phantom, a creature made of sunlight and energy, ephemeral, intangible—

Oscar was laughing. Was it Oscar? He put his hand on the small of her back. Was it Oscar? His hand went straight through her. She screamed. Did she? Was that really her? She jumped up and ran toward the house, white light streaking off her slowly disintegrating body and trailing across the yard—

Cat? Cat? Are you okay? It was Miranda, eyeless. She was bleeding from the mouth. A zombie—no, her lipstick was smeared. Her eyeliner had smudged. *Oh, fuck you, Oscar, you are such a fucking asshole. I can't believe you'd do that*—Miranda disappeared. Cat could still hear her voice. *At least warn her!* Cat pushed into the house. She wanted to find her purse, her purse with her comm slate and her house key and her bank card. She wanted out of this party. She wanted away from Oscar. She wanted . . .

The house was dim and cool and the dark walls were lined with family portraits that all rose out of their frames, eyes glowing. Cat refused to look at them. Her purse. It was lying on the floor next to the dining room table. She wound the strap around her arm. Concentrate. She needed to concentrate. She took slow, hesitant steps out of the house, that house filled with floating eyes. Out onto the warm, quiet street. She picked a direction and walked, into the darkness, away from the noise of the party and the weight of those floating, glowing eyes. She wasn't sure of the direction of her own home—she didn't recognize the street signs. They looked electric.

Cat sat down on the curb. She was still expanding like a star. She could not stay out here all night. She could not call home. *Finn.* Contact Finn. He didn't have a slate, but she didn't have to call him. He was a computer. She saw it so clearly now, light radiating off her skin. He was a *computer.*

She pulled her slate out of her bag and set it down on the curb next to her. She tapped the screen and it lit up pale blue. It was hard to see through the clouds of light her fingers were giving off. But the slate could connect directly into the computers in the house, including the one she wanted more than any other. All the information was stored in the slate's memory, she just needed to work her way through it—numbers. It was all numbers from here on out. They wiggled and twisted in front of her. She rubbed her eyes. Light blossomed everywhere. She had done this a thousand times before, with the computers in the kitchen and in her bedroom, and Finn should be just the same, she just needed to find Finn, just needed to find Finn among all those numbers—

She had it.

Finn, she typed. *Finn are you there? It's Cat.* She watched the cursor blink, blink, blink. It matched the beat of her heart.

Why are you contacting me like this?

Because I can't tell my parents! I need you to come get me! I'm falling apart! She paused, distracted by the light coming off her fingers. Then: *Don't tell my parents!* Then: *Please?*

I will have to lie.

Cat didn't know what to say to that. She wrote *Please?* again.

The cursor blinked for a long time. No answer. Then:

Wait where you are. Keep slate with you. Be there soon.

DON'T TELL MY PARENTS, she typed, one last time. He never responded. Cat fell back against the grass, her feet kicked out onto the street. Overhead the stars were moving. The constellations danced, Orion waltzing with Cassiopeia. Cat seeped into the soil, lighting it up—it was beautiful but she was scared, scared she would dissolve completely, she would be devoured by the world, she would become nothing, nothingness—

A pair of headlights swept over her. Cat pushed herself up even though it was difficult in her diaphanous state. The car stopped, its engine idling, and Finn stepped out.

"Finn!" she sighed. "Finn, my atoms are flaking off."

"Your atoms seem quite normal to me." He held out his hand and Cat grabbed it and he pulled her to her feet. She closed her eyes, opened them. Finn was staring at her.

"What have you done to yourself?" he asked.

"Wasn't me." She wobbled as he guided her back to the car. "Oscar . . . that prick." She slumped in the seat and looked out the window and saw that the place where she'd lain was now illuminated in the shape of her body. "I can't go home like this," she said. "They'll know. I'll light everything up." She looked at Finn. "Let's go to the park." Finn reached across the car and put his hand on Cat's chin and turned her face toward him. He looked straight at her eyes. Cat didn't dare move. His eyes vibrated and then flashed silver. He blinked. "Oh," he said. "I see." His hand dropped to his side. "It generally takes six to twelve hours to wear off. You shouldn't do this again. Repeated usage can lead to permanent side effects."

"I'll bet." Cat nestled herself in the curve of the car seat. "To the park, Finn!"

He did as she requested, driving to the old rotting playground at the park's center. The swing set and the merry-go-round were grown over with kudzu. The jungle gym was rusted and breaking into pieces. Cat stumbled out of the car and ran to the merry-go-round and sat down on the edge and tried to make it spin but the kudzu held it tight. Finn sat down beside her. Cat felt calmer now, less afraid of falling apart, even though the stars were still dancing overhead, even though she still lit up the darkness.

Finn stayed with her all night, watching her with the calm detachment of a scientist. She wandered all over the playground, passing her hands over the flowers curled up tight for the night, watching the shimmer of stardust that flaked off her skin. At one point she was overwhelmed with exhaustion and so she wandered over to the place where Finn sat on the merry-go-round. She laid her head in his lap. The surrounding darkness settled over her like a blanket. He rested his left hand on her shoulder. She closed her eyes. She thought she felt his fingers stroking her tangled hair but maybe it was just the tingle of energy as she lit up the darkness. She couldn't be sure of his touch but the idea of it soothed her.

When Cat finally began to come down, just as the sky was turning pale pink, Finn drove her home. Her head was still gauzy and confused but she told him to wait in the woods for a few hours so they wouldn't come in together—the things she learned from her friends at school.

"Just act like you were hanging around outside all night," she said. She was less worried, in that moment, about getting in trouble herself—she could probably talk her way out of any serious punishment. Really, she wanted to protect him. She wanted to protect him because he had protected her.

Cat slipped in through the kitchen door. The house was silent. Her parents were still asleep. She splashed her face with cold water from the sink and then went upstairs, peeled off her sweaty, smoky clothes, and slept, dreamlessly.

*   *   *   *

Cat's parents never said anything. Maybe they genuinely didn't hear her come home; maybe they preferred to remain in a state of denial. Either way, Cat was relieved.

Her slate was full of messages from Miranda and Oscar. She deleted them all without reading them. She had the entire weekend before she had to go back to school and deal with the repercussions of the party, and so she put Monday out of her mind. She wanted to pretend her friends didn't exist.

She spent a lot of time in Finn's room, weaving while he worked on his computer. She didn't care what she made—she needed to do something with her hands. Sometimes Finn watched her.

"May I try?" he asked.

"Do you know how to do it?"

"Theoretically."

Of course. He knew everything theoretically. Cat gestured for him to sit beside her on the bed, and pushed the table with the loom over in front of him and handed him the shuttle.

"Go at it," she said. "I'll tell you if you're screwing up."

"Thank you." Finn picked up the shuttle.

Cat leaned back against the wall. His movements were clumsy, like he wasn't used to the feel of the yarn, but he did everything correctly. It calmed her, watching him. She'd been on edge all day. Distracted. Anxious. *Betrayed.*

"Finn," she said as he hunched over the loom. He looked up at her expectantly. "Thank you. For picking me up. That was . . . kind. And thanks for not ratting me out."

"It was no problem."

Cat laughed. "Oh my God, you almost didn't sound like a butler for a minute there."

"Dr. Novak wrote a new linguistic program for me. He's attempting to incorporate more idioms into my speech patterns."

"Idioms are a bitch."

Finn stopped weaving and looked out the window above his desk. Cat watched him in profile. He looked so much like a person. A person she would notice if she saw him at school or at one of the shows at the VFW hall, if she'd never met him. Then he glanced back down at the loom, back over at her.

"That was also an idiom," he said. "It wasn't included in the list Dr. Novak provided for me. I've added it."

"It was an idiom about idioms."

"Yes." Finn smiled.

Cat looked at the fabric Finn had woven. The stitches were perfect. They did not look handmade. They'd been done by a machine.

"This is very enjoyable." Finn nodded toward the loom.

"I know," said Cat. "You can do it as long as you want." She laid her head on his shoulder without thinking. He turned his face toward her and his hair tickled across her forehead and she laughed and he went back to weaving. She watched the movement of his hands and for the first time in a long time she considered the mystery of Finn: the mystery of the clockwork inside his tall slim body, the circuit boards and memory processors. She knew they were there. She'd heard her father talking about them with his scientist friends, his colleagues from the university two towns over. She had memorized Finn's specifications years earlier: the only information she'd ever been able to wring out of her father about Finn's history. She used to recite those specifications to herself when she couldn't sleep, a string of meaningless numbers and abbreviations.

Meaningless, Cat thought. Meaningless to her. Finn combed the weft thread across the loom. Meaningless to her, but not to him.

*   *   *   *

Cat broke up with Oscar underneath the tree in the courtyard. All their friends watched from the branches, like wild cats. She did it first thing in the morning because the minute she saw him—his long knotted hair, his ratty old band shirt—her heart began to pound and she tasted wax on her tongue. Predictably, he called her a bitch. Cat fled the courtyard before he could say anything more hurtful, about her father, her family, Finn.

Miranda found her at lunch, hiding in the muggy cafeteria, surrounded on all sides by a wall of noise. She slid onto the bench across from Cat and folded her hands on top of the table.

"I heard you broke up with Oscar," she said. "Good idea. I totally beat him up for you at the party. I guess you got home okay?" It was hard to see the concern beneath all her eye makeup.

"Finn came and picked me up."

Miranda nodded. Cat stirred the lumpy gravy on her plastic tray. It was unrecognizable as food.

"So what'd you think?" Miranda leaned forward over the table and lowered her voice. "I mean, obviously it's better if you're prepared for it. But—"

"I don't want to talk about it." Cat stood up, took the tray to the stack next to the trash cans, and walked away.

Some days went by, then weeks. Cat avoided Oscar despite the smallness of the school, and she didn't talk to Miranda as much as she used to. The days grew longer and hotter. It didn't rain. Every time Cat went outside the sky was a clear wash of bright blue, utterly cloudless, but after a while that cloudlessness felt oppressive, like there was nothing between Cat and the blinding sun. The grass dried up. The garden withered. The river turned into white rocks.

One day Finn knocked on Cat's door while she was lying under the fan and listening to music. He came in and sat down in the chair at her desk.

"I was thinking," he said, "about the question you posed to me."

"What question?" Cat swept half of her hair to the side and began to comb it into a braid.

"You asked if I thought you were pretty."

"What?" she said. "Oh my God, that was like two years ago." She had forgotten it—mostly. At night sometimes, or soaking in a cool, lavender-scented bath—then she remembered, how he didn't answer.

"It was a difficult question," he said. "It's not something I'm generally called upon to consider. Previously, I had only contemplated the concept of beauty with regards to works of art."

Cat finished braiding the other side of her hair. She sat up and stared at him.

"If you're going to say no," she said, "I don't really want an explanation."

"I'm not going to say no."

Cat's heart stopped beating, and then started again, fluttery and strange.

"I realized, after you asked me, that I needed to work with a different algorithm. The definition of beauty in a human being is different from the definition of beauty in an object. This is a philosophical question, of course, and philosophy is difficult for me. It's too abstract. I still have problems with abstraction." He paused. His eyes shook. "I considered facial shape and the writings of Vitruvius. I also took into account my own experiences with you. I find it . . . pleasant to be around you." He looked at her then. Cat's skin warmed.

"So my answer to your question," he said, "is yes. I do think you are pretty."

All the breath left Cat's body. Since the night she'd asked Finn that question, she had been called pretty—by boys at school, by friends of her parents. She had, in fact, been called a myriad of adjectives for that same concept. Beautiful. Gorgeous. Hot. But all other compliments were thoughtless compared to this one. This was the only time such a statement had any thought behind it.

"Thank you," she said finally.

"You're welcome." He regarded her with his dark eyes. Cat crawled forward on her bed and reached across the chasm between them to pull the chair, with him in it, closer to her. It was heavier than she expected. She took one of his hands in her own and he looked down at it, their hands holding, but he didn't say anything.

There was something electric in the air, like static or lightning. It shimmered against Cat's skin. Her room was so bright. The inside of a lightbulb. It made her dizzy. The only thing she could clearly see was Finn's face: everything else receded into the distance, blurring away at her periphery. She heard the sound of her own breath. She heard the fan clicking overhead.

She leaned forward and pressed her mouth against his. At first he did nothing. Cat did not give up. When three or four seconds had passed, his head tilted and his mouth parted. Cat wrapped her arms around his shoulders, leaning across the space between the bed and the chair, pulling him close. His mouth was dry and tasted vaguely metallic. He kissed as though he knew how. His hands looped around her waist. They pulled their faces apart and looked at each other. Cat could barely breathe. He moved forward, out of the chair, and sat down on the bed beside her and resumed the kiss, seamlessly. She put one hand against the side of his face. That soft skin. She touched his hair, lightly, and it clung to her fingers as she moved her hands through it.

His hands stayed at her waist, pulling her in tight, pulling her in close.

Cat ran her hand over the top of his head, around to the base of his neck. He seemed to stiffen slightly in her arms, but she kissed him more intently, afraid he would pull away, and her hands found something just above his hairline, an imperfection in the skin, like a—

Finn suddenly slumped over, dead weight on top of her. Cat

screamed. Finn didn't move. She put her hands on his shoulders and shimmied out from underneath him. "Finn?" she whispered. Panic rose up in her throat; her mouth was dry as cotton. She pushed his hair out of his eyes. They stared blankly at the wall across the room. "Oh God, Finn, oh God, oh God. What the fuck happened?" She nudged him, and then shook him hard, but nothing happened. He didn't even look like a person anymore. He looked like a mannequin. He looked like a doll. He looked like the empty shells of cicadas she found clinging to trees.

Cat backed away from the bed. She stared at Finn so long and so intently that she was certain he'd moved—but no. It was only the fan blowing his hair.

"Get up," she whispered. "Please."

Nothing. The sweat prickling up out of her skin felt like ice. Cat stumbled out of her room. "Dad!" she called out. She ran downstairs, looked for him in the living room and the kitchen. Not there. She went down to his lab and found him standing in front of a computer, frowning at the screen. She ran in without knocking. "Daddy! Something's happened to Finn!"

"What do you mean?"

"He just . . . We were talking and he just . . . slumped over and he's not moving and—"

"You were just talking?" He hit a keystroke on the computer and started walking toward her. "Where is he?"

"Upstairs, in my room."

Her father pushed past her and jogged upstairs. She followed him. When he saw Finn slumped over on the bed he took a deep breath and turned back toward Cat, who leaned against the doorframe, her hands in her pockets, not wanting to look her father in the eye.

"You were just talking, were you?"

"Yeah." Cat tucked her hair behind her ears and widened her eyes.

"I see. Well, it looks like he got shut off somehow."

Cat didn't say anything. There was a sickening weight at the bottom of her stomach. *Shut off.*

Her father walked over to Finn. He gently lifted up Finn's head and slipped his hand underneath the hair at the back of Finn's neck. Finn's eyes flashed silver and then faded back into black. He sat up abruptly and looked around the room.

"What happened to me?" he said.

"Cat said you were talking," her father replied, in a tone that suggested he didn't believe it.

"Oh yes," said Finn. "Yes, I remember now." He looked over at Cat and she wanted to shrink up into the shadows in the hall, her cheeks burning. "We were talking. Something—" He stopped.

"Right," said Cat's father. "Finn, go down to the lab. I want to check to make sure nothing's damaged. Cat . . ." He walked up to her and leaned in close. "For God's sake, be more careful," he whispered. "And don't tell your mother."

"We didn't do anything!"

"Save it." He pushed past her, turned to look over his shoulder. "Come on, Finn." His heavy, angry footsteps faded down the hallway. Cat ran up to Finn before he could follow.

"I'm so sorry," she said. "I didn't know." She resisted the urge to touch him. "You're not mad at me, right?"

"I understand," he said. "You didn't do it on purpose."

"No, God, I would never do that! That would be a . . . a violation."

"Yes," he said. "A violation." His eyes vibrated. "But how could you know that? You can't be shut off."

Cat stared at him hopelessly, not knowing what to say. She wanted to kiss him again, wanted to do it over. She felt a surge of desire, thinking about it. She could keep her hands away from the back of his neck. She could use them to explore every other part of his body.

But he only nodded at her, and left the room.

*   *   *   *

Her father never said anything about Cat accidentally shutting off Finn. Not to Cat, not to her mother.

The kiss was never repeated. Cat was too embarrassed to ask after it, embarrassed and shy, and Finn never said anything about it, either. Things went back to normal, more or less. She spent less time weaving fabric and painting pictures in Finn's bedroom. She went back to eating lunch with Miranda and even attended the occa-sional house party, although she always guarded herself carefully at them and avoided Oscar as best she could.

In her last year of high school she took the various standardized tests needed to get into college, the only one of her friends to do so. Her math scores were abysmal. This didn't surprise anyone.

"I suppose," her mother said, "some people just aren't cut out for college."

They were eating dinner. Cat pushed the food around on her plate. She wanted to go to college. She liked learning—she just didn't want to study engineering. One of the academic counselors at school had told her about an old-fashioned liberal arts university in the city, where they studied in the classical style, reading works of literature and philosophy spanning three thousand years. To Cat, it sounded like her childhood, reading Homer with Finn. She had applied that day, not telling anyone, spending two hours in her room writing an essay about the nature of personhood. She wrote about Finn.

"Have you thought about trade school?" her mother said. "You could learn to be a lab technician, maybe."

"No," said Cat.

"Helen, just leave her alone," her father said. He was working at the table, on some contract from China that Cat understood was vaguely related to the space program. But right now he looked up from his computer in earnest. "I'm sure you'll find your way, sweet-heart."

Cat sighed and stabbed a green bean.

Her senior year passed uneventfully. She went to a football game for the first time and sat for three hours on the grass-covered cement bleachers, drinking a Coke that tasted of cardboard. She finally built a functioning circuit board in one of her engineering classes (although Finn helped her, a little). Miranda convinced her to go to the prom as her date, since Miranda had sworn off boys and all their perfidy for the time being. Miranda drove the two of them into the city to buy dresses, and on prom night Cat's mother took pictures of them with their arms linked together underneath Cat's citrus tree in the garden, the yellow sun catching the highlights in their hair, making them both glimmer. They gave each other corsages but danced with other girls' dates at the dance.

Then, Cat received an e-mail notice that she had been accepted to the liberal arts college. It was waiting for her when she woke up one morning, sunlight washing out the computer screen almost entirely. Cat read and reread the e-mail: they were even offering her a scholarship. She brought up the e-mail on her comm slate and ran downstairs. She went to the laboratory first, sticking her head into the doorway and shouting, "I got into college!" before ducking back out. She found her mother out in the garden, pulling weeds.

"Mom," Cat said, pushing through the wrought iron gate. "Mom, I got into college."

Her mother looked at her, dropped a clump of weeds to the ground. "What?" she said. "Where? Your scores weren't high enough—"

"Just my math scores. My qualitative scores were almost perfect. Here." She thrust out the acceptance e-mail. Her mother slipped off her gloves, took her comm slate, and read it.

"Oh, Cat, this is one of those pointless rich kid schools. You're not going to be able to get a job—"

"Who cares?" snapped Cat. "They gave me a scholarship. And I am a rich kid."

Her mother sighed and drew her hand across the top of her forehead. "Cat, you don't understand how the world works. You're too sheltered. You're going to wind up a housewife or a secretary, going to a school like that. Women can do anything they want now."

Cat snatched the comm slate away. "I'm going."

The screen door slammed, and her father and Finn appeared at the gate of the garden.

"Now, what's this I hear about college?" her father said.

"I got in!" Cat ran up to him, showed him the e-mail. "They're giving me a scholarship and everything."

"That's wonderful!" Her father encircled her in his arms, drawing her up to his massive chest.

"Congratulations," said Finn.

Cat thought about hugging him, too, but just smiled shyly instead.

"Where's the school located?" Finn asked.

"In the city," said Cat's father. "Not far from here. Still." He paused and stroked the stubbly beard that had begun to appear over the last few days. "Still, we're going to want you to come back and visit. And that'd be a lot of easier if you had your own—"

"Car?" said Cat. "You're finally going to let me get a car?"

"I think you only deserve it." Cat shrieked and threw her arms around his shoulders. He laughed and picked her up off the ground, the way he did when she was still a little girl. Her mother stayed in the garden. She pressed her hands to her hips and smiled weakly, but her features darkened, and Cat's celebratory mood, for a moment, wavered.

FOUR

One night at the end of Cat's first year at college, they all went out to the bar—Cat and her roommate, Lucinda, and some of Lucinda's friends, as well as Cat's recently acquired boyfriend, Michael, a pale, intense boy who was obsessed with folk music and mid-twentieth-century office supplies—to watch the landing of the first manned mission to Mars.

The bar was the same dim, ruby-lit bar they always went to after class. Usually it was half-empty, and so sometimes the owner let them smoke cigarettes inside while they listened to the lo-fi bands that played there during the week. But on that night, the night of the Mars landing, the room was crowded with students from both the liberal arts school and the school of technology down the street. The bartender had turned on the huge in-wall monitor, and everyone was hushed and still as they watched, like they were sitting in the pews of a church. Cat and her friends crowded around a tiny, wobbling table and ordered a round of imported beer. Michael pulled out a cigarette and stuck it in his mouth but didn't light it. He leaned back in his chair, trying to look nonchalant.

Up on screen, a newscaster interviewed a trio of scientists who had worked on the project. Cat thought she recognized one of them, from her parents' dinner parties. A tall, thin man with a puff of brownish gray hair. The other two were Chinese, subtitles flashing as they spoke. Cat pulled out her comm slate, set it in her lap under the table, and sent a message to Finn: *Are you watching?*

He responded *yes*. Cat smiled to herself. She had spoken to him a few days ago over video chat, sitting in the empty bathtub with her slate propped on top of her knees so Lucinda couldn't listen in.

"Your father was contracted by the Chinese government to work on the Martian exploration project," he'd told her. "I helped him."

"Seriously?" asked Cat. "When?"

"Your sophomore year of high school, I believe."

"Wait—that's what you were doing back then? I thought you were just repairing the satellites or something. Why didn't you tell me?"

"I didn't think you were interested."

"Oh, come on, Finn! Freaking Mars!" She ran her fingers through her hair. She didn't want the conversation to end. "This drunk aeronautical engineering student told me some company's thinking about building a station on the moon. Like, a dwelling. Where people can live. But he also said the moon smells like cordite and I have no idea how he'd know that, so . . ." She shrugged.

"I didn't know that about the moon's scent, but your father mentioned the lunar station two months ago. He may accept a contract offer."

Cat laughed. "Well, I want you to tell me about it this time, okay? If he does decide to do it?"

Finn smiled a programmable smile and nodded.

Cat thought about that smile as she sat in the crowded bar. She folded her hand over the screen of her comm slate. Michael leaned over in his chair and looped his thin arm around her shoulders and squeezed.

"Who were you talking to?" His still-unlit cigarette bounced across his lower lip.

"No one," Cat said. "Someone I used to know as a kid." She slipped her comm slate into her purse and then set her purse on her lap. Michael smirked at her. He plucked out his cigarette, then leaned forward and kissed her on the mouth.

All the sound in the bar seemed muffled, as though they were caught in a snowstorm.

Michael sat back in his chair. Up on the monitor, the shuttle had just landed. She pulled away from Michael, leaned eagerly across the table. Michael shifted in his seat beside her.

The video's color was brighter than Cat expected, brighter and laced through with silver veins of static. Both of the astronauts had cameras mounted into their helmets, and the screen was split, one side for each astronaut. They looked at each other: two mirrored helmets, reflecting each other. And then they looked out onto Mars. *Mars.* It looked like pictures Cat had seen of the Midwestern Desert, only rockier, with a dusty yellow sky, and no sad, decaying farmhouses. Nothing moved. Not in the landscape on-screen, not in the bar on Earth. Cat held her breath and thought about Finn: he'd made something, some tiny thing—a chip, a jumble of wires, something—that helped propel that shuttle to another planet. But of course her father had taken the credit. He had to.

Someone sitting a few tables over from Cat and her friends started clapping, and then suddenly everyone was clapping and cheering and hollering. A couple of Cat's friends, despite all their neo-Beat technophobia, lifted their beer glasses up to the air. Even Michael looked pleased with the human race: a rarity for him, Cat had learned in the short time they'd been together. The cameras panned across the ocher landscape. The astronauts spoke to each other in Mandarin, their voices rippling with static. Cat pulled her slate out and wrote, *Everyone's clapping for you.*

Afterward, Cat and Michael and all the others spilled out of the bar into the cool, balmy night to have a smoke. Michael lit Cat's cigarette for her, leaning across the old wooden picnic table the bar had set up on the patio. He dropped his lighter into his shirt pocket and exhaled smoke up toward the starless, light-polluted sky.

"So there's another planet we can fuck up," he said.

Cat didn't say anything. She pulled her slate out of her purse. Finn had messaged her: *Why would they clap for me?* Her cigarette dangled from her lower lip as she tried to come up with a witty response.

"Or they'll build, like, space highways." Everyone laughed.

Cat wrote, *Because if it weren't for you, they'd never have gotten there!* Hit send. Slid her slate back into her purse.

"Don't be a slave to the machines," Michael said.

"Who's a slave?" Cat pretended to blow smoke into his face. He laughed and wrapped his arms around her and pulled her in close to his chest. Cat nearly dropped her cigarette on him in surprise. He was her first boyfriend since she'd come to college, and he was constantly surprising her with unannounced kisses and touches or unpredictable outbursts of emotion. He was nothing like the boys she'd known in high school—he was smarter, wilier, and Cat could never grasp hold of him, or of what he wanted from her.

He wasn't like Finn, either. "You check that fucking slate more than anyone I know," Michael said, his hand pressing into the curve of Cat's waist. Michael didn't even own a comm slate, just a beat-up disposable phone that he folded up in his wallet.

"It's because I'm more important than you," Cat said.

Michael laughed, leaned in, kissed her.

*　*　*　*

Later that night, Cat drove Michael back to his apartment. He was drunk from taking whiskey shots with a group of electrical engineers who'd been slumming it down at the bar, and the entire way home he kept leaning his head on her shoulder, singing old folk songs into her ear, songs about death and loss. His two favorite subjects.

Cat shook her head so that her hair flew across his face. "Stop," she said. "You're making me depressed."

Michael leaned away from her, against the passenger-side door, and laughed. "I don't fuck much with the future." His voice slurred. "You do it too much. That way lies only sorrow."

Cat fixed her gaze out the windshield. The lights of the city twinkled and flashed as she drove along the misty freeway.

"Well?" said Michael. "What do you say to that?"

"I don't know what you're talking about." She drummed her fingers against the steering wheel. They hadn't dated that long but she already knew he got like this whenever he was drunk.

"Oh, you know. The Disasters were a warning. We let things get out of hand and everything went to seed but we're up to our old tricks again, like we never learn. We're sticking humans on Mars! That's not going to end well. And all the automatons I've seen around town. It's borderline slavery—"

"You weren't alive for the Disasters," said Cat. She wanted to change the subject. The topic of automatons was not one she ever wanted to discuss with Michael—and she certainly didn't want to discuss it tonight. "How would you know what it was like before?"

"Let's not fight," Michael said. "I'm just saying there's beauty in analog, is all. You liked that mixed tape I gave you."

At this, Cat smiled in spite of herself. The damned mixed tape. Michael had shown up at her apartment, the mixed tape in one hand, a bouquet of sunflowers in the other. He'd wrapped the mixed tape in homemade paper—his trademark, she later learned from Lucinda. *Watch out for the homemade paper,* Lucinda had told her. *It means he's trying to get in your pants.* But she let Cat listen to the tape on her restored tape player anyway.

"You *did*." Michael laughed, kicked his feet up on the dashboard. "I *knew* it."

"Oh, shut up."

Michael laughed again and refolded his legs under the seat. Then he leaned across the car and kissed Cat on the neck. She swatted him away. The car swerved between lanes, but there was no one out on the road. The headlights danced across the mist.

Michael slid back down in his seat and started singing again, softly, under his breath. Cat drove until they came to the exit. She recognized the song. It had been on the mixed tape he made for her: all ancient music, nothing recorded after the 1940s. Another trademark of his.

The streetlights blinked red and amber. The sky was violet with light pollution. Cat drove Michael back to his apartment, but it was not Michael she thought about.

* * * *

A few days after the Mars landing, Cat went down to the vice stand where she worked as a vice girl. It was fashionable at the time, if you were pretty enough and didn't actually need a job, to work as a vice girl. (Those girls who did need jobs, who didn't have parents who were engineers or corporate CEOs, tended to work in the university archives.) Cat worked only part-time. She told her parents she was a receptionist for the philosophy department.

The vice stand was a little one-room glass building set into a wide, black parking lot that ran up against the interstate. The back walls were lined with mirrors and rows of overpriced and overtaxed cigarettes. Cat worked at night, and she started her shift as the sun set: on that particular evening the air was charging up for an early summer storm. The palm trees in the parking lot whipped back and forth in the wind. The sky was a peculiar yellowish purple, and occasionally the entire world whited out for half a second from the sheet lightning.

Cat didn't feel particularly safe in her little glass box on the interstate, sitting perched on a stool in the center of the room, wearing a bright, backless dress and a pair of heels. She was supposed to roll cigarettes as she waited for a customer to pull up in front of the stand—roll cigarettes and wave at the cars driving by. Instead, the storm churning up outside, she surreptitiously checked the weather report on her slate, holding it underneath the table laid out with canisters of tobacco and rolling papers and elaborate, designer cartons. The storm was expected to pass over the city without doing any major damage, and there was no call for a curfew. Yet.

By the time the rain began to fall, smearing the freeway lights and the neon across the panes of glass, any nervousness and excitement from the storm had faded away. Working in the vice stands was boring. None of Cat's friends who sat scattered across the city in their own glass boxes talked about this boredom. Cat rolled another cigarette and slid it into a slim cardboard carton, watching the pattern of rain slip and slide down the glass. She let one of her shoes drop off her foot. A car, sleek and black and reflecting the vice stand's bright neon lights, pulled up outside. The customer bell chimed.

Cat jumped up, felt around with her bare foot for her lost shoe. She picked up the umbrella they kept next to the table and popped it open. The doors slid silently open, and a spray of rainwater splashed across her face. She smiled anyway. The car's driver's-side window dropped down, and a man with messy hair, wearing an expensive-looking black suit, leaned out and squinted against the rain. An LCD monitor glowed on his dashboard—it was one of those expensive programmable cars. Completely automated.

"Pack of Lucky Strikes," the man said, handing over his bank card. "How're you doing this evening? Keeping dry? You look cold."

Cat smiled. It was colder outside than she expected, and the sound of rain beating against the asphalt much louder. The man smiled back. "I hope to hell you have someone waiting at home to warm you up," he said. "It'd be a shame otherwise."

"I might." Cat laughed the way she'd seen other girls do it, the way that was becoming more and more natural as time went on: she tossed her hair, flashed her teeth, and made certain her eyes lit up all the while. Otherwise, her laughter sounded forced and fake. And fakeness was the sort of thing the vice stands worked to avoid. When Cat was first hired, her manager sat her down at one of the headquarter offices and said, "If people wanted to buy cigarettes from a machine, we'd save a whole lot of the money we lose off human error, and stock these things with robots. So you better act interested in every fucking customer." And Cat had blinked and wrung her hands under the table and wondered what she had gotten herself into.

The man shooed her back toward the stand. Cat tottered inside, oily rainwater splashing up around her ankles. The dress was so thin it felt as though she weren't wearing anything at all. She plucked a pack of Lucky Strikes off the shelf, ran his card through the computer, and took a deep, preparatory breath before going back out into the rain. The misty wind blowing off the freeway whipped her hair into her face as she handed the cigarettes and the card over to the man.

"Thanks, darling." The man fell back against his car seat, slapped the pack against his palm a few times, slid two cigarettes out. Handed one to her. "Hope that keeps you warm till you get home," he said.

"Thanks," said Cat. "I hope I can light it in this weather." She laughed again and pushed her hair out of her face. It was a stupid joke. She tucked the cigarette behind her ear and went back inside. They always gave her free cigarettes. She kept them in a cheap metal cigarette holder, saving them for when she went out to the bars, so she wouldn't have to pay the exorbitant taxes on a new pack.

So it was a boring job, but it had its perks.

Around midnight, Michael's rattling Volvo pulled up outside the stand. The rain still fell steadily across the freeway. Cat had rolled so many cigarettes she could no longer feel her fingers. She didn't feel like talking to him right now. It was exhausting, being someone's girlfriend. But his car sat idling in the lot, and for that reason alone she picked up the umbrella and went out into the storm.

"Working hard?" Michael leaned out into the shimmering neon haze. The lights from the stand smoothed out the gaunt features of his face. He almost looked like Finn, pale and dark-eyed. Cat ruffled his hair.

"Are you going to buy something or not?" she asked.

"I don't know if I can afford to buy cigarettes right now. Really just came to see you." He grinned.

"I'm not giving you anything for free." As she spoke, Cat was suddenly overwhelmed by a dizzying rush of sadness. She took a step backward, held out a hand to steady herself. She missed Finn. She missed him with a strength and a ferocity she had not thought possible. Where had that come from? Michael looked too much like him. He looked too much like him even though he didn't act like him at all. And the Martian landing had her thinking about him more. Cat wrapped her arms around her torso. Out on the freeway the cars zoomed by, kicking up a froth of dirty rainwater. Occasionally, someone honked, flashed their headlights. She heard the neon sizzling in the sign overhead.

"You okay?"

"Yeah." Cat smiled. Her eyes did not light up. "Just damp."

"Yeah, I can imagine." Michael ducked back into the darkness of the car and reemerged brandishing a flask. "Gentleman Jack. Drink up."

Cat took a sip. It scalded the back of her throat. But she did feel a momentary warmth in her core. She handed the flask back to Michael.

When Cat came home from work later that night, Michael was sitting on the couch in the living room of her shabby apartment, watching videos on her laptop. Lucinda had let him in. Cat stood in the entryway, shaking the water droplets from her hair. He closed the laptop and gazed at her, leaning his head back against the wall. He didn't look like Finn anymore. Cat slipped off her shoes and sat down beside him and immediately he began to kiss her, slowly at first and then more urgently. "Lucinda went to bed," he told her, kissing along her neck. Cat closed her eyes. She had not stopped thinking about Finn all evening: the kiss in her bedroom, the moment right before she accidentally found the switch on the back of his neck. She had thought about that moment so often during the past few years it had dried out. It was stale, like old, odorless potpourri. But she still went back to it, because it was the only one.

What she wanted, what she really wanted more than anything, was for Finn to kiss her, and not the other way around.

Michael pushed her down so she was lying on her back. She slipped her hands up inside his sweater. He jumped.

"Your hands are cold," he whispered. Cat didn't say anything in return.

Michael kissed her more and more urgently. He peeled off the layers of her clothes. Cat felt a distracting twinge of guilt, as though she were caught in an act of betrayal. Only she was not certain whom she was betraying. If it was Michael, or if it was Finn.

*   *   *   *

After that first out-of-season storm, the usual May heat crept back around the college campus, making the bougainvillea and jasmine that hung off the old, broken-down telephone poles wilt and wither. The college was in a part of the city that hadn't been destroyed during the Disasters, and so it hadn't been reconstructed, either, like the neighborhoods Cat had visited as a child.

The air buzzed, the way it always did in the summer.

On one especially sunny afternoon Cat decided to ride her bike to the little clapboard snow cone stand on the corner. It was just hot enough to be a crazy idea, but Cat was in a crazy mood: nostalgic and wild. The sort of mood where you eat snow cones and pretend you're ten years old again.

As she rode down the sidewalk, the hot wind blustering across her face, she wove around the detritus of the past: the crumbling concrete, the abandoned houses overgrown with wild grass and dandelions. Only half a mile away all the buildings gleamed with reinforced metal and hurricane-proof glass, their sleek lines cutting silver gashes across the canvas of the sky. Only half a mile away the entire world was brand-new.

There was no line at the stand, and after Cat received her snow cone from the automated machine, she wheeled her bike to the little city park across the street. She let her bike drop down in the silky bluegrass, and then she sat on a cement bench overlooking a tangle of wild morning glories wilting in the heat. She nibbled on her snow cone, the condensed milk eating away holes in the sugary, blackberry-flavored ice. It was all turning back into syrup faster than she would have liked. Sweat dripped down the back of her neck.

As she ate, Cat heard giggling coming from behind a row of hibiscus bushes. A rustling. Then the bushes ripped open in a flurry of leaves and bright pink and orange flowers, and a little girl burst out, her face and hands streaked with mud. The little girl giggled again. She turned back around to face the bushes, which still rustled and shook and vibrated.

An android stepped out.

Cat nearly dropped her snow cone on her knees. The android clapped his gleaming metal hands together. He laughed. The newsfeed had been talking about this all year, how androids built from the updated schematics of the old post-Disaster automatons were becoming more affordable, how middle-class families snatched them up as nannies. But Cat had never seen one before today.

The android looked old-fashioned. He had narrow, lithesome limbs, but he still moved with a strange jerky motion, one Cat noticed in the mass-produced androids she had seen in history videos. When he laughed, though, a light seemed to switch on beneath the thin metal of his face. This made the little girl jump up and down and screech with delight.

The android was like Finn, and he was not like Finn.

Finn. Cat sighed. She used her spoon to crunch the snow cone's melting ice up with the condensed milk, but when she took a bite she could hardly taste it. She was too distracted by the android and the little girl, wishing she could watch them but not wanting to seem rude. So she listened instead. The android kept laughing. Finn had never laughed that much when she was a child—when she was that little girl's age. Still, she had considered him her best friend.

There was a butterfly flurry of yellow fabric as the little girl blazed past Cat's park bench, the android trundling along behind her. Cat looked up from her snow cone. The android paused, looked at her, and tilted an invisible hat in her direction.

"Ma'am," he said. His voice had a metallic twang to it, like a steel guitar.

Cat smiled, lifted up her snow cone cup in response.

When the android turned away from her to follow after the little girl, Cat saw a string of numbers emblazoned across his back. A manufacturer's label. 7829H-23. The twenty-third android out of a set of a hundred. Or was it a thousand? It was standard, but Cat could never remember the base amount.

Finn didn't have a manufacturer's label.

Cat had looked for it once. When she was maybe thirteen, fourteen. She had convinced Finn to go swimming with her in the river, the water cold and green-black-gray and tipped occasionally with white froth from the rocks jutting up out of the bed. Finn had removed his shirt. When he waded out into the water, Cat hung behind, looking at the ridge of his spine. It looked just like her own spine, only paler. No numbers.

"Finn," Cat had called out. He turned around. Cat put one foot in the water, jumped back at the surprising coldness of it.

"Yes?"

"You don't have a number across your back," Cat said. "Like the Disaster automatons."

Finn blinked at her. For a moment Cat thought a shadow had gone across his face, like a cloud sliding across the sun. But then she decided she had just imagined it.

"No," he said. "I don't."

Cat carefully put another foot in the cold water. She inched forward. "I thought most robots had a manufacturer's ID."

"I don't have one," Finn answered. "I believe I'm one of a kind."

Cat closed her eyes and splashed forward in the water, wanting to get all the cold over with. She shrieked as her skin prickled into goose bumps. Finn stood motionless, his own skin still smooth.

"So you don't know who ma . . . where you're from?" She was glad he didn't have a manufacturer's ID—she didn't like to think of him as being *made*, even then. Still, sometimes she asked her father for details. He never supplied them.

"I'm from Kansas." The stock response.

I'm from Kansas. The last words she remembered from that day before the cold shocked her system out of order. Back in a city park in the middle of a very hot afternoon, Cat closed her eyes and thought of all the times she had asked her father about Finn's background. *It's of no concern to little girls.* Or, when her parents had started acting weird about her friendship with Finn, right before they sent her off to that high school in the town: *He was made by a colleague of mine. That's all you need to know.*

All you need to know.

Cat sighed, stood up, dusted the loose grass off the back of her shorts. She pitched her half-finished snow cone in a nearby trash can, disguised by the city with honeysuckle, got on her bike, and rode back to her apartment. She felt listless, distracted. Bored. Her boredom made her want to have sex. So she called Michael. After all, he was her boyfriend.

* * * *

Cat was sprawled across her bed, listening to one of the scratchy, old-fashioned bands Michael always talked about. The current song faded out and before the next began Cat heard her slate chiming faintly in the bottom of her bag. It was her father. The video was turned off on his end—voice only. Strange.

"Kitty-Cat?" His voice sounded distorted and frail. Like maybe he'd been crying. Cat had never seen her father cry. Her stomach clenched up. Something was wrong.

"Daddy? Are you okay? Did something happen?"

"Your mother. It's . . . she . . ." He took a long breath. It sounded like shuddery, disjointed static over the slate. Cat's heart pounded. "Oh, Cat, there was an accident . . . She, she, oh God . . . She's dead."

In that moment, the weight of the Earth fell away from Cat. She floated above the dusty apartment floor, and she could no longer hear Michael's twangy music, only a rushing sound in her head like the ocean. "What?" she whispered.

Her father started crying again.

"Daddy," she said. "Daddy, tell me what happened. I'll come home right now. I'll—"

"Cat?"

"Finn." She gasped his name like she'd been holding her breath. "Finn, do you know what happened?"

"Your father is very upset," he said. "You should come home immediately."

"Do you know what happened?"

For a long time, he didn't answer. She gnawed on the crescent of nail hanging off her pinkie finger—she needed to hear the sound of his voice. She was drifting apart, molecule by molecule. The mechanical evenness of his voice would bring her back together. It was the only thought she had. *I need to hear your voice.*

"It was a car accident," he said finally. "This morning. She was turning onto the highway."

The rushing in Cat's ears grew louder. Something curled up tight inside her, so tight it disappeared completely.

"I'm leaving now," she said flatly.

Then she threw the slate across the room.

FIVE

Cat drove through the night, out of the city and its glimmering suburbs, down the wide, brightly lit highways surrounded on all sides by forests and gas stations. She didn't tell anyone where she was going: not Lucinda, not Michael. She simply picked up her bag, walked out to her car, and left.

She stopped once to use the restroom and buy a cup of bad coffee. The station buzzed with anemic fluorescent light. As Cat washed her hands, she stared at the mirror, trying to recognize herself.

She had not cried once. She had not even been on the verge of crying.

When Cat pulled up the drive of her parents' house, a thin, sickly band of sunlight appeared at the horizon, turning the rest of the sky gray. She stumbled up the front porch stairs and collapsed on the swing. The chains creaked. She could already feel the inevitable heat of the day.

The front door's screen slammed against the house's siding. "I heard your car," said Finn. Cat glanced over at him. "Your father is sleeping." He paused. "You should sleep, too."

"It's nearly daylight."

"You should still sleep." He moved closer, his footsteps loud and hollow on the wood of the porch. "Or would you prefer to eat something? People from town have been bringing food."

"Of course they have." Cat rubbed her eyes, itching from lack of sleep. She wasn't hungry. Finn knelt down beside the swing and put his hand over hers. This sudden touch jarred her. She didn't want it to end.

"Come inside," he said. "I'll bring your things in."

"I didn't pack anything."

They went into the house together. Finn held her hand, awkwardly, his long narrow fingers wrapped around her own. She was glad of it, because she didn't know if she would have had the strength to walk inside alone, into that dark dusty foyer choked with memories. Cat shuffled past the closet filled with old coats and rain boots, into the cavernous living room, dim from the drawn curtains. Finn led her into the kitchen, where the dawn illuminated the dishes of casseroles and pies and baked dips that had been brought over, Cat supposed, by the church ladies from town. The sight of all that food made her dizzy.

She wanted to lean against Finn but instead she steadied herself against the doorframe, pressing her forehead against the slick, painted wood. Finn did not drop her hand. She did not drop his.

"I don't want any of this," she said.

"You need to sleep," said Finn. This time, she didn't protest; she let Finn walk her up to her old room, where she curled up on her bed alone and fell asleep.

*　*　*　*

She woke up to a sunset, the room turned gold and pink from the liquid light spilling in between the slats in the blinds. Cat felt made of charcoal, like she left streaks of gray in the vividness of her room. She crawled out of her bed and took off her clothes, musty with the scent of travel and sleep, and put on an old sundress she hadn't worn since high school. She sat down at her vanity and brushed the curl out of her hair. She thought about putting on some mascara but decided not to. She sprayed perfume and watched the atomized droplets of fragrance dissolve in the room's golden light. It reminded her, sharply, of the night of the prom, her arm linked in Miranda's, her mother—*her mother*—snapping pictures of them out in the garden.

Cat knew nothing about the bureaucratic procedures of dying. She knew nothing about wills and testaments, nothing about funeral arrangements or the collection of life insurance. If it had been someone else's mother who died, she wouldn't even have thought to bake a casserole. *My mother is dead*, she thought, but she didn't believe it.

She went downstairs, looking for Finn or her father and finding Finn. He sat at the kitchen table in front of one of the portable computer stations, typing quickly, his eyes jerking back and forth.

"Dr. Novak asked me to arrange the funeral," he said. "It'll be in two days." He looked up at her. "I hope you're all right."

"I'm fine." *No, you're not. You still haven't cried.* "I just wanted to get something to eat."

Finn smiled. It seemed empty. *Had his smile always seemed empty?*

Cat went into the kitchen and filled a plate with scoops from each of the casserole dishes, not caring what any of it was. She microwaved the entire thing and took it out on the back porch to eat. She leaned back in the rickety plastic chair and watched twilight settle over the yard and the woods. The casseroles all tasted like cigarettes.

The stars came out. She had forgotten what they looked like. Cat went back inside and dropped her plate in the sink. She sat down at the dining room table and watched Finn type.

After five minutes, he stopped, his hands hovering above the computer. "Do you need anything?" he asked kindly.

Cat shook her head. She felt hollow. "Just let me watch you," she said.

"Watch me?"

Cat nodded. She wondered if Michael had tried to call her yet, or if he had shown up at her apartment. Lucinda would say, *I thought she was with you.* Cat was too numb to deal with them at the moment. Her comm slate was buried in her bag in her room, switched to silent. Maybe Michael was calling her right now. She didn't care. She just wanted to slump down at the table, her eyes heavy and dry, and watch Finn work.

*   *   *   *

Cat didn't speak to her father until the morning of the funeral. She didn't have anything black in her closet so she put on the dark blue dress she used to wear on the rare occasions she went to Mass. She dug out an old pair of flats, and then, without thinking, breezed into her parents' bathroom and took out her mother's jewelry box. She was fastening the necklace of pearls at the base of her throat when she realized she was stealing her mother's jewelry as though she were still alive.

"Cat?"

Her father materialized in the doorway, wearing a suit and a tie but looking faded and sleep-worn, his eyes sunk low into the contours of his face. The pearl necklace dropped to the counter. "Finn told me you were here. I'm sorry I hadn't seen you yet—" He stopped. "Her pearls," he said. "I gave those to her. On our first anniversary. I thought they were lost—she never wore them anymore." He walked up to where the pearls lay curled on the pale blue tiles, and then he lifted them to the light. "You should wear them."

Cat nodded because she didn't know what else to do. Her father was mourning. She could tell by looking at him. She could see in the lines of his face that he couldn't quite fathom how all the knowledge he had accrued in his lifetime—the knowledge of circuitry and diodes, the tangled arteries of wires—could not be applied to stop his wife from dying.

And Cat knew she looked the way she always did. Not distraught. Not half-dismantled. Her eyes weren't red from weeping. But she took the pearls her father offered her, and she followed him down the stairs to the living room where Finn sat in his ill-fitting suit. He stood up when they walked in, his face as dispassionate as Cat felt.

Finn drove them to the church in town, Cat sitting alone in the backseat of the car, her forehead pressed against the window. She watched the blur of trees. She watched the town appear building by faded building: the post office, the high school, the rows of clapboard bungalows. When they pulled into the grassy lot next to the church it was already full of cars and old women in dark dresses.

"Thank you," said her father, turning to look at Finn. Cat watched them from the backseat, the yellow sunlight casting their profiles in silhouette. "Thank you for taking care of this."

"You're welcome," said Finn.

"Everyone's staring at us," Cat said.

"Would you expect anything less?" said her father.

They stepped out of the car. Cat's father wrapped his arm around her shoulders as they walked through the grass to the open doors of the church, down the sunlit aisle to the front pew. The coffin was up on the altar, shut tight and covered in flowers. Cat closed her eyes. She could hear her father breathing beside her, and Finn whirring on her opposite side, and beyond that, the rustle of fabric and whispers.

The service began.

Cat sat still throughout, her hands folded in her lap, sitting and standing and kneeling by rote. She tuned out the cursory speeches given by some of the church ladies, irritated by the way they dabbed tastefully at the corners of their eyes. When her father went up to speak she felt the roar of blood in her ears, and for a moment she was back in her apartment in the city the day he called her, floating weightless above the floorboards. His cheeks glistened as he spoke. Cat curled her fingers around Finn's hand.

Did Finn glance over at her as she sat in the pew, shimmering with disbelief? She couldn't say. But he didn't drop her hand from his side, and Cat still felt hollow.

Afterward, they rode in silence to the cemetery—the cemetery Cat had once taken Finn to see, when she was a child and still convinced he was a ghost. Her mother had always loved it. She used to bring Cat there during the buzzing, indolent two-week spring to pick bouquets for the dining room table. There were no flowers now. It was too late in the season, and the summer sun had already begun to burn all the growth away.

Even this early in the day it was too hot, and so not as many people came out to the cemetery as they did the church. The few ladies who did brave the sweltering heat sniffled in the background, wiping at their eyes. They wept as they threw carnations down the hole in the ground. Cat threw an entire bouquet, yellow roses and bursts of baby's breath, but she did not cry. She was as dry as the weeds in the cemetery, as dry as the leaves shriveling up in the trees.

She still did not believe her mother was dead.

* * * *

In the weeks after the funeral, Cat rarely saw her father. He retreated down into his laboratory and emerged at strange hours—four thirty in the morning, two in the afternoon—looking disheveled and sleepy. He carried microwave dinners downstairs by the armful, never bothering to eat the meals Cat prepared and then shoved in the back of the refrigerator to be forgotten.

There was a deep resounding emptiness in the house, a vacuum where sound should have been, like the interior of a bell. It made Cat's teeth ache.

Finally Cat drove back to the city to pick up the clothes she had left behind. She played her music so loud on the way that when she walked up the stairs to her apartment her ears would not stop ringing. She unlocked the door and went in. Michael was there. He and Lucinda were sitting close to each other on the couch, and Lucinda jumped up when Cat walked in.

"Cat!" she said. "Oh my God, how do you feel? Are you okay?"

Cat stared at her levelly. People had been asking her this question for weeks, and she still didn't know the proper answer. *I feel empty. I feel fine. I think she's just on vacation.*

"Sad," she finally said. She glanced past Lucinda at Michael. Back at Lucinda. Lucinda seemed upset.

"You're cheating on me," she said. She was looking at Lucinda but she saw Michael flinch out of the corner of her eye.

Lucinda's eyes widened. She opened her mouth.

"It's fine," Cat said to her. "I'm not angry." And she wasn't, although she couldn't tell if this was because she never cared about Michael or if it was because she was so thoroughly numb. She looked over at Michael. "I can't deal with a boyfriend right now. So this is convenient."

"I always loved your open-mindedness," Michael said. "I'm so sorry about your mom." But there was a flatness in his voice, as if

Cat, in her grief, had abandoned him, tricked him into a compromising position with her roommate.

"I wasn't—we weren't—sure how long you were going to be gone," Lucinda said.

"I'm not staying. I just came to get my things." Cat looked over at her bedroom, the door hanging open the way she'd left it. "I need to stay with my dad. You know. For the summer. I'll pay rent or whatever. If you find someone to sublet—" She waved her hand in a circular motion. She didn't want to think about these things now. She had quit her job at the vice stand the day after the funeral, when she made all the calls to her friends, explaining what happened. She wanted everything to slip away. All her attachments.

Lucinda nodded again, her expression serious, even though Cat could tell she was pleased to have the apartment to herself for the next few months.

Cat left the city that day, in the hottest part of the afternoon, her clothes in a pile on the backseat. She threw the apartment key in her glove compartment and forgot about it. She turned the air conditioner on high but still her legs stuck to the car seat.

The summer wore on. Cat stopped going outside during the day. She downloaded old shows from her childhood and let them play in the background as she swept the hallway and wiped clouds of dust off the ceiling fans. Noise. There always had to be noise in the house. The silence was painful otherwise. When the summer storms started up, earlier than usual and more violent, Cat still hadn't cried. She and Finn spent a day between storms undertaking the annual ritual of fortifying the house. They locked the storm shutters down tight and checked for loose shingles on the roof. Cat watched Finn as he examined each of the generators, handing him any tool he needed. It was familiar and monotonous—the generators' dark hum, Finn's quick, assured movements. Even the desire bubbling up inside her was tedious, almost dull. Every year since she was a little girl she had watched him climb among the generators, a wrench dangling from one hand.

It felt so normal. That was the danger of monotony. It was so normal she could almost forget she should even be crying at all.

After the house was stormproofed, Cat's days fell into a languid rhythm, like the breath of someone sleeping. She herself slept whenever the hot sun came out, in the glaring afternoons, and stayed wide awake during the wild storms and the silent, silvery witching hours. She swept the floors. She scrubbed out the mold in her father's bathtub. She wiped away the toothpaste splatters from the bathroom mirrors. *The house will be clean when she gets home*, Cat thought while mopping the kitchen floor. *She'll be so happy.* Every week she emptied the refrigerator of all its leftovers so she could fill it back up again. She made vegetable curry and meat loaf, étouffée and roast chicken. She ate very little of any of it.

One rainy, humid afternoon Cat decided she should learn how to make pies from scratch. She opened up the kitchen computer and typed in *Joy of Cooking* and picked the most recent edition, settling on a recipe for lemon meringue. She walked barefoot into the gray drizzle to pick lemons from the tree in the garden, and when she pushed open the creaking, heavy gate something twinged in her chest. A loss of breath. She remembered the day, years ago, that she planted the lemon tree, digging out the dirt while her mother pruned the roses growing across the fence. Her mother had worn thick gloves but still her upper arms had been covered in tiny red scratches from the thorns.

Cat leaned against the garden gate. The dampness of the air soaked through her shirt, and the memory passed, leaving her clammy and disoriented. She took a deep breath. Then she walked past the spiny roses and the overgrown, unflowering jasmine, and plucked a trio of misshapen lemons, each the size of a fist, off a low-hanging branch of the tree. Her hair clung to the back of her neck, the side of her face. She went back inside.

She burned the first two crusts she made. The third crust she checked too frequently, paranoid, and it came out patchy and uneven, half-golden and half-beige. She filled the trash can with unwanted piecrusts, until finally she pulled one out of the oven and it was the color of almonds and its sweet, buttery aroma drowned out the acrid scent of burnt flour from her earlier attempts. She set it on the counter to cool and took her lemons and the flat metal grater out onto the screened-in porch so she could listen to the sound of the rain falling through the trees as she grated the peels into zest.

Finn was there, sitting in the chair where she had first seen him as a child, his narrow fingers moving across the screen of his computer tablet. She stopped in the doorway. His head turned toward her.

"I'm making a pie," she said.

"Why?"

Cat shrugged. She sat down on the porch's damp floor and scraped the lemon across the grater, stopping now and then to pull the yellow pulp away from the notches in the steel. She dropped the zest into the bowl next to her feet. She could feel Finn watching her, and she wanted to say something to him but she wasn't sure what. She felt suddenly self-conscious, the way she had when she was younger, in that time after her wild, forest-scented childhood but before she started high school. That awkward in-between place.

Her cuticles stung from the lemon juice.

"Can I help?" Finn asked. "Surely I can do that more quickly than you—"

"I'm fine." Cat rolled the lemon against her palm. "It's relaxing, kind of." She grated for a few moments longer and then set the lemon in the bowl, next to the pile of zest, and stood up. She wanted to look at Finn but she didn't.

Her heart was thrumming when she went back into the kitchen, and she set the bowl on the counter and glanced out the window as she washed her hands. His shadow appeared through the porch's gauzy screen, his fingers the only part of him moving. For a moment, Cat wondered who exactly she was learning to make a pie for.

"I wish you could eat," she said to the image in the window.

Then she mixed up the lemon filling, added the zest and the cream and the butter to a saucepan, and stood next to the stove, stirring idly, waiting for it to bubble and thicken. She poured all of it into that precious piecrust and tossed a towel over it to protect it from gnats and flies while she prepared the meringue.

"The meringue may not set properly." It was Finn.

"What?" Cat turned around and smiled at him, trying to cover up her voice's weird, nervous breathiness. "How do you know?"

"The weather," he said. "The humidity index is near one hundred percent."

Cat frowned.

"Meringue requires a certain amount of dryness in order to set."

"Okay, so how do you know *that*?" said Cat. "Do you seriously have the *Joy of Cooking* in there?" She tapped at her temple.

"I'm connected to all the databases in the house." He paused. "You know that."

Cat shrugged.

For a moment they stood in silence, and the room began to feel too hot and too humid, as though the outside was seeping in through hidden cracks in the windows and doorways. Cat touched her hair: she could not stop touching her hair. It had curled into ringlets from the weather. She needed to distract herself. So she turned to the refrigerator and took out the eggs.

Finn sat down at the table in the corner. "You're going to watch?"

"It's interesting to me."

Cat took a deep breath. She tried to pretend he wasn't there, tried to pretend his mechanical eyes were not tracing her steps across the kitchen. She followed the meringue recipe in the *Joy of Cooking*, sifting out the yolk through the sieve of her fingers. She worked steadily, conscious of the egg splatters across the kitchen counter, of the web of sugar glittering on the inside of her wrist. Still, she had trouble getting the eggs to whip, as Finn had warned her, and she asked him to help. He stood over the bowl and whipped the whites into peaks of airy foam like the tips of waves. His arm moved so quickly it became a blur. The sight of it hypnotized her. She felt as though she should be bothered by it, this reminder of his inhumanity, but she didn't want to stop watching.

When he finished, she uncovered the pie, smoothed the meringue out to the edges, and then ceremoniously placed the whole thing, wobbling from her shaking hands, in the oven.

"Can you set a timer?" she asked Finn.

"I already did. According to the recipe, we'll need to wait twelve minutes."

Cat slid into the chair across from him. He reached over and took her wrist in his hand and dusted off the sugar. It seemed to chime as it fell across the table. Cat shivered. She looked up at him.

He looked back at her.

"How's Daddy?" she said. "He stays downstairs all the time. I'm worried about him."

"He and I are working on a contract. He's worried about you."

"Me?"

Finn nodded.

"Oh, come on. I'm totally fine." *Liar.* "I'm baking pies. So normal."

Finn didn't say anything, and even in the shadows created by the storm clouds coalescing outside Cat could see his irises vibrating. Eventually, he said, "I am . . . concerned for you as well."

Cat did not know what to say to this. Her heart beat faster than a human heart should. She laid her head down on the table.

"Why?" she whispered.

"You seem to be denying . . . what happened to Mrs. Novak."

She isn't dead. She'll be home soon. There will be pies and clean ceiling fans waiting for her. "I don't feel anything," she said, so softly she wasn't sure she even said it out loud.

Finn's hand enveloped her own. Sheet lightning lit up the kitchen for one white second and then Finn said, "Twelve minutes." Cat stood up rotely, used a towel to take the pie pan out of the oven. The heat burned through the towel, singeing her skin. The meringue looked a little too brown on top. She carried the pie over to the table and set it in the center, halfway between her and Finn.

"It needs to cool completely," he said.

"I know." She leaned back in her chair. The rain fell across the yard with a rising chatter. Thunder cracked. Something was welling up inside her, drop by drop. Not grief. Something much more tumultuous. "Finn—"

There was a crackling in the walls, a low mechanical thump as the electricity failed.

Finn's eyes gleamed in the darkness. "Wait here," he said. "I can repair this."

"No." She threw out her arm in the direction of his eyes, felt the solidness of his arm. "Dad's generators are all working, right? Just leave it."

"You wish to sit in the dark?"

"Not really, but I don't want you to leave."

The glow in Finn's eyes brightened enough to cast light on the table, on the lemon meringue, on the place where Cat was clutching Finn's sleeve.

"Remember when I kissed you?" she said.

Silence. Then Finn said, "You're upset." He paused. "No, that's the wrong word. I don't—"

"I'm not upset," said Cat. She wrapped her fingers more tightly around his arm and pulled her chair around so she was sitting close to him. She didn't want to lose her contact with him, afraid that if she stopped touching him he would disappear as suddenly and inexplicably as the house's electricity. "I think there's something wrong with me."

"I wouldn't say—"

"I don't feel anything," she said. "I should, right? I don't feel sad or angry or guilty or any of the things you're supposed to feel. I'm just . . . here." She shook her head. "Why am I telling you all this? It's not like you'll understand."

Lightning flashed and for half a second she saw his features in the light, his blank face full of sadness.

Darkness.

"Can I kiss you again?" she said. "I promise I won't—"

"Yes," he said.

And so she did, cautiously at first, pressing her fingers lightly against the side of his face. She kept her hands away from the back of his neck. He wound his arms around her shoulders. The smell of him, clean and electric, nearly overwhelmed her. And for the first time since the start of that summer, she felt something: not grief, not mourning, but desire, and it twisted up inside her like a flame until that was all she was, a pillar of lust.

"Finn," she whispered, breathless. His mouth was at the side of her throat, his hands at the scoop of her waist. "Finn, how human are you?"

He pulled away, and her entire body rioted against it. She grabbed ahold of his hands, pressed them to her chest. *Never let him stop touching you.*

"I don't understand," he said.

"Sex, Finn. I want to know if you can have sex."

There was a long computational pause.

"I was built to resemble a human being in every way."

"Don't be coy."

Another pause. Then: "I'm not sure it would be appropriate."

"Appropriate?" Cat leaned in close to him. She heard the trees thrashing outside, the hail pinging against the roof. She was burning up. "Who the fuck cares?"

"I *can* do it," he said slowly. "It's part of my store of information—"

"Good," she said, standing up, pulling him along with her. She kissed him again, and he drew her close, his fingers slipping under the waistband of her skirt.

"We should go to my room," he said. "Dr. Novak could come up—"

"You're right." His room was the most private, tucked away in the rafters of the house. Cat curled up against his side, her arm slung around his waist, and they walked through the dark, still hallways, his eyes lighting the way, and Cat never once stumbled on a piece of wayward furniture or the uneven attic stairs. They went into his room and she climbed backward onto his bed, the bed he never slept in because he did not need to sleep, and pulled him on top of her. She took off his shirt, kissed his pale hairless chest. He had no heartbeat but she could hear something spinning inside of him. She was entranced by it. Like white noise, like the recorded sound of stars.

He cupped her face in his hands. There was a long pause, when they didn't move. Finn's body, warm beneath the cool, dry veneer of his skin, pressed against her own. Up here in the attic bedroom the sound of the rain and the hail was louder than in any other part of the house. It sounded as though the sky were falling in fragments all around them. Finn kissed her again. He took off her shirt, slipped her skirt down over her legs. She wrapped one leg around his waist, and his hand moved down between her thighs. The tiny golden hairs there stood on end. Cat gasped.

When he finally slipped inside her Cat cried out at the unexpected intensity of it: How long had she wanted this, without realizing it? How long had she wanted to feel him pressed against her? To understand the shape of his body? She buried her face in his shoulder and whispered his name as they rocked together. He made no sound, only nuzzled the top of her head as her hand trailed up and down the path of his electronic spine. She could feel a tension building inside her. Before that moment she had slept with a couple of boys, and none of them, not even Michael, made her bloodstream spark and boil like Finn was doing now. And now, and now—she shrieked. The world slid away. She dug her nails into the skin of his back.

In his arms, she shook and shook and shook.

*　*　*　*

Afterward, Cat lay flat on her back, Finn stretched out beside her. The tips of her fingers grazed the back of his wrist. The storm had moved farther on, away from the house, but the electricity was still out.

"Was that acceptable?" Finn asked.

"Yes," said Cat, the word drawn out of her as though on a tapestry needle. Something inside of her—her calcified heart, her numbness—had cracked in two, and she was trembling and she thought, *Here, this, this is what it feels like to feel something.*

She began to cry.

At first she just felt the slickness of moisture in the corners of her eyes, but then that moisture became tears, real tears, tears that rolled down the incline of her cheeks, that pooled in the crevices of her collarbone. She covered her face with her hands and immediately she sensed Finn leaning over her, felt his hands pressing lightly against her arms.

"I'm okay." She dropped her hands to her sides and looked up at him. Her tears threaded through her eyelashes. "I mean, it's not you. You were . . . everything I wanted. Amazing. It's—" She wept harder, and sat up on the bed, naked, not caring. The light coming in through the windows was the color of amber. She wrapped her arms around him, buried her face in his throat. He held her close.

"She's dead," Cat whispered. "She's dead."

Finn stroked her hair. He didn't say anything. Cat cried harder as the terrible realization of her mother's death grew, as all those things she had willed herself to forget came forward: Her mother was not on vacation. She would not come home to a clean house and a full refrigerator. She would not come home at all.

All summer Cat had been in a fugue. She had been made of mist and moonlight. Now, for the first time, she felt like herself again, like a person, a human, cast out of flesh and blood and muscle and bone. She leaned against Finn's chest, and her tears dropped onto his skin. All her sorrow gushed out of her. "Thank you," she told him, her voice scratchy and wet. She twisted around so their noses touched. Put one hand on his face. "Thank you for that."

"You're welcome."

"I'm so tired." It was true. As if she hadn't slept in days. She let her head drop, and Finn scooped her up like a kitten. He was so much stronger than he looked. She wrapped her arms gingerly around his neck and let him carry her down the stairs to her room, where she crawled naked under the cool sheets. Her eyes were wet. Finn sat by the side of her bed, and she stretched out her hand so that their fingers touched, and he said nothing, and she said nothing.

She cried until her tears turned to salt on her cheeks.

Finn never left her side.

PART TWO

SIX

Cat drove to her apartment after her shift ended at the vice stand. She'd managed to get her old job again when she moved back to the city after the summer of her mother's death. Now that she was older, she worked the day shifts, even though she still wore the same clicking high heels and low-cut sheath dresses. The sky above the city was steely, the exact color of the cement on the freeways, the exact color of the narrow roads winding through the old falling-apart neighborhood in which she lived. She parked her car on the street. The gutters were lined with piles of wet brown leaves that pasted themselves to the bottoms of her shoes.

It was nearly the end of winter. Cat was nearly twenty-eight years old.

Cat trudged through the damp, cold grass toward her apartment—a duplex converted out of a two-hundred-year-old house. Cat lived on the first floor. Someone was sitting on the front porch, next to the old table lamp Cat kept out there ever since the porch light fizzled out nine months ago in a shower of white sparks. Cat stopped in the middle of the yard and lit one of the cigarettes she'd gotten as a tip, her coat dangling off the crook of her arm. The person on the porch stood up and stuck his head out into the gray sunlight.

"Hello, Richard," Cat said. "You're off work early."

"I missed you, baby." Richard jumped over the porch's redbrick banister. He shook out his shaggy blond hair and frowned at the swirl of cigarette smoke. Cat walked up to him and turned her head to the right, politely, to exhale. Richard kissed her on the cheek.

"Seriously," said Cat. "It's only—what? Five thirty?"

"Halfast sent me home. She said I needed to take a break. That I work too much."

"You do work too much."

"I do what I have to do." He grinned. "I thought we could go eat somewhere. Mo Mong, maybe?"

Cat dragged contemplatively on her cigarette. Mo Mong. That name sounded familiar. It was one of those trendy fusion places he'd taken her when they first met. Sleek white robots instead of waiters. Expensive, as she recalled—every place he took her on those first few dates was expensive. "I'll need to change. Otherwise everyone will think I'm a call girl."

Richard laughed. Cat walked up to her front door, the thud of her shoes echoing dully across the hollow wooden porch. She dropped her cigarette into the teacup she used as an ashtray. Her keys jangled against the glass doorknob. She'd never given Richard a copy of her apartment key. He used to hint at it, but she always deferred, changing the subject to a topic less terrifying than the prospect of Richard being able to come into her apartment whenever he wanted. Eventually he quit bringing it up. This did not stop him from periodically waiting for her on the porch, without calling first.

Cat's apartment was small and threadbare and filled up easily with dust. The wooden floors gapped in certain places, wide enough that Cat routinely lost rings and tapestry needles into the darkness beneath the house. The panes of thick glass didn't fit snugly against their window frames, and the doors didn't always lock. It was the best she could afford on her vice girl's salary. The commissions from her artwork came too sporadically to justify moving anywhere with a higher rent.

She tossed her coat over the sagging couch and went into her bedroom to change. Richard trotted behind her, and when her dress dropped around her ankles, he applauded. Cat looked over her shoulder at him, winked, wiggled her hips. Then she pulled a sweater out of her closet, shivering in the draft seeping through the cracks in the windowsill.

Cat had been dating Richard for almost two years. They met on the day he sold a company he started in college for an unfathomable sum of money. He and his roommate turned business partner stopped at the vice stand on their way out to the bars to celebrate their wealth, only a few hours old at that point. Neither of them even smoked. Cat tottered out on her high heels. The cold wind blowing off the freeway whipped her hair into her eyes.

"Your most expensive hand-rolled," said Richard. He wore a gray suit but no tie. The car, Cat remembered, smelled of whiskey. When she took his credit card he winked at her, and that old roommate, who had since moved to Ontario and whose name Cat could never remember, leaned across his lap and shouted, "When do you get off? You're fucking beautiful."

"Thanks, honey," said Cat.

"Ignore him," said Richard. "He's an asshole."

Cat completed the transaction, running the card through the computer, boxing up the cigarettes she'd rolled herself earlier in her shift. She could hear their muffled shouting. Only once did she glance up. They flashed their headlights. She waved.

After that, Richard came to the vice stand regularly. He always bought the same cigarettes he bought that first night, although she never saw him in a suit again, just thread-worn sweaters and nondescript T-shirts. He asked her if she'd like to hang out some time. She said yes because he seemed like the sort of person her mother had wanted her to be. On that first date, she and Richard ate tapas and drank wine and went dancing at a rooftop club downtown. Richard couldn't dance. They went on another date and then another, and then they were a couple. Richard started a new company, not yet profitable, that dealt with artificial intelligence.

Cat still worked at that same vice stand where they met. She spent most evenings at the artists' studio she shared with a few friends, working on her tapestries. That was the thing about dating Richard:

he worked so much, sometimes weeks went by before she saw him again in person. It was an arrangement she liked, but this week he'd been coming around. This week, he wanted to take her to Mo Mong.

When Richard wasn't looking, Cat slipped a change of underwear into her purse. She suspected he would want her to spend the night at his apartment as well.

*   *   *   *

On Cat's next day off—a Tuesday, the sky that same unending gray, the air humid and cool—she rode the light-rail down to the yarn shop in the Stella. She was looking to start a new project. Another tapestry, maybe. Her last commission had been with a finance company, a series of abstract lines meant to suggest ticker tape. She'd enjoyed the project well enough, and was certainly grateful that it had become trendy in recent years for companies to display heirloom artwork in their lobbies and waiting rooms, but finishing up that tapestry had put her in mind to make one of her own.

Cat walked the two blocks to the yarn shop, her skin clammy from the weather, and slipped in through the side door. She headed straight for the shelves of mohair and cashmere. The prices were more than she could afford, but she wanted the tactility of that overpriced designer yarn. She picked out a handful of skeins from the pile, looking for any color that caught her eye: pale green, cream, gunmetal gray. Gossamer strands of fiber tufted out from the skeins. They looked as though they were shrouded in halos. The cashmere was soft against the skin of her arms.

She bought all of it, the entire armful. The old woman behind the counter recognized her, asked her about the finance company commission.

"Oh, you know," said Cat. "I'm having to deal with the repercussions of being a sellout." She rolled her eyes and grinned.

"That friend of yours was in here," said the old woman. "The flamboyant one."

"Miguel," said Cat. "He wants to learn how to knit." She dropped her voice conspiratorially. "He's hopeless at it."

The old woman laughed. She dropped the skeins one by one into a thin, transparent bag, one of those new bags made of synthetic material that dissolved harmlessly into water. "What are you making?"

"I don't know yet." Cat hated that question. They always asked it.

The old woman told Cat the total cost with a mercenary twinkle in her eye. Cat went dizzy for a second or two. It had been a long time since she'd come down to this yarn shop without some corporate account number. She handed over her credit card.

Cat left the shop and walked over to the studio—a converted warehouse that somehow survived the storms and the floods of the early part of the century, that apocalyptic time before Cat was born. As she walked she sweated underneath her thin coat. The air was choking on its own moisture. The brief winters seemed shorter and shorter the older she got.

Cat shifted her purchase from one hand to the other and wondered what she could make with all this designer yarn. Something personal, of course. No commissions. She had been in a strange mood lately, her sense of self tatted together like a piece of lace. Delicate. Barely held together. Richard had been stopping by her apartment too much. She knew without knowing that whatever she ended up weaving on the enormous floor loom in the corner of the studio, nestled between Felix's potting wheel and Lucy's scraps of installation art, would be as diaphanous as she felt. A cobweb, full of loops and gaps.

The sort of fabric that when you hold it up to the sun becomes solid.

*   *   *   *

Cat set up the warp threads on the loom, a canvas of white striated linen, but found she couldn't proceed. A few weeks went by. A month. Greenery started budding out on the tree branches. She stared at the loom, her mind blank. Eventually, she always ended up sitting beside Felix as he threw clay.

"How's the reg?" he asked her.

"Fine." This was Cat's stock answer to any question regarding Richard; in truth he had been acting strange. On her days off he messaged her constantly in the mornings, trying to convince her to have lunch with him—and Richard never took lunches. He left the office unimaginably early, running mysterious errands around the city. And although Cat never asked what he was up to, he repeated over and over again that he couldn't tell her.

He'd been the same way right before he began gathering venture capital for his new start-up. Right after he'd met her father for the first time. Her father, and Finn.

"You should dump his ass," said Felix. He drew the clay up into a long, slender silhouette, and then pressed it back down again. "He's a boring bourgie nerd."

"It'd be more trouble than it's worth," said Cat. It was the truth. Her relationship with Richard, such as it was, didn't particularly impinge on her quality of life.

Felix peered over at her, his face speckled with droplets of clay. "You're using him right up, you little slut. For his money. You're a . . . what's the word? A gold digger."

"Takes one to know one."

Felix dipped his fingers in the bowl of gray water he kept beside his feet and flicked them at her. She shrieked and slid behind the battered old dim sum cart, the shelves sagging with crusty brushes and half-empty cans of turpentine. Lucy's mess of platinum curls appeared from behind a support column.

"I'm not cleaning that up," she said. "Not like last time."

"The hell are you talking about?" asked Felix.

"The paint fight," said Cat.

"Oh, Jesus," said Felix. "That was like three years ago."

"I hold a grudge." Lucy glowered at them, her pixyish face curled up tight as a seashell. "I was up for three hours while the rest of you slept on that nasty-ass mattress Miguel kept in here."

"I remember that mattress," said Cat. "It was an STD farm."

"Which is why I burned it." Lucy ducked back over to her space on the other side of the warehouse. Cat lay against the studio's cold cement floor. She remembered that night: they'd all had Mexican martinis down at the cantina on 52nd Street. All of them except Lucy, who didn't drink, smoke, or eat candy, three activities she thought introduced too many impurities into her body. Then they came back to the studio and used up all of Miguel's cheap acrylic paint by hurling globs of it at one another. Cat remembered curling up on Miguel's thin, stained mattress afterward, the paint drying into stiff patches on her hands, and messaging Finn, telling him the entire story. She missed him and she was drunk enough to think he missed her back.

She missed him most days, really. Even those days she saw Richard. Especially those days she saw Richard.

Cat sat up and went out on the studio's stoop to smoke a cigarette. She had a few Marlboros left in her holder, a few hand-rolled, a single fuchsia-colored Fantasia. She took out one of the Marlboros. How long since she last saw Finn? In person, not through the distortion of the camera in her comm slate. Christmas. Three months ago. They had sat in front of the spindly, crooked tree. The lights glimmering in the darkness made the living room look like the inside of an aquarium. Her father was asleep or working. They didn't speak for a long time, just sat close enough for their thighs to touch. Eventually, Cat leaned over and kissed Finn on the mouth. He slipped her sweater up over her head. The house had smelled of pine and sugar cookies and dust.

Cat dragged on her cigarette, watched the smoke swirl out over the narrow, potholed street in front of the studio. She wondered if she could convince Finn to borrow her father's car and drive to her apartment this week. It was so much easier for him to drive now, ever since those fully automated cars came on the market. Designed for use by humans and robots both. Humans could program in their destination, robots could hook directly into the car's computer. Her father had bought one last year.

Cat pulled her comm slate out of her purse. She pulled up the string of code that connected directly into his mind. Like she was whispering in his ear.

Can you drive here? she wrote. *To see me?* She hesitated. She wanted to write, *I miss you* but wasn't sure she should. The wind rustled the thin, silvery green leaves of the trees. The wisteria was already blooming.

Her comm slate flashed his response.

I'll be there this weekend.

* * * *

The night before Finn came to visit, Cat went out to dinner with Richard. He took her to a sushi bar that had just opened. They sat at their table and watched the sushi roll by on a silent conveyor belt. The arrangements looked like orchids.

"I'm going to be busy tomorrow," Cat said. "I'm having Felix and Miguel over to do gallery submissions."

Richard looked up at her, his eyes wide, his mouth full. He swallowed and nodded. "When do you think you'll be done?"

"I'm not sure," said Cat. She dipped a piece of pink tuna into its pool of soy sauce. "Miguel's been putting it off for like a month."

Richard wasn't listening to her. He kept glancing around the bright room, tapping his fingers against the counter, pushing his hair away from his forehead. He picked up a California roll and then set it back down.

"Are you okay?"

"I'm fantastic." Richard leaned over the table. "I'm cooking something up. It's going to be huge. But I can't tell you yet." He put one finger to his mouth, as though to shush her.

The next day she woke up early and alone, having sent Richard home after dinner, reminding him of her imaginary submission party with Felix and Miguel. The lemony morning sunlight fell in a triangle across her face. She opened up all the windows so the air, sweet from the honeysuckle and the wisteria growing along the power lines, could erase the staleness of her apartment. She cleaned the sink in the kitchen. She swept the dirt off her porch. She tried on dress after dress in front of her bathroom mirror, finally deciding on a flimsy vintage thing she found in a thrift store years ago. In the bright spring daylight, she could see the faint outline of her underwear. She put on mascara.

When Finn finally arrived, pulling up to the curb in her father's dusty car, Cat was sitting on the porch, waiting for him. She had smoked one cigarette after another for the last thirty minutes. Finn stepped out, his hands dangling at his sides.

"You were able to make it," she said.

"Yes." Finn walked across the green yard. "Dr. Novak has been busy, but he told me it was all right for me to take a break." He came onto the porch and sat down beside her. Cat tapped her cigarette into the teacup. Finn frowned.

"You know that's not good for you."

"People do lots of things that aren't good for them."

She watched Finn consider this. She reached over and put her hand on his. What passed between them, these times they were alone together, was always unspoken. Cat did not know how to discuss the intricacies of desire with someone made of circuits and wires. She was afraid of the damage she might do. And he never spoke of it directly.

"Let's go inside," Cat said softly. The wind picked up as she spoke, rippling the grass in the yard. They stood up at the same time.

The light in the apartment was slanted and filled with dust. Cat had never shut the windows, and her gauzy curtains billowed like ghosts. Purple wisteria blossoms scattered across the floor and stuck to the soles of her bare feet. She let the wind slam the apartment door shut, and then she turned to face Finn. She lifted her hair up off her neck.

"I'm glad you could come," she said.

"So am I."

She dropped her hair back down and entwined her arms around his shoulders. He rested his hands on the curve of her hip. She kissed him, and he kissed back. Finn reached down and slipped the dress over her shoulders. He kissed places on her skin that made her shiver. Cat didn't care that the windows hung open, that she could hear cars driving by in the alley behind the house's yard. Her hands were at the zipper of his pants. He picked her up as easily, as carefully, as he would a circuit board out of a machine and rocked her back and forth, slowly, against his body. She entangled her fingers in his hair, clenched her eyes shut, moaned against the side of his neck. Later, he carried her into the bedroom, laid her across her clean bedsheets, and kissed a trail from her mouth, over her belly, into the V of her thighs.

Time dripped by and all the oxygen in Cat's blood flowed out of her: through her mouth, her eyes, the space between her legs. The light changed, turned amber and then violet and then blue, and the warm breeze of evening fluttered through the window, the scent of wisteria fermenting the air. She became so dizzy she nearly lost track of him. Of course, he didn't come. He never did. He had told her it was impossible, once.

Eventually, Cat was too exhausted to do anything more. She stretched breathless and flushed across her rumpled bed, Finn beside her, their hands barely touching. He turned his head toward her. His eyes gleamed the way they did in darkness. Cat let out a long contented sigh, and then Finn slid off the bed and disappeared into the dark hallway. She heard the sound of his footsteps moving through the apartment.

"Don't leave yet!" She stood up, wrapped a sheet around her waist, and followed him into the apartment. Her steps were shaky and uncertain. She found him in the kitchen, gazing into the refrigerator.

"I wasn't going to leave." He looked over at her. "I thought you might need to eat."

Cat laughed, touched. "How do you remember stuff like that?"

Finn looked back at the refrigerator. The light made his pale skin the color of frost. "I observe."

"I can just order some Chinese food." Cat pushed the refrigerator door shut. Finn looked at her. Cat was suddenly aware that she was naked, that the sheet had slipped down low on her hips. Her heart thumped in her chest. It was not desire. She'd burned up all her desire hours ago. It was something else, something that could not be reciprocated.

Her breath came out shallow, like puffs of steam.

A few hours later, Cat fell asleep. She curled up like a cat on top of her bedspread, her head leaning against Finn's smooth, pale chest, listening to the familiar absence of a heartbeat.

"Promise you won't leave until morning," she said, her words blurred with sleepiness.

"I won't leave."

She closed her eyes and then she dreamt of smudges of light

filtering between the branches of black trees, of curls of kudzu twisting around her bare waist. She dreamt of circuit boards.

She slept for a very long time.

* * * *

Cat sat straight up. Her entire body vibrated. When she breathed, her breath materialized on the air in front of her. "Finn! What's happened?" Cat realized she was cocooned in quilts and woven blankets she had made years ago, things she kept stashed away in the linen closet because she'd never been able to sell them to a gallery. She pulled the blankets back up around her neck and drew her legs up tight against her stomach. She called out Finn's name again.

The windows in the bedroom were still open. Ice fringed the sills. The curtains rattled in the wind. Cat shivered and then Finn appeared in the doorway, unfazed, wearing the same short-sleeved shirt he had on yesterday.

"God, you didn't close the windows!" Cat pulled the blankets more tightly around her shoulders.

"I'm sorry," said Finn. "I didn't realize—I only saw you shivering while you slept." He strode across the room and pulled the windows shut and the bangs reverberated through the apartment, fading into twinkling, starlit echoes.

"What's going on?" Cat asked. "It's freaking April." Her teeth chattered. "Get over here and warm me up."

"It's still March. It won't be April for another two days. Please, let me close the rest of the windows—"

"Okay, right. Sure." Cat pulled the layers of blankets over her head, blocking out the pale, milky sunlight. The windows slammed shut, one after another, like gunshots. She heard Finn's footsteps come back into the room. She poked her head out.

"Get into bed with me."

And he did. She threw the blankets around him and pressed herself tight against his chest. He wrapped his arms around her. His skin was cold but a faint heat emanated from his body's core. Cat brought the blankets over both their heads.

"I'm sorry," he said. "I thought the blankets would be enough." He paused. "It's rather enjoyable listening to the wind blow in. That is why I didn't close the windows."

Cat smiled in spite of the cold. She knew what he meant. Whenever northers blew in, the trees rattled outside her bedroom window, and the sound always comforted her. It reminded her of Christmas.

"I still can't believe it got so cold. It's spring. Everything was blooming."

"The weather patterns are still very difficult to predict," said Finn. "Even for me."

They lay there, pressed close to each other, until Cat warmed up. She directed Finn toward her closet and told him what clothing she wanted, and she dressed under the covers. Then she padded into her living room to turn up the heat, her breath condensing on the air. The heater shuddered on, smelling faintly of burning dust. When she came back into the bedroom Finn was staring out the window. The air around his face was empty, no clouds of breath curling like mist out of his mouth.

"What's it like out there?" she asked. She walked up beside him, her eyes on the profile of his face. She pressed her hands to the glass, turned her head, looked out. Her heart skipped a beat.

Spring had frozen. All the flowers, all the delicate green leaves on the trees, all the curling, fragrant vines—everything was encased in ice. The wisteria blossoms outside the window caught the sunlight and glittered. The grass had turned to diamonds.

Cat's breath fogged up the glass while the section of window in front of Finn stayed transparent as always.

Already, the ice that formed along the inside of her apartment had begun to melt. It dripped down the walls and formed glassy pools along the baseboards. Cat hooked her arm into Finn's and leaned against him.

Someone knocked on the front door. "Ignore it," Cat said.

More thumping. The house's frozen walls rattled. Cat's comm slate trilled from the table beside her bed. She picked it up, saw the backlit picture of Richard. "Shit," she said softly.

"Should I leave?" Finn was staring at her. The soft silver light brought out the shimmery highlights in his hair.

"It's just . . . It's Richard."

Finn turned back to the window. "Oh," he said. "I see."

A twinge of guilt twisted through Cat's belly. But then Finn glanced at her, and his face was calm and dispassionate. Not jealous at all. She told herself he didn't mind.

Finn and Richard had met twice before. The first time Richard sat down beside Finn and asked if Finn would open himself up so Richard could see the mystery of Finn's clockwork. Finn refused, but three days later, Richard announced his new business venture. Artificial intelligence. He wouldn't say anything more about it.

The second time, it was Thanksgiving, at Cat's father's house, and Richard stared from across the room as Cat and Finn played Scrabble without him.

"I don't think he's going away." Cat dropped her comm slate on the bed. "He's been so weird lately."

"I should go back to Dr. Novak's house," Finn said. "We have quite a lot of work to do. Your father has a contract with STL. For the lunar base."

Cat walked up to him and kissed him one last time. His mouth was cold against hers. It warmed at her touch.

The knocking stopped, replaced by a scratching noise outside the bedroom walls. Cat took a step away from Finn and then Richard's face appeared in the defrosting window, his cheeks red from the cold. He knocked on the glass. Waved. His gaze flickered between Cat and Finn.

"I find him off-putting." Finn turned to Cat. "I hope you don't mind me saying that."

"I don't mind." Cat looked at Richard through the glass. He blew into his hands, stomped his feet on the ground. She never cared when her friends made fun of him. Still, she supposed she loved him, because she couldn't bear the thought of his anger being directed at her. Also, whenever he was around, she felt normal, like a normal part of the world. His normalcy was contagious. Her mother would approve.

Cat followed Finn into the living room. She unlocked the door. Cold air blasted across her face, the wind biting and sharp. It nearly knocked the door off its hinges. The outside world smelled like the inside of a freezer. She almost slammed the door shut, but Finn had already stepped out onto the porch. Richard came around the side of the house.

"Hey, Finn!" he said, his words turning into steam. "What're you doing round here?"

Finn regarded Richard with his dark eyes. Cat couldn't stop shivering but Finn didn't move.

"I was visiting," Finn said.

"Oh," said Richard. "Right. Part of the family. I get that." He held up his hands, palms out, and then shoved them back into his pockets. "Can I come inside? It's fucking freezing out here."

Cat nodded. Richard bounded up the steps to the porch, slid through her apartment door. He stuck his head out. "You're not coming in?"

"Let me walk Finn to his car."

Richard wrinkled his forehead. Finn was already walking down the sidewalk to the curb where her father's car was parked. Cat ran after him. Before he could climb inside, she put her hand on his upper arm. She wanted to kiss him but she didn't.

"Thank you," she said.

Finn stared at her. The cold wind ruffled his hair.

"You should go back in to Richard." He nodded. "Good-bye."

"Bye," Cat whispered. She leaned back on the heels of her shoes and watched as Finn started the car. She folded her arms over her chest. The frozen wisteria vines clinked overhead. The entire world sounded as though it were made of glass.

Finn drove away, and Cat stood for a moment longer, letting the cold seep through the fabric of her clothes, before going back inside.

"So how'd it go with the Wonder Twins?"

Cat stopped in the doorway. Richard leaned against her couch.

"Who?" she said.

"You know. Felix and Miguel. You were doing . . ." He waved his hand around.

"The sub party." The lie felt tasteless on her tongue. She shut the door. "It went well."

Richard nodded. He ran his fingers through his hair, and it stood on end. His eyes were bright and glossy, as though he hadn't slept. He dropped down on the couch and patted the seat beside him. Cat walked across the room and sat down and Richard kissed her, suddenly and more passionately than she expected. After an entire night of kissing Finn it was sloppy, unclean. Overly wet. Whenever Richard pulled her close to him she could feel his heart beating against her chest, and it always disconcerted her, the feeling of another heart beating out of time with her own.

"This weather is crazy, isn't it?" Richard kept his hands on Cat's shoulders. "I was up at the office when it blew in. I swear I thought the glass was going to shatter."

"I didn't hear it," Cat said. "When I went to sleep, it was still spring."

Richard grinned. "Did Finn listen in? You think he even noticed?"

Cat hesitated, unsure of the best way to answer. But Richard had already distracted himself.

"This weather is making me crazy," he said. "It's making me do crazy things." The tenor of his voice had changed. It was higher pitched, breathier. "Do you want to know what sort of crazy things it's making me do?"

Cat didn't move. The correct answer was yes. She knew this. She nodded slowly.

"It's making me buy shit."

"What kind of shit?"

Richard laughed, a drawn-out, nervous, staccato laugh. She had seen him do this before giving speeches to investors. He ran his hands through his hair again. Looked her straight in the eye.

"Caterina, I'm going to be honest. I tried to figure out how to make this romantic."

Romantic? Cat thought. She heard her blood rushing in her ears.

"Yeah. But everything I came up with was just so . . . cheesy. Insincere." He smiled and reached into his pants pocket. He kept his hands folded over whatever it was he pulled out.

Cat sat very still, as still as a statue.

"And then last night, I'm up there working, it's three in the god-damn morning, and there's this howling all around me and I swear I can almost see the ice forming on the glass. I thought, *Caterina would love this shit*. It was so, you know, artistic. And I wished so hard that you could have been there with me." His words came out too fast, a blur. He held out his hands, unfolded them like a flower.

And then Cat saw the black velvet box resting in the palm of Richard's hand, and then that was all she saw. Her apartment fell away. Richard fell away. The black velvet box was a black hole, drawing into itself everything that made up Cat's life. She went numb.

"Caterina Novak." She was vaguely aware that he had slipped off the couch, onto one knee. She heard the rustle of his clothes, the thump of bone hitting the floorboards. "Caterina Novak, will you marry me?"

A black hole, and its center, at its core, was a glittering shard of light.

SEVEN

She told him she would have to think about it.

His cheeks flushed, but he grinned and bobbed his head. "That's fine," he said. "I talked to Halfast. She said I should give you time."

Cat nodded. Outside the wind howled and crawled across the windows. Richard lifted her hands up from her side, his skin cold to the touch. He dropped the box in her right palm and curled her fingers over it.

"I don't expect you to wear it," he said. "If you don't want to. I just . . . want you to have it."

"Of course."

Richard stood up. He shoved his hands in his pockets and bounced in place on the balls of his feet, as though he were trying to warm up. Cat realized he hadn't looked her in the eye, not once, not since he asked. She tightened her grip on the ring box. It felt normal, now that she held it, now that she knew it was tangible. She wanted to give it back. She wanted to tell him no. She kept thinking about the night before. *Finn.*

"I was going to go to the studio," Cat said.

Richard nodded. "I should go back up to the office." He peeked up at her through the fringe of his hair. She met his eyes and he looked away, toward the window. "Call me." He wagged a finger at her. "And don't take too long deciding."

Cat flinched, but it looked like a smile.

Cat kissed Richard on the cheek before he left, and she stood on the porch as he shuffled down to his car, her fingers turning numb from the cold. The ring box exuded its own uncomfortable warmth. When she went back inside she locked the door behind her and dropped the box on her kitchen counter.

When had Richard become interested in marriage? The friends of his she had met at parties always joked that they were married to their jobs. That even the days without sleep, the diet of pizza and overly caffeinated soda—it was healthier than a wife's constant nagging. This was why you dated someone like Richard Feversham. Because you were assured that he'd never, ever propose.

Cat left the ring sitting on the counter. She went into her bedroom. The cold air had evaporated all the scent out of the room. Even the cocoon of blankets, glimmering with rows of silver thread and scraps of designer brocade, looked innocent. Cat sighed. She slid back into the bed and curled up on her side. The foundation of the old house creaked, the frigid air slipping inside, mingling with the dry heat rattling the vents in the ceiling.

She rolled onto her back, trying to force any thoughts of Richard from her mind. The image of him on one knee, that ring glinting in the overhead lights—she clenched her eyes shut. The memory evaporated and was replaced with Finn, Finn standing in her front yard, staring at her as she smoked on the porch, her desire burning her up from the inside. Cat wiggled down into the blankets on her bed. She ran her hands down the sides of her thighs. *Finn. Finn.*

A residue coated all her thoughts. That memory of Richard on one knee.

Cat's eyes fluttered opened. She sighed. Tilted her head. Something glimmered on one of her pillows, not the one she slept on. A black hair.

Cat picked it up between her thumb and forefinger and held it up to the light. It must belong to Finn—it was too dark to be her own. Or Richard's.

Suddenly, she wanted to drive to the studio and work on the tapestry. She carried the hair into her kitchen and placed it in a sandwich bag, then folded the bag over on itself and tucked it in her pocket.

Cat drove to the studio slowly, uncertain of how to deal with so much ice on the roads. Occasionally she reached down and touched the sandwich bag, wanting to assure herself that it was still there. Fortunately, no one else was out, and when Cat's car hydroplaned at a blinking red stoplight, the wheels shooting her out into the intersection, there were no other cars to hit. The studio was empty, too, all the lights turned off, the air as cold inside as it was out. Cat exhaled long white breaths. She switched on the lights, all of them, even the antique string of electric Christmas lights wrapped around the doorframe. She dug a space heater out of the utility room, her fingers already aching from the cold, and set it up next to the loom. She turned it on, watched the coils burn bright red. Then she laid out all of her yarn across one of the drafting tables.

Cat chose a pale, moon-colored silk yarn first, because that pale grayish white had begun to creep into the edges of her vision, the cold was so pervasive. She dug through some of Lucy's fiber art supplies until she found a spool of shimmering silver thread, and she twined the two together, trying to approximate the look of ice. She thought she might introduce some green a little later, but the ice, the coldness, would be her base. It took a long time to wind the weft threads back and forth across the loom, because her fingers were stiff from the cold and she had to keep stopping to crouch beside the space heater to warm them up. It wasn't long before her stomach rumbled and she felt the beginnings of a headache creeping into her temple. She dragged herself away from the loom and called the guy who delivered homemade soup out of the back of an old van. He would be there in an hour—it was a busy, extraordinary day. Winter sunlight in April (no, March), flowers made of ice. She understood.

Cat worked steadily, losing herself in the rhythm of the loom, no longer a woman but an extension of this ancient machine. She forgot the emptiness in her stomach. She didn't notice when her back began to ache. Everything dropped away.

Including Richard's proposal.

When her soup was delivered, she almost didn't hear the door buzzing. She thanked the soup guy and gave him an extra tip because he looked more harried than usual, his hair sticking out from under a knit cap, dark circles under his eyes. She ate standing in front of the loom, staring at the narrow strip of fabric she had just created. The heat of the soup—creamed tomato, flecked with oregano and thyme—went straight into her bloodstream. After she finished, she went back to work. The sun moved higher in the sky, shone through the ice still clinging to the windows. While she worked, Cat thought of nothing. She changed yarn colors by instinct.

Cat had not worked this hard on anything since she graduated from college. Not for her commissions, those bland corporate-approved tapestries with their subdued blocks of color, and certainly not at the vice stand.

When she had woven a strip of fabric almost three inches wide, Cat pulled the sandwich bag containing Finn's hair out of her pocket. She picked up the weft yarn—pale, shimmering white cashmere—and, flexing her fingers against the cold, plucked Finn's hair out of the bag and wound it around the yarn. Then she wove it into the tapestry.

That single action didn't take long, but when she had finished, when Finn's hair was completely incorporated, she went outside for a smoke. As she exhaled, her breath pale and arabesque from the cigarette and the cold, her mind burned with a feverish intensity, as though she had woken from a dream. The world had begun to melt during her time in the studio, even though to Cat, a child of the South, the damp air was still unusually cold. She listened to the drip of ice from the tips of the blossoming trees and watched the embers of her cigarette flare out in the wind. She thought about the evening before, her legs wrapped around Finn's waist in the bedroom. Finn going through her empty refrigerator to find something to feed her, because he thought she might be hungry. Did he even know what that meant? To be hungry? It was impossible. She remembered how her father told her once that his kindness was a program. She hadn't believed it as a child, but she was older now, and she knew how computers worked. He was a computer who acted as if he loved her, and even though she ought to know better, that fact made her heart flutter hopelessly inside her chest.

She thought about Finn's touch, but she did not allow herself to think about the deviancy of it. Only damaged people slept with androids. People who couldn't stand a human embrace. Cat wasn't like that.

So she didn't think about Finn, but she didn't think about the ring sitting on the counter in her kitchen, either.

Cat finished her cigarette. She worked until the sun set, until the stars came out, and then she went home.

*   *   *   *

Cat didn't hear from Richard for three days. The ring stayed in its place in her kitchen, a black velvet speck against the cream-colored tile.

Then, one night when Cat came home from work, she found a sleek white box propped up against her front door. It was crowned with an enormous silver bow, *Wing On* running down the center of the ribbons in black brushstrokes. The Hong Kong department store from downtown. Cat stared at the box, the light from the lamp casting long melancholy shadows. The cold air of the freeze had disappeared completely, and so the night was balmy against the bare skin of Cat's back. She picked up the box and carried it inside. Unwound the silver ribbon. Pulled off the lid.

It was a dress.

She peeled aside the sheets of thin, flimsy tissue paper and picked the dress up so it unfolded in front of her, fluttering as it moved. It was made of gray silk, so light against her fingers it felt like gauze, with a narrow belt at the waist and an elaborate, pleated drape across the hips. She laid it across her couch. Her hands shook. It had to be from Richard. No one else would buy her a dress. She pulled out the rest of the tissue paper from the box, looking for a note, but there was nothing but layers and layers of paper. Cat sank down beside the dress, laid out so perfectly against the couch it looked like the woman who had once inhabited it had disappeared, leaving just her clothing behind.

Cat noticed a tiny triangle of white poking out from the dress's V-neck collar. She tugged at it. The price tag.

The dress cost two months' worth of her rent.

"Jesus Christ, Richard," she murmured. Her head spun. She couldn't accept something like this. Not if she turned him down. But she hadn't turned him down. Not yet.

Cat rubbed the price tag between her thumb and forefinger but she didn't tear it off. Eventually, she tucked it back down in the collar. Then she carried the dress into her bedroom, dug out an empty hanger from her closet, and hung the dress from the knob of her bathroom door, where it rippled like a ghost in the air generated by her ceiling fan.

When Cat went to the studio the next day Felix was there, throwing clay and listening to loud, clanging music. For a moment she sat staring at the tapestry stretched out, unfinished, on her loom. She found the dark line of Finn's hair. Ran her fingers over it.

"Wow, Cat, that's really gorgeous."

Cat jumped and snatched her hand away from the loom. She looked over her shoulder. Felix was leaning against the support column, his hands shoved in his pockets. "Is it a commission?"

Cat shook her head. She turned back to the loom. "It's a gift." As soon as she spoke she knew it was true, even though the thought had not occurred to her until then. A gift. *For Finn.*

"Seems pretty involved for a gift," said Felix. "Please, in the name of all that's holy, tell me it isn't for the reg."

Cat smiled. "It isn't for the reg."

"Thank Christ." Felix walked up beside her, crossed his hands over his chest. His face had a particular expression it adopted whenever he was examining the work of anyone who helped pay rent on the studio—like he didn't want to look at the piece at all, like he was afraid he might have to say something negative and increase the rent shares. He tilted his head to the side.

"I think you could sell this easily," he said. "You know. If you change your mind."

Cat nodded but didn't say anything.

"How is the reg doing?" Felix asked. "Does he know you spend all your time making presents for other people?"

Cat tugged at the hem of her skirt. She pulled her metal cigarette case out of her pocket but didn't open it yet. "He bought me a dress."

"Okay," said Felix.

Cat extracted a long, slim cigarette and slipped it into the side of her mouth. She wanted to tell Felix about Richard's proposal but she couldn't bring herself to do it. If she told him, he would tell everyone. Then she would be forced to think about it. She would be forced to come to a decision.

She didn't want to marry Richard. But the dress almost made her want to say yes. She had fallen into a pattern of normalcy with Richard, one her mother would have approved of. An entrepreneur working twelve-hour days on the promise of the future. A ring. A dress. So it wasn't what Cat wanted for herself—that didn't matter. Because when Cat thought of what she wanted, of the person she wanted, she knew it was impossible, she knew she was acting like a silly, petulant child.

"By the way," said Felix. "Miguel's having another rent party on Saturday. You should come." He reached over and stole one of Cat's vice girl cigarettes. "Ten bucks at the door, BYOB, no regs." He winked, pulled out his lighter, mimed drawing a cigarette down from his mouth. They walked outside to the front stoop, both knowing better than to let the scent of cigarette smoke get entwined in Cat's work. Felix lit her cigarette and then his own.

"Can I bring someone?" she asked. "Not Richard." She squinted against the sunlight. The scents of jasmine and wisteria and honeysuckle stained the air around them, the blossoms lush and bright despite last week's freeze.

"Who else do you know?" asked Felix. "Everyone's gonna be there. Miguel's made up flyers. Jane's band's going to be playing."

"He won't know about it." Cat dragged on her cigarette. "The person I want to bring."

"The recipient of your artwork in there?" Felix arched an eyebrow.

Cat tilted her head down. She ashed her cigarette. She let herself feel silly, petulant. Like a child. But she didn't say anything at all.

* * * *

The day of Miguel's rent party, Cat dropped the box containing the ring into her silverware drawer before digging her comm slate out of her purse and calling Finn. She actually called him—called the main line of the house computer, rather than connecting directly into his brain. Finn answered. *Novak residence. Dr. Novak cannot take calls at the moment. How may I help you?* He sounded like an automated answering machine.

"Finn," said Cat. "I know it's you. Stop working."

On the other end, a slight pause. "Why do you think I'm working?"

"You're always working. I want you to go to a party with me."

"I wasn't working."

"Awesome! So you have no excuse."

"Why do you want me to go to a party?"

"Because it's a fucking hipster rent party and I want someone there with me who won't spend the entire time talking about their performance art at the Partisan."

There was a long silence on the other end. Cat dug her nails into the fabric of the couch and wondered what she would have to say to convince Finn to drive into the city to see her. Because she needed to see him. She knew if she didn't see him she would forget who she was.

It was desire, but a different sort than usual.

"I'll leave now," Finn said finally. "What time does the party start?"

"I don't know, ten or so. You'll make it." She paused. "Thanks, by the way."

"You're welcome."

Cat tossed her comm slate aside. Sunlight poured in through the windows, heating up the apartment like a convection oven. It made her sleepy—she felt as though she hadn't slept in days, not since Richard proposed. A few days ago he'd sent a message to her comm slate. *The offer still stands.* Cat had stared it for a long time, her heart vibrating in her chest, before deleting it.

Many hours later, after the sun had set violet and red into the horizon, Finn rang the doorbell to her apartment. Cat was sitting at her desk, wearing the gray silk dress—the tag removed—and a pair of cheap cowboy boots, idly distracting herself with her laptop.

The silk tingled against her skin. The laptop's tiny fan hummed like a purring cat. "It's unlocked!" she shouted. The door clicked open, his shoes thudded against the floor. Cat snapped her laptop shut and looked up, and when she saw Finn warmth rushed through her, a flush in the layers of her skin. She jumped to her feet and threw her arms around him and laid her head on his shoulder and didn't say anything. He was there, solid as always. He was real.

For a long time, she held him, she breathed in the scent of him, a scent like winter afternoons, cold and mechanical. He set his hand in the small of her back.

"Would you like me to drive to the party?" Finn asked.

"What?" Cat said. "Oh, no. It's in the Stella. There won't be any parking for like five kilometers. We can take the light-rail."

Finn's fingers twitched.

"I don't like going out in public," he said. "Not anymore."

Cat split herself away from him, looked up at his dark eyes. "What happened?"

Finn's irises vibrated. He didn't answer.

"Finn!" Cat wrapped her hands around his and thought about the news reports that occasionally found their way onto her comm slate during slow periods at the vice stand: Androids were becoming inexpensive and therefore ubiquitous, and the protests kept increasing. From the Fundies. From the labor unions. People like Erik Martin. God, she hadn't thought of him in years. *An abomination.*

Finn's irises were still shimmering.

"Do you not want to go to the party?" she asked. His eyes focused on her.

"The party's fine." One of his computational pauses. "The other guests—they're your friends."

Cat pressed her palm against Finn's chest. He looked down at her hand. His eyes were still vibrating. Cat stared at him appraisingly, head tilted to the side.

"Do you have any idea how human you look?" She paused. "You aren't . . . like the others, the mass-produced ones. Not really."

His eyes didn't stop vibrating. It was the only motion in his body.

He didn't blink; he didn't move his limbs. He didn't twitch his fingers. The air-conditioning didn't even tousle his hair.

"I mean it. No one who just sees you for two minutes on a light-rail is going to think, *Oh my God, a robot*! They aren't going to do anything to you."

And as it turned out, the ride on the light-rail was uneventful—she kept her arm looped through his and no one looked at them twice. They were traveling into the part of the city known for strangeness. At one point Cat glanced at their reflection in the light-rail mirrors, and all she saw was a handsome dark-haired man and a girl wearing too much eye makeup who smiled waveringly back at her.

She did not think about Richard.

At their stop, Cat went into the liquor store on the corner and bought a bottle of whiskey and a bottle of Coke and gave them both to Finn to carry as they walked through the neighborhood to the party. It was darker here than in other parts of the city, even the part where Cat lived. Half the streetlights were burned out. The darkness made their footsteps' echo against the cement seem louder than it was. Cat kept the tips of her fingers pressed against Finn's wrist. They did not speak.

Cat didn't know the scruffy, bearded man guarding the door to the party, collecting covers. She handed him a pair of wrinkled bills she'd withdrawn earlier that day and nodded toward Finn and said, "I'm getting both of us."

"You friends of Miguel?" the man asked.

"I knew him in college." Cat smiled dazzlingly, and the man looked expectantly at Finn.

"I've never met him," said Finn.

Cat took Finn's hand and pulled him into the noisy, smoky, dimly lit house. Old, scratchy music played on an antique record player, set up like a centerpiece in the middle of the living room. People stood around and smoked cigarettes and laughed. Cat threaded herself through the crowd, dragging Finn behind her, toward the table in the dining room sagging with the weight of alcohol. Cat poured herself a whiskey and Coke. Finn stayed close to her side and looked thoughtfully out over the party.

"Are you okay?"

He nodded.

Cat sipped her drink. It tasted syrupy and bright, and she wanted to drink it as fast as possible. The music wailed long and low. Something fluttered against Cat's left shoulder.

"Well, well, if it isn't the mad scientist's beautiful daughter."

It was Miguel, Miguel who was short on rent that month. Cat hadn't seen him in nearly half a year but he looked the same: same dark curly hair, same lopsided grin. She rolled her eyes. He always called her that in college. The mad scientist's beautiful daughter.

"That's a fantastic dress." Then: "Who's your friend?" He raised an eyebrow. "Boyfriend?"

"This is Finn," said Cat. Finn nodded mechanically at Miguel and held out his hand and Miguel shook it.

"It's very nice to meet you, Finn," said Miguel before leaning in close to Cat's ear. He smelled of aftershave and alcohol. "This is the one, isn't it? Who your thesis was on? Jesus Christ, Cat, I thought you were making it up."

Cat hushed him, but Finn was already staring at her with what she imagined to be alarm. "You wrote about me?"

"You shouldn't be upset," Miguel said to Finn. "It was gorgeous. You should make her give you a copy."

"Why did you write about me?" Finn asked.

"I wrote about the nature of consciousness," said Cat.

"Through the lens of an android."

"Shut up, Miguel."

Miguel laughed. "I do work with the Automaton Defense League now, did you know that? I may have passed out a few copies."

"Jesus, Miguel." Cat's face burned.

"I'll take your name off. God, I thought you'd be flattered." He threw his arm around her shoulder and squeezed. "Here, I'll make it all better." Then he turned toward the liquor table, and Cat gulped her whiskey and Coke. She glanced back at Finn. "I'm sorry," she whispered. Her cheeks were flushed and hot. "I didn't give specifics. I didn't name you or anything."

"It is all right," said Finn. Unexpectedly, he pushed a piece of her hair away from her face. His hand lingered there, and for a moment Cat stared at him, her heart pounding, the place where his skin touched hers burning up. "I'd like to read it sometime."

"Okay, sorry to interrupt you two, but here." Miguel held out two tumblers of a pale pink liquid. "Rose-petal liqueur. Grew the roses myself. Felix helped me ferment it."

Cat took one of the glasses. He offered the other to Finn.

"I can't drink anything," said Finn. "But thank you."

Miguel smiled. "I always like to offer anyway." He knocked back the liqueur and set the tumbler down on the table. "All right, I'm out. Cat, thanks for helping the cause. Finn, you don't know how happy it makes me to know you're real." Miguel laughed again and disappeared into the party's dark crush. Cat sipped the rose-petal liqueur. The sweetness made her head spin. She almost didn't realize how alcoholic it was. Almost.

"Is it . . . good?" asked Finn.

"It tastes like flowers." Cat finished her glass and poured another. The room brightened. Finn began to glow. Cat realized she had forgotten to eat before coming to the party. She wrapped her arm around Finn's waist and pulled him into the backyard. No one was out there except for a few girls setting up amplifiers on a plywood stage in the corner of the yard. She lit a cigarette. The moon was huge against the violet sky. Cat stared at it.

"Do you see a rabbit or a face?" she asked.

"I don't understand."

"In the moon."

Finn looked up. He took a long time to answer, his eyes shaking, the moonlight dusting across his features. Entire decades had gone by since Richard proposed. It was a memory now. Harmless. Nothing she would ever have to think about.

"I see a face." Finn looked over at Cat. "It's laughing."

"Yeah, I always thought so." Cat sipped her liqueur. She couldn't stop drinking it. She dipped a finger in and stirred it around. The liqueur clung to the pores of her skin. She said Finn's name. He glanced over at her. She slipped her finger into his mouth, felt the artificial dampness of his tongue.

"Can you taste it?" she asked. Finn nodded. He closed his eyes.

"What do you think?" She let her hand drop to her side.

"It tastes of fermented sugars."

Cat drained the rest of her drink, threw the tumbler into the soft grass, and kissed Finn, hard, in public, surrounded by the moonlight and the girls in the band. She pulled away from him.

"Come dance with me," she said, hearing the slur in her voice. Her entire body pulsed with desire. Richard Feversham had cast some sort of suburban spell on her, with his ring and his proposal, his expensive dates and expensive gifts, his normalcy, and Finn had broken it.

They danced for two hours. The party filled up the house and once people got drunk enough the band started playing and everyone danced, flailing around arhythmically. Someone took the doors off the hinges and created an uninterrupted passageway between the inside of the house and the backyard, a corridor of sweat and music and flushed fevered bodies. Finn danced better than Cat expected, and she realized, drunk though she was, that he was copying the movements of the people around him, combining them to create something new. This was always how Cat danced as well. He did it more efficiently.

Cat laughed so much that evening, she grew tired of laughing. She spilled beer down the front of the gray silk dress and she shouted, "Shit!" but, really, she didn't care—really she was glad the dress was ruined. It was a dangerous thing, to own something so expensive. The party wore on. People trickled out. Cat felt herself sobering up, but she was tired of drinking, tired of the taste of beer and whiskey. The band stopped playing and someone turned the record player back on. Cat threw her arms around Finn's neck and swayed to the music's slow, droning violin. No one stared at them. No one said anything. If only this party were the real world. If only Finn could take her on dates to trendy and expensive restaurants. If only Finn would drop down to one knee and give her a ring in a box of black velvet.

Cat stopped. She stopped and Finn didn't and he stepped on her foot, his heavy black shoe grinding into the toe of her old cowboy boot. Cat yelped.

"You're not dancing." Finn pulled away from her and put his hands on her shoulders.

"I'm tired." She placed a hand on his elbow. They were back inside, and there was no one else in the room with them—the few people left at the party had migrated into the kitchen to play some stupid drinking game. Every now and then, their laughter burst out over the crackling music.

"Would you like to go home?"

Cat shook her head. She dragged her finger through her tangled hair, damp with sweat and the moisture in the air.

"Finn, can you fall in love?" she asked.

Finn froze. On the record, one song faded out and another began. Laughter from the kitchen.

"What." He didn't say it like a question. His voice was strange, distorted. Then he blinked. "You're not the first person to ask me."

"I'm not?"

"No. The preacher came to Dr. Novak's house not long ago. He asked me the same thing."

"Oh, Finn," said Cat. "No. No . . . I meant." She stopped, bit her lower lip. "Please don't think—"

"Think what? It's a reasonable question." He paused. Cat's heart pounded. Her head ached, the start of a hangover. "No, I don't believe I can. Love is far too ill defined a concept to work within my current parameters. It's too . . . abstract."

"Oh." Cat took a faltering step back. "It's too hot in here," she said, and she stumbled backward, out into the backyard. The air was damp with dew. Music throbbed out of the walls of the house. Her heart had splintered into a thousand shards of glass. *His kindness is a program. A program.*

A program. A computer.

Finn came outside. For a moment he stood in the doorway, haloed by the light of the party. His skin wasn't flushed red, his hair wasn't matted down with sweat. Then he glided toward her.

"Is everything all right?" he asked. "I'm sorry if I upset you. It seems to be an upsetting issue for some—"

"Richard asked me to marry him," Cat said.

Cat could barely see Finn except for the silver of his eyes, reflecting the moonlight.

"I see." He didn't say anything more for a long time.

Then: "Congratulations."

Tears welled up behind Cat's eyes. She took a deep breath. It passed.

He is a program.

"I haven't said yes yet."

Another long pause. The music changed. Cat could barely hear it now.

"Why not?" said Finn. "Don't you want to get married?"

"I don't know." Cat collapsed onto the wet grass. Her head no longer seemed attached to her body. "Would you marry me?"

The words left her mouth even though she didn't mean them to. They hovered in the air between Cat and Finn, chiming like tree branches covered in ice. Cat slapped her hand over her mouth. She suddenly wanted to throw up. Rose-colored vomit.

"I believe you understand that's not possible," Finn said. "I can't get married."

"You don't feel anything," said Cat. "You're a machine." Finn didn't say anything. He knelt down in the grass beside her. Cat was going numb. She was icing over. If Finn kissed her, if Finn touched her, she would shatter.

"I am a machine," he said. Cat closed her eyes.

They rode back to Cat's apartment in a taxicab. The lights of the city flashed over the windows and moved in long liquid lines across the contours of Finn's body. Cat watched him out of the corner of her eye. He stared straight ahead.

There was an ache in her limbs, a twisting in her belly. When they came home she took off her cowboy boots and left them lying in the doorway. She combed her fingers through her hair, sticky with sweat and cigarette smoke. Finn regarded her silently from the corner of the room. She pulled the dress up over her shoulders—in the light of her apartment she saw the beer stain closely for the first time, a streak of darkness running down the front—and threw it across the living room floor. For a moment she stood, one hand on her thin cotton underwear, hair falling across her eyes, feet bare and sticking to the hardwood floors, and tried to breathe.

"Would you like me to stay with you?" asked Finn. She heard him take one step forward. Another. With all her strength she lifted her head. She twisted her torso around, looked at him over her shoulder.

You can't have him.

The way the shadows had fallen across his face, he almost looked concerned.

No. You can have him and not have him, at the same time. She nodded.

*   *   *   *

Two days later, Cat dug Richard's wedding ring out of the kitchen drawer and carried it into the living room. She sat down on the edge of her couch. She flipped open the lid, stared down at the ring. The curtains were drawn and so it didn't catch the light like before. She shut the box. Picked up her comm slate from the coffee table. She pulled up the messaging program and then shook her head. No. She should call him.

It only rang twice before he answered, his voice guarded when he said her name: "Caterina." No *Hello.*

"Richard," she said.

"I thought you'd blown me off."

Cat looked down at the ring. "I did," she said. "I guess. I had to . . . had to think about some things." She paused. "I decided on yes, if it's not too late."

There was silence on the other end. Cat wasn't sure he would accept her acceptance, so long after the proposal; she wasn't sure she wanted him to. She felt hollow.

"Are you still there?" Cat said.

"Yeah, I am." Richard laughed. "I'm just . . . I'm stunned, Caterina. I really thought I'd never hear from you again."

"Sorry."

"Are you wearing it?"

"What?"

"The ring. Are you wearing it right now?"

"Oh." Cat glanced down at the box, the lid shut tight, the ring hidden away. "Of course."

Richard laughed again. "This is ridiculous," he said. "Why aren't we together right now? Get over here. Or I'll go over there. Are you at your apartment? Stay there. We need to celebrate." Then she heard him shout, away from the comm slate's speaker: "I'm fucking engaged! She finally said yes!"

Cat sighed, stared at the curtains flattening themselves against her living room window. Richard was saying something to her: the ring. He was asking how the ring looked. She didn't have an answer. She flipped open the box, pulled out the ring, slipped it on her finger. It fit perfectly.

EIGHT

Cat knocked on Felix's door, clutching a bottle of expensive wine by its neck. Trickling through from the other side of the door was the faint murmur of voices, the occasional starburst of laughter, the hum of music. She rubbed at the place on her finger where Richard's ring should be—currently, it resided in the bottom of her purse—and felt an immeasurable gulf between herself out in the hallway and her friends in the apartment.

The door swung open. Felix, his hair fashionably mussed, had one arm slung around Miguel's shoulder.

"Miguel," said Cat, surprised to see him.

He grinned at her. "Nice dress."

"You look like my fucking mom," said Felix.

Cat glanced down: she was still wearing the dyed linen sheath dress from the engagement party at Richard's condo. Another dress she hadn't bought for herself.

"I have a bottle of Château Margaux," she said. "You want it or not?"

"Oh shit, are you serious?" Felix straightened and dropped his arm to his side. "Where the hell did you get that?"

For a moment Cat's heart thumped inside her chest. *My*

engagement party. But she only shrugged, lifted the bottle up in the air, and glided into Felix's apartment. The same worn-out beige carpet as always, the same ugly floral-patterned thrift store couch. He'd switched out the pottery lining the bookshelves, though.

"So what brings you around on this lovely Friday night?" Felix walked over to the dry bar, pulled out a trio of wineglasses.

"The better question," said Cat, "is what brings Miguel?"

Miguel slouched on the couch, kicked his feet up on the coffee table. "We're an *item*." He rolled his eyes. Over in the corner, Felix laughed.

"Seriously?"

"Since the rent party." Miguel took a wineglass from Felix. "We made enough to pay for two months, by the way. So fucking grateful."

Cat smiled. Felix plucked the wine bottle out of her hand and tucked it under his arm. "I want to go out on the balcony." He walked across the room and slid open the glass door. Miguel shrugged at Cat. They both stood up, followed Felix outside. The air was warm and dry from the early summer sun. Cat sank down on a sagging patio chair. Felix opened the wine.

"I'm assuming," said Felix, as he filled up each of their glasses, "that you got this from the reg."

"The one and only." Cat swirled the wine, so dark it looked like ink.

"What's the occasion?" Miguel asked.

For a long time Cat only stared down at the surface of her wine. When she glanced back up, Felix and Miguel both watched her.

"Sweetie," said Miguel, "is everything okay?"

"I'm engaged," said Cat.

Neither Felix nor Miguel spoke. They didn't move. A wind picked up, blowing heat and car exhaust across the balcony.

"Shut the fuck up," said Felix.

"Where's your ring?" said Miguel.

Cat sighed and slumped back in her chair. "In my purse." She flicked her head toward the balcony door. "If you want to see it, you can go get it." She sipped from her glass. The Margaux tasted like wine, maybe a little better than the cheap sort they served at parties in college. The alcohol burned the back of her throat.

Felix set his glass on the balcony cement and pulled out his pack of cigarettes. He slid out two, lit both of them, handed one to Cat. She accepted without question.

"Congratulations," said Miguel.

"Thanks."

Silence settled around them, heavy as heat. Felix and Miguel sat down on the cement, their backs pressing against the metal grating.

Cat finished her wine and poured another. So did Felix; so did Miguel. They drank until the bottle was nearly empty.

"Okay," said Felix as he finished his glass. "So Cat is getting married." He lit another cigarette, and smoke curled like a halo around the crown of his head.

"Are you going to move out to the suburbs?" Miguel asked. He and Felix looked at each other and laughed.

"So are you going to have the three and a half kids they tell us to have?" Felix said. He dragged contemplatively on his cigarette. "Would you rather have the bottom half or the top half?"

Cat allowed herself a smile before draining the last of the wine in her glass. "I have no idea. The top, I guess."

"My question was serious," said Miguel. "You don't seem like the suburban type."

"Well, she does in that dress," said Felix.

Cat ignored him. She wanted another cigarette. She stretched her legs out in front of her, remembering the engagement party—Richard's condo made balmy and hot from the crush of too many bodies, sweat pooling at the base of her spine as he stood her up in front of all his friends and employees for a toast. *This will be a dry run for our wedding*, he'd told her as they laid out the catered hors d'oeuvres before everyone arrived.

"So what I want to know," Miguel said suddenly, "is how your android friend is taking this. Finn."

"Android?" Felix perked up. "Did I miss something?"

"You're not supposed to know about him," Cat said. "You might sell him off to the government for a billion dollars."

Felix gasped. "Don't even," he said. "Do I look like your fiancé?"

They all laughed, although Cat's laughter sounded like an engine failing in the middle of a freeway. She looked down at her hands.

"He wouldn't do that," she said. "He . . . likes robots. He treats them like people."

Miguel frowned. "Doesn't have a problem selling them off, though."

Cat didn't answer. Felix looked between Cat and Miguel. "Seriously," he said. "How come I didn't know about this?"

"Because I didn't tell you," said Cat.

"He was at my rent party," said Miguel. "She danced with him for like four hours."

"Wait, that was an android?" Felix lit another cigarette. "Okay, that is *not* what the androids at your meetings look like." He paused. "It looked . . . human. You know. Real. Not creepy."

"*He* looked human," said Miguel gently, placing one hand on Felix's wrist. Cat felt uncomfortably warm. *Too much wine*, she thought. *The heat from the cigarettes.*

She knew that wasn't it.

"Anyway," said Miguel. "You never answered my question."

"What question?"

"How's he taking it?"

"What are you talking about?" She smiled like she was made of plastic, her blood rushing through her ears.

"You know. You getting married and all."

"He doesn't care. He doesn't feel anything."

"That," said Miguel, "is bullshit."

Cat fumbled for another cigarette.

"I can tell these things," he said.

"Yeah, you know so much about robotics," said Felix.

"Hey, we're discussing human consciousness here. You go sit in the corner with your pottery. Let the big kids talk." Felix dove toward Miguel with a lit cigarette, pretending to burn him. Miguel laughed and shoved him away. Cat walked up to the railing. When she picked up Felix's cigarette pack, her hands shook. She looked out over the city. The freeway stretching off into the distance was a river of light. She smoked her cigarette down to the filter and then flicked it out into the darkness. Her heart raced and raced.

Miguel and Felix shrieked behind her, their voices rising and falling and then silencing completely. When she glanced over her shoulder, Felix nuzzled Miguel's shoulder. They didn't notice her.

She picked up her dirty wineglass and let herself back inside, where the air-conditioning swallowed up the heat and the bright lights swallowed up the darkness. She could not stop shaking.

*   *   *   *

Just after the summer storms started up Cat drove Richard down to her father's house. It was the first time she had seen her father (or Finn) since she'd accepted Richard's proposal, and the drive seemed to take longer than usual. At one point Cat reached over to switch on her music but Richard asked her to turn it off.

"I'm sorry, sweetheart, but I really need to concentrate." The light from his comm slate reflected two white pinpricks in the center of his pupils. He tapped the screen, glanced up at her, and smiled.

"What are you doing? Are you talking to Ella?"

"We've got this huge deployment two weeks from Tuesday. Huge. World changing."

He talked about all his business ventures that way—*world changing*. Cat didn't say anything. They drove in silence for a few minutes longer, the sound of the tires spinning against the asphalt pulling Cat into a fugue state. Then: "Don't you want to know what we're deploying?"

"What?"

"You never ask about what I do."

"I thought you were bus—"

"It's a fully automated housekeeping system."

"They already have those."

"Not like this. It's a house. A sentient house, sort of. We think we've found the sweet spot between sentience and autonomy—so you can have the benefits of sentience without worrying about exploiting a robot or whatever."

Cat stared at the road disappearing to a point in front of her. Richard tapped against his screen.

A few hours later the car pulled into the gravel-lined driveway of her childhood home. It had been too long since she'd come back. Everything was unfamiliar. An arabesque pattern she swore she had never seen before twisted around the porch railing. They climbed out of the car. Cat smelled the rainstorms on the horizon and she was jolted with the shock of nostalgia, thrown back to the time right before she started high school, slipping across the muddy banks of the river, her hands pressed against the damp cypress trees for balance—

"Kitty-Cat! You made it!"

A trio of bangs from the front porch: the screen door slapping against the frame. Cat's father leaned over the railing and waved. The sunlight slanting through the trees made him glow like an X-ray. He looked different. Thinner.

Cat waved back, and when she dropped her hand to her side, Richard took it up in his own. Cat shifted her weight from one foot to the other, suddenly uncomfortable.

"So I hear you proposed." Cat's father strolled across the yard, his hands tucked into his pockets. His clothes hung loose on him. He squinted up at Richard, flicked his eyes over to Cat. Back to Richard. "Never thought anybody'd be able to convince my little girl to take the plunge."

Richard beamed, threw his arm around Cat's shoulder. "Definitely looking forward to our merger here." Richard laughed.

Cat looked down at her feet. The grass was still crackly and golden from the recent drought, although a tinge of green grew up from the roots. The storms.

"Well, I managed to whip up something to eat—and by whipped up I mean bought. You like fried chicken?"

Richard nodded, though Cat knew he didn't eat fried foods.

Her father turned and trudged back to the house. "Jesus," said Richard. "He's looking pretty rough."

"He's fine."

"Sure hope so. I'd hate to think he'd miss the wedding. Plus I wanted to hear his thoughts on our deployment." A strong damp wind pushed through the trees in the woods, picking up the dried-out leaves. The sky was gunmetal gray and hung lower than normal, like the oppressive ceiling of an old office.

"Please," said Cat. "Let's not talk about work."

* * * *

The storm rumbled in while they all sat down at the dusty table in the dining room, a box of fried chicken from the run-down restaurant in town propped open like a centerpiece, buttery yellow biscuits piled up beside it.

"Sorry I didn't cook." Cat's father pried the cap off a beer. "But, you know. Never learned."

"You look like you haven't been eating at all," said Cat.

"This is fine." Richard picked up a piece of fried chicken, dabbed the grease off with one of the flimsy napkins. "Looks great."

At the other end of the table, next to Cat's father, Finn sat with his hands folded in his lap.

"So, Dr. Novak." Richard peeled the battered skin off his chicken and draped it over the edge of his plate. "You working on anything exciting? SynLodge has got something really spectacular lined up." He grinned. "It's a secret."

Cat sighed.

"What?" said Richard. "I was just asking."

Cat's father took a swig of beer. "I'm doing work on the lunar station."

Richard's eyes widened. "The lunar station!" His mouth opened and closed like a fish. "The one STL is funding?"

Cat's father nodded.

"Ho-lee shit." Richard crossed his arms and looked at Cat's father in the casually appraising way he used when sizing up potential rivals. "Robotics, I'm assuming?"

Cat's father set down his piece of chicken and wiped his hands on his napkin. "No," he said. "I don't do work with robotics anymore."

Cat went numb.

"May I ask why not?" Richard glanced at Finn. Only for a second.

"Politics," said Cat's father.

Silence. Richard nodded. Cat's father picked up a biscuit. "I'm just working as a contractor," he said. "Developing a circuit for the shuttle—just a tiny thing, an offshoot of what we made for the Mars landing."

"We?"

Cat's father nodded. "Finn and I."

Richard peeled more skin off his chicken. Outside, the wind picked up, and the tree branches tapped against the windows.

"I didn't know that," said Cat. "That you were both working on the lunar station." When she spoke, she spoke to Finn.

"I didn't think you were interested," said Finn.

"So what do you think of those activist groups out on the coast?" Richard leaned toward Cat's father. "I'm guessing that's why you got out of the field. I don't blame you. Lot of tension."

"Yes. Tension."

The windows illuminated and went dark.

"Is the storm going to be a bad one?" Cat tugged at the greasy napkin lying in her lap. She was still looking at Finn.

"Yeah," said Richard. "I mean, I mostly agree with them, but some of the wording in that legislation is pretty strong."

Cat wound her napkin around her fingers. She said Richard's name so softly it was nothing but an exhalation.

"Take Finn here," Richard said. "He helps you out, but you can't pay him."

"Right," said Cat's father. "Finn's my lab assistant, yes . . ."

Richard grinned so wide he showed all his teeth, and outside the trees beat against the walls of the house. The rain still hadn't started.

"Exactly! You don't have to pay him, you don't have to worry about him getting hurt . . ."

Finn stared at Cat from across the table.

"Where are you going with this?" Cat's father wrapped his hand around the neck of his beer bottle.

"All I'm saying is, there are benefits to having a bot do a human's job, yeah? But those activist groups are saying it's slavery, right, so you gotta find a way around the whole sentience question." He glanced at Finn. "I'm sorry to phrase it that way. I really don't want to suggest—"

"Richard," said Cat. Finn was still staring at her, his eyes refracting silver. "Richard, please, let's talk about something else—"

"No," said Cat's father. "I'm curious what he's building up to."

Richard laughed. "This is what SynLodge's been working on. That sweet spot between intelligence and sentience. You can have one without the other. Then you can get around that moral question of whether or not it's slavery. Plus, those laws are all going to pass eventually, so you get around them, too."

For the first time all dinner, Finn's eyes moved off Cat.

He stared at Richard, unblinking, unmoving.

Cat's father sipped his beer. "I certainly hope they pass."

"So do I," Richard said.

"I do offer Finn recompense," Cat's father said. "Not that it's any of your business."

Richard paused. "I'm sorry." He sounded sincere. "I would never suggest enslaving *sentient* bots is a good thing. I'm just saying, maybe there are some problems with sentience. Not always, but sometimes." He leaned back in his chair. "You know, like what happened with Ishiguro and McHugh—"

"I'm familiar with the case," said Cat's father.

"As am I," said Finn. "There were extenuating circumstances."

Richard grinned and threw out one arm toward Finn. "Look at that! That's exactly what I'm talking about."

"I don't understand," said Finn.

"Neither do I," said Cat.

"That's because you're an artist, sweetheart," said Richard.

"Cat understands the nature of consciousness," said Finn. "I read her thesis."

"You did?" Cat's breath caught in her throat. She and Finn stared at each other from across the table. She could feel Richard watching her. Finn nodded.

"When?"

"I'm sure it was a brilliant paper," said Richard. "But it's not what I'm talking about. Nobody's denying Finn has consciousness, or saying he shouldn't have rights because of it. What I'm saying is—people don't *want* consciousness in a bot. That's really the basis for all the protests, right? I mean, those bot-rights activists still want intelligent computers. I'm just saying, you get rid of sentience, you get rid of the whole slavery issue entirely."

"Richard," said Cat. "Please shut up."

She was answered by a trio of clicks, then a long, low *whomp* as though the house had sighed. The lights flickered once and went dark.

Cat's father cursed. The silvery glow in Finn's eyes brightened, casting enough light that Cat could see the outline of his fingers pressing against the table. "I can fix this," he said. His illuminated eyes pushed backward and then rose up.

"That really isn't necessary," said Cat's father. "We can wait till the storm's over at least. Cat, there are still some candles left over from last year—"

"It's no problem," said Finn. "I don't mind."

Lightning flickered across the windows, and in that sudden flash of whiteness Cat saw Richard scowling. She pushed away from the table in disgust and felt her way out of the dining room and into the kitchen. Trees thrashed against the window above the sink, water sluicing over the glass. Finn followed her, cutting across the kitchen to the screened door.

"Finn, I'm sorry."

But he was already outside.

Cat opened and then slammed shut one drawer after another until she found a pair of half-melted orange-scented candles and an old disposable lighter. She lit both candles and carried them into the dining room. In the gloomy light, Richard and her father sat at their seats, not looking at each other. Cat sat down beside Richard, pushed aside her uneaten fried chicken, and watched the candle flames dance and hop in the darkness, the spicy scent of orange curling into the air.

Five minutes passed. Cat's father sipped his beer. Richard drummed his fingers against the table. Cat tried very hard not to think about anything in particular.

The lights came back on.

"You can thank Finn for that," Cat's father said.

"I really am sorry. I know I can get worked up sometimes, and I shouldn't have . . ." But Richard's apology was met with a glare. Cat didn't bother to blow out the candles. She waited for Finn to come slamming through the kitchen door, water dripping off his clothes and his hair. She wanted to ask him when he had read her thesis. How he'd read it. She wanted to apologize on behalf of Richard, again.

But the storm raged on and Finn never came back inside.

* * * *

Cat wheeled her old bicycle out of the storage shed. The world glimmered silvery wet from the storm, which had passed through as Cat and her father and Richard sat eating the last of the congealing chicken. Now dinner was over and the sun was setting behind the leftover storm clouds. After he had helped her dump the chicken bones in the trash, Richard disappeared upstairs to take a video conference with Ella Halfast on his computer: Cat could see his silhouette in the window, pacing back and forth across the square of yellow light, hands gesturing wildly. For a moment, she stood on the driveway and leaned on her bicycle, watching him. Her anger with him had faded; he was like a little kid sometimes, getting so excited about his work that he didn't understand when he was putting off the people around him. And he really was trying to help people with SynLodge. She knew he found the idea of exploiting sentient robots distasteful, even if he wasn't the best at getting his point across.

Besides, his views lined up with the rest of the world's. He was the normal one here. Not her, not her father.

Cat rode her bike down the muddy road to the cemetery where her mother was buried, the breeze cool across her face. She jumped off the bike and left it lying in a patch of damp grass next to the gate. She hadn't been back to her mother's grave for so long. She used to come regularly, every few months, whenever the stress of faking normalcy became too much of a burden. Every few months she'd drive down to her father's house, she'd collapse into the comfort of Finn's arms, she'd ride her bike to the cemetery.

"Mom," she said when she walked up to the sleek black gravestone, glistening with rainwater. "Mom, I'm engaged." No response but the whispering of the trees in the forest, the insects in the trees.

"It's Richard. I told you about him? He owns his own company? Well, he asked me to marry him during the spring freeze. I don't know if you knew about the spring freeze, did you? I don't think the ground froze that far down, but well—there was the freak freeze in April. Everything glassed over."

Cat stopped. She lowered herself into the wet grass, draping over the headstone of Mrs. Patty Longbotham, dead at eighty-five a hundred years ago, and once dearly loved, dearly missed.

"Can I tell you a secret, Mom?"

The storm clouds had dissipated and already Cat could see the pinprick of stars against the black sky, the moon hanging like a thin-lipped smile in the northwest corner.

"I don't want to marry him."

All the insects in the world buzzed and buzzed. "Don't tell him, okay? Don't send him any . . . portents. But I mean . . ." Cat looked at the grasses shimmering in the starlit wind.

"It's a business arrangement," she said finally. "An acquisition. He's very sweet but he sees everything in terms of business, you know? But he's . . . It would be secure. And I won't have to work anymore. I know you don't like me being a vice girl."

Cat leaned her head against Mrs. Longbotham's gravestone. She twirled a piece of her hair around her finger and stared at her mother's grave. The flat ground was covered with a pelt of dried-out grass. During the two weeks of spring, black-eyed Susans grew there, an enormous clump of them, their heads nodding against the slightest hint of a breeze.

"I love you," said Cat. "I'm sorry my life isn't what you wanted it to be. But I really am trying."

She stood up, wiped the mud from the back of her pants. Her bike waited for her in the grass outside the gate, and she rode home in the darkness, mud splattering up along her spine from the rear wheel. Crickets chirped and lightning bugs blinked on and off in the distance. By the time Cat pulled up to the storage shed, she was coated with a splatter of mud and a thin sheen of sweat from the storm's humidity. She put her bike away and scraped at the filthy residue coating her skin. Richard was still in her bedroom, pacing back and forth in front of the window. She had always found Finn after visiting her mother's grave, because afterward she felt empty, and Finn's touch filled her up again.

Tonight, she wanted a bath.

Cat slipped into the downstairs bathroom, the big, airy one with the window that looked out over her mother's old garden—the garden her father had let go to seed after her mother's death. She pulled her old silk bathrobe out of the linen closet and draped it over the sink. Turned on the water. Dropped in a spongy capsule of lavender oil. The tub was ancient: claw-footed, the porcelain patchy and worn thin. The surrounding tiles were stained from years of dripping bathwater.

Cat took off her clothes, dropping them into piles on the floor. She took off her engagement ring. While the water filled up the tub, she opened the window, breathed in the woodsy, rainy scent from the garden. Then she slipped into the bath, dropping down until her head was completely submerged, her knees poking out of the silky, lavender-scented water. She opened her eyes. The antique light fixture overhead wavered like a ghost.

Cat exhaled a long stream of bubbles. When she pushed herself up out of the water, it was only because she needed to breathe.

Finn stood in the doorway.

Cat stared at him. Water streamed through her hair, over the sides of her face, into the crevice of her collarbone. She didn't know what to say so she slid back into the water, kicking up one leg and then the other.

Finn didn't move except for his eyes, following the motion of her body as she straightened up and leaned over the side of the tub.

"I missed you at dinner," she said.

"Did you?"

"You know I did."

"You're getting married."

Cat hesitated. "Why didn't you come back from the storm?"

He didn't answer right away. His irises vibrated. Then: "I felt that my presence made Mr. Feversham uncomfortable."

"No," said Cat. "His presence made you uncomfortable." She held her breath.

"I can't experience discomfort."

"Oh. Right." Cat sighed and slid back into the water. "I forgot."

"I wanted to tell you," said Finn, "that I found your thesis fascinating. Remarkable, even."

Her thesis.

"Oh?" she said. "How'd you even get a copy of it?"

Finn smiled. "I have access to all networked computers in the house. I found a copy."

"Jesus, I forgot I put it on there." Why had she put it on the network anyway? Maybe she'd wanted him to find it.

"It doesn't bother you, does it?"

Cat shook her head, tilting her gaze to her abdomen. She skimmed her hands across the top of the water. "As long as you thought it was fascinating."

"I did. You approached something I hadn't previously considered." He paused. "There are some points I disagree with, of course. I don't think it would be possible for you to be wholly accurate regarding my condition, but—" He stopped. His eyes vibrated. "It's difficult for me to express what I'm trying to say."

Cat leaned forward in the water, listening.

"There is nothing else like me in the entire world," said Finn. "That's what you wrote. I'm the only one."

"I know."

"I can't tell you what it means to be the only one of my kind," he said. "I can't . . . There is a lack in myself. But your thesis almost filled it in. It was . . . a start."

"You're lonely," said Cat. As soon as she spoke, she knew it was true.

"I . . . I am not sure."

Finn stared at her from his place in the doorway. Cat was aware of her nakedness. She wondered what Richard would do if he wandered back downstairs, went looking for the bathroom.

"I guess you couldn't wait to tell me all this," she said, her voice shaking, "when I wasn't in the tub."

A pause so long time lost all meaning. "Would you like me to be honest?"

"I thought you were incapable of dishonesty."

"I'm capable." Finn's eyes whirred. "I wanted to watch you."

Cat's heart thrummed. "Watch me take a bath?"

"Yes."

All the skin on Cat's body tingled. She lifted up her arm. She watched the water fall in a line across her breasts. So did Finn.

A warm wind blew in through the open window, tousling Finn's hair.

Cat thought about Richard's shadow, pacing back and forth in front of the yellow light of her bedroom window.

"Close the door," she said.

"Of course," said Finn.

He slid the lock into place.

Cat stood up. Water rushed over her body and into the bath. Finn didn't move. Cat took one step out of the tub, then another and another. Water pooled on the floor. She left a trail of shining footprints behind her.

"You're lonely," Cat said. "So you came to find me." She put one hand on his chest. He slid his arm around the small of her back.

Outside, the wind picked up, damp with rainwater, and blew through the screen in the window, bringing inside the wild, overgrown scent of the garden.

"I came to find you," said Finn.

NINE

The day of Cat's wedding the sky was cloudless and so blue it sagged beneath the weight of its color.

At the chapel, the sunlight illuminated clouds of golden dust that lifted up in bursts off the statues of saints. She dressed in the choir room, Lucy and Miguel and Felix hovering around her like bees. The bodice of her dress was encrusted with fake jewels and pressed tight against the bones of her chest. It felt as though it weighed a hundred pounds. Richard had picked out the dress a few months earlier, using his preferred tactic of purchasing the most expensive item in the store. Cat found something endearing about that, the way he believed in capitalism so much he extended it to personal relationships. She admired anyone who could navigate the world with that much self-assurance. She certainly couldn't.

Cat barely recognized her reflection in the full-length mirror. The bodice flickered and blinked in the sunlight, but all the color in her skin had drained away hours ago.

"Are you sure that hair's secure?" Felix asked. He held a tiny bottle of hair spray at his hip, cocked and ready, like a gun.

"If you spray that one more time I'm smashing your potting wheel," said Lucy. "I'm not even joking."

"Stop bickering, the two of you." Miguel offered the veil to Cat, and Cat flipped it over and rested it on top of her head. "Are you nervous?" Miguel asked, his voice low.

Cat nodded. She hadn't eaten anything for nearly thirteen hours. Her cheekbones looked hollow from the blush Lucy had applied earlier; her eyes were bigger than usual and fever-bright from the eyeliner and the mascara. "It'll be fine," Miguel said. There was a disapproving tightness in the skin around his eyes. "You'll be beautiful, if nothing else."

"Yeah, you look really amazing." Felix tossed the hair spray aside. Lucy nodded in agreement.

Someone knocked on the door. All four heads turned toward it. The door slid open. Richard, in his sleek black tuxedo. He smiled at Cat and threw his arms out wide.

"You aren't supposed to be in here!" Lucy said. But Richard ignored her.

"Let's do this thing," he said.

And Cat's world turned to mist.

The wedding ceremony had all the logic of a dream. Cat walked for ten hours down that never-ending faded pink carpet. Roses and baby's breath grew out of the wooden church pews. For half a second her father appeared, his face looming in close to hers. He was smiling; he was crying. She smiled back at him. Then he kissed her cheek and disappeared. Up in their alcoves, the statues shifted and whispered among themselves as Cat recited her vows. She heard only sounds as she spoke, guttural and ancient.

The chapel smelled like the inside of a freezer in a flower shop, damply cold and sickly sweet.

At only one point during the ceremony did Cat's focus sharpen. The mist melted away. She was in a church, surrounded by statues, wearing a heavy white dress and too much makeup. There were two rings on her finger: one with a diamond, the other a narrow band of gold.

Cat blinked.

Then she handed her bouquet to Lucy, as she had been instructed to do in the rehearsals. She turned back to face Richard on the altar and, in those few moments when her eyes belonged only to herself, she glanced out over the church. Her side was half-full, dotted with old scientist friends of the family. Finn sat in the front row next to her father. Her father's cheeks were wet. Finn looked straight at her. He was the most beautiful man she had ever seen. And then Cat was gazing at Richard, and Richard was taking her hand in his own, and she was back in that fog, that haze, that mist that persisted until the moment they walked down the aisle with their arms linked, organ music billowing out behind them, and emerged into the bright, burning world.

*　*　*　*

At the reception, Cat's head cleared.

There was a sit-down luncheon, of course, the smell of which made Cat's head spin and her stomach grumble. Pomegranate soup and artichoke hearts simmering in pools of butter, chicken roasted with honey and pine nuts. Cat ate all of it with huge, greedy bites, not worrying about wine-colored splatters across her dress. White lights twinkled overhead and in halos around the tables: the reception hall was windowless and dark except for the occasional moments when someone slipped outside and sunlight flooded through the open door and across the neat arrangement of round tables.

After lunch, people from SynLodge stood up to make toasts and speeches. The last person to toast was Ella Halfast. At the microphone, she set down her champagne glass, a frosted pink lipstick kiss on the rim. "I have to say," she said, "I never thought I'd see it. Caterina—" At the sound of her name, Cat jerked her head up and looked Ella in the eye. "Caterina, congratulations. I'd *love* to know your secret." Then she picked up her glass, lifted it above her head. "To the Fevershams," she slurred.

"The Fevershams," the audience shouted back, their glasses held aloft. Richard laughed. Cat wanted to slide under the table and disappear in the billowing folds of her gown. But before she could move, Richard grabbed her upper arm, pulled her in close, and kissed her on the mouth.

Later, they cut the cake with an oversize knife, Richard's fingers wrapped around the knife's handle, Cat's fingers wrapped around his. The cake was covered entirely in flowers made of icing: sugar-spun marigolds and morning glories, amaryllis and alstroemeria. As the knife slid through the cake, the flowers all muddied together, turned back into icing.

Richard slipped a piece of cake between Cat's lips, neatly, leaving his fingers in a little longer than he should have. Everyone applauded. It sounded like rain. Cat and Richard danced, though it was difficult for Cat to move in that heavy dress. Her skirts swished across the floor, across her bare feet—she had slipped off her shoes as soon as the reception started, left them lying underneath the table where she'd eaten lunch.

The afternoon wore on and Cat drank glass after glass of champagne until her thoughts were made of air. She didn't stop dancing, even though the arches of her feet ached and burned, even though the weight of her dress pressed down on her chest. These minor inconveniences of the body were preferable to sitting down at the light-draped table at the center of the room. Cat didn't want to be the center of attention, the focal point for every single person at the reception, the place where their eyes naturally turned. That role exhausted her more than dancing ever could.

Eventually, Cat had danced with everyone willing, all the awkwardly suited young men from SynLodge, a handful of her father's friends. She broke away from the dance floor and drifted out among the twinkling tables strewn with champagne flutes, making sure to keep moving, a fluff of dandelion seed caught on the wind. She drifted over to where Finn was sitting.

"Dance with me," she said, and he looked at her with his black eyes. Miguel sat next to him, his tie loosened, and Cat saw him watching her with an expression of drunken amusement.

"Was he bothering you?" she asked Finn.

"Not at all."

Miguel winked conspiratorially at her. Cat had drunk too much champagne to care. She grabbed Finn by both hands and pulled him to standing. He wore the same ill-fitting suit he had worn to her mother's funeral. They walked out to the dance floor and the music changed, became something old and slow and sad, too sad to be romantic, too sad for a wedding. No one else was dancing. She put her arms around Finn's neck, and he put his hands on her waist. The dress's weight disappeared. She moved her face close to his, and he didn't pull away. They were close enough to kiss.

The song lasted three and a half minutes. For three and a half minutes, Cat lived a completely different life. For three and a half minutes, she had married Finn instead of Richard. For three and a half minutes, the version of her life that rolled out in front of her did not fill her heart with dolor.

For three and a half minutes, Cat understood joy.

When the song ended, Cat felt something rushing out of her, as though she had been holding her breath underwater. Finn pulled away, his hands at her elbows. Cat looked dazedly around the room. It was late in the afternoon, and no one was paying any attention to her. Richard loitered by the bar, laughing raucously with his friends. Felix and Lucy and Miguel leaned against one another at one of the tables, passing a bottle of vodka between them. Her father, sitting alone by the door, looked toward the annihilated wedding cake, his hands folded neatly in front of him. Cat turned back to Finn. His eyes vibrated.

"Thanks for the dance," she said.

"You're welcome. Congratulations on your marriage." A pause. "Mrs. Feversham."

* * * *

When Cat stepped outside the reception hall, the glare from the sun flashed up off the jewels on her dress and blinded her. She threw up one hand, eyes fluttering, pupils contracting into tiny pinpricks. She saw nothing but white light.

"Time to go." Richard's voice was in her ear; his breath was at the nape of her neck. The heat of his hands pressed against her lower back, pushing her into a shower of birdseed. Cat lifted up her skirts, tilted her head down. In the miasma of sunlight she spotted the shine of Richard's car. Everyone was cheering. She couldn't breathe.

She climbed into the car, hoisting her skirts up around her. It was pointless even to try to buckle the safety belt. She slipped off her shoes and tucked her legs up underneath her and peered out the window at everyone peering back at her. She didn't see Finn.

"We're fucking married." Richard threw his arm around her shoulder and pulled her across the shift stick. Kissed her. "I have a surprise for you."

"A good surprise or a bad surprise?" The last thing Cat wanted today was a surprise. What she wanted more than anything was to sleep.

He smiled. "A good one." He started the engine and pulled out of the parking lot. A cheer erupted behind them. Cat watched the reception hall disappear in the rearview mirror.

Richard pulled onto the freeway. He reached down and turned on his music player, drummed his fingers against the steering wheel.

Cat almost said, *You're in a good mood* before she stopped herself, realizing, *He just got married. He married you. You're married.*

She took a deep breath.

They weren't driving in the direction of the condo; they were, in fact, driving out of the city. Everything here was brand-new, reconstructed in the last few years. This part of the countryside had flooded, many years ago, before Cat was born. Three hurricanes in a month, with winds strong enough to shoot off strings of tornadoes like Christmas lights.

"Where are we going exactly?" Cat pressed one hand to the window. The thin strips of grass lining the freeway were greener than the grass in the city.

"I told you, it's a surprise." Richard guided the car off the freeway, onto a road surrounded by sound walls the pearly color of conch shells. He turned down one street and then another. Huge suburban houses flashed by. A stone sank to the bottom of Cat's stomach. She didn't like the look of these houses. They were more normalcy than she was prepared to handle.

Richard pulled up to a guarded gate, pressed his ID card to the glassy computerized reader. A dot of ice-blue light blinked three times, and the gate slid open. Richard drove through twisted, curving streets, leaning back confidently in his seat. The houses here were bigger than in the other parts of the neighborhood, each one surrounded by trees and a swath of empty, impossibly green yard. Richard pulled into a cul-de-sac.

Cat's heart hammered. Heat built up behind her eyes. "I bought you a house," Richard said. The car rolled to a stop. He turned off the engine.

"Oh my God."

Richard grinned. "It's this one." He pointed through the windshield to a house made entirely of glass. Cat stared. She could see straight through the walls to the blinding blue sky.

"You bought a house?" She looked at Richard. "I thought we were just going to live in the condo—"

"Oh, hell no," he said. "Do you like it? I know I should have asked for your input. I mean, I know this really should be a decision we make together, but—" He bit his lip earnestly. "I wanted to see the expression on your *face*, you know."

"It's lovely," said Cat. "Um. Thank you."

Richard laughed. He pushed the car door open, stepped out. Cat followed, not bothering to put her shoes back on. The grass was cold beneath her feet. The wind blustered through the trees, and Cat's veil streamed out behind her, fluttering at the ends. Her skirts billowed around her legs. Richard walked up the narrow stone pathway to the front door. Cat didn't follow him. She just stood at the edge of the yard, her veil tugging gently at her temples. Cataracts of white light fell off the angles of the house.

"Well?" Richard called out. He gestured for Cat to join him on the porch. "You want to see the inside or not? It's completely outfitted with Robocile."

"What?"

For a second, Richard's eyes narrowed. Then he swiped a card across the door. Cat lifted up her skirts and walked across the yard.

"This is a new subdivision." Richard leaned against the door to hold it open. "Pretty trendy. Lots of big names designed the houses. I mean, I didn't recognize any of them, but I was told they were big names." He paused as Cat stepped on the porch. Faint lines of disappointment traced around his eyes.

Robocile. Of course. His AI program.

"So I'll finally get to see what you were working on all those late nights," she said.

Richard beamed and gestured for her to step inside. There was no foyer—only an enormous room, full of sunlight and empty of furniture. The ceiling extended above her head for two stories.

"So everything's automated?" Cat prompted.

"Yep," Richard said. "Well, most everything. The computer's built into the structure of the house, although I don't think it's been turned on yet. And of course you talk to it." He paused. Cat gazed around the room. There were no clouds of golden dust to catch the sunlight. "You're going to be the first person outside the company to test it. You can let me know if you think we faked the sentience well enough."

"All right."

"Let me show you around." He wrapped his arm around her shoulder and pulled her close. "I like how everything's open, you know? Here, let me show you the bedroom." He led her down a wide, sunny corridor, a pair of discreet control panels set into the walls. All the lights on the panels were dark and still. The master bedroom was around the corner and encased in alabaster white walls, although a square of blue sky was visible through the ceiling.

"Isn't it fantastic?"

"It's beautiful." Cat pulled away from him and walked back out into the corridor, ran her fingers over the control panels. The house was silent save for the *swish swish swish* of her dress. She followed the corridor into the main room, where she found a sliding glass door leading out to a stone patio. She tugged the door open with the pads of her fingers and stepped out onto the smooth, cool stone. There was no grass in the backyard, just tilled-up dirt. The yard was surrounded by a ring of fast-growth pine trees that looked plastic. Cat gathered up her skirt with both hands and stepped off the patio. Her feet sank into the soil. The hem of her dress dragged across the dirt.

"Oh," said Richard behind her. She looked over her shoulder at him. "Yeah, they haven't laid the grass out yet. Sorry."

Cat didn't say anything. She walked to the center of the yard. The wind whipped up her dress like a bit of cloud. She turned around and looked up at the glittering house, at Richard standing in his tuxedo in the doorway.

"Smile," said Richard. "You're home now."

TEN

Six months into her marriage, Cat discovered a coffee shop she liked. Ever since the honeymoon she was alone most of the time, and the coffee shop was the sort of place that favored aloneness. It was in an old wooden house in a leafy, gentrified neighborhood on the edge of the suburbs, the rafters strung with tarnished silverware that clinked and jangled whenever someone opened the door. Cat liked to sit at the same table next to the window, drinking a caffè breve and looking at the wildflower garden growing in the backyard. Hidden speakers played sad, whispery music. Dusty beams of sunlight fell through the skylights.

One of the baristas was an android.

Not quite like Finn. The android was vaguely female and moved more stiffly and possessed a more limited vocabulary than Finn did. Her facial features didn't change as much. But like Finn, she was truly automatous. She was not like the computer in Cat's glass house in the suburbs; she wasn't even like the army of electric servants that now paraded up and down the streets of middle-class neighborhoods, children and dogs in tow.

"Hello," the android said when Cat drifted through the door one balmy autumn afternoon, setting off the chiming chain reaction of the silverware overhead. The android's mouth and eyes lit up electric white. "Caffè breve?" she said.

"Yes, please."

"Coming right up."

Cat paid and then slouched near the table covered with sugar canisters and pitchers of cream. Behind the counter, the android slid a metal filter packed with espresso into the coffeemaker. Milky steam clouded up into the air.

"Do you like working here?" Cat asked.

The android turned around, steam curling around her expressionless face. "Oh yes," she said. "Mr. Rodriguez hired me." *Rodriguez* slurred slightly, the final *z* sounding more like an *s*.

"Is he the owner?"

The android nodded, a quick jerk of her head. *Finn can nod, really nod.* Cat smiled, hoping she looked trustworthy. The android poured the steamed cream over the espresso. "He found me. Long ago. At McCallister's." The android's mouth lit up again. She slid the caffè breve down the bar toward Cat.

"McCallister's." Cat tried to place the name.

"Yes."

"Oh my God. That's the junkyard, isn't it?" She remembered Lucy talking about it—she used to jump the fence on rainy nights, when the guards would be curled up with their computers inside the little shack next to the gate, to scrounge around for found-art objects.

"Yes."

"Who would—"

"I was de-fec-tive." The android's mouth did not light up.

Cat didn't say anything. The android stared at her for a moment longer, but then the silverware rattled along the ceiling. A trio of college students walked in, their faces pink from the sun.

Cat carried her coffee over to her favorite table. Loose granules of sugar glittered in the sunlight. It was too hot for a caffè breve, but Cat drank it anyway. The college students sat nearby and erupted periodically into screeching laughter, the legs of their table clicking against the wood floors. Cat always felt like she was the same age she had been in college, but the college students here seemed so young. They were children.

When Cat finished her coffee she went out into the wildflower garden and lit a cigarette in the shade of an enormous magnolia tree. The sun's glare made it difficult to see through the coffee shop windows, but every now and then pale white lights would blink inside.

*　*　*　*

Cat didn't work at the vice stand anymore. She still went to the artist's co-op, where she would weave a few rows on her project, the yarn unfamiliar against her skin. The drive there from the suburbs was long, though, and often slow with traffic, and sometimes the co-op seemed more of an artifact of her past than a reality of her present. But every month she paid in her portion of the rent, and at least twice a month she roused herself out of bed to make the trip and work at her loom.

Even so, the mild sun-kissed winter transformed nearly unnoticed into the mild, sun-kissed spring and Cat's life took on a uniform sameness.

She exercised most mornings, doing Pilates off the screen in the living room. The house always chimed to remind her, even though she couldn't remember asking it to. She reread the books of her childhood, all those stories Finn recited to her from memory: *Metamorphoses* was still her favorite. These many years later she was still enamored of the idea of things becoming other things, of bodies changing into other bodies.

Richard worked his usual long hours—even longer now that SynLodge was on a meteoric rise toward capitalistic greatness. It had finally begun to turn a profit, he told her on one of his rare Sundays at home. Another AI company, Noratech, was talking about incorporating it. Cat nodded along to all this business chatter but rarely listened; when she listened, she didn't care.

During the blur of days, Cat looked forward to her long evening walks. She followed the meandering cement paths cutting through the neighborhood, the houses twinkling in the twilight. Even though the days were already uncomfortably hot, the evenings still held on to a faint strain of coolness. Many of the neighborhood houses didn't draw their curtains, and Cat liked to peer in through the illuminated windows at the families set up like tableaux inside: a housewife with frosted blond hair, children in school uniforms, a service android—they were all androids out here; anyone who could afford these houses could afford a robot that looked like a person—washing the dishes or mixing up cocktails. Sometimes she lit a cigarette, away from the house's computer, which always read the smoke as a fire.

She wondered if anyone walked past her glass house at night. She wondered what they saw, what conclusions they drew about her, curled up on the low-slung divan with a reading slate and a glass of red wine. No service android. They wouldn't know that the house itself was veined with artificial intelligence.

Cat had also begun to donate money to the Automaton Defense League.

She didn't tell Richard. She'd made the first donation at Miguel's urging, down at the co-op, with no intention of making another. But then a few weeks later she had sunk so deep into her suburban haze her waking life felt like a dream. Halfway through one of her walks, she stopped beneath a pine tree drooping with heat, pulled out her comm slate, and signed away a portion of Richard's money to an organization that wanted to shut down his company.

The donation cleared her head. After that, when the neighborhood closed in on her, she donated. It helped, sometimes.

One humid evening in May, Cat came home after a futile afternoon at the co-op to find Richard drinking a glass of orange juice at the breakfast table. When she walked in he leapt up and threw his arms around her shoulders, pulled her down onto his lap.

"Where would you rather live," he asked. "The beach or the mountains?"

Cat teetered on the edge of his knees, steadying herself against the table. "The beach, I guess."

"Excellent," said Richard. "Because if this purchase goes through, that might just happen six months out of the year." He winked. "And I've got something else up my sleeve, too."

"What?" She didn't particularly care.

"It's a secret."

Cat slid off his lap. Richard drained his orange juice, stood up, kissed her, and then scurried out of the kitchen, toward the office in the back of the house, where he could continue working even though he was at home.

"Well," said Cat to the empty kitchen. "What was that about?" When there was no response, she added: "Computer?"

"Mr. Feversham is pleased about an impending financial contract involving SynLodge." The computer had a chiming voice that always sounded insincere. "I can request more information from Mr. Feversham if you would like."

"No," said Cat. "Forget it. It's not important." All conversations with the house's computer went the same way: It repeated what Cat already knew. It mistook her small talk for serious inquiry.

Nearly a year in the glass house. And although Cat had grown accustomed to the automation easily enough—the toilets cleaned themselves, the walls released armies of vacuum bots every other day at exactly two p.m.—the computer's voice still unnerved her. It didn't sound like a robot, but it didn't sound like a person, either. The voice had a hollowness to it, an emptiness, like the bottom of a well. When the computer had first been turned on, a few weeks after they'd moved in, Cat had wandered uneasily from room to room, waiting for the computer's polite chime. Even now she sometimes jumped when she heard it.

Cat dug in her pocket for a cigarette, found one, slipped it between her lips. She didn't bother to light it. Not with the computer recording every impurity in the air. Cat pulled out one of the uncomfortable metal chairs and sat down. She leaned her head against her hand. She tried to look outside, but the sun had set and all she saw was her own reflection in the glass wall.

* * * *

The next afternoon Cat asked the house computer to bring up the chat monitor. She was in the house's office; Richard was at work. He was always at work. She punched into the keypad the string of numbers to connect her to the computer in her father's house—the old dusty one, the one he'd set up in the dining room after her mother died.

Her father's face appeared on the screen, startling her. "Daddy," she said. "I . . . How's it going?" Her father never answered when she called this computer. She wasn't sure he left his laboratory anymore. He'd gotten so frail lately, his skin sallow, his face gaunt. "You look . . . Are you eating enough?"

"I'm fine." He drawled the *fine* out into an unconvincing twang. "You don't need to worry about me." He smiled. "How are things in the glass house?"

"They're good."

"I'm sorry I haven't made it out there. We've been so busy, Finn and I, what with this lunar station and all." He smiled gently. "But you weren't calling to talk to me."

Cat's cheeks warmed. "I was just calling home. To talk to anyone."

"Let me get Finn. Cat?" He peered at her. With the changes in his face and the glassy quality of the video chat monitor, she barely recognized him. "I love you. I hope you're happy."

Before Cat could answer, her father disappeared. On the screen, she saw the dining room windows, the sheer curtains hanging lank and still. Her air-conditioning switched on. The foundation of the house groaned. The oleander bushes outside clicked against the glass.

Finn came into view.

"Cat," he said. "How are you?"

"I miss you." Every time she called, she asked him the same question. "Would you like to come visit?"

"You're married." Always the same answer.

Cat listened to the creaks and moans of the house. She always felt like the house computer was eavesdropping on their conversation. Recording it.

"Daddy looks so thin," she said. "Is he all right? Is he eating?"

Finn paused. His skin looked too pale through the camera. "Yes," he said. "He's fine. You don't need to worry about him."

Finn's eyes twitched away from the camera, back to her. She'd never seen him do it before she married. But now, every time she spoke to him, she counted the number of times his eyes flickered away from her.

She didn't know what it meant.

"You're just busy," said Cat. "With the lunar station."

"Yes," said Finn. "The lunar station."

"How's that going?"

"Well."

"Are you sure you don't want to come visit? Or I can come visit you."

He looked away, looked back. "You're married."

Always the same answer.

"I should go," said Finn. "Lots of work to do."

"I understand."

The monitor flickered black, then bright blue, then switched to the screen saver of floating, iridescent jellyfish. Finn had severed the connection from his end. He was gone. Her father's house was gone. Replaced by jellyfish that looked like ghosts.

Cat went out to the front porch, to get away from the house computer. She lit a cigarette. She smoked more now that she could afford the taxes on the cigarettes and didn't have to cull a stash from customer donations. Next door her neighbors, several decades older and from families that had been wealthy before the Disasters, were sitting on their porch. She heard the lilt of their voices, their twinkling laughter.

Cat walked through the yard, smoking, the sound of Finn's voice ringing in her ears. *You're married.* Next door, the neighbors stopped talking. Cat looked up at them, and they lifted their drinks in greeting. The wife smiled, pressed one hand against her silver hair. Cat waved with a cigarette pressed between her fingers.

That was the extent of Cat's interaction with her neighbors.

She finished her smoke and went back inside. The house echoed with its emptiness. She wandered into the living room. Turned the video screen on manually. It was still set to the twenty-four-hour news feed Richard watched in the mornings while he lifted weights. Cat watched the screen for several seconds before she realized she was looking at the view from the lunar station: grainy, crackling footage of the moon's surface in more or less real time. Robots that looked nothing at all like people crawled in and out of the shot. Cat turned up the volume.

About to send the first manned mission, said the voiceover. *The tests all look great. Everything's coming together ahead of schedule.* The image of the moon flickered and was replaced by a pair of newscasters and an older woman who looked like a scientist. She seemed vaguely familiar; Cat wondered if she had come to her wedding.

We'll be cycling through, once a year, she said. *Our hope is to understand how humans cope, psychologically, with life on the moon.*

Life on the moon. A life of barren soil and silvery breathlessness. *I'd live on the moon,* Cat thought, dots of sunlight scattering across the living room floor. *Couldn't be any worse than here.*

* * * *

One day Cat found a stack of boxes in one of the spare bedrooms. She'd planned to go to the co-op that day, but the weather had turned cold and rainy, and she knew the traffic would be terrible. The gray light seeped through the glass walls and settled over Richard's sleek Danish furniture. Cat was restless. She couldn't weave, but she still wanted to do something with her hands.

Cat sat down on the spare room's cold tile floor. The rows of track lighting set into the walls burned steadily against the rainy darkness. She pulled down the first box: it was full of tufts of yarn and scraps of expensive, designer fabric. Cat pulled out a handful of yarn. It reminded her of her project at the co-op. The gift.

Cat slid the box aside and pulled down the next one, which was full of more art supplies, these even older: dried-out tubes of oil paint, a bouquet of paintbrushes with crusty, hardened bristles. A few canisters of undeveloped antique film. High school stuff, junk that had been shoved into the back of her closet at her old apartment.

Something glossy and flat was tucked down at the bottom of the box. A photograph. Cat eased it out, trying not to smudge the print with her fingertips. Charcoal dust billowed into the air.

It was the photograph she had taken of Finn over a decade ago, his eyes boring straight into the camera. It could have been taken the last time she saw him, last week, when they spoke through the video chat, when Finn reminded her that she was married.

Cat deflated. She crawled across the floor until she was leaning against the bedroom wall, the photograph of Finn balanced on her knees. So he didn't age. He looked the same as he had the first time she saw him, when she was five years old—and he would look the same long after she had disintegrated into the soil of the cemetery, when the only trace left of her would be a string of molecules in the wildflowers above her grave. She wondered why knowing this did not make her feel revulsion or fear or malignant curiosity, why all it did was add to her pervasive and unending sadness.

Cat dropped the photograph back into the box. The rain picked up, rattling against the roof. She stood up, put the lid on the box containing Finn's photograph. Maybe the traffic in to the co-op wouldn't be *that* bad. She hadn't felt this strong a desire to work in a long time.

"Computer," said Cat, walking out of the room and into the dark hallway. "If Richard comes home, tell him I went into the city."

"Of course, Mrs. Feversham. However, may I advise you of the extreme weather forecasts for this afternoon—"

"Not necessary, Computer. I've driven in a thunderstorm before." Cat grabbed her purse and slipped on a pair of flats.

"If you insist, Mrs. Feversham."

Cat drove for nearly an hour through the rainstorm. The traffic was miserable, and the glow of brake lights blurred and streaked as though it were made of rainwater.

The studio wasn't deserted when Cat finally arrived. She parked her car along the curb. Felix stood huddled under the narrow overhang jutting out over the stoop, the ember from his cigarette glimmering in the darkness. Cat pushed out of her car and ran splashing through the puddles up to the door.

"Holy shit," said Felix. His voice materialized as smoke on the wet air. "Or as my auntie Lynn would say, *As I live and breathe.* I thought you were dead."

Had it been that long since she'd come to the co-op?

Cat realized she couldn't remember.

"Seriously, though," he said. "It's great to see you. Did you come to say hi or . . ." He waved his cigarette around.

"I wanted to work on the tapestry."

"Oh thank *God*," Felix said. "Lucy has been harassing me non-stop about that fucking loom. She wants to try her hand at weaving again." He rolled his eyes. "I caught her sneaking over to it the other day with a pair of scissors. Nearly kicked her out of the co-op. I told her it was a *gift* and she needed to back the fuck down."

"Yeah." Cat tugged at her hair. "I'm sorry about that. About not coming. The time got away from me—"

Felix put a hand on her shoulder. "It's fine. As long as you're sending me that monthly rent check, your work is safe with me."

The inside of the studio smelled like turpentine and old clay. Rain pounded against the tin roof. The damp air seemed to hang in clouds near the ceiling. Cat tossed her purse aside, shook out her wet hair, and walked over to the loom. The silvery green threads of Finn's tapestry fluttered unfinished in the breeze from the metal fan next to the sink.

Cat pulled up a chair and began to weave. The rhythm of it was simple and instinctual, the way it had been before she married. Felix came back inside and sat down at his potting wheel without saying anything. They worked in silence.

After two hours, Cat took a break. She stepped outside for a smoke, watching the rain fall in sheets over the street. Droplets sprayed across her face, clung to her cheekbones and eyelashes. She smoked only half her cigarette before she flicked it out into the storm and went back inside.

Felix had disappeared. The potting wheel sat empty; he must have gone to the kiln room, in the back of the studio. Cat ran her fingers over the completed portion of the tapestry, rolled up tight in front of her. It seemed flat. Lifeless. She knew, suddenly, the problem: there wasn't enough of herself in it. Miguel had told her that once, a long time ago, when they first met.

"If you make a gift for someone," he had said, "particularly someone you love, you have to put part of yourself into it." It was

Christmas. They were at some Stella bar. Strings of lights twinkled around his head.

"You do?" said Cat, half-drunk, playing along. Miguel looked so serious.

"Of course. Otherwise, it's just a lopsided candy dish from fifth-grade art class. It's junk. I mean, they'll take it, if they're polite, and then they'll wait till you're gone to toss it in the trash." The legs of his chair slammed down on the bar floor, and Miguel picked up his beer, knocked it back. "Making gifts is not something to be taken lightly, Mad Scientist's Daughter."

Now, years later, Cat plucked out one of her hairs and wound it together with the weft thread. It glinted reddish gold in the studio lights. Cat wove the weft thread through, combed it down. Worked back the opposite direction. When her hair was firmly woven in place, Cat stood up. She took a deep breath. Her legs shook. It was only a hair woven into a tapestry but she felt drained, exhausted.

The back door slammed and Felix walked into the studio, raised an eyebrow at Cat standing, shaking in front of the loom.

"You okay?"

Cat nodded. She slid back down in her seat, picked up the weft-ing thread. And then she worked for another three hours, as the storm abated, as the moon came out from behind the clouds.

* * * *

"Where the fuck have you been? I've been calling you." Cat dropped her purse on the floor. Richard barreled up to her. He wore a tie and a jacket. Cat stared at him for a moment, trying to figure out why he wasn't in his usual jeans and T-shirt.

"Oh my God," she said.

"Great, now you remember."

"The Noratech party. It was tonight."

Richard jerked his head up and down. Cat knew he was nodding *yes* but it didn't really look like it.

"When were . . ." Her voice faltered. She had completely forgot-ten the party. The rain, the photograph, the loom: they had made her so melancholy she had slipped into the recesses of the past. The present had become the future, and therefore not worth bothering with.

"Thirty minutes ago. Why the hell didn't you answer your slate?"

"I didn't hear it."

Richard glared at her. Cat kicked off her shoes, headed toward the bedroom. "Let me throw on a dress," she said. "And pull my hair back. I can do my makeup in the car—"

"Why didn't you hear your slate? Where were you?" Richard caught her by the upper arm, whirled her around. Cat shook off his grasp. "Were you—" He stopped and took a deep breath. "Just tell me where you were."

"At the studio with Felix. The roof's metal so with the rain I didn't hear you calling." Cat stomped into the bedroom. "Jesus, where did you think I was?"

"I don't know." Richard stayed in the hallway. Cat shimmied out of her clothes, stiff with dried rainwater, and pulled a black cocktail dress out of the closet. She checked her hair as she dressed: the rain had curled it into ringlets. She probably didn't even need to pull it back. Cat twisted her arm around behind her to jerk up the zipper.

"Are you sure you're gonna go like that?"

Cat stopped, half-zipped. She looked over her shoulder at Richard. "Like what?" she said.

"I don't know, your hair's a little wild."

Cat pulled up her zipper the rest of the way.

"We're thirty minutes late," she said. "My hair's not that important."

Richard shrugged. "I know," he said. "It's just . . . There'll be photographers there."

"So?" Cat grabbed her makeup bag, filled it with a tube of mascara and a couple of shades of lipstick.

"Well, I mean, you need to look good, you know. It makes me look good if you look good."

Cat stared at him. "Seriously?" she said. "Do you want me to go to this party with you or not? I'm sorry I was late, but I lost track of time—"

"Forget it." Richard smiled. "You look beautiful. And you're right, we need to get going."

Richard drove, the air in the suburbs steaming from the rain and fragrant with pine trees and potted plants. Cat put on her makeup by the flickering light of the street lamps. Red lipstick, black mascara, yellow light. She refused to allow herself to think about anything but eyeliner. Even so, constantly in the back of her mind, was this: *Finn's tapestry.*

Finn. Finn. Finn.

Cat finished putting on her makeup. She felt like a seashell, pretty enough but empty and easily broken.

The party was at a hotel overlooking the glassy, manmade lake on the edge of the suburbs, not far from the tree-lined business park where Richard was thinking about relocating his offices. When they walked in, a few bored-looking photographers snapped their pictures. They floated up to the party in a glass elevator. Cat put her hand on Richard's biceps and held herself up tall and straight because this, going to parties in a designer dress, was the only thing she really had to do in her marriage. Her one responsibility was to be a pillar of light, thrusting Richard out of the darkness.

She smiled as dazzlingly as she could to all those strange faces in the party's soft golden glow.

They stayed for only a couple of hours, long enough for Richard to cycle through the investors, shaking their hands and charming them with flashes of white teeth. Cat peeled away from him and found herself in a huddle of corporate wives, all in dresses that looked like hers, their hair ironed flat or wound up in elaborate bouffants, their laughter sharp as diamonds.

"Caterina Feversham," one of them said, holding out her hand limply. Cat shook it. "We've heard a lot about you. You're an artist, right?"

"I pretend to be," Cat said. They all tittered like they didn't quite get the joke. Cat took a long drink of champagne. She glanced at her reflection in the window and for a moment she couldn't see herself: just another corporate wife in a cluster of corporate wives.

A wife in a slinky green dress tilted her head and tapped one manicured finger against her chin. She frowned. "Feversham," she said. "I know that name."

"My husband owns SynLodge," said Cat.

The wife shook her head, her brow furrowed. The other wives shifted their weight and tossed bored glances at one another.

"She's an *artist*, hon," one of them said. "That's probably where you've heard of her."

"No, it's not that." Then the wife in green snapped her fingers. "Of course! I've seen that name on the ADL donation roster."

Cat did not move. Her champagne glass hung beside her, bubbles drifting to the surface.

"ADL," she said.

"Aren't they involved with the whole robot-rights thing?" asked one of the sideline wives. The rest picked up their heads, alert to the possibility of gossip. "Haven't they been protesting the merger?"

The wife in green narrowed her eyes. "My husband works for Noratech," she said. "And so do I. ADL makes all their donation records public."

Cat sipped her champagne.

"It doesn't reflect very well on your husband," said the wife in green, and she smiled, curling up her lips to reveal a row of perfect teeth.

"Excuse me." Cat turned away from the cluster of wives. It occurred to her that this revelation should be more distressing to her than it was: she had been keeping the donations a secret from Richard but she no longer cared what his reaction would be if he found out. Cat's heart beat normally, as though she had been discussing the weather, the quality of the food.

After the party, Richard and Cat drove home in silence. The freeway was nearly empty. Cat stared out the window. She slipped off her shoes, and when they arrived at the house she walked in her stockings up the damp stone sidewalk, her skirt swishing around her knees. The porch light switched on. She could smell the oleander growing along the side of the house.

"Well?" she said to Richard. "I say we got there fashionably late. No harm done." She spoke only because she couldn't bear the silence any longer.

But Richard didn't answer. He walked away from the bedroom,

in the direction of his office. Cat heard the sigh of the door shutting behind him.

She went into the bedroom, took off her stockings and then her dress, tossing them both down the laundry chute. She lay across the bed in her underwear and looked up through the glass ceiling at the pale scatter of stars.

You're married.

This was her marriage. This was her life.

ELEVEN

Cat followed Miguel through a dark, narrow corridor, past a law office, the glowing sign in its window missing a handful of letters, and a noisy banh mi place. They were in an old storefront near the center of the city. The floor was dusty from disuse and the storm tape in the windows hadn't been taken down since the last hurricane. Cat hadn't seen storm tape since she was a child—most buildings came equipped with automatic shutters these days.

"Are you sure we're in the right place?" Cat kicked a pile of broken glass with the toe of her shoe.

Miguel turned toward her. "I come out here twice a month, Mad Scientist's Daughter."

Cat smiled; she hadn't heard the nickname in years. Miguel grinned, then whirled on his heel and followed the corridor until it dead-ended into a pair of double doors, a handwritten sign reading AUTOMATON DEFENSE LEAGUE propped up against the wall.

Miguel held the door for Cat. She smoothed the skirt of her dress; she smoothed the loose pieces of her hair. She hadn't wanted to come to the meeting at all, but Miguel had insisted, telling her that her donations were a tremendous help to the group, that everyone wanted to meet her. Cat thought back to that party a month ago, the Noratech wife knowing she had given money to an organization working against everything Richard had worked for. Sometimes Cat wondered if Richard knew. She wasn't sure that she cared.

There were about fifteen people at the meeting, sitting in folding chairs and eating from the potluck dishes spread out on a table near the door, and five robots of varying degrees of complexity. None of them as complex as Finn.

Everyone, even the robots, turned to look at Cat and Miguel standing in the doorway. Cat felt herself curling up like a morning glory in the heat of the afternoon. Then a man near the front of the room raised a hand in greeting, and Miguel called out a cheerful, "Hey, everybody!" and there was a murmur in return and then all the faces turned away. Cat let out a long, slow breath. It was harder and harder for her to be looked at these days. All that time spent under glass.

One of the robots, an android, male-identified, filled a paper cup with punch and brought it to her. His movements were fluid, graceful, but his skin had a glossy plastic sheen to it and his eyes possessed the flatness of computer monitors. Cat accepted the punch. It was too sweet, like syrup, like medicine.

"Welcome." The android's voice reverberated with electronic feedback.

Cat nodded. "Thanks." She looked down at the surface of the punch, swirled it in its cup.

"Would you like some information about the organization?" the android asked. He smiled at her, rows of too-small perfect teeth. Cat shook her head.

"I already donate."

"Oh! Are you . . ." For a second his eyes went blank, like a turned-off screen, and then he blinked. "Caterina Feversham?"

Cat nodded, feeling suddenly shy.

"Thank you." The android grasped Cat's free hand and she jumped, because his touch was cool and dry and felt exactly like Finn's. "Thank you so much. You don't know how grateful we are—" The android stopped, dropped his hand to his side.

"You're welcome." Cat hesitated. "What would you like me to call you?"

"Oh! I'm sorry, I forget myself sometimes." The android smiled. "I'm Alastair."

Cat repeated the name to herself, letting it ripple over her tongue. *Alastair.*

"I gave it to myself after I was emancipated," he said. "I didn't have a name before."

"That's a shame."

"Just a numerical designation."

Cat nodded. She sipped her punch. When she looked at Alastair and met his steady mechanical gaze, a numbness wrapped tight around her heart. Her entire body sagged. She didn't know what to say.

"Best of luck to you," she murmured, and Alastair smiled again. He was constantly smiling. For a moment Cat wondered what sort of work he had been programmed to do before. She assumed it impolite to ask.

The man at the front of the room called the meeting to order, banging his fist a few times on an old wooden podium. Miguel waved at Cat, and then pointed at a chair up front. Cat excused herself from Alastair. Everyone was taking a seat, coming together in clumps, humans and robots both. Cat sat down next to Miguel.

"Welcome to the July fifteenth meeting of the Automaton Defense League, chapter number 4938." The man ran one hand over his hair, slicking it away from his face. He was tall and thin and middle-aged, his life etched out in arrows from the corners of his eyes. "We'd like to extend a welcome to any visitors here today." Cat was relieved he didn't look at her. "The ADL welcomes both humans and robots in its membership, and works to change legislation dealing with the rights of manufactured life forms at both the local and national level."

The man continued his speech, running through recent legal victories—another rights law passed on the West Coast, an increase in vocal support for full mandatory emancipation. Cat closed her eyes, his voice running over her like a river, like the river that slipped past her childhood home, where she swam with Finn in the cold green water.

Cat liked robots, but being in this room with them, all free of their duties, all free to program themselves into whoever they wanted to be, twisted her stomach. It was like being a child again, like she'd broken one of her mother's inscrutable rules. She couldn't quite place where the feeling came from.

" . . . thanks to the donations of Mrs. Caterina Feversham. Let's give her a round of applause."

Cat opened her eyes. The applause sounded like raindrops pattering across the roof of the glass house. Miguel nudged her, and Cat stood up and turned around so that she could look out over the members of the Automaton Defense League, chapter number 4938. She waved. Smiled. The five robots sat scattered among the rows of chairs, and she felt as though she had let them down somehow. She felt like a fraud.

The applause died away.

"Thank you all," she said. "Very much." She paused. Miguel nodded at her, encouraging her to go on. Strange to think the Miguel she knew from college was so involved with the rights of robots. Or maybe not. He had always been conscientious. Not like her. "It's very important to me that robots are granted the rights of human beings." She smiled waveringly. "We're all people."

More applause. Cat sat back down.

"You did good, lady," whispered Miguel. But knots still tied up the inside of Cat's stomach.

Forty-five minutes later, when the meeting ended and the humans filled up paper plates with piles of fruit salad and French onion dip, Cat sat at her seat and transferred a thousand dollars to the ADL donation account. She did not tell anyone that she did it. Not Miguel, not Alastair, not the chapter's president. It was that haze again, only this time it was thick with unplaceable guilt. She had felt it every time Alastair smiled.

*　*　*　*

One morning, Cat woke up early, the sky above the ceiling a pale pinkish gray. The space of bed beside her was empty and unrumpled, just as it had been when she fell asleep the night before, Richardless.

This had been happening a lot lately.

Cat crawled out of bed, the heat of the day already pooling around the glass. She didn't bother putting on her robe, just shuffled into the hallway in her panties and tank top, running her fingers through her sleep-mussed hair. When she came into the kitchen, Richard was sitting at the breakfast table, his eyes rimmed with red, his skin the color of old dishwater. His computer was sitting in front of him but he didn't look at it. Instead, he stared at the back-yard, where birds squabbled in the patchy grass. The grass, planted a month after they moved in, had never taken to the thin soil. Cat poured a cup of coffee, squinted at the bright sunlight reflecting off the countertops. "Looks like somebody stayed out all night," she said.

Richard lifted his head but didn't turn his eyes away from the birds out in the yard. "I've been here since midnight." He looked over at her then, twisted his entire body around, the chair scraping against the tile. "Not that I expect you to notice. You live in this house and suck up all my money, but you don't give a shit about where it comes from."

He jerked away from her.

Cat stirred her coffee slowly, not sure if she should acknowledge his outburst or creep back into her bed. She sipped at her coffee. It was lukewarm, burnt, old-tasting.

"What are you talking about?" she said.

"Forget it." Richard slammed his computer shut. "You don't care."

"I do care." It sounded insincere even to her. She knew she should try harder. "Tell me what's wrong. Did something happen?"

"Did something happen?" Richard tipped back in the chair and laughed. Cat stared at the back of his head. "Did something *happen*? Do you pay any attention at all to what goes on outside of your fucking art studio?" When Cat didn't respond, he shook his head. "This is what I'm talking about. You just—" He pushed his hands through his unwashed hair. "SynLodge is losing money. All those goddamned robot-rights protests. They want rights for all AI, sentient or not. So of course the investors are pulling out." His hands dropped to the table. "Noratech doesn't want to buy us anymore."

"Oh." The air in the kitchen was too thick to breathe. "I'm . . . I'm sorry."

Richard stood up and faced her. Cat pressed the small of her back into the countertop. Richard's hands had curled into two tight fists. Cat pulled her coffee mug against her chest like a shield and waited for him to say something about the ADL donations. He had to know.

"I'm sorry," she whispered. "And you're wrong—I do care. About what happens to you."

Richard leaned close enough to her that Cat could see the spider-web of pink veins crawling across the whites of his eyes, smell the smoky alcohol he'd drunk last night.

"You don't care about anything," he said.

Cat looked away from him, down at her sludgy coffee. Richard exhaled, pushed his hands up into his hair. "See?" He took a long step back from her, toward the picture window. "You don't even try to deny it. I married the fucking ice queen." One backward step. Another. He passed the refrigerator; he passed the kitchen island. The house was silent, frozen in the white-hot sunlight.

"Richard," Cat said carefully. But she didn't know what to say to him. She suspected his accusation was true. Why else did she feel like a fraud at the ADL meeting? Why else did she let herself be preserved like an experiment subject beneath the house's glass ceiling?

"Don't even try."

"Richard, I'm sorry for . . ."

Cat didn't know how to finish the sentence, but it didn't matter. Richard lunged across the room and picked up one of the metal chairs from the kitchen table, hoisted it above his head, and flung it into the window. For a moment, the million shards of glass hung silent in the sunlit air, throwing off miniature rays of light. Then the chair landed in the grass outside, and the room filled with an unmistakable ringing chorus as the window showered across the kitchen tile. Cat dropped her coffee mug. It broke into four pieces. Coffee oozed across the floor. Richard stalked out of the room, his head down, his eyes on the floor.

* * * *

A week or two went by. It might have been longer. The days, all so sunny and hot and clear, blended together too seamlessly now. Cat couldn't keep track.

Almost all evidence of Richard's violence that morning had been eliminated by the house's automation. The bots even carted in the chair from outside while Cat was tucked away in one of the back bedrooms. The only thing the house couldn't repair was the missing glass in the window. Cat left it uncovered despite the sweltering heat and the computer's hourly complaints. *The cold air is escaping. Dust is accumulating in the kitchen.* The computer had filed a work request, but the contractors hadn't shown up to fix it.

"Richard broke the window," Cat said. "It's his fault. Let him deal with it." She wanted to believe this; she didn't want to believe that what he told her was true, that she didn't care about anything, that she was soulless, empty, like the shell of a cicada.

Cat began to notice the natural world making its way into the sterile, sun-dried house: disintegrating pine needles and rotting flower petals, swirls of dirt, butterfly wings, tiny black beetles. One morning Cat came down to the kitchen and found a line of ants marching across the gleaming counters, onto the floor, out into the backyard. They had, in the night, found the place where she'd spilled a teaspoon of sugar while fixing a plate of strawberries, and now they carried off her messiness, granule by granule. She stood in the opening in the glass and watched them work.

The computer chimed. "It is predicted to rain tomorrow. It would be advisable to cover the empty pane. The contractors are still delayed."

"I know." Cat sighed. "I'll find a tarp or something this afternoon."

Then she went upstairs and showered and dressed and went about her long, empty day.

A little after four o'clock, someone rang the doorbell. "No one is at the door," announced the computer.

"What are you talking about?" asked Cat. "It just rang."

"No one is at the door."

Cat tossed her reading tablet aside and walked to the door. For a moment, in her fugue, she didn't understand what she was looking at. Finn. She saw Finn through the glass, his hair falling across his eyes.

Maybe it didn't matter anymore that she was married. Maybe she had completed enough unspoken penance to earn back his affection.

"Finn!" she cried. "You stupid machine," she said to the computer. "Somebody is there! It's Finn."

"No one is at the door."

Cat laughed and slid open the door. Finn blinked. "Cat," he said, and the way he said her name made her breath catch in her throat. Had it always sounded like that? Her name in his voice?

"Finn," she said. "Oh my God, come in—I can't believe you finally showed up! Did you call? Sometimes I don't hear my comm slate, the house is too big."

"I didn't call." He paused. "I wanted to surprise you."

"Surprise me?" She laughed. "Well, you certainly did that."

The corners of his mouth turned up in a sad, unusual way.

Cat couldn't resist the urge to kiss him, even though he stood in the doorway, where the neighbors might see them together, so she brushed her lips against his cheek, pulled herself away before it went further. He stared at her.

"Let me show you the house," she said.

"That won't be necessary."

"Oh, come on, it's made of glass. That's crazy, right?"

"It's certainly . . . strange . . . to live in a glass house."

"I think the neighbors spy on us."

"That's unfortunate."

Cat laughed. She felt transformed. Leavened. When she laughed she imagined a string of bubbles drifting up toward the transparent, sun-filled ceiling. She forgot about the hole in the kitchen and she forgot about Richard and she even forgot about the computer lurking silently in the circuitry of the house. She floated into the living room, and Finn followed her.

"You seem well," said Finn.

"I'm okay." Cat collapsed into the expansive folds of the couch. "It's good to see you."

"Yes." Finn stayed standing. "It's good to see you as well." Cat crossed her legs and tugged on her skirt. Finn watched her. The weight of his eyes on her was heavier than she remembered. Maybe it had been too long since she'd seen him: in real life, not through the distortion of video chat. He looked the exact same. He would always look the exact same, until the end of time.

But even so, something had changed. "What's wrong?" she said.

"Nothing's wrong."

"Something's happened." A pain in her heart. "Is it Daddy?"

"Nothing has happened to Dr. Novak." For a second, Finn didn't speak. "You shouldn't worry about him. He wouldn't like it."

"Then what is it?"

Finn looked out through the transparent wall, where the oleander bushes pressed against the glass. The sky was bleached white from the heat.

"I'm no longer the property of your father," he said.

"What?" Cat pushed herself forward on the couch. He still wouldn't look at her. "You were never anybody's property."

"I am now." Said so softly it sounded like a disruption in the white noise of the air conditioner.

Cat stared at him, a cold horror gnawing at the edges of her stomach. She wiped her palms against the couch. The light in the room was suddenly too bright. Finn turned his head toward her.

"I believe it was on the news."

"What are you talking about?"

"The auction. I auctioned myself off."

Everything in the world went still. Cat could no longer feel her lungs contracting and expanding. She could no longer feel her heart beating.

"What?" she whispered.

"I decided," said Finn, "that I no longer wished to belong to your father. And so—"

"You didn't belong to him!" Cat shrieked. She put one hand to her forehead. *Stay calm, stay calm.* Tears welled up at the base of her lashes, and she tried to blink them away. "You belong to yourself."

Finn smiled in that same sad strange way. "That's what Dr. Novak said. I contacted all the parties involved myself. Of course the money went to him, but . . . I have no need for money."

A tear escaped the cage of Cat's eyelashes and slid down her cheek. She didn't bother to wipe it away. "Why?" she asked.

Finn looked at her. Impassive. *Always so goddamned impassive.* "It's . . . difficult to explain." His eyes twitched away from her. That movement again. The sight of it made her sick to her stomach.

"That's not fair," she said. "You can't just . . . do something like that. And not have a reason."

"I have a reason." His gaze settled at a point above her head. "I just can't tell you." And then he moved across the living room floor and sat down beside her on the couch. He tilted his head and picked up her hand and she let him, because now more than ever his touch electrified her.

"You can tell me anything," she said.

"No," he said. "I can't."

His words stung her. Cat looked down at their hands, at their fingers entwined together. For a moment, they sat unspeaking, the room hot and bright and still. Outside, the oleander scraped against the glass.

"I was purchased by Selene Technologies," he said. "STL."

Cat froze. She tightened her grip on Finn's hand. "The lunar station," she whispered.

"Yes."

"You're going to the moon." She thought about the videos she'd seen on the news programs. Bots crawling across the lunar surface. Like little remote-control cars.

He nodded.

"The *moon*?" Cat slumped against the couch. She gripped Finn's hand, her sweat beading up in the space between their palms. The moon. Of course. He didn't need to breathe, he didn't need to sleep, he didn't need to eat. He would not go mad from loneliness or isolation.

"You can't do this," she said. He regarded her with his black eyes, and she shook her head. "No, you can't. They just . . . You'll be like a slave. They're just using you—"

He jerked his hand away from her. Cat stopped. She'd never seen so violent a movement from him.

"Yes, I already know what that's like."

"What do you mean?" Cat stared at him. "Daddy never—"

"I am not," said Finn, "talking about your father."

An airplane flew overhead, and the sunlight in the room flashed as though reflected from a mirror. For a split second Cat went blind. Finn's words carved out her heart. *The fucking ice queen.*

"I have to go," Finn said. "I have preparations to make."

"When do you leave?" Cat jumped up and grabbed his upper arm and tried to pull him close to her. He was heavier than she expected when he resisted. She couldn't make him move.

"For the lunar station? In two weeks. However, they're shipping me to Florida tomorrow—"

"Shipping you?" Finn stopped.

"Yes."

"They can't put you in a plane like you're a human fucking being?"

"I am not a human being. This method is more cost effective. And safer."

Cat tried to protest but the words caught in her throat. For the first time in a long time she felt something other than dull, weary malaise. She felt panic.

She cupped his face in her hands and leaned in to kiss him on the mouth. It was the only thing she could think to do. But he pulled away from her. She faltered.

Cat thought her heart had stopped beating.

"Finn," she said, because she didn't know what else to say and she didn't know what else to think. Only his name. *Finn. Finn. Finn.*

"I have to go," he said. He turned away from her.

"Wait!"

He stopped.

"Is there a way . . . a way I can contact you? Like when I was in high school?"

Finn turned his head just enough that she could see his profile.

"No," he said.

The front door hissed open. The heat from outside washed over

Cat, and instantly sweat prickled out of her pores. Finn turned and looked at her over his shoulder. The sunlight cast him in silhouette. Like the first time she ever saw him. A silhouette, a shadow. A ghost.

"Don't go." Her voice cracked in two.

"Good-bye, Cat," he said.

He stepped outside and the door shut and through the glass Cat watched him walk down to the auto-taxi idling on the curb. He pulled open the door and stepped inside. His arm reached across the front seat to program in his destination.

Cat forced herself to move. She ran out through the door, into the blazing dried-out yard, just as the taxi pulled away. It was so hot. She was the only living thing in the world.

She walked barefoot onto the asphalt, the soles of her feet burning, and jogged halfheartedly down the street. She smelled the electricity from the taxi. But it was gone.

The sun burned the tops of her bare shoulders. A hot wind picked up, tossing her hair away from her face.

And although she wanted to, she didn't cry. All her tears would have turned to steam anyway.

TWELVE

"It was his decision," her father said.

"I don't believe it," said Cat. "I don't believe he'd just . . . decide something like that. What happened?"

She sat in the house's office. Her father ran his hand over his thin white hair.

"You got sick of living here, didn't you?"

"He can't get sick of anything," Cat said. "At least, that's what he would say."

Her father laughed sharply. Cat frowned. "It's not funny."

"Cat, I can't tell him what to do." He looked away from the camera. "I don't like it, either."

"I wish you'd just tell me what happened."

The house computer chimed. "Welcome home, Mr. Feversham."

Cat sighed.

"The hell was that?" said her father.

"The AI," Cat said. "Richard programmed it to do that."

"Charming."

"I should go." She heard Richard rustling around in the bedroom. "He'll be fine."

Cat nodded, unconvinced, and said good-bye. She flicked off the camera and walked into the hallway. Richard stuck his head out of the bedroom door, his shirt unbuttoned.

"The computer just told me I need to cover up the hole in the kitchen," he said. "I thought you were going to take care of that?"

His voice sounded far away, even though he was only one room over.

Cat leaned against the hallway wall, her arms crossed over her chest. "I've been distracted," she said. "I guess I forgot about it."

"Jesus, hasn't it been chiming at you all this time? You know I programmed it to direct all household matters to you." He appeared in the doorway again. Shrugged out of his shirt. He had gotten a haircut a few days ago and his hair was shorter than usual, his scalp peeking through. He looked so unlike someone Cat would ever want to speak to, much less marry, that she wanted in that moment to enrage him.

She herself felt numb.

"I told the computer it should take it up with you," she said. He looked at her, an eyebrow raised. "It was, after all, your fault."

"Cat, I really don't need this right now."

"Need what?"

Richard closed his eyes. "Please don't be a bitch."

"I just want you to cover the window, Richard."

He looked at her. He was glowing with the orange light of the sun setting into the subdivision. "I want to point out here that, of the two of us, *I* have a job. A shitty job at the moment, but it's still a job. I'm sure you can take ten minutes out of your busy fucking schedule doing Pilates and gossiping with the goddamn AI to cover the hole in the kitchen." He moved closer. "Don't think I haven't noticed all the dirt and shit that's gotten in. The house can't clean it up that fast."

"The mess," Cat said, "came from a hole. That you made. When you threw a fucking chair through a fucking window."

Richard's chest rose and fell. He clenched his hands into fists. His eyes burned straight into hers. She kept her gaze steady. Dealing with his anger was easier this time. She soaked it up without damage. She was merely a receptacle, and if she wanted she could throw his anger back at him like a mirror reflecting light.

"And I don't spend all day doing Pilates," she said. "God knows I have to keep my schedule clear in case you decide I need to get my hair done two hours before we go meet a bunch of corporate assholes."

Richard's eyes narrowed.

"It takes a lot of time keeping myself pretty for your investors."

"Seriously?" Richard's jaw moved. The muscles in his neck tightened. "Because I'm not seeing it."

Cat dug her nails into the palms of her hands, her skin tingling.

Richard pushed past her. "There are plenty of secretaries I could fuck, you know," he said. "Five in my offices alone. God knows how many in the building."

"Oh please, like you can get it up for anything other than a venture capitalist writing a check."

Richard's hand slammed into the wall above the computer console. There was a crack, the sizzle of short-circuited electricity. The computer chirped. He turned his back to her, the muscles rippling in his shoulders. Cat shrank against the hallway wall. Richard turned and glared at her, his face flushed red, his eyes burning like two stars going supernova. "Get out," he said. "Get out. I can't look at you."

"What? I live here. It's my house, too."

"No, it's *my* house, I fucking bought it, and I'm telling you to get. The fuck. Out."

The computer continued to beep.

"Fine," said Cat. "I can't stand looking at you anyway." She slid past him, and even though she made sure their skin didn't touch, static electricity sparked between them, forcing the hairs on the back of her neck to stand on end. She picked up her purse and slipped on a pair of shoes she kept next to the door. She could feel his rage in the way he watched her leave.

And then she was outside. It was still too hot to breathe. The storms hadn't shown up yet but she felt them on the air. She climbed into the car and flew out of the driveway. She didn't bother to switch to the fully automated mode. She wanted to direct her energy, her anger, her grief, into driving. Two days since Finn disappeared into a taxicab parked outside her house. He would be in Florida by now, surrounded by orange trees.

Cat fumbled in her purse, trying to find her cigarettes. They weren't there. Neither was her comm slate. The suburbs shimmered as she drove out of the subdivision and onto the freeway. She was too inflamed to stop at a vice stand. She clutched the steering wheel so tightly her fingers tingled as she sped past the cars dotting the road. The city lit up the horizon, turned the rim of the sky violet.

She drove to the studio.

Lights glowed in the windows when she pulled up to the curb. Felix's car was parked out front, but no one else's. Cat put her car into park but didn't turn off the engine. She left the air-conditioning running, wanting the cool, dry air to blow across her hot face. She took a deep breath. All of the anger from before had evaporated on the drive into downtown, and now she was deflated, dried out.

Wind rustled the pecan trees lining the street. Cat turned off her car and walked to the studio. In the city the air felt different: wilder, hotter, more toxic.

She rang the buzzer next to the door, her key still at the glass house. Felix's laughter drifted through the cracks in the foundation. She heard his footsteps. The door swung open.

"Holy shit, it's Cat!" He looked at her and said, "What's wrong? Get in here and tell me everything."

Cat stepped inside. The studio was flooded with soft white light. The loom sat patiently where she'd left it. She realized with a jolt of sadness that she had nearly finished the tapestry for Finn. And he'd never see it.

Felix wasn't alone in the studio. Miguel sat on the floor beside the potting wheel, drinking from a bottle of apple schnapps, and when he saw Cat he raised the bottle and called her the mad scientist's beautiful daughter. And for half a second Cat was back in college and Finn was only a few hours' drive away and she had never met Richard.

"You look upset." Felix took both of her hands and pulled her over to the potting wheel. Miguel handed her the bottle of schnapps. She took a long, burning drink.

"Richard kicked me out of the house." Said aloud, in the light of the studio, it sounded absurd. She laughed and took another drink.

"Isn't it supposed to be the other way around?" said Miguel. "Did you sleep with your secretary or something?"

"I need a cigarette," said Cat. "I left my pack at home."

Felix pulled his pack off a nearby table. "It's my last one," he said, handing it to her. "And I won't make you go outside." He paused. "Just this once."

"I'll buy you an entire case." Cat drew the smoke into her lungs, and that deep toxic breath almost made her feel normal. She closed her eyes and saw the afterimage of the studio lights fractaling against her lids. Inhale, exhale. It didn't matter if the smoke caught in the tapestry.

"So," said Felix. "Do you need a place to stay?"

"I don't know. Probably. I don't want to think about it."

"Seriously, I want to know what you did to him." Miguel leaned forward, a smile teasing up the corners of his mouth. "Did he find out about the ADL donations?"

Cat shook her head. "I insulted his manhood. At least, I think that's what did it. Everything sort of blurs together."

"His manhood?" Miguel and Felix looked at each other and laughed.

"I'm sorry," said Felix. "It's not funny."

"No, it is," said Cat. "I told him he could only get it up for a venture capitalist."

This made Felix and Miguel laugh even harder, and Cat laughed a little, and then a lot, and then her laughter edged over into hysteria. She knew it wasn't only because of Richard. She wiped the tears away from the edges of her eyes and finished the cigarette. Dropped it into the sink stained with paint and clay.

"Also," she said slowly, looking down at the veins in her hands. "Finn went away."

"Who the hell's Finn?" Felix said.

"Shut up, Felix," Miguel said. Then, to Cat: "Where'd he go?"

"The moon." Cat picked up the bottle of schnapps and drank. It tasted awful, the way turpentine smells. She sat next to Miguel, and he put his arm around her shoulder.

"Is that some sort of . . . metaphor?"

Cat shook her head. "We're talking about the android," she said to Felix, and then she told them how Finn had come to her house unannounced, how he'd sold himself off, how he was about to disappear into the night sky. Miguel held her tight the entire time, and when she finished, he pulled her into a hug.

"That's pretty fucked up," said Felix.

"Insightful." Miguel put his hands on Cat's shoulders and peered up at her between the parted curtain of her hair. "I don't envy your situation," he said.

Cat shut her eyes. She would not cry. Not here.

"I talked to him at the wedding," Miguel said. "I like him. I don't like your reg of a husband, but hey, you didn't ask me." He leaned back. "It's a shame you couldn't marry Finn. I told him that, by the way."

Cat's head jerked up. "Why?"

Miguel smiled at her. She looked back down at the dried clay dusting the floor, and then she asked, "What did he say?"

"I don't remember. Nothing. It was during your first dance with what's his name. He watched you the whole time. I saw his eyes moving around the room." Miguel shrugged. "I think he agreed with me."

"That's not possible."

"You keep telling yourself that." Miguel stood up. Cat looked between him and Felix. Everything swirled together. She was exhausted or drunk or maybe both.

"Come back to my apartment," Felix said. "Worry about it in the morning. You can sleep on my couch." He jerked his head toward the door. "I'll even drive."

Cat smiled. It didn't feel right, smiling, but she did anyway, and she followed Felix and Miguel out to the car, and she curled up in the backseat to the sound of their voices. The neon street signs filled the car with color. The windows fogged up from the heat and the humidity.

It was easy, in that moment, to forget everything.

* * * *

Cat went back to the glass house the next afternoon. Her hair hung lank and greasy against the back of her neck, and her rumpled clothes smelled of cigarette smoke and sleep. She parked the car in the driveway. Richard's car was in the garage.

Seeing it, she felt a twinge of guilt.

When she walked into the house the computer was still chirping the way it had when she left. Otherwise, the house was wrapped in muffled quiet. Cat dropped her purse on the floor and crept into the living room. Empty. She went into the dining room, the kitchen. Both empty, although a blue tarp had been tacked over the hole in the glass. Cat stopped when she saw it. The wind pushed against the tarp so that it billowed out into the kitchen, then flattened itself up like a sail. The computer beeped and beeped. The tarp snapped and fluttered.

Cat left the kitchen. She walked down the hallway and saw the dent in the wall next to the console. She took a deep breath and pushed into the bedroom.

Richard was laid out facedown on the bed in his underwear, snoring faintly, the comforter balled up under his feet. The room was hazy with afternoon sunlight. Cat sat down on the edge of the bed and watched him sleep. His bottle of whiskey sat on the bed-side table, the tumbler beside it stained amber. She stood up and the bed creaked and Richard opened one eye.

"Caterina?" His voice was thick, as though he was still drunk. He pushed himself up on his arm. "I'm so glad you came back."

Cat walked over to the closet. She wanted to get out of yester-day's clothes.

"I'm sorry," he said. "I'm so, so sorry. You're beautiful. You're beautiful right now. I should never have told you to get out—"

"It's fine." Cat stared at her clothes. "I'd like to change."

"Come to bed." Richard rolled over onto his back. "I want to apologize."

"I need to take a shower."

"Whatever. So do I."

He sat up. Cat unzipped her skirt and dropped it to the floor, lifted her shirt over her head.

"C'mon," he said. "You can't skip the best part of a fight."

When Cat laughed, it came from outside herself.

Richard crawled out of the bed and wrapped his arms around her, buried his face in her hair.

"You smell like you," he said. "You smell human."

"You smell like whiskey."

"I covered the hole in the kitchen."

He said this as though it were a confession, a secret, and that made Cat weaken. She shouldn't have baited him; it wasn't his fault Finn went away. He slipped his hand under the band of her bra. What did she care? A touch was a touch. Soon there would be no one left on Earth whose fingers could electrify her.

Richard drew her in for a kiss. She kissed back. He pulled her into the bathroom and turned on the shower. The sound of running water drowned out the computer's steady beeping, and while the steam swirled up around them it was like the fight had never happened.

* * * *

The white-hot days went by.

Cat found a website showing the shuttle launch that would take Finn into space. She watched it outside, early in the morning, sitting in the shade of the pine trees, with a cup of coffee and a cigarette. *Launch of unmanned shuttle*, the website said. *Carrying equipment and supplies*. Cat set her laptop in the grass and walked out into the yard and squinted up at the sky, wondering if she would be able to see a streak of burning darkness across the hazy golden clouds, heading toward the unfathomable thermosphere—but no, of course not.

A few days later the contractors arrived to fix the kitchen window and the broken computer. Cat wasn't sure what to do with these strangers in her house, so she followed them from room to room, trying to make conversation. The younger of the two talked with her while he worked, and the elder ignored them both. It was all nonsense, what Cat said, what the contractor said. The inanity of flirtation. Cat laughed the way she used to with boys in college. She offered them blackberry lemonade she made herself. Only the younger accepted, and he leaned against the counter while the elder repeatedly, pointedly, checked the time on his slate.

"I'd love to take you out sometime," the younger said.

"Forget it, Josh," the elder said. "You want to keep this job?"

Cat smiled, tilted her head, shrugged. The rules of this particular game had been set years before she was born. But she knew she wasn't going to do anything.

Then the summer storms started up. Finally, the sweltering heat transformed into dark, angry clouds that rolled in over the suburbs every afternoon and deposited a solid wall of rain. Lightning arced between the roofs of the houses. Cat took to lying flat on her back in the middle of the living room so she could watch the rain pool and streak against the glass ceiling. She had never thought to look up, through the roof of her house to the sky, until now. She found the roof was filthy, covered in pine needles and broken branches and bird shit. Cat asked the computer to send the cleaning bots out twice a week.

On the rare occasions when Richard was home, Cat withdrew into herself. Richard had been in a better mood lately—in the evenings he sometimes sought her out and chatted idly about SynLodge, how he thought he'd found a way out of the financial sinkhole. Cat didn't have the energy to pretend she cared. She didn't have the energy to be hurt by the fact that he had once accused her of feeling nothing.

"You never talk to me anymore," Richard said one evening over dinner.

Cat looked up from the curry she'd made that afternoon. She didn't know why she had made it. The weather was too hot for curry, even with the storms.

"I don't have anything to talk about," she said.

Richard poked at his food. "Well, work has been busy. But busy's good." He glanced back up at her. "This isn't about Finn, is it?"

All the breath left Cat's body.

"You did hear about that, right?"

For a moment, Cat considered lying, but she could not bear to hear the news a second time. She nodded.

"Three billion," he said. "Fucking hell. We talked about trying to get in on it, you know, thinking it'd restore the investors' trust, but there's no way we could have competed."

Cat's hands shook. She dropped her spoon into her bowl and folded her hands under the table. *Three billion.* She was dizzy. Of course the price was high. But he was priceless.

She realized Richard was staring at her from across the table.

"That's right." His face was unreadable. "We tried to buy him. We would have treated him well, too." He paused. "I can't believe your dad auctioned him off like that. I thought he was into all that robot-rights stuff."

"He didn't sell Finn," Cat whispered. Richard was too calm. It unnerved her.

Cat picked up her spoon, gripping the handle tight to keep her hand steady.

"You were close," Richard said. "Weren't you?"

"Close?"

"To Finn."

Cat's skin prickled. "He was my tutor."

"Oh, I know." Richard looked down at his bowl. "That's always what you say, when I ask about it. Your tutor."

Cat ate a bite of curry. It tasted like salt.

"Did he tutor you in . . . everything?" A pause. "The, ah, birds and the bees?"

Cat looked up at Richard. He was not smiling. His eyes were two small burning-blue dots.

"Are you implying something?"

"Well, you seem to be quite the fan of the, ah, *biologically impaired.*" He paused. "Aren't you?"

The air in the dining room was thick and humid, from the rainstorms, from other things. Cat let her spoon drop. Curry splattered across the table. Richard did not stop staring at her. She jutted her chin out, held her head up haughtily. Dared him to say something.

He didn't. He just picked up his bowl and carried it into the kitchen, his steps heavier than usual.

Cat shook.

THIRTEEN

It was the hottest day on record. The world had dried to tinder. Cat woke up covered in a thin sheen of sweat, her mouth parched. The sun flooded through the ceiling, lighting everything on fire. She slept so much lately, unable to shake her exhaustion.

"Computer." Cat peeled off her damp nightgown. "Could you tint the windows or something, please?"

"Tinting the windows would ruin the architectural effects of the glass walls."

"I don't care," said Cat. "I used to be an artist, and I don't care. The architectural effects are cooking me alive."

The computer chimed. Immediately, the light in the bedroom dimmed as though a cloud had passed over the sun. Cat thanked the computer and drank a glass of water. She took a cold shower, her skin rippling with goose bumps. When she stepped onto the bathroom tile, dripping and shivering and awake, the house was still so hot she warmed up immediately.

She asked the computer to set the air-conditioning as low as possible while she ate a mango at the dining room table. She stretched out on the couch in her underwear, the tinted windows giving her a peculiar sense of freedom. She could do anything she wanted. No one standing on the sidewalk could see through the house and watch all her actions and her secrets and her insignificant transgressions.

For nearly two years, she had lived under glass, like the exhibit of extinct animals at the Natural History Museum, the mannequins of tigers and red wolves and condors frozen in midleap and midflight.

Cat sat up, swinging her legs through the heavy air. The coolness from the AC was just beginning to creep into the larger rooms of the house. She heard the faint, persistent whine of the cleaner bots as they rolled up the outside walls and over the roof. It was odd not to see their shadows moving over the furniture.

She was struck by a sudden sadness.

Cat blinked, startled. For the past month she hadn't felt anything. She couldn't quite put her finger on this sadness—she didn't want to cry, but she felt weighed down by sorrow.

She wanted to talk to Finn.

It was impossible. She knew this. But the heat makes people do crazy things, and on that day, the hottest day on record, the heat convinced Cat that Finn had lied to her before disappearing into an electric cab. Surely she could whisper a message to him through ether and wires. Surely the many thousands of kilometers between the two of them did not constitute a gulf so wide she couldn't even say hello.

Cat walked into the office, dark with the tinted windows. She slid the touchscreen up from the desk and typed in the string of numbers that spelled out Finn's name. She'd forgotten how to tell whether she was connected to him or not, but she poised her hands to type anyway. Whatever she said, it should be perfect.

Someone once told me the moon smells of cordite. Is this true? She stopped, leaned back. She read those two sentences over and over. Her hair clung to her scalp. Sweat slid down the furrow in her back. She hit the keystroke that sent the sentences away.

And then she waited. And waited.

And waited.

"Fuck," she whispered. She snapped the screen back into its snug cubby in the desk. The air conditioner droned on in the background. It hadn't worked. She couldn't speak to him. He had told the truth after all, the way he always had.

She pushed away from the computer so she wouldn't write more: *Do you remember when you caught me in the rain? Do you remember when you knocked the sugar off the inside of my wrist? Do you remember the citrus tree in the garden?*

No response.

Cat stalked into the kitchen to retrieve the cigarette pack she kept hidden behind the jars of flour and sugar. She turned on the oven. At the wet bar in the living room, she pulled out a bottle of whiskey and two tumblers. Then she sat down at the head of the dining room table. Poured her glass up halfway. Lit a cigarette.

"Computer," she said. "This smoke isn't from a fire. Do you understand? I'm cooking something and it burned."

The computer chimed. "I understand."

"Good." Cat dragged on her cigarette. "Do you have a name?"

"I am a Sunlight AI, model number three two seven—"

"Stop." Cat blew the smoke up at the dark glass ceiling. The shadow of a bird moved across the blacked-out sky. "No, I mean, do you have a name? Something I can call you?"

"You may call me Computer."

"That's not a name. How about Arianne? You seem like an Arianne."

"I do not understand."

Cat stiffened, her cigarette poised next to her head, her fingers pressed against the rim of her glass. He always said that to her. *I don't understand.*

"Is there anything with which I may assist you?" said the computer.

"I just want to talk." Cat picked up the glass of whiskey. "Tell me something about yourself."

"I am a Sunlight model—"

"That's not what I meant." Cat took a drink. The whiskey was expensive, smooth against the back of her throat. She barely tasted the alcohol anymore. "Who made you, Arianne?"

"I was manufactured by SynLodge, in the Pine Hills laboratory in the Central Texas area. My make and model—"

"I know your make and model," Cat snapped. "Who designed you?"

"I don't know."

"Do you know why you were made?"

"That consideration isn't part of my programming. Would you like to watch a movie? Shall I provide you with a list of available options?"

"No, I told you, I want to talk."

"Shall I bring up possible contacts from your address book?"

"No." Cat used the dying embers of her cigarette to light another. When she dropped the butt in the second tumbler it sparked and smoldered. "I want to talk to you."

"I do not understand."

"Please don't say that," Cat said. "You're an AI. I knew an AI once, and he used to talk to me."

"I'm not programmed for extended discussion. If you are confused, I can provide you with a list of simple commands that I will recognize. Please describe what task you're trying to accomplish."

Cat laid her head on the table. A line of ash fell across the polished mahogany.

"If you are unwell," the computer said, "I can contact Mr. Feversham—"

"Oh God, don't." Cat sat back up and rubbed her forehead. "And if I was unwell, why would you contact him? Why not 911?"

"I'm programmed to contact Mr. Feversham in case of an emergency."

Cat rolled her eyes and slumped against the back of her chair. "Of course you are." She felt Finn's absence as surely as she felt the heat of the hottest day on record, as surely as she tasted the whiskey on her tongue. "Computer," she said. "Could you bring up the dining room monitor, please?"

Two panels in the metal bookcase on the opposite wall slid apart. The monitor flashed on. Its background that same restored blood red Rothko painting all the house monitors had.

"I want you to search for news stories for me." Cat paused. "I'm looking for any instance of the use of androids on the lunar station."

"Please wait."

It took longer than Cat expected.

"I have found fifty-three instances of the use of androids on the lunar station."

"Any videos?"

"There are ten videos dealing with instances of the use—"

"Okay," said Cat. "Thanks. Show me the longest one." She lit another cigarette. "No, scratch that. Show me one that was actually taken on the moon." The monitor turned black. The screen flashed the STL logo: that gray pockmarked moon, a city shooting out of its surface. The video started. Soundless at first. Only a slow, grainy pan across the surface, showing the lunar station against the backdrop of the perpetual night sky. Then a cut to the station's interior. A pair of astronauts, one man and one woman. Their mouths moved silently for two or three seconds. The sound started. *We've been here a few weeks now, and everything's going fine.* The woman waved, said hello to her children, her words several seconds behind the movement of her lips. *We want to show you some of the equipment we're using here at the STL Lunar Station.*

Cat tightened her fingers around her tumbler.

Let's introduce you to some of our robot friends.

"Oh, for fuck's sake," Cat said.

Robots that looked like spiders and tiny cars and photo processing machines paraded across the screen, blinking and whirring, shoveling gray dust, calculating atmospheric conditions.

And then there he was.

He stood on the gray soil. Half of Earth rose up behind him. She saw the top of Asia, a swirl of white clouds. He wore a jumpsuit like those the astronauts wore. He smiled politely. He waved. Her breath caught in her throat. Her heart pounded. Off camera, the male astronaut said, *This is George. George can do all the things we can do, only without a space suit or a helmet. We're very grateful for all of George's help here at the STL Lunar Station.*

Cat eyes fluttered. A single tear landed on the table. She was unraveling.

"Turn it off." She stabbed her cigarette into the tumbler. "God, turn it off." She stumbled away from the table. The house was too dark. She put her hands against the wall to steady herself and it was cool to the touch, foggy from the constant rush of the air conditioner. The condensation left her fingers damp. She took a deep breath. Her heart slowed back to normal. Calm. She was calm.

She was numb.

* * * *

Richard took Cat out on a business dinner: one of the investors and his wife. Cat wore a blue belted dress and a pair of white pumps, and she had her hair styled at a salon. She applied her lipstick on the way out the door.

As they drove into the city, Richard tightened and loosened his tie. He drummed his fingers against the steering wheel. Cat kept her hands folded in her lap and stared out the window. It had been a week since she'd tried to contact Finn and seen that video at the dining room table; she'd been in a fog since. Always wanting to sleep, her limbs aching.

"You look nice." Richard glanced over at her and then back at the road. "Really classy."

"Thank you."

Richard didn't say anything. She knew that when they arrived at the restaurant he would step out of the car transformed, as smooth as glass. Since their fight, she was more aware of his vulnerability, of his weaknesses. She was aware of the way he buried them so neatly in the rituals of business.

Nothing could touch Cat. Nothing could hurt her. But Richard— she looked at him and she knew how easy it would be to twist a knife into his heart and let all that insecurity flow out.

They arrived at the restaurant. The investor was so old it hurt to look at him. His wife was Cat's age. She wore the exact same shade of lipstick. When the four of them met in the restaurant's lobby, Cat and the investor's wife stared at each other in the candlelit darkness without smiling. Then the investor's wife tucked her clutch purse under her arm and limply held out her hand.

"It's lovely to meet you," she said.

"Likewise," said Cat.

All of the tables were full, but their party was whisked away, without any wait, to a quiet back corner. A pair of candles burned steadily in two red-dyed cracked jars. Richard pulled out Cat's chair, but as soon as she sat down he turned to the investor.

"You have no idea how excited I am about this new product," Richard said. "It's a game changer."

Cat shut him out, sipping her glass of wine. The investor's wife drummed her fingers against the table, flicked her eyes from Richard to Cat.

"I like your dress," she said finally. The candles on the table flickered, and the investor's wife looked as insubstantial as a ghost.

Cat smiled politely and thanked her. "It's a Dior."

"Ah." The investor's wife tugged at her earrings. They looked like sparks of electricity. Her own dress was a drapey black thing, rather avant-garde, the sort of dress Cat had admired through boutique windows when she was in college.

"Yours looks like a . . ." She held out one hand. "Let me guess. I love guessing."

The investor's wife waited.

"A Yamamoto," said Cat.

The investor's wife laughed. "You're right," she said. "Are you in fashion?"

"Sort of," Cat said. "I used to work in textiles." She thought of the last time she had touched a loom. How she had woven a piece of herself into that tapestry for Finn. It was still unfinished. It would never be finished.

"Textiles?"

"Yes," said Cat. "Weaving."

The investor's wife smiled politely, one of those subtle social cues Cat had learned to recognize during the course of her marriage to Richard. It meant she wanted to change the subject.

Cat glanced over at Richard. He leaned forward over the table, nodding intently to whatever the investor was saying. They were talking about money. Cat didn't have to listen to the conversation to know. She could barely understand the investor anyway. He slurred his words in the manner of men from the swamps. It took him forever to say anything. *A self-made man*, Richard had told her a few nights before, over dinner. *More money than God.*

Cat wished she could light a cigarette on the table's candle. Instead, she passed her fingers over the flame. The heat warmed her skin.

"So how long have you known Richard?" the investor's wife asked.

Cat looked up at her. She realized she couldn't say. It felt like a lifetime. All that time before Richard had been a dream. Finn. Finn was a dream.

"A few years," she said.

"I met Michael three years ago." The investor's wife looped her arm in her husband's and he glanced at her, interrupting the conversation with Richard. The lines of the investor's face melted into a smile. Richard looked annoyed.

"Ah yes," said the investor. "I remember that day well." He tapped the side of his head. "I bought a pack of cigarettes."

"I was a vice stand girl," the wife said.

Cat laughed. The dream-life. "So was I. In college." She paused. "And for a few years afterward."

"Oh, a lifer, huh? What stand did you work?"

"The one in Juniper Park." Cat sipped her wine. "I guess it's still there. I haven't been back to check."

"I was out on the interstate," the wife said. "Awful. I heard the in-town stands were much nicer."

Their food arrived. The waiter walked over, a tray hoisted high above his head. Only the most expensive restaurants were staffed by human waiters rather than robots. "Mahimahi glazed in ginger-sake sauce," he said. "The plate's very hot."

Cat looked down at the cut of fish displayed across the white china.

"Ain't this nice," the investor said. Everyone except the waiter turned to him. Steam curled up from his plate. "Not too often you get served by a human anymore." He grinned at the waiter, who nodded stiffly, asked if everything was to their satisfaction.

Richard frowned, furrowed his brow. The investor laughed.

"Oh, don't look like that," he said. "Lord knows we still need those things. But sometimes it's nice to go back to the old ways of doing business."

Richard relaxed, his shoulders slumping beneath his crisp suit.

The investor cut into his fish, and silence fell as everyone ate. Cat pushed the mahimahi around in its thick sweet glaze.

"So, Mrs. Feversham," said the investor. Cat looked up at him, startled. "You've been living in the Sunlight House. What do you think?"

"I'm sorry?"

"He's asking for your opinion," said Richard. "Darling."

The investor nodded. "I like the sound of it," he said. "All the benefits of an AI and none of the legal hassles. I was just wondering what it's like to live there."

Cat felt Richard staring at her.

"I appreciate its convenience," she finally said.

"Ah. That's it? What do you think of your husband's AI? Does it work as well as he claims?"

Cat took a bite of fish so she wouldn't have to answer.

It melted on her tongue like a communion wafer.

"It works fine. Doesn't it, honey? Helps you keep track of your appointments." Richard slung his arm around her shoulder rough enough that he hurt her collarbone. "She's self-employed. An artist."

The investor laughed. "Artists. The vice stands are lousy with 'em. Same with the damn robot-rights groups—"

His wife's fork clattered against her plate. "Michael," she said. "Please don't start—"

"I'll talk politics if I want." The investor turned to Cat. "I'm sure you're not involved with all that nonsense, though. You got a good head on your shoulders." He winked. "I can tell."

Cat felt the movement of her blood through her veins. She felt her heart pumping in her chest. In the moment, she was ashamed of her humanity.

"Actually," she said, "I donate regularly to the Automaton Defense League."

The entire world went silent. Cat kept her gaze straight ahead so she would not have to look at Richard. The investor set down his knife and fork and rubbed his chin, and his wife's lipsticked mouth froze into a lovely, crystalline smile.

"Well," he said. "That's a bit unexpected."

"Why do you say that?" Cat's voice came out calm and sweet as syrup.

"They've tried to shut down SynLodge," said the investor. "Haven't they?"

"More than once." Richard's voice rang out across the table.

Cat dropped her head, heat flushing her cheeks. She twisted her napkin around her right hand.

"I take it you didn't know about this, Feversham?"

Richard sat up straight. "You shouldn't take her seriously." He tilted his head toward Cat. When she turned to meet his eye, she did not recognize what she saw there. "She's joking."

Cat smiled weakly and smoothed the napkin over her lap. Richard pressed his mouth into a grimace.

"See?" he said. "A joke."

"A joke." The investor looked from Richard to Cat. "Something tells me that ain't no joke."

"It was. She jokes all the time. Very wry. Right, sweetheart?"

"I suppose." Cat turned back to the investor. She was calm; she was lighter than air. "And to answer your question," she said, "about the AI? It works very well."

"Don't you worry about its . . . *rights*?"

"The Sunlight AI has no consciousness," said Cat. The investor leaned back and stared at Cat with a dark, appraising expression. Cat stared back at him. She knew this was a man who'd made his fortune off the sorrow of others. Then he laughed, short and barking.

"Yeah," he said. "No consciousness."

"That's how we avoid the legality issues, of course." Richard said quickly. "But, I assure you, we've found the sweet spot between—"

"But don't you think the lack of consciousness takes away what makes these things so exciting?" the investor asked. "I always like my AIs to have a personality, myself."

"That's the sacrifice," Richard said. "They work much better. Personalities in a household bot are overrated." His eyes flicked over to Cat. "They get insolent. They form activist groups. You know George, on the lunar station?"

Cat's fork dropped from her hand. Her calmness solidified in the pit of her stomach.

Stop, she thought.

"The creator was Cat's father."

Stop.

"The thing was like an obnoxious grad student, I swear to God."

Stop stop stop stop—

And then Cat realized that Richard *had* stopped, and moreover that he was glaring at her, and that the investor and his wife both watched her from across the table, the wife looking engaged with her surroundings for the first time that night.

Cat had been saying it out loud. *Stop. Stop. Stop.*

She wanted to dissolve into the darkness. Instead, she picked up her fork.

"You don't understand what you're talking about," she said to Richard.

"Of course I don't," Richard said. "How could I? I just run an AI company. I'm just an evil corporate shill trying to enslave a bunch of poor automatons. Right?"

Cat didn't answer. Her cheeks burned. From across the table, the investor smiled.

"She was a little too attached," said Richard. "If you know what I mean."

"Not something I want to think about," the investor said. Cat picked up her glass of wine and drank it down without tasting anything. Richard's eyes seared straight into her.

"A little too attached," he said.

*   *   *   *

After dinner ended, the investor and his wife breezed down the sidewalk into the gleaming lights of downtown. Cat and Richard stood outside the restaurant waiting for the valet to bring their car.

"That was a fucking disaster," he said.

Cat dug her nails into the side of her clutch purse.

"Do you have any idea how much money was riding on that dinner? How much you just lost me?"

"It's all true," Cat whispered. "I wasn't joking."

The valet pulled the car up to the curb. Richard paid without speaking, then stalked around to the driver's side. Cat stepped in carefully, thanked the valet in his red suit, laid her head back against the seat.

"No fucking shit. I've seen the bank statements." Richard jabbed his fingers into the autoprogramming screen. "Although why you felt the need to tell the goddamn investor is beyond me."

The car pulled away from the curb, and Richard sucked in his breath through his teeth. He kept his eyes on the road ahead of them. The city threw off sparks of light. Cat pulled a tissue out of her purse and wiped off her lipstick.

They rode the rest of the way home in silence, Richard simmering beside Cat. She could smell him, the acrid tang of his sweat. She turned on the air conditioner. She could tell he was making a concentrated effort not to look at her, not to see her. Cat slipped off her shoes and kicked her feet up on the dashboard, pushed her seat back, stared at him.

He said nothing.

When they arrived home, Richard slammed the car door and stomped into the house before Cat had a chance to put on her shoes. She walked languidly across the moonlit yard, through the front door. All the lights were off. Everything was in black-and-white from the moon. Cat couldn't bear the thought of the moon tonight.

"Computer," she said. "Why's it so dark in here?"

The light by the door flickered on. Cat walked across the living room, the house's illumination following her. Wherever she went, light followed, brightening her steps. She threw her shoes down next to the couch. She found Richard in the dining room, pouring a glass of whiskey. When the lights switched on, he barked: "I said keep all the lights off!"

The lights switched off.

"You're a fucking slut."

Cat stood there barefoot in the darkness and the moonlight.

"Why do you say that?" she asked.

Richard looked up at her, slowly. "Don't act like you don't—" He stopped, drained his glass. "Did you fuck him?"

"Who, the investor?"

Richard hurled his glass at Cat, so quickly she didn't have time to react. He missed. The glass shattered on the wall beside her head. Her muscles tensed but otherwise she didn't move.

"You know what I'm talking about."

The moonlight spilling in through the roof was everywhere, and Cat had been anticipating this conversation since the day she first said *yes* to that glint of diamond in the black velvet box.

"I really don't. And I don't appreciate you throwing things at me."

Richard jumped to his feet and drew back his arm. The bottle went flying, whiskey arcing out of its neck. This time Cat dropped to her hands and knees. The bottle exploded where her head had been. The glass wall cracked. Whiskey splattered across her back and seeped through the fabric of her dress. The smell of it reminded her of the old dive bar where she went drinking in college. It made her head spin.

Now her heart was pounding.

"You are a fucking deceitful bitch," he said. "And I'm sick of your ice queen bullshit."

He stepped toward her. Cat looked up at him through the curtain of hair that had fallen across her eyes. When she stood up, she stepped on a piece of broken glass. She bit down on her tongue to keep from crying out.

"There's something wrong with you," said Richard. "Something not right. Growing up out there in the woods all alone with nothing but a madman for a father and a goddamn *robot*." He lunged at her. Cat jumped away, slipping on the blood from her foot. Richard grabbed her by the arm and pulled her close to him.

"What was it like?" His nails dug into her arm. His breath was hot and damp on the side of her neck. "Look at me." He grabbed her by the chin and jerked her face toward him. "You think I'm stupid? You think I didn't figure it out? Baby, this isn't about the ADL. I mean . . . I saw the way you looked at him. The way you *defended* him."

"Please let me go."

He slapped her.

Everything in the house froze. Cat. Richard. She felt the imprint of his hand across her cheek, the individual lines of his fingers, hot and stinging. She tried to step away from him, but he didn't let go of her arm. For a moment of moonlit lucidity Cat wondered what sort of violence the man she married had repressed all these years. She felt it coming to the surface. She felt it in herself, reflecting back at him. And fear, too, shot through it all. But none of it belonged to her. It was all his. "Richard," she said.

His face contorted: sneering, angry. The scent of whiskey. The moon reflecting off the glass walls. Cat tried to steady her breathing.

At the edge of her vision, she saw his hand balling into a fist.

Get away. You have to get away. She reached up and began to pry his fingers away from her arm and then he swung at her and she ducked down, hit him in the stomach. He grunted, doubled over, grabbed at her hair. She turned and ran as best she could with her bleeding foot through the living room. He caught her at the waist and pulled her around and when his fist slammed across her right cheek she screamed. She couldn't help herself.

A sickening crack. A blossom of pain. The room went bright and then dark. Cat slithered away from him. He caught her by the wrist and hit her again, in the nose. Warmth slid over her face, down over her clavicle. She swung at him, knocked him in the side of the head. Not even hard enough to hurt her own hand. She was too shaken, too confused.

"Computer!" Cat shrieked. She tasted something slick and metallic. "Turn on the lights!"

The house flooded with illumination, bright and clean. The light showed a trail of impossibly red blood snaking out of the dining room. Richard froze. His eyes went from furious to terrified. His jaw dropped. He backed away from her.

"I'm sorry," he said. "I drank too much. I'm sorry . . ."

Blood welled up in Cat's mouth, and she turned her head and spat a comet's tail of red that splattered across the glass walls. She turned to look at Richard.

"Get out," she said.

Her voice was dark and deep. She wiped her hand across her mouth. More blood. Her right eye felt heavy and swollen.

"Caterina . . ." Richard backed away from her. "God, Caterina, let me call an ambulance. I'm so sorry, there's so much . . ."

Cat ignored him. She stumbled away, toward the bedroom. Her head was ringing. She had told him to get out but she knew she couldn't stay here. She knew she couldn't ever come back to the glass house. She hobbled into the bedroom and told the computer to lock the door. She dragged the suitcase out of the closet and threw in clothes, not paying attention to what she packed. A cocktail dress. A pair of ratty old shorts. She dumped in a pile of underwear and clicked the suitcase shut. She avoided looking at herself in the wall's reflection. She didn't want to see that she needed to stay and clean up the blood.

She had to get out.

Richard still stood in the living room, cradling his bloodied hand to his chest. When Cat walked in, he looked at her and started crying. She stepped into her white pumps and bit back a scream at the sudden burst of pain in her foot.

"Don't leave," he said, his voice broken and wet. "Cat, I'm so sorry. You know I'd never do anything like—"

"You just did." Cat dragged the suitcase to the front door and stopped. Picked up her purse, the keys to her car. She didn't look at him. Her foot burned and her face ached and her heart was worn out from all the sorrow of her life.

"Please—" he said.

Cat walked out the door.

She drove all night. She stopped once, on the side of the highway, and used the napkins in the glove compartment to wipe at the blood crusted on the bottom of her foot. Most of the blood on her face had flaked away and spilled into her lap, and she stood up, dusting off the front of her dress like sweeping the dirt off the patio of her old apartment. The pine trees lining the road rattled with the dryness of autumn heat. Cat leaned against the side of the car and looked up at the sky, the stars, the moon. *Finn.*

She got back in the car.

Cat watched the sun come up through the front windshield. Strata of pink and orange and pearly gray. The sun rose higher in the sky. The car warmed up. Cat turned on the AC. The woods grew thicker. Cars lay abandoned on the side of the road. She turned off the main highway and drove along the rough Farm-to-Market road that passed through the town where she had gone to high school. Nothing sparked in her memory. Nothing made her gasp with nostalgia. There was only the steady, aching throb in her foot, in her face, in her fingers.

And then she arrived at her childhood home. She parked the car behind her father's. She stepped out. Pain shot through her foot and up her leg. Her ankles wobbled in her shoes. The yard seemed made of dust. The garden was a pile of dried-up vines and spindly tree trunks and curling dead leaves. The paint on the house flaked and peeled. Cat pulled her suitcase out of the trunk and dragged it up to the porch. The door was unlocked. She went inside. She didn't think about anything. Her heels clicked unevenly against the floorboards, and the wheels of her suitcase rattled and echoed through the hall. She limped down to the laboratory and stood in the doorway.

Her father looked up from his workstation. Computers blinked all around him like lights on a Christmas tree. For a second Cat thought he might scream. She wondered what the bruising was like. The blood. She wondered what he saw of her.

And then Cat let go of her suitcase. It slammed against the floor. Her entire body shook. All those computers. The whole world was made of light. She could pass right through it like a ghost.

"Daddy," she said. Her voice cracked.

PART THREE

FOURTEEN

Cat combed down the warp thread, pushing it gently into place. She worked slowly but methodically, focusing only on the tapestry stretched out in front of her. It would be finished soon. She didn't know what she would do with herself then, because she had discovered, in these months since she'd come home, that the times she worked were the only times she didn't think.

She turned the warp thread. Blue thread now, a deep rich blue, the color of the sky at twilight, right before the stars come out.

It was strange working from her father's house, without the familiar sounds of the studio ricocheting around her. None of Felix's laughter, none of Lucy's chatter, none of the wild twangy music they let loose through the cheap speakers. Just the creaks of the old house settling into its foundation, the wind rustling the pine trees, and silence. She had set up the loom in the upstairs guest room—the room where Finn had tutored her, so long ago—so she rarely heard her father puttering around in his laboratory or the kitchen.

Sometimes it made her lonely, but mostly she found the isolation soothing.

Cat wove until she came to the end of the warp thread, then

rested the shuttle on the loom frame and stretched her aching fingers. Dusty sunlight spilled through the window. Only a few more rows and it would be done. Of course, it was a gift for someone currently residing on the moon, and a gift that cannot be given remains incomplete. Cat ran her fingers over the completed portion of the tapestry, smoothing the soft downy fibers, and stood up. No sense in adding new yarn to the shuttle, since she didn't want to add those last few rows today. Cat walked to the window and pressed her face against the warm glass.

The woods looked far away. She dropped her hand to her belly, something she did frequently, without thinking.

The first few weeks back in the house, when her face was still swollen and painful to the touch, she had thrown up constantly. Her father made her take the test. It came out positive. She did not remind herself that it was Richard's baby.

The doctor had told her she was nearly two months along.

Cat turned from the window and went downstairs. The house was filled with sunlight. She walked through the kitchen and into the yard, buzzing with cicadas and the scent of pine trees. She pulled the package of peppermint sticks out of her dress pocket and slipped one into the corner of her mouth. For a long time she stood leaning against the banister, sweetness coating her tongue, wishing she could have a cigarette.

"Cat?"

Cat turned around. She pulled the peppermint stick from her mouth and dropped it to her side. Her father stood in the doorway, propping the screen door open with one hand, his body thin and bony. The sunlight illuminated the lines in his face.

"What's up?"

"I heard you clomping through the kitchen. Thought I'd come out and check on you, see how you're doing." He squinted at her. "You doing okay?"

"I'm doing fine."

He looked at her as though he didn't believe her. He had good reason.

"Well, in that case . . ." Her father eased himself out onto the porch, letting the screen door slam behind him. "Would you mind going into town for me?" He thumped the walls of the house. "Got a lot of work to do, you know, and I'm craving some of Maybelle's key lime pie." Maybelle. Cat shuddered at the name. Maybelle owned the little pie shop in town. Her father adored Maybelle's pies—and they were delicious-enough pies, certainly—but every time Cat went into Maybelle's the air crackled with all the unspoken town rumors and gossip about her, about her return home, her divorce from Richard. "Sure, I can go into town."

"You want to take my car?" her father asked. But Cat shook her head. She was already walking toward the shed to pull out her mother's old bicycle. She'd had her own car towed back to the glass house a few days after she came home, afraid of being beholden to Richard. He had called her when it arrived, leaving sorrowful messages on her comm slate. He'd left hundreds of messages during those first few weeks, most of them mournful and incoherent. Eventually he disconnected the comm account, and Cat started a new one, under her name, using money she borrowed from her father. Now she rode her bicycle into town on days when it was not too hot. She liked the feeling of the wind pushing her hair back from her face.

Cat coasted down the hill leading into town, resting one hand on the handlebars of her bike, leaning back a little in the seat. The doctor had told her it was important that she exercise and stay active. A thin sheen of sweat had already formed on her skin, not so much from the air's heat but from the sun beaming down on her as she rode along the asphalt. She felt that usual prickle of electricity, the insistence in the back of her mind that everyone was talking about her. *The mad scientist's daughter,* they were saying in their lazy honey-drawl voices. *The mad scientist's daughter, back from the dead.*

*   *   *   *

At Maybelle's pie shop, Cat sat at the two-person booth by the swinging kitchen doors, waiting for the gray-haired waitress to box up her key lime pie. Maybelle had installed a sleek, modern monitor in the wall above the cash register. It looked out of place in the run-down pie shop. They kept it tuned to one of the twenty-four-hour streaming news sites, and as Cat watched a pair of pundits argue about robot rights, she absentmindedly rubbed her bare ring finger. The blinding engagement ring and the wedding band were both gone, shipped to Richard in a plain manila envelope, with no return address, no letter inside. That was the day Cat contacted the lawyer about her divorce.

The waitress emerged out of the kitchen, a pie box dangling from one hand, wisps of hair falling out of her updo. She tossed the box aside and glanced up at the monitor. There was a new law pending, one that would grant autonomy to any machine that attained a certain level of sentience. There had been a great deal of support for it; everyone was sure it would pass. Miguel had invited her to an ADL party celebrating its introduction, but Cat had declined.

Richard's AI houses were not covered under the new law, of course—no doubt Noratech had already bought him out. That particular idea of his must be worth billions. Cat didn't care. But she did wonder about Finn.

"Things sure do change fast," said the waitress, her eyes on the monitor as she slid the pie expertly into the box. She looked at Cat. "Can't believe it'd ever come to this, you know? They're talking about granting 'em full rights! As people."

"I know." Cat studied the etches in the tabletop, declarations of teenage love and teenage existence that were already wearing away. When she looked back up, the waitress was watching her.

"You're the Novak girl, ain't ya?"

"Yeah."

The waitress nodded. She folded the box flap on the pie, slipped the box into a bag. Cat stood up and pulled out her bank card.

"Whatever happened to that robot your daddy had? The one he used to call his assistant?"

"He's gone."

The waitress ran her card. The monitor played footage of a sad little protest staged by a fundamentalist organization. Hand-painted signs marched through a gray drizzle. If the law passed,

Finn would no longer be the property of anyone. Not her father. Not STL. But she knew he wouldn't come home either way.

"Still think it's a slippery slope." The waitress handed the pie across the counter. Cat knew better than to respond. She went outside, slung the bag over the handlebars of her bike, and rode back to the house.

* * * *

The next day, Cat slept late, waking up after lunch. She went downstairs and chatted with her father about his work. He asked her if the baby had kicked yet, but she shook her head, still waiting to feel that ripple inside herself. She drank a glass of orange juice. Her father told her the weather had cooled off a little and so she wandered out to the garden. She didn't feel like going up to the loom. Let the tapestry stay incomplete for just a bit longer.

The black paint had chipped off the garden gate, and the metal had rusted. Cat tugged hard on the gate's handle to force it open. A breeze trickled in from the north and changed the scent of the air, blowing over the pine trees in the woods rather than the Farm-to-Market road. Her citrus tree towered over her despite the garden's neglect. Its branches stretched against the cloudless blue sky.

Maybe it's a daughter, Cat thought.

Where did that come from? She stopped, wrapped her arms around her chest. Goose bumps prickled up along her calves. She should have grabbed one of her sweaters before coming outside— did she even pack any sweaters? Already, she'd brought down the boxes of clothes she wore in high school, plus some boxes of her mother's clothes, because half the things she'd brought from the glass house—stiff pencil skirts and gauzy blouses and satiny, stylish dresses—had proven to be useless. She didn't have any need for pencil skirts out here. There was no one to see her wearing them.

A little girl with dark hair and dark eyes who could tell stories from memory.

Cat went back inside, leaving the garden gate hanging open. She dug a faded black sweater out of the hall closet. She hadn't been out to her mother's grave since coming home. But right now she needed to pretend she had a mother.

She rode her bike down the old dirt road, the wind whipping up her hair behind her. She never liked seeing the cemetery in the fall, when it was covered in stalks of yellow grass rather than spring's effulgence of wildflowers and grasshoppers. Golden dust billowed up on the wind. Cat wheeled the bike off the road and leaned it against the twisting oak tree. She shoved her hands in her pockets to warm them and walked to her mother's headstone.

"Hi, Mom," she said.

She sat down cross-legged in the dirt. Her hair blew into her eyes, her mouth. She didn't push it away.

"I'm pregnant."

Cat knew she was alone in the graveyard. She didn't imagine her mother as a ghost curling around the stalks of grass, watching and listening. But it still felt like a confession. It was easy to confess things to the crackling golden countryside.

"I'm pregnant," she said. "It's Richard's baby." Cat covered her face with her hands. Autumn crept around her, a chill dusting across the hairs on her arms. "I wish it wasn't. When I first found out, I almost didn't keep it. Because I couldn't stand the thought of a little Richard growing inside of me." She cocked her head to the side. "I'm still not used to the idea. Of having a kid. I don't feel pregnant, you know? But just now, I was in the garden—not much of a garden now, Daddy's been terrible about keeping it up—anyway, I was in the garden, and I started thinking . . . What would it be like, you know? To have a little kid." She looked up at the sky and watched a wisp of white cloud move over the pale imprint of the moon. Just a sliver right now. "To have a little . . . me."

Cat leaned back in the grass. She'd never understood until now why she chose to flush down the toilet, one by one, the pills that would have cast out the baby. When she first found out she was pregnant, when she first came home from the doctor, she thought she should take the pills. But she couldn't. She didn't want to punish the cluster of cells growing inside her for her mistakes and Richard's violence.

"Richard couldn't make me normal," Cat said to the gravestone. "And really, Finn was a better choice. I mean it." She stood up and dusted the soil off the backs of her legs. "But he's gone now, too. Everyone's gone." She sighed. "I hate coming here out of season. I should have brought flowers."

Still, Cat wandered the perimeter of the cemetery the way she did in the spring. She collected strands of grass and wheat and curls of Spanish moss. An autumn bouquet. A bouquet of falling-apart things. But lovely still.

When Cat finally rode her bike back to the house, the sun had sunk below the tree line, turning the sky orange. She cut across the yard and looked up at the moon, the way she always did when she came outside in the evenings. In a few days she wouldn't be able to see it at all. She hated those times.

When she came inside, her father was at the kitchen table eating a bowl of watery soup, broth dribbling off the side of the spoon. He glanced up. "Everything okay?"

"Why wouldn't it be?"

He shrugged and turned back to his soup. Cat slid into the chair across from him. The kitchen lights were sallow and thin against the encroaching darkness.

"You seem . . ." He paused. "Distant." He looked at her with clear eyes. "I wanted to make sure you haven't had any . . . problems. You know, with the . . ." His voice trailed off.

"The baby's fine, Daddy."

He smiled, dropped his spoon back into his bowl. Cat looked out the window at the backyard, the ground littered with dead leaves.

"I wish Finn were here," she said.

Silence. Cat looked over at her father. He wouldn't meet her eyes but she thought he looked sad. Thinking of Finn made her inexplicably tired, as though her body couldn't withstand the memory of him.

"He made his decision," her father said. "It's just you and me."

Just you and me, thought Cat. *No, it's me. It's just me.* But aloud, she said, "I know."

* * * *

The next day, Cat decided she would finish the tapestry. She woke up late, after sleeping dreamlessly for nearly twelve hours. The sun flooded the room, and she stretched out beneath her thin, cool bedsheet, feeling her blood pumping out to her extremities. Her fingers tingled. The tapestry was a gift for Finn. In the golden sunlight of her bedroom she allowed herself to believe that, if she finished it, Finn would come back.

For an hour, she wove the spindle through the warp threads and combed the wefting threads down with her fingers, over and over again, the movement as rhythmic as a heartbeat. Then she came to the end. Cat stopped and wondered if the image of the tapestry in her head would match the thing she'd created.

She went downstairs and dug a pair of scissors out of the junk drawer in the kitchen. But then she stopped, standing in front of the sink, scissors dangling from the crook of her finger. She never liked cutting warp threads alone. Usually Felix watched her, urging her on, telling her it was okay. But Felix wasn't here.

She knocked on the door of her father's laboratory. "Come in!"

Cat pushed on the door with her shoulder so the weight of her body swung it open. Her father stood in front of a computer monitor, his fingers moving shakily across the console. He looked up at her expectantly.

"Hi, Daddy." Cat slipped into the lab. She knew the place had been updated many times over, but it still seemed the exact same as when she was a little girl, all blinking lights and electronic humming. The only difference now was the lack of Finn.

"What's up?"

"I need you to do me a favor." Cat looked down at the cement floor. "It's silly, but . . . it's important, too. If you don't mind."

"Of course! What is it?"

"I finished the tapestry I was working on." She hadn't told him it was for Finn. "I need to cut the warp threads and tie it off and roll it out and . . . well, I have this kind of superstition, where I don't like being alone . . ."

Her father laughed and held out one hand. "I understand. Give me a second. I'll meet you upstairs."

Cat nodded, then ducked out of the laboratory. She took the stairs two at a time. She heard her father moving through the house, more slowly than he used to, as though he were a windup toy on the verge of stopping.

In the room, in the dusty sunlight, Cat took one last look at the rolled-up tapestry, alone.

Her father appeared in the doorway and nodded at the loom. "All finished?" he asked.

Cat nodded. She stepped over to the loom. Held up the scissors like a gun. She took a deep breath and on the exhale she snipped the first string, only one, and when the entire thing didn't unravel she cut cleanly through the rest. The tension in the tapestry sagged. She tossed the scissors aside and began the slow process of unrolling the tapestry.

The gift.

Her heart beat quicker. The tapestry grew too large for her to hold, and Cat looked at her father and gestured with her chin toward the pile of knotted yarn overflowing her arms. He took hold of one end and held it up so the tapestry didn't drag across the dusty floor. As she unrolled, Cat watched the tapestry wrapped around the warp beam. It appeared in fragments, strips of green and gray and silvery white. She remembered the cold snap that had first inspired her. How she'd sat straight up in her bed, her breath forming a cloud around her face. How Finn had left all the windows open so he could listen to the north wind. How he'd wrapped her in blankets, how his hands had kept her warm as she shivered and shook.

"Wow." Her father's eyes shone. "You did this? It's beautiful."

"Thanks." Cat laughed. "I've been working on it forever. Since before . . . since I lived in that old duplex."

Cat finished unrolling the tapestry. She untied the warp threads. For a moment she and her father stood with the tapestry cradled awkwardly between them.

"We need a table," she said. "Or a bed."

"Right."

Carefully, they shuffled into the hall, toward Cat's bedroom. They laid the tapestry over her unmade bed, her father straightening and smoothing out all the wrinkles and folds.

Cat lost her breath.

The tapestry glimmered in the sunlight streaming through the windows. Its image was an abstraction, but it still reminded Cat of the way the world had looked through the window, after her breath fogged the glass.

The stitches were loose, twined together into a web of loops. Cat slipped her hand underneath and lifted it up, the cashmere and silk luxurious against her skin. She found the strand of Finn's hair, that narrow line of darkness. Her own hair was lost in the weaving.

"What about the ends?" her father asked. "The loose threads? Do you leave those?"

Cat shook her head. "I'll tie them off. I've got a tapestry needle somewhere." She smiled dimly at her father. "You don't have to stick around. I know you're busy. It's just . . . cutting the threads makes me nervous."

Her father smiled. His skin was as transparent as paper. "I can't believe my daughter made this. This is what you do. I can't believe I'd never seen it before." He enveloped her in a hug and Cat closed her eyes, pressed her face against his new thinness, the bones in his chest pushing up through his T-shirt. "I'm sorry," he said.

"For what?"

"For not taking enough of an interest."

Cat laughed. "I'm glad this is the first thing you ever saw. It's . . . it's the most special to me."

Her father nodded.

Cat found a tapestry needle in the top drawer of her dresser. She pulled a chair up to the edge of her bed and began tying off the warp threads so that the tapestry would not unravel. Her father watched her for a few moments longer, then set his hand on her shoulder before he walked out the door. His footsteps echoed all the way down to the laboratory. Cat knotted off the warp threads as deftly as she could—for some reason, her hands would not stop shaking. As she worked, she thought about Finn. Then she thought about nothing at all.

The sunlight in the windows turned burnished gold as the afternoon wore on.

When she finished knotting the threads, Cat stood up and stretched. The tapestry lay waiting and sparking in the sun. She folded it up, neatly matching the corners. She folded it in half, in quarters, in eighths. It was complete; it was unfinished. She sat back down in her chair. She had expected to feel different afterward, the way she used to feel whenever she donated to ADL. She didn't.

She could put it in his old room. But she hadn't been to his room since she came home, and she couldn't bring herself to go up there yet.

Cat clutched the tapestry to her chest, the fibers of the yarn intertwining with the hairs of her arms. Then she opened her closet door and set the tapestry on the shelf above the clothing rack.

Someday, she would go upstairs to the attic bedroom, she'd lay the tapestry on his empty desk, she'd do the best she could.

*   *   *   *

Two weeks passed. Cat carried on, working in the garden in the cool mornings, sleeping in the afternoons. She scheduled another visit to the doctor and began to practice the breathing exercises—even though she hadn't decided whether she wanted a natural birth or not.

She found she enjoyed working in the garden. She pulled out weeds and piled them along the side of the house for compost. She trimmed the unwieldy jasmine vines and twisted them around the fence. Pruned the citrus trees. Planted a row of rhododendrons to add color amidst autumn's brownness.

One morning she decided she would set about the task of uprooting the rosebushes, now dead, that had once grown along the perimeter of the fence. She pulled on a pair of thick woolen gloves to protect her hands, but the thorns still scratched up and down her arms, trails of pink etched like tattoos across her skin. After an hour, she pulled off the gloves and wiped the sweat beading along her brow. It wasn't hot outside but the work warmed her up. She filled a glass with water in the kitchen and then sat beneath the lemon tree and admired her work, the row of dark, waiting gouges in the garden's soil. She'd read that you should plant roses in February.

And then she felt it, a flutter of movement below her stomach, like a hand touching the surface of water.

Cat went still, waiting to feel it again, to ensure it wasn't her imagination.

There. Another ripple. Cat pulled up her shirt and laid her hand against her bare stomach, her skin smooth beneath her fingers. She felt it again. Proof of life.

Cat leaned against the narrow tree trunk and looked at the clear, cloudless sky through the tree's branches. She thought about her baby—her son, the doctors had told her at her last visit. A little boy.

She thought constantly of names. They came to her without any reason, like a song that had wedged itself into her consciousness. *Jordan. Henry. Frank. Salvador.* Name after name after name.

She always pictured him with dark hair and dark eyes. She always pictured Finn.

Cat spread her hand across her stomach and closed her eyes. *Finn.* Although of course Finn had never been born. He'd only sprung to existence somewhere in Kansas, the product of intelligence rather than desire, delivered by strings of code rather than doctors. And that, Cat realized, was all she knew. All this time and all she knew about his origins was that he came from Kansas, a place that had turned to desert a long time ago.

That had been the secret in this house throughout her entire childhood. Where Finn came from. Her father refused to divulge any information when she was younger. By the time she was an adult, she had stopped asking. She didn't like what that said about her.

Cat stood up. She left her gloves and her garden spade and her glass of half-drunk water sitting in the garden, and she walked down to her father's laboratory and went in without knocking.

"Cat!" Her father was hunched over a computer. "What brings you down here?" He glanced up at her, glanced back down, glanced back at her. "What's wrong?"

"I want to know about Finn. Where did he come from?" The question shimmered on the air.

Her father straightened, ran one hand over his head. "That's . . . abrupt." He peered at her. "Are you okay? What happened to your arms?"

Cat glanced down. "Oh, I'm fine. I was pulling out the roses in the garden. You know, the ones that all died." She smiled. "The baby kicked. And I started imagining him, you know—" She stopped herself. "I just started wondering where Finn came from. You never told me."

Her father shuffled his weight from one foot to the other. Scratched at his arm. "Cat," he said slowly. "I'm not sure this is the best idea—"

"You told me once you didn't make him," she said. "Then who did? Why did you bring him here? Did you have anything to do with his . . ." She fumbled for the right word. She wanted to say *production*; she wanted to say *birth*.

Her father hesitated. Then he hit a keystroke on his computer and walked around the long low table to Cat's side. "Marginally," he said. "I was marginally involved. A colleague of mine, Judith Condon—he was her project." He grimaced a little. "I hate talking about him like that."

"Judith Condon." The name was unfamiliar on Cat's tongue. Heavy. "So Judith Condon is his . . . So she made him?"

"She took the credit. She had a whole team of people." Her father looked at her. "Do you really want to know this story?"

"There's a story?"

"There's always a story." He paused. "Here, sit down." He gestured at the cheap rolling chairs he kept shoved under the table. They both sat. Her father tapped his fingers against the table's Formica veneer. "I met Judith when I was in grad school. I'd see her at conferences and so forth. She was brilliant. That's what everyone said. I was a little scared of her." He laughed. "She had this intensity . . . I don't know. I didn't know anyone else like her. Anyway. This was back at the tail end of the Disasters, and we were all idealistic about saving the world and doing all these amazing things, like we'd suffered and now was our chance to start over new. And we did do a lot of amazing things back then. Some of us are still doing them. But Judith . . ." He leaned back and looked at the ceiling, his hands folded into a steeple beneath his chin. "She started to drop off from what the rest of us were up to. She was older than us, not old enough to be senile but we attributed it to that anyway." He shrugged. "She called me right after I met your mother. Wanted me to help her with some circuit design. She didn't tell me what it was for, though. Just said she was working with artificial intelligence, but that meant something different than it does now. She didn't say an artificial *human* intelligence."

Cat listened, one hand clenching the other in her lap.

She thought she felt the baby's heart beating.

"Anyway, I did the work for her, but then I got involved with this huge NSF grant so I had to bow out. I didn't hear from her for a long time. I basically forgot about her, honestly. She had fallen completely off the radar. Then one day I get a call from Dr. Ramirez. Do you remember him? We used to have him over for dinner."

Cat nodded. Distantly, she recalled the warm golden glimmer of the dining room lights, the hum of music in the background, her mother's forearm reaching across the table as a silver bracelet jangled against the bone of her wrist.

"You were very young," her father said. "He's passed on since then, of course. Well, he called me one night. Told me he'd been working closely with Judith for pretty much the entire duration of the project. He was damn near hysterical. Asked me if I knew what it was, started shrieking that they'd made a life—wouldn't give me any details. Just made me promise I'd fly out to Judith's workshop the first chance I got. Apparently she'd set up something in the desert, the Midwest. Wanted total isolation." He grinned and shook his head. "People call *me* the mad scientist."

"Is that when you found Finn?" Cat asked. "When you flew out there? That was the life they'd made, right?" She closed her eyes. She wanted to picture everything in her head. A laboratory in the middle of the desert. Finn when he was brand-new. In her mind, Judith Condon looked like her own mother, just with dark sleek hair and black, black eyes.

Her father nodded. "John—Dr. Ramirez—met me at the airport. Looked like he hadn't slept in a week. As he's driving me out there, he pulls a goddamn bottle of Jack Daniel's out from under the seat and starts drinking it straight up. Then he tells me that Judith has gone total psychopath, and that she wants to kill it. That's what he keeps saying, over and over. *She wants to kill it, she wants to kill it.*"

Her father looked at the air above Cat's head. "One time, one time he said *him*. That she wanted to kill *him*. We were almost to the house at that point. The Jack Daniel's was basically gone."

"You saved him," said Cat. "Finn."

Her father's face turned very serious. "I suppose you could look at it that way."

"What . . . What was it like? When you saw him for the first time? What'd you think?"

"He was shut off."

Cat's throat tightened.

"John led me straight to the workshop. Said something about how we didn't have much time. The whole house was a mess. We walked through the living room, and I just remember everything was covered in dirt from outside. You could taste it in the back of your throat. The workshop was *spotless*, though. It was remarkable. And lying there, right in the center of the room, was Finn."

"Shut off." Cat remembered how he looked the first time she kissed him, crumpled up and empty.

"Yeah, shut off. I didn't understand what I was looking at. Something like Finn—even now it feels like magic, sometimes. Like something that shouldn't exist. I thought it—he—was some sort of model. I had no idea what she was up to. But then John went over and reached behind Finn's neck and his eyes opened. God, I'll never forget that. Those eyes lighting up. He looked *right at me*." Cat's father bit his lower lip, and Cat had the sudden sense that he wasn't speaking to her anymore.

She wondered when he had last told this story. If he'd ever told it at all.

"He sat up and looked around the room. Looked at John. Greeted him, you know how he is. *Hello, Dr. Ramirez.* But then"— his voice trembled—"then he asked how he'd gotten there. He didn't . . . didn't seem to understand that he'd been switched off. And it bothered me. It bothered me that you could act upon him and he wouldn't realize it." He took a deep breath. "God, I hadn't thought about that in so long . . ." He closed his eyes. "Shit."

"Daddy?" Cat put her hand on his forearm. He opened his eyes and looked at her like he was surprised to find her sitting there. She asked him if he was all right.

"I'm sorry, sweetheart," he said. "It was a strange experience."

"If you don't want to talk about it . . ." But she wanted him to keep going. She wanted to know everything.

"There's not much else to tell. Not much else that's important." His eyes flicked away from hers: that tic. He was lying. She didn't push it. He looked too frail in the sallow laboratory lights. "John led him out to the car. Told him 'Mother' was sick and he was going to stay with Dr. Ramirez. I realized later he was talking about Judith, but—well, it's not important." He shook his head. "I knew John didn't want to keep him, though. We drove straight on into Texas. John probably shouldn't have been driving but I had to examine him. Talk to him. Learn how he worked."

"Is this when you brought him home with you?" Cat asked. This part of the story, bringing Finn back to Texas, was as gauzy as lace. But her heart still hammered in her chest because Finn's world had opened up for her a fraction wider. *Judith Condon.* She had a name. Her father shook his head.

"No, that was a few months later. John told me he couldn't . . . he couldn't see past all the circuits he'd built. He was afraid he'd get cruel." Cat's father shrugged. "I couldn't imagine it. He was a wonderful father. But I accepted it, of course. To be honest, it was too good of an opportunity—scientifically speaking—for me to pass up. Plus, I'd enjoyed speaking with him when we drove back to Texas."

Cat's father leaned back in his chair. Cat considered asking him if Judith Condon was still alive but she decided against it: he was lying; he always lied to protect her. There was something comforting about it, his lies of omission, and she knew she could learn more on her own.

When her father stood up, he trembled. Cat leapt up and put her hand on his back. He swatted her away. "I'm fine," he said. "I need to get back to work."

"Thanks for telling me all that."

He smiled. "I should have told you sooner. Your mother—she didn't approve."

"Of Finn? No shit."

"Well, of the particular combination of you and Finn. Finn by himself, I think she could have managed." He laughed, then took Cat by the chin and looked her in the eye. "It bothered me, when you were younger. Because you were younger. But now—" He stopped. "I could have handled things better. I just wanted . . . I just wanted you to be happy. Both of you."

Cat hugged him. Now she had a purpose, a goal: she would find Judith Condon and through her she would find Finn, the part of Finn she had heretofore been much too selfish to even know existed.

FIFTEEN

The next afternoon when her father was in the lab, working and wasting away, she went into the dining room and sat down at the computer set into the otherwise unused table. The room was full of dust and sunlight. She brought up the list of all the networked computers in the house and stared at it for a long time, her fingers tapping the table.

Which computer held the information she wanted? Not the antiquated learning slabs tucked away in boxes in the hall closet, not the cheap laptop where her mother had filed all her recipes. One of the laboratory computers. Maybe the one Finn had kept in his room. Cat scrolled through the list until she found the lab computers, until she found one labeled with nothing but a string of numbers. Finn wouldn't have bothered giving his computer a name.

She tapped the icon. It was Finn's computer: here was a robotic diagnostic program, here was the video chat program he had used when she went away to college. A folder of unfinished code she only half understood. A collection of images saved from the Internet: ballet dancers and Barnett Newman paintings, photographs of the city skyline lit up at night, a shot of the band that had played at the

Stella rent party, so long ago it may as well have been another lifetime, when Cat made the decision to marry Richard.

She flicked through the images, each one adding to the others to form a picture of Finn. It was a picture she didn't quite understand.

Cat closed Finn's computer and began searching methodically through the lab computers. Files for her father's space-exploration contract work. She went back farther. Notes on earthbound robots—the files used the old word *automata*. Cat frowned, furrowed her brow. She went back even farther, from computer to computer, tracking in reverse the trajectory of her father's career.

And then she found it. A directory of files labeled "Finn." Cat's breath caught. She touched her belly without realizing it and watched the file list load on the dim old monitor. Everything about him in one place.

She tapped on a file labeled "Schematics," and an entire universe blossomed onto the screen. She leaned closer. The text, amber on black, blurred together. She only understood bits and pieces, left over from her high school engineering classes. She knew enough to know: This was him. This was every part of him, translated, laid out in front of her.

I am a machine.

Cat closed the file. Her hands trembled. She walked over to the window and pulled aside the curtain, the fabric worn thin from moths and sunlight and time. The window looked out into the backyard, out at the tree line of the forest.

"All right, baby," Cat said. "Do you think I'm doing the right thing?"

She waited. Movement fluttered through her womb, like butterfly wings dusting across the back of her hand. "I'll take that as a yes." She remembered how she used to eavesdrop on her father's video conferences so she could learn bits and pieces of Finn's specifications—the size of his memory processors, the speed of his electronic brain. Scraps of mostly meaningless information that she knitted together and memorized. Now she wanted to cry. Here was an entire directory of files, stored on a computer in the house, not even hidden behind a password, and she hadn't bothered in all this time even to glance at them.

Cat sat back down at the computer. "Schematics" was still high-lighted. She scrolled down, looking for something she could understand.

There. "Contact." Cat touched the link.

The folder was mostly empty. The files were labeled with dates. The first brought up some saved e-mail files, exchanges between her father and Dr. Condon. *I need some of that famed Novak genius, Daniel*, Dr. Condon wrote. *You didn't win that grant for nothing, did you?*

There were no details. Dr. Condon never mentioned the specifics of her project: Only that there was a project, that she had relocated to the desert.

I've brought in some artists to do shell work. They love the light out here. They won't stop raving about it. I dunno, I just like the isolation. I need it. Just like I need the artists even though they're pissing me off.

Cat went to the next file. It was an electronic copy of an old magazine article, dated toward the end of the worst of the Disasters. *Dr. Judith Condon*, read the article title. *Forerunner in the Automata Revolution.*

There was a black-and-white picture, the lines blurred, the capture grainy. Dr. Condon looked young, not much older than Cat, and intense, the dark smudge of her eyes staring straight into the camera, her hair swept away from her face, her mouth unsmiling. Cat stared at the picture and something sparked inside her, electricity rushing from one circuit board chip to another, forming a half second of connection. Here was the woman who made him. Here was the woman who cast him out.

Just like I did. Cat closed the article, wiping the monitor clear.

One more file. Another set of e-mail exchanges, this time between Cat's father and Dr. Ramirez. Cat read through them all, trying to jostle Dr. Condon's dark staring eyes out of her memory. Friendly banter, most of them, how-are-yous, invitations to dinner. She read for a long time. And then she found something.

Over twenty-five years ago, Dr. Ramirez had sent an e-mail to Cat's father in which he listed the address of Dr. Condon's desert laboratory.

Per our conversation, he wrote, as though discussing a business proposition, *here's the address in case I can't meet you.*

Cat hit print screen. Then she collected the e-mail from the rickety old printer set into the telephone alcove, folded the printout into fourths, and slid it into her pillowcase like a love letter.

* * * *

After Cat found the address, she set about making clandestine preparations to travel into Kansas. Drought had transformed the Midwest into a desert long before Cat was born, and then human innovation had transformed that desert into a source of energy for not just the country but the entire continent. Windmills grew instead of corn. It was not a place people lived. Nor a place they visited. Cat learned she would have to apply for a travel permit if she wanted to go farther than the city on the desert's edge.

It could take months to get approval. Still, Cat filled out the form on the website in a flush of excitement. A screen came up after she submitted it, telling her the expected date of her permit's approval; she would be nearly seven months pregnant then. She should still be able to travel.

After that, she could only wait. She went about her days as best she could, preparing for the baby, cooking meals for herself and her father, working in the garden. She felt the itch to weave again, and so she contacted some of her old clients, one of whom was delighted to commission a new piece from her. She borrowed her father's car and drove into the city for her supplies and began the tapestry that evening. It was an accounting firm, and they gave her free rein to create what she wanted: so she wove the night sky, constellations of stars glittering against an indigo background, the moon stitched in bone-colored silk.

Because it was coming into winter and the days had cooled to a bearable temperature, she wove in the mornings and relegated her garden work to the afternoon, when weak sunlight slanted through the tree branches. The air was tinged with the cold-weather scent of metal, and Cat scooped up the soil, hard and cold in her fingers, digging up the virulent honeysuckle vines that had grown over the fence. Her fingers turned red but she was warm enough from work-ing that she didn't notice.

When she finished clearing away the honeysuckle she carried the vines in armfuls to the compost pile set up next to the old air-conditioning unit. She walked back to the garden, which rustled forlornly, and shoved her dirty hands in her pockets. She tried to imagine how it would look when her baby was born: heavy with flowers and greenery, indolent with extra oxygen. Maybe she would plant some vegetables.

Tires crunched along the driveway. Her father was down in the lab, too involved in his work to leave the house. She walked onto the porch and followed it around the house's perimeter. When she came to the front, her heart stopped.

Richard's car.

She recognized it immediately, sleek and dark as a beetle. He sat in the front seat, staring at the porch. He saw her. Cat's entire body prickled with sweat. Out there on the porch, it was as though she were back in the glass house and everything she did was on display.

The driver's-side door swung open, and he stepped out. His hair was longer than she remembered, and he wore a thin black coat that flapped around his knees as he trudged through the yard. He held something in his right hand. A slim, dark brown comm slate, the sort lawyers used.

"Caterina," he said. "I need to talk to you."

"No," she whispered. Her hand dropped down to her stomach. She was showing a little, probably not enough for him to realize she was pregnant. She snatched her hand away. *Don't draw attention to it.*

He clomped up the steps to the porch. "Damn, it's cold out here."

"What do you want?"

"Don't be like that." He looked her up and down. She curled her hands into fists.

"You look radiant," he said. She didn't respond.

"Can we go inside?"

"Why are you here?"

Richard looked down at the tablet like he couldn't imagine how it had found its way into his hands. He sighed. "You need to sign this. Slap your thumbprint on there. It's not the final papers, so . . ." His voice trailed off. "Seriously, I'm freezing my ass off. Can we go inside?"

Of course. The papers. The lawyers still called them that even though nothing was on paper anymore. Vaguely Cat recalled the last conversation she'd had with the lawyer. She always lost track of everything he said, but he had mentioned needing her signature, her thumbprint. Cat sighed, ran her hands through her hair. Cold dirt clung to her scalp.

"Why didn't you just send it?" she said.

Richard stared at her. "I wanted to see you. I miss you. Cat—"

She pushed the front door open so roughly it slammed against the doorstop and bounced back, almost clicking shut again. She caught it with the tip of her toe. "Come in." She looked over her shoulder at him. "You're not staying."

Richard frowned. The lines in his brow were deeper than she remembered, his eyes paler. She remembered how she used to care for him, how she used to find those transparent eyes compelling. His normalcy had been so appealing: he had been an antidote to Finn, one that failed utterly. Thinking on it made her stomach ache.

She led him into the dining room. Her father was still in the basement. No need to let him know what was happening. Richard sat down but Cat stayed standing. For a moment he stared at her. She crossed her arms in front of her chest, trying to ward him off.

"Caterina," he said. "I'm sorry. You have to know that. I didn't mean—"

"Let's get this over with."

Richard sighed and handed her the slate. Cat sat down at the table, two seats away from him, and turned it on, blinking at the flash of light from the screen. For a moment she pretended to read over the block of words she was too tired to understand. Then she plucked the stylus off the side of the tablet and carved her name into the electronic signature line. The screen went gray, and Cat saw the ghost of her signature. *Caterina Novak.*

"We don't have to do this," Richard said.

The screen brightened. It wanted her thumbprint. Cat pressed her right thumb against the glass.

"You hit me." She handed him the tablet and stood up. "What else is there after that?"

He stared at her.

"Please leave."

"I drove all the way out here—"

"When you could have just sent it. Don't try to guilt me into letting you stay."

He shook his head. His eyes had iced over. "You were fucking that robot, weren't you?" he said. "That's why you donated all that money to ADL. It wasn't because you actually cared."

The room suddenly seemed too small and devoid of air. Of course he'd always known, but hearing him say it out loud, Cat was struck with a flare of anxiety in the center of her chest. She could never be normal because she *wasn't* normal. She had kept Finn secret for so long because of that deviancy. Now she was pregnant. It wouldn't affect only her anymore.

Cat willed herself to keep her expression blank and dispassionate.

"I'll take that as a yes. I can't believe this." Richard looked her right in the eye. She held his gaze. "It's sick."

"What? Donating to ADL?"

"You know what I'm talking about."

"You hit me. I don't think you have the right to pass judgment on anyone."

Richard slid his chair away from the table and stood up. He tucked the tablet under his arm. Cat ran her hand, unthinking, across her stomach and then dropped it to her side. He didn't seem to notice.

"I came here," he said, "to apologize for that."

"Fine," said Cat. "Accepted. Now get out."

Richard's hands curled into fists, and the room jolted. Cat took two steps back. Her fingers went to the spot beneath her right eye that had hurt the most in those weeks that followed. But then Richard let out a muffled grunt and stalked out of the dining room. Cat followed him, keeping her distance. He stopped in the foyer and turned around.

"Why aren't you keeping anything?" he said.

"What?"

"You're so weird," he said. "You don't even want my money, at least?"

"You *hit me*."

Richard seemed to recoil, as though a moth had fluttered against the tips of his eyelashes. Then he said, "Ella warned me. She didn't get why I'd marry someone like you. I should have listened to her."

"You think *I'm* weird because I don't want your money and your horrible fucking house?" Cat laughed. "What, am I supposed to do that? Because I'm a woman? Because you're rich?" Her laughter tinged on hysteria. She was so relieved the conversation had turned to money, to material possessions, instead of the fact that she was an ice queen who could only be with a robot. Richard glared at her. He pulled against the door, and a rush of cold air filled the foyer. Cat couldn't stop laughing.

"You're planning something," he said. "You and that lawyer of yours."

"I don't want your money, Richard." Tears formed in the corners of her eyes. She hoped he wouldn't notice. "I know that's a difficult concept for you to grasp, but there it is."

"Bitch."

He said it almost tenderly, and then he turned away from her, stepped through the door and out to the porch, out to his car, away.

Cat pushed the door shut and leaned against the cold wall and listened to the sound of his car engine starting up and disappearing down the driveway. When she heard only silence she looked at her hands. Dirt stained the crescents of her nails.

Ella was right. He should never have married someone like her. She used to think that he was using her in their marriage—as a decoration on his arm, as a test subject for his AI—but she understood now that she had used *him*, that he had loved her and she never once reciprocated despite claiming otherwise, over and over again. When he gave her the ring that day of the freeze, her thoughts had been with Finn. She should have said no.

Cat stared through the window at the void where his car had

been. She felt as though Richard had pricked her and all her energy had flooded out.

She left the living room and sat down at the dining room computer, where she pulled up the directory with Finn's information. She opened the schematics file. The schematics reminded her of threads on a loom. She ran her finger across the monitor, tracing the path of one electronic neuron to another. She wished more than anything that she could decipher them completely, that she could understand Finn through the logic of engineering, if nothing else.

"Cat?"

Cat jumped and switched off the monitor. "What were you looking at?" her father asked.

"Nothing."

Her father pulled up a chair beside her and turned the monitor back on. Finn's schematics flared into place.

"Oh, Cat," he said.

"There wasn't a password or anything."

"I know. It isn't that . . ." Her father rubbed his forehead. His fingers looked like sticks. "I thought I heard talking. Is everything okay?"

"Yes," said Cat. "Richard came by—"

"What? He didn't hurt you, did he?"

"No. He just brought the papers. Or one set of them, anyway. The last set before everything's finalized." She spoke in the direction of the schematics. "It doesn't matter. I'm an adult, I can take care of myself." She turned off the monitor.

"I know that."

They sat in silence. Her father ran one hand over his thin hair. Scratched at his arm. Their reflections moved in the darkened screen.

"This is my fault," he said.

"I should never have married him."

Her father shook his head and kept his gaze focused on a spot on the floor, halfway between them. "I'm not talking about Richard." He bit his bottom lip. He still did not look at her. "I know why Finn left."

Cat's mouth went dry.

"I did something to him." He took a deep breath. "Do you

remember when you were a little girl and you made that scarf for him?"

She nodded.

"He kept it, you know. All these years. Strange, huh? Do you remember what I told you, when you came looking for him so you could give it to him?"

"I don't understand what you're getting at."

"I told you he was just a program. That he couldn't feel anything."

"Yes." Cat's heart clenched up.

"I lied." He laughed, shook his head. "Sort of. He could feel things. I just think he—it—was different. His ability to feel things was . . . repressed. A protocol that was meant to make him obedient. Like a perfect child. Certain intense emotions were overridden. And so I wanted to . . ." He stopped and closed his eyes. Leaned back in the chair.

Cat felt cold. A weight settled at the bottom of her stomach.

"I wrote a program," her father said, "that erased all that. His programming, his circuitry, it's all extremely complicated. Baroque, really. I figured out a way to hack past some of it, get a few synapses firing that hadn't been firing before. So to speak. Anyway, I'd been working on it for a few years, you know, in my spare time, but after your wedding—"

"My wedding? What does my wedding . . . ?" But she knew.

Her father looked up at her. "I saw you dancing with him," he said. "I realized it wasn't fair. It wasn't fair to you, and it wasn't fair to him."

"I don't understand." She clenched her hands around the hem of her skirt, her nails cutting into the skin of her hand.

"You love him," said her father.

Love was a word Cat had heard so many times that it no longer held any meaning. Boyfriends had told her they loved her and she had said it back and it was like any number of words. It was like *hello* or *I'm fine.* But here, as she sat on an uncomfortable wooden chair in her father's dining room, the cold northern wind slapping against the glass in the windows, the word *love* sounded like a revelation.

"No," she said. *Liar.*

"Oh, Cat. I saw the way you looked when the two of you danced. It damn near broke my heart, knowing you couldn't marry him." He leaned forward in his chair. "It's okay," he said, his eyes bright and sincere. "It's okay to love him."

She couldn't breathe. She thought about Finn staring at her, saying to her, *You're married.* His expression had been cold and she hadn't allowed herself to see it at the time. And when he came to her before he went away to Florida, there had been a change in him, like something inside him had switched on or off. The transformation in how he spoke her name, his sudden sharp movements, the way he wouldn't look her in the eye. She had refused to acknowledge what she saw. All this time, she had blocked it away, this one simple fact: Richard wasn't the only man she had used in her life.

"The program worked," she said flatly.

"Yes." Her father looked away from her. "He was . . . upset. Afterward. He went out to the woods and didn't come back for a long time. I actually went out to try and find him. I thought . . . I don't know. I don't know what I thought. There aren't a lot of precedents for something like this."

"No," said Cat. "I can't imagine that there are." Her entire body was numb. Her father had given Finn a gift, and she had ruined it by treating him like a machine. She had beaten up Erik Martin in the courtyard of her high school for less than what she did herself.

"Cat," said her father. She looked at him. He smiled sadly. "I think it was too much for him. To feel everything all at once. He wouldn't tell me, which is strange, you know, he was always so forthcoming, but . . ." He shook his head. "Nothing we can do. He made his decision."

"Can you talk to him?"

"I'm sorry?"

"At the lunar station. Can you contact him? To, you know, check up on him?" *To apologize to him.*

Her father looked at her strangely. "He belongs to STL now."

Cat slumped against the couch.

"I'm so sorry." His voice shook.

"It's not your fault," she said. "Daddy . . ." She leaned over and wrapped her arms around his neck, laid her head against his shoulder. He wiped at his eyes. "Thank you for trying."

"He seemed to give you happiness."

Cat sat back in her chair, legs shaking. She nodded. He *had* given her happiness; he *had* taken her pain away. But he was not a machine designed to eradicate her sorrow. For the first time, she understood why he ran away.

For the first time, she didn't blame him at all.

*　*　*　*

That night Cat couldn't sleep. Her thoughts were too heavy. She lay in her bed with her hands resting on her stomach. After a while, she pulled her comm slate off her bedside table and checked the status on her travel visa to the Midwestern Desert. It hadn't gone through yet. Now more than ever she wanted to fly to Kansas and see where he came from, even if it was just an abandoned house in the middle of the desert, coated in dust and infested with snakes and scorpions. She couldn't apologize to him on the moon, but she wanted to find his history, she wanted to learn everything about him.

She wanted to prove to herself that she could see him completely.

All the room's shadows were silver. Her closet door hung open, the tapestry glinting in the moonlight. Eventually, she crawled out of bed and put her jacket on over her pajamas. She slipped the tapestry off the closet shelf and crept into the hallway, in the direction of Finn's old room.

Since moving home, she had pretended that the door leading to the attic stairs opened into a linen closet. That the attic room never existed. Sometimes when she walked past she felt a spark in the hairs of her arms, like static electricity.

But tonight, she wanted to see the room and breathe the stale dusty air. She wanted to set the tapestry on the foot of his bed and pretend he would find it when he came home from his trip to the moon. She had started the tapestry on a whim but now she knew it was a gift of contrition, recompense for not seeing the emotions lying dormant inside him.

The attic stairs were covered in dust. She left smeared, indistinct footprints as she walked to the bedroom, her shoulder pressed against the wall to guide her in the watery darkness. A strip of moonlight seeped from beneath the door to the room, a silver fan feathering out across the stairwell. She nudged the door open with her shoulder. Put one bare foot on the cold floor and then another. The air in the bedroom was unmoving and warmer than the air in the rest of the house, though Cat still shivered beneath her thin jacket. The curtains on the window were pushed aside, and the moon was visible through the glass, huge and flat-looking, lighting the room. Dust floated everywhere. Cat sat down on the edge of the bed. The room looked abandoned even with the few touches that had marked it as Finn's: the electric fan Cat had carried up the stairs behind her mother the day Finn came to stay. The unused sheets stretched across the bed in the corner. The computer was missing from the desk. Cat set the folded-up tapestry in its place. Her body burned.

She stepped away from the desk and opened the door to the closet, where she found his clothes lined up neatly on their hangers, all the plain T-shirts and jeans. A pair of black boots. That scarf she'd made hanging from a hook on the door. She took it off and wound it around her neck. Then she walked back to the desk and sat down. She rested one hand on top of the tapestry, let her fingers sink into the fabric. *I know it's not enough,* she thought. *But I hope you like it.* She squinted through the window at the moon. She saw the man and she saw the rabbit and she wished she could see the lunar station. Even though she'd seen pictures of it on the Internet, she still imagined it to look like an old power plant, a web of amber lights, white steam belching into space. But of course you couldn't see the lunar station on the surface of the moon from a room in a house here on Earth.

Cat pulled open the top drawer of Finn's desk. A nest of wires, a black external hard drive the size of her thumb. She opened the next one down. Empty. The next one. She stopped.

That third drawer, that last drawer, contained a stack of paper Cat recognized as the sort she used to sketch on, back before she started high school. She pulled it out and laid the first paper down on the desk. A drawing, charcoal, not one she had done. It was a drawing of her, probably from when she was in college: she stood beside the citrus tree in the garden, pulling a lemon off one of the branches. It was technically proficient, but it took Cat's breath away because she knew Finn had drawn it. She turned to the next sheet of paper. Cat asleep, her hair tousled over one shoulder. The next one. The bathtub in her old apartment, her legs and her arm draped over the side, her eyes peering over the tub's edge.

Cat blinked and tears welled up in the corners of her eyes. She gathered up the papers and placed them back in the drawer. Her heart beat painfully in her chest. Her body ached from thinking about the pain she had caused him. *Pain.* How could she be so stupid, so self-involved, to not see that she had caused him pain during all those years they were together and not-together? He never said anything, but that was no excuse. She should have known better than anyone else on this Earth.

She took off her jacket and crawled underneath the blankets of his bed. She buried her face in the pillow but it didn't smell like him. It didn't smell like anything.

The baby moved. She dropped her hand down and lay still and felt that tiny motion shimmer back and forth. She turned her head toward the window so she could see the moon, so she could see where he was.

"Hello, baby," she whispered. "This used to be your daddy's room."

* * * *

A month went by. The baby grew, and so did Cat. One day she looked in the mirror as she stepped out of the bathtub and she didn't recognize herself or the curve of her stomach. She had been going to the Lamaze classes at the sun-filled studio in town, learning the breathing exercises, visiting the doctor, buying tiny cotton onesies and packages of disposable diapers off the Internet, running through lists of names. But the fact that she would give birth was unreal to her until that moment when she saw herself, and she thought, *I am going to be a mother.*

The idea that she would be responsible for another life left her unsettled. Her own life remained unsorted. Her divorce with Richard had not yet gone through—he was delaying things, tying up the lawyers. She still could not escape the guilt that seemed to hang over her as she worked on her commission with the accounting company and planned her trip to the Midwest, reading advice for how to travel safely through the desert, looking into hotels and flight times even though she couldn't book anything yet. She checked her visa status every day.

She also began teaching herself to read Finn's schematics. It wasn't the same as learning about him as a person, but it was the closest she could come.

She downloaded engineering and robotics manuals to her reading slate and studied them in the evenings, winter curling its dry hands around the loose, rattling windows. She brought up the schematics files on her personal computer and attempted to decipher those diagrams stretching like the lines of yarn across a loom. She started at the tips of his fingers, with the intention of working her way up the corded circuits to the epicenter of his existence. His brain. His heart.

One night, when her father was working late in the laboratory and the icy wind seeped through the cracks in the house, she carried her computer and reading slate up to Finn's room. It was the warmest place in the house. She sat at the desk and worked through the schematics of his touch. She had moved on from his fingers to his palm, to the point where everything connected, twining together into his arm. It was here that the code became complicated. She thought of her father's word—*baroque*. She worked for a long time, night wrapping around the house like a blanket. She tapped in notes to herself on her reading slate, but she still didn't understand. Each finger, individually—that she could picture in her mind. But she didn't understand how his hand became whole.

It grew late. Even the lamp seemed exhausted. Cat pushed her computer away, knocking it against the window that looked out over the night-drenched yard. She had been reading these manuals for nearly two weeks, but nothing clicked into place for her. She didn't understand. She couldn't understand.

Cat stumbled away from the desk and curled up on Finn's bed. For the last few hours she'd been reading about him as a machine, because it was the only way she had to be close to him, but now she thought about him not as a system of circuits and code, but as a person. She spun through her memories. She passed over the obvious ones, the ones where she used him—the ones where he touched her, the ones where he kissed her—and then she was thinking of a time in high school, several months after the fight with Erik, long before the night Oscar gave her a poisoned kiss. It was summer, the Fourth of July. They had driven to the parking lot of the old Walmart, one of the last to close down in that time before Cat was born. The sign was still plastered against the side of the building. Nothing had ever moved in to take its place, and the parking lot was a huge scar of black cement, marked with faded gray lines, glittering with broken glass. The rows of darkened streetlamps looked like palm trees. They drove out there, just her and Finn, to watch the fireworks. She must not have told her parents; she vaguely recalled the weight of that omission hanging between the two of them. Even though Finn didn't approve, he would have done it anyway.

They lay on the car's hood as the fireworks exploded overhead. The noise always bothered her, that crackling thud like weapons in war movies. She and Finn didn't touch; they weren't at the point of touching yet. The air smelled of gunpowder. The night sky filled with smoke and reflected the light of the fireworks and their colorful, fiery rain. The smell had lingered in her hair even after they came home. A drunk astronomy student had once told her that the surface of the moon smelled of cordite. That the dust that looked matte gray in photographs, like the earth's soil in black-and-white movies, glittered silver. How could he know that? Cat wondered at the time, but now she thought of Finn drifting unencumbered across the moon's surface, barefaced, his hair and his clothes unmoving. She wondered if he smelled cordite and remembered the fireworks bursting overhead. She wondered if the silver moon dust reminded him of broken glass in the parking lot of a chain gone bankrupt.

She wondered if he thought of her, ever, at all. Not because of the complicated design of his machinery, but because she'd hurt him. Because he couldn't bear to think of her.

Cat began to cry. She pulled the blanket under her chin. The fabric was old, too thin and worn to keep her warm, but she liked the weight of it against her clothes, her sweater and jeans. She cried until her eyes ached. She cried because it was her fault he didn't think of her. She cried because she'd finally begun to understand that for all the times she spent with him, stretched out naked across the cheap mattress of the bed in her old apartment, she didn't understand him in the slightest. She hadn't allowed herself to, because understanding him would mean giving up the convenient lie that he didn't care.

All of Cat's tears ran out. She stared at the computer on the desk, at the reading slate lying useless beside it. She didn't want to read about his schematics anymore. She wished she could read about *him*.

But it was impossible.

She signed idly in to her e-mail account, looking for a distraction. She expected it to be empty.

Instead, there was a single e-mail: *Congratulations*, it said.

You have been approved for travel to the Midwestern Desert.

SIXTEEN

The airplane was small and, Cat suspected, old. It rattled and creaked as they puttered through the cloudless sky. She picked at a long thread unraveling out of the seam of her seat and wound it around her finger. Her belly stuck out enough that it rested across the tops of her thighs. The woman sitting beside her glanced over and smiled.

"How far along?" she asked.

Cat jerked up her head. "A little over six months."

"I have two of my own," the woman said. "Are you excited?"

Cat nodded, but at this particular moment she was more nervous than anything else. A curl of dread rested constantly at the bottom of her stomach—dread and anticipation. She still couldn't believe she was on this plane, flying to the stretch of desert that had once been Kansas.

"In fact," said the woman, "I'm going to visit my oldest. Sarah. She's in college now. Agricultural engineering. Working an internship this semester." She turned to the window and the sunlight fell across her face, and her expression softened, became wistful and undefined. "They'll make you so proud of them."

Cat smiled politely and looped her headphones back on. The

woman glanced at her and then looked back out the window. Cat leaned against the seat's headrest. The plane vibrated and dipped down, jerked back up. So few people flew to the Midwest that the airlines chartered tiny private planes rather than send the sleek, modern jets that flew so high up in the atmosphere they were almost spaceships. Cat listened to the steady thumping of her music and wondered if she would find anything out there. What if Judith Condon still lived in her house? Cat wondered what she would say to her if that was the case: The truth, that Cat was in love with Finn? Most likely she would go the easy route and claim she was some interested researcher.

The e-mail, creased and soft with constant handling, was tucked away in the bottom of her purse, although she'd entered the address into her comm slate as well. She'd made arrangements to rent a car to drive from the airport into the middle of the desert. She had not told her father what she was doing—just, *A vacation. I'm going on a vacation before the baby's born.* But she also didn't cover her tracks.

The airplane finally landed, dropping down in jerks until it touched the tarmac. Cat looked past the woman with the daughter named Sarah, out at the flat, brown landscape. This close to the ground the sky was yellow from the dirt. The woman unbuckled her seat belt and stood up. She looked down at Cat.

"Congratulations," she said. "And good luck."

Cat dragged her suitcase down the plane's narrow aisle—the bedraggled attendant said good-bye to Cat's stomach—and then out into the tiny, nearly empty airport. Country music played over the loudspeakers, and Cat bought a bottle of water from a faceless robot at the coffee shop next to the bathrooms. She followed the signs directing her to the car rental kiosk. Her footsteps echoed in time with the steady revolutions of her suitcase's plastic wheels. Every now and then she passed another human being.

At the kiosk, Cat punched in her rental number and fed her ID card and driver's license to the attendant bot. The computer beeped and whirred, informed her the receipt had been e-mailed to her, and spat out a slim plastic key. It told her the make and model in its pleasant mechanical voice, then informed her that she could find the map to the car's current parking spot in her e-mail.

"Thank you," said Cat, out of habit.

The rental cars were housed in a dim, cavernous parking garage where giant metal fans circulated the thick, dusty air. Cat hadn't stepped outside once since her arrival but the dust was already coating her skin and clothes, matting her hair. When she found her car, the headlights flashing helpfully, she noticed that it was the color of champagne, and her fingers came away from the door handle dirty.

"Baby," Cat said. "Here goes nothing."

*   *   *   *

Cat checked into a motel situated on the edge of Halcyon, the last town before the land became unlivable. The Windswept Motel. Halcyon was little more than a sprawling power plant, built for the rows and rows of wind turbines out in the desert, and Cat spent the rest of the afternoon halfheartedly reading the baby books she'd downloaded onto her slate, the heating unit beneath the window rattling and whining. Cat left the hotel to find dinner after the sun set, and in the darkness the town had transformed completely from its tangle of dirty white buildings to a net of twinkling amber lights. Like a city of ghosts and fireflies. Cat ate some bad Mexican food at a cantina in the town's windy downtown. She watched hockey on the monitors hanging above the bar. She wished she could order a shot of tequila; she wished she could sit outside in the cold dust and smoke a cigarette. Instead, she drove back to the hotel and ran a bath that turned to mud the minute she slid into the water. So she turned on the shower and rinsed herself off and then she sat dripping on the side of the tub and watched the dirt swirl down the drain.

Afterward, she crawled into the king-size bed, which felt empty and cold in the buzzing silence of the motel. To warm herself up she thought about Finn, and slipped her hand between her legs, and cried out as though he were there.

She woke up early the next morning to the insistent chiming of the hotel alarm. Weak wintry sunlight filtered through the orange curtains. She didn't get up, just lay in the bed, her hand resting at the apex of her belly. The baby kicked his tiny feet against her womb as though he were sending her a message in Morse code. *Long. Long. Short.* She fluttered her fingers against her belly in response. *I'm here, Baby.* She hadn't decided on a name. None of the ones her father or Maybelle suggested felt right. The last time she spoke to Miguel, he said, "As long as you don't name it Richard I'm totally cool with anything you decide."

Eventually, Cat pulled herself out of bed. She dressed in black maternity tights and a black skirt and a dark blue cashmere sweater that still fit. She regretted bringing it, considering the dirt, but she wanted to look nice in case she met Judith Condon. She buttoned her coat to her throat, pulled her hair back in a ponytail, and brought up the map to the laboratory on her comm slate. It was a four-hour drive. She checked the list of dust storm warnings but conditions were calm, so she climbed into her car and left. The landscape outside of the town was unchanging.

For the first hour she plugged her music into the car's stereo until she couldn't stand the sound of it any longer. She switched to the radio. The car didn't have digital, and so she listened to a Pentecostal preacher ranting about the sins of technology, the sorrows of the modern world. His voice shimmered with static until it faded out completely and there was only the rushing sound of wind.

Eventually she arrived at the wind farms, turbines spinning like pinwheels in tandem. Cat pulled the car onto the side of the road and stepped out. Immediately dust flew into her eyes. She ran around to the passenger side of the car so she wouldn't be standing so close to the road—not that she'd seen very many cars out here, only a few filthy trucks from the power plant—and wiped at her face. The wind calmed. She squinted up at the turbines. They were bigger than she would have guessed from the pictures she'd seen—like lazy-armed colossi—and spread more widely across the landscape. Swirls of dirt lit up in the sun, flowing around the turbine's slow machinations. The baby kicked. Cat crawled back into her car and drove on.

She drove and drove. She tried not to fall asleep. The wind farms disappeared; the flat, brown landscape returned. She stopped again, her comm slate telling her she was forty-five miles from the laboratory, to squat clandestinely beside her car to pee.

She drove.

And then she saw an imperfection on the smooth, flat line of the horizon. A dot of color against the choleric sky. She pressed her foot down on the gas and drove faster, following the arrowshot of the road. The land here was so flat she knew the dot was twenty miles away, but she also knew this was the house where he was born. As she approached, she saw the color came not from the house but from a garden. The green was so vivid she nearly lost her breath. There was an orchid tree and a line of hibiscus bushes and many more plants and flowers she didn't recognize. The house flashed from behind the vegetation: a tawny brown, nearly the same color as the landscape. She pulled her car off the main road and drove over the loose soil, stirring up clouds of sediment too thick to see through. When she activated the window cleaner, it only smeared the dirt across the glass. She parked the car a few meters from the edge of the garden and stepped outside. She knew if she dwelled on what she was doing, she would turn around and drive away.

In the open, the air smelled of dirt and metal.

Cat bent her head low as she walked through the gate into the garden. The plants blocked most of the loose dust as they shook in the wind. She heard a noise that reminded her of wind chimes, a kind of metallic twinkling, but she couldn't place it. There were no wind chimes in the garden.

She walked up the narrow stone path and rang the doorbell. She waited. No one answered.

Cat cursed beneath her breath. The house didn't look abandoned, not with so vibrant a garden blossoming around it—

No, thought Cat. *It's winter.* But the garden was in bloom. A pomegranate tree drooped with the weight of its brilliant red flowers. Wisteria curled around the gate. Daffodils swayed in the biting wind. Cat stepped off the tiny concrete porch and followed the path through the lush, twinkling garden. Sunflowers taller than her stretched toward the sky. The orchid tree she had seen from the road rippled and shimmered, its delicate, insectlike flowers hanging low and heavy on the branches. All that excessive growth only reminded Cat of how cold the air was.

"Who the hell are you?"

Cat jumped and, turning, tried to find the source of the voice. It was an old woman's voice, scratchy, deep throated.

"My name is Caterina—Caterina Feversham." It was the first name she could think of that wasn't her own. "I'm a postdoc in . . . electrical engineering." Was that even the right subject? She didn't care. A shadow moved past the trunk of the orchid tree. Cat took a few steps forward. "I'm looking for Judith Condon."

A woman stepped onto the path. She'd let her hair go gray and the lines in her face ran deep, but she stood up straight and haughty, and her forearms, poking out of the pushed-up sleeve of her sweater, were wiry and strong.

"What do you want?" she said. "And, perhaps the more interesting question, how'd you find me?"

Cat considered her options. "I worked with Dr. John Ramirez—"

"Bullshit. You're too young."

Cat fumbled over her words, trying to work out what to say. The woman—Dr. Condon—stomped her boots on the path, knocking off clumps of sticky earth.

"I met him through Dr. Novak," she said. "Daniel Novak?"

"And how did you meet Daniel?" Dr. Condon crossed her arms over her chest and peered at Cat. Her gaze was unflinching. "Save you some trouble: if you say 'university,' I'll know you're lying."

Cat tried to remember those meaningless acronyms from years-old dinner conversations. "NDIL," she said, hoping she had the letters in the right order.

"Mmhmm," said Dr. Condon. "I don't think I believe you."

Cat sighed. The wind picked up, rustling the plants' leaves. The sky had turned a darker shade of yellow, like burnished gold. Dr. Condon glanced up and frowned.

"I'll give you one more chance to tell the truth," she said. "Else I'm chasing you off with a shotgun." She pointed at the sky. "And there's a dust storm coming. You won't want to get trapped in that."

Cat didn't doubt her. Dr. Condon seemed like the sort of woman who owned a shotgun. A strange charge crackled in the air, heavier than the thunderstorms Cat was used to, and more foreboding. Cat took a deep breath. She rested her hand on top of her stomach. She couldn't feel the baby moving inside her but she knew he was there.

"I'm Dr. Novak's daughter," she said.

Dr. Condon raised an eyebrow and rested her weight against the trunk of the orchid tree and said nothing.

"When I was five years old he brought a robot—an android—named Finn to our house." Cat watched Dr. Condon's face. It remained completely expressionless. "I grew up with him. He was my tutor for while, and then later . . . we were friends. We were . . . quite close."

Dr. Condon pushed a strand of hair out of her eyes. Her hand shook. "Finn." She laughed. "That wasn't Finn. That robot your father brought home? Not Finn at all."

Cat didn't say anything. Dust coated her skin, and she could smell it on the inside of her nostrils. She didn't want to get run off and stranded in a storm.

"I don't like to talk about it," said Dr. Condon. "I'm warning you now. I'll let you stay till the storm blows over, but I don't much like discussing my failures." She jerked her head toward the house. "Shall we? Before it gets too thick to breathe?" She breezed past Cat, toward the front door, and Cat had no choice but to follow.

Inside, the house was dim and warm and smelled faintly of cinnamon. Dr. Condon tapped against a control panel set into the wall. The lights flickered and turned a peculiar golden color; Cat heard the guttural sound of a generator kicking on somewhere in the back of the house, heard the *snick* of guards sliding over the windows.

"You can sit down if you want," said Dr. Condon. "No sense standing when there's a perfectly good couch." She strolled away from the console and settled herself into an old easy chair, pulled off her muddy boots. "How's Daniel doing? He know you're out here?"

Cat shook her head.

"Didn't think so. You have the look of subterfuge about you."

Cat didn't know what to say to that. She took off her coat and sat down on the edge of the couch. "Daddy's doing fine," she said.

"Still doing all that contract work?"

"I believe so, yes." Cat shrugged. "I never really kept up with it, to be honest. He was doing stuff for the lunar station—"

"The lunar station, huh? Yes, I think I heard something about that." Over the sound of the generator was the sound of the wind, howling and shrieking. Cat had waited out plenty of storms in her life but never had she heard wind that sounded like that, like a woman screaming. Goose bumps prickled up the sides of her arms, and she rubbed at them through the fabric of her sweater.

The two of them sat in silence. Cat wanted to broach the subject of Finn but Dr. Condon looked so harsh and unyielding in the weird sallow light. Dr. Condon rocked back and forth in her chair, and then, just when Cat didn't think she could stand the sound of the wind anymore, Dr. Condon stood up, and announced she was going into the kitchen for a drink.

"You want anything?" she asked, as though she had only a vague memory of how to treat a houseguest.

"Water would be fine."

Dr. Condon disappeared through a doorway into the back of the house. Cat looked around the living room. All the furniture and decorations were old-fashioned, out of style. Dusty. The pictures sitting on the mantel weren't even digital. The only thing that looked like it had been produced in the last twenty years was the console in the wall.

Cat stood up and stretched her legs. She was tired of sitting. She walked over to the photographs. One was of Dr. Condon at about Cat's age, her hair thick and black, her cheekbones sharp. She was laughing, sunlight radiating out behind her head. Beside it was a photograph of a little boy with serious green eyes. He looked familiar. Cat leaned in close, squinting. The picture was old, taken long before she was born, and yet—

It hit Cat like a punch in the chest. *It's Finn.* But of course it wasn't Finn. Finn was never a little boy. But she saw the resemblance nonetheless: the pearly skin, the dark hair already falling across his forehead. In the picture, the boy who was not Finn cradled a white kitten to his chest. He looked straight at the camera. The room spun.

"Oh, so you're snooping now?"

Dr. Condon appeared at Cat's side holding a bottle of beer and a glass of water. Cat took the water and drank. It tasted of dirt. She felt Dr. Condon watching her. When she finished, she looked over at her. "Who's that little boy? He looks exactly like—"

Dr. Condon's face darkened. "He was my son."

"Was?" said Cat weakly.

"Yes. He died."

Cat felt her own son spinning inside her. She put her hand on her stomach. "Finn," she said. "My Finn . . . He was a . . . he was a . . ."

"It was a copy. I told you I won't talk about this."

"Please," said Cat. "I'm in love with him."

All the air went out of the room. The wind screeched and hollered outside. Cat drew herself up, held her back straight and tall. Dr. Condon sipped from her beer and looked Cat up and down.

"Oh, really?" She tilted her beer at the curve of Cat's stomach. "It knock you up, too?"

"I mean it," Cat said. "I love him." She had never said it aloud before. She closed her eyes. She imagined him standing in the room with her. "I love him."

But when she opened her eyes it was just Dr. Condon. "You do mean it." The beer bottle tipped up, obscured her face. "Fuck me."

Cat stumbled over to the couch and sat down. Sweat prickled up all over her body. Dr. Condon sat down beside her. "Why'd you come here?" she said. "You know I didn't want it. It would have told you that, I imagine. It or your father."

"Daddy told me." Cat rubbed her forehead. "Finn's gone. I'm not . . . I'm not sure why, but he auctioned himself off. Like a piece of property. And now he belongs to STL—the lunar station—and I haven't spoken to him in months. I just want to know more about him, you know? I just wanted to see where he came from."

"Jesus, honey, don't start crying." Dr. Condon set her beer on the floor and patted Cat's shoulder unenthusiastically. She grimaced in a way Cat suspected was meant to be a smile. "I'm not sure I can help you," Dr. Condon said.

"How did you make him?"

Dr. Condon sighed. She looked at the ceiling. "You don't want to know that," she said. "It's impossible to love something you know's made out of wire and metal." She dropped her head down. Turned to Cat. "You ever see inside him?"

Cat thought about the schematics she had studied so diligently in the drafty rooms of her house. "I've seen him switched off."

"Not the same." Dr. Condon stood up. Her eyes glinted in the loamy house lights. "I think you should know what you're getting yourself into."

"I already know what I'm getting myself into."

"No, you don't."

Dr. Condon walked toward the back of the house and this time Cat followed, listening to the low mechanical whine of the generator. The hallway was so dark she could barely see in front of herself. Dr. Condon stopped, and Cat ran up against her. She heard the chime of a card key unlocking a door. Light flooded the hallway.

"My lab," said Dr. Condon.

Cat stepped inside. The lab looked like the inside of a greenhouse: ropes of honeysuckle and wisteria, green, leafy stems scattered across the counter. Cat ran her fingers across the vines curling next to the door, not quite understanding.

"Ah yes, the big secret of my garden." Dr. Condon grabbed a handful of honeysuckle and pulled. It didn't snap off in her hand. The green peeled away and a bouquet of copper wires spilled out from between her fingers.

"The whole thing's like that?"

"What, you thought I actually got something to grow out here?" Dr. Condon laughed. "No, it's just . . . this is all I know how to do. And plants can't . . . plants can't disappoint you." She dropped her hand and the vivisected honeysuckle twisted back and forth, its exposed wires catching the light.

Dr. Condon strode across the room. Cat stayed standing next to the honeysuckle. She touched her fingers to one of the yellow blossoms. Now that she knew it was a machine, the texture felt unusual—slicker, slightly rubbery. Something chimed. Across the room, Dr. Condon pushed a metal door across the wall, its edge scraping against the cement floor. She looked over her shoulder.

"Well, get over here," she said. "You wanted to know about my work."

It was a hidden bookshelf, set into the wall. But there were no books, only a tangle of electrical engineering junk—wires, circuit boards, soldering irons. Dr. Condon pulled out a black, old-fashioned laptop. "Hope this still works," she muttered, setting it down on the table in the center of the room. The computer beeped and rang off a series of electronic notes. Cat walked around the table and stood next to Dr. Condon as the computer booted up. "These are the plans," Dr. Condon said. "I stored everything on here. The circuit maps. All the programming. The shell designs. Everything."

"You talk about him like he's a computer." Cat thought of snow dusting across the top of her head. *Why?*

"He is a computer," said Dr. Condon. "That's what I'm trying to tell you."

Cat frowned. "I've seen his schematics already," she said. "The code and stuff. I don't think of him as a computer."

Dr. Condon ignored her.

The laptop was old enough that it still had a built-in keyboard and a mouse track pad, and Cat listened to the click of the keys as Dr. Condon typed in a series of passwords and then a series of commands. "Here," she said, swiveling the screen around so Cat could see. "Your *lover*." It was a circuit diagram, much more complicated than the schematics she'd already examined. It was so complicated it looked like a work of art. Like an Oriental rug, a postmodern painting. Cat squinted against the screen's backlighting, trying to sort out what she was looking at. It was unfathomable to her, as unfathomable as the models of the human circulatory system she had once seen in a science museum.

"This is him?" she said. "What part of him? I don't recognize it."

"It's just a circuit," said Dr. Condon. "For the brain." Her fingers flew across the keyboard. "Here, look at this." The diagram was replaced by a photograph. *Click, click.* The photograph filled up the screen. Cat gasped in spite of her best intentions to stay calm.

It was Finn, it had to be Finn, but the figure in the picture had no head. The torso was split open. Below that, the narrow hips, the top of the pubis—it was familiar. Dr. Condon watched Cat and smirked, and Cat forced herself to keep her eyes on the picture. She looked at the open torso. The inside of him didn't look the way she expected. It didn't look like the inside of a computer or a lightbulb or a car. The wires were transparent, silvery, and seemed lit from within.

"It's not so terrible," said Cat.

"Liar," Dr. Condon said. "Let me show you something else." She walked back to the row of shelves, pushed aside a stack of cardboard boxes. The muscles in her back rippled through her shirt. "I built some test parts," she said. "They don't work, but . . ." She turned around, cradling a hand. The skin tone was pinkish and fake-looking. She set the hand on the table next to the computer. Cat remembered the schematics she'd been able to decipher. This looked more like Finn's hand than they did. Cat put her own hand on top of it and compared its stillness to her trembling.

The hand didn't feel like Finn's hand at all. It felt like plastic.

"The skin's wrong," she said.

"Yes," said Dr. Condon. "I hadn't brought in my prosthetics guy yet. I was more interested in getting the fingers to work properly." She flipped the hand over, palm-side down, and tugged at the skin. "Every time you let it touch you," she said. "Every time it pushed that perfect hair of yours out of your face, that was my work."

"And were you the reason he knew to do all those things in the first place?" Cat snapped.

Dr. Condon didn't answer. She peeled the skin away from the hand to reveal the rows of transparent wires, as thin as threads. They were dimmed and dull, reflecting the tawny color of the underside of the skin, but there were thousands of them, twisting around one another on their way to the fingers. Cat was entranced. She imagined the way they would look inside of him as he ran his hand down the side of her body in the dark: Illuminated. Luminous. Beautiful.

"This is the reason you couldn't love him?" Cat could hardly believe it.

Dr. Condon slid the skin back into place. "It's not flesh and blood," she said. "It's not normal." She picked up the hand and threw it on the shelf. The sudden clatter of plastic against metal made Cat jump.

"Show me more." Cat's heart beat as fast as a hummingbird's. "Show me everything."

"Everything?"

"I want to know everything about him."

"How selfish. Knowing everything about one's lover never works out in the long run."

Cat scowled. "I want to know how he works," she said. "Not how he thinks. Not how he feels—"

"It can't." Dr. Condon's voice was dark. "That was the whole problem. I couldn't get it to feel. Not if I wanted it to be a son, a perfect son."

"I thought the problem was the wires and the circuit boards."

"It was both." Dr. Condon pushed the computer over to Cat. "You want to know how it works? You know AktOS?" She leaned back against the wall, her arms folded over her chest. Cat pushed the screen around so she could look at it while she typed. The high school had had AktOS installed on some of the computers in the lab, but she hadn't used a manual keyboard in so long. She sifted through the files clumsily, trying to determine what she was looking for. *Anything, anything at all.* She found more elaborate schematics: the inside of his forearm, the length of his conductive spine.

"There," she said. "What's that?"

It was another new schematic, one not as complicated as the others. Cat whispered the commands under her breath, trying to picture what it was describing. Some kind of reaction. It seemed familiar.

She looked at Dr. Condon. "Is this another way to . . . to switch him off?"

Dr. Condon raised an eyebrow. "Of all the things," she said. "Of all the things you'd pick up on." She slid forward, took the computer out of Cat's hands, hit a couple keys. "Here's the second part of it." She shoved the computer over the table. On the screen was a list of body parts: *left neck, sternum, forehead, right cheekbone, left shoulder*. Then, at the end: *deactivation*.

"I don't understand."

"It was a joke," Dr. Condon said. "I brought in a couple of grad students to help me. They wrote it in, hid it. I didn't find out about it until later. You touch him in a certain way and then press the deactivation switch and he . . ." She did not look at Cat. "One of them fancied himself a poet. He called it the second little death. The first little death being normal deactivation, I suppose."

The little death. "Orgasm," said Cat. The word was sharp and clinical and didn't sound at all like what it was. *Desire. Ecstasy.* "He can—"

"Mmm." Dr. Condon closed the laptop and pushed her hair away from her eyes. Fidgeted.

"He told me it was impossible."

"In the biological sense, it is."

"But—" Cat stopped. "Does he not know? Does he not know he has that . . . capacity?"

Dr. Condon shrugged. "The storm's almost passed over." She shoved the laptop back on the shelf, dragged the metal doors shut. "You'll have to ask it yourself."

"Stop calling him it!" Cat shrieked, heat inching up her face. Dr. Condon pressed one hand against the metal door that hid the beginnings of Finn.

"I'll call it whatever I want," she said. "I made it." She looked over her shoulder and her gray hair fell in her eyes and for a moment it could have been Finn looking over at Cat so reproachfully. "Don't think because you let it feel you up in the back of your daddy's car you know anything about why it exists. It shouldn't exist."

"Please don't say that," Cat whispered.

"My son," said Dr. Condon. "I just wanted my son to grow up." She slammed her hand against the door, and the metal rang out. The dangling electronic vines shook. Cat jumped. She took a few hesitant steps toward the door. Dr. Condon had turned away from her but Cat could see her distorted reflection in the metal door: hair wild, eyes dark smudges against her pale skin. Her shoulders shook almost imperceptibly.

"Thank you," Cat said. "Thank you for letting—"

"Please leave." Dr. Condon didn't turn around, didn't look up.

Cat walked backward out of the laboratory and into the silent house. She hadn't noticed earlier that the winds had stopped shrieking and pounding against the walls but now the lack filled the rooms with an unbearable emptiness. The computer console in the wall blinked bright green. Cat walked over to it. *Release storm guards?* A yes or a no. Cat tapped the yes and listened to the clank and whine of the house unfolding. Grainy sunlight filtered in through the windows. Cat turned the knob on the door, pushed it open slowly. Dust spilled out across her feet. It got into her lungs and she coughed and sputtered but there was still no sign of Dr. Condon. Cat thought of her weeping silently against the metal door. She thought about the serious little boy in the picture on the mantel. She thought of Finn, her Finn. He had told her he was a machine but she thought of him as a man, she had always thought of him as a man.

She had even used him like a man.

Outside, everything was still. The vivid colors of the garden were muted by a layer of brown grime. When Cat walked down the path her steps stirred up little typhoons of dust that clung to her tights. The taste of dirt filled up her mouth. It was inescapable.

At the gate, Cat stopped and ran her hand across the climbing roses that twisted around the fence. Dust fell away; a few slivers of green appeared. She wrapped her hand around the branch, ignoring the quick stab of pain from the thorns, and bent her wrist sharply. The branch snapped but didn't break: beneath the woody exterior was a rope of wires. Cat wondered what would happen when the dirt got inside those tiny machines. Would they wither up and die? Had Dr. Condon made them that realistically?

Had she made Finn that realistically?

Cat's car bled into the landscape. She wiped away the dust from the windows with her jacket, then wiped off the handle and unlocked the car and climbed in. When she slammed the door, dust billowed up across the front seat. She threw the filthy, probably ruined jacket into the back. She sat for a moment, looking at that tiny house in the middle of the desert.

There it is. The house where you were born.

Cat turned on the car. The engine sputtered to life. She plugged her music player into the stereo and flipped through the songs until she found one that always reminded her of Finn.

And then she drove in the direction of home.

SEVENTEEN

After coming home from her trip to the desert, Cat went outside at night more and more, particularly on nights when the moon was heavy and bright in the sky. One night Cat cut across the backyard into the woods, an electric flashlight bouncing unused against her hip; the moonlight was enough to see by, even through the new growth of the trees. She could feel that moonlight like a glass of ice water pressed against hot skin.

Cat walked all the way down to the river. It trickled thinly over the rocks, gray in the moonlight. It hadn't rained much this spring. The drought had lasted since last summer. Cat heaved herself down the side of the bank, her knees knocking up against her stomach. The baby kicked, protesting maybe, or excited at this sudden burst of movement. She still hadn't thought of a name for him. When she came to the scatter of smooth white stones at the shore, she sat down with a sigh, legs stretched out in front of her, ugly pink maternity dress hiked up around her thighs. She leaned back and looked up at the veins of stars. The moon. She ran her hands over her stomach. "Baby," she said. "What do you think your daddy is doing right now?"

The river whispered an unintelligible reply. "I think he's taking soil samples," she said. The baby fluttered and rippled. "He can go out on the surface without any protection." She closed her eyes. "He can breathe the useless air. You won't be able to do that, of course, but neither can I. No shame in it."

She paused, listening to the river and the creak of the woods. The humidity made the air as gauzy as a butterfly net. Her eyes slid open. She looked at the man laughing in the surface of the moon. There were still those times when she wanted nothing more than to pull out her comm slate and type the string of numbers and letters that once tethered her to Finn. She wanted to talk to him, to apologize to him, to see his words to her appear on the screen. But that code tied her only to the house now.

More and more, though, she found that the urge to call him had faded, that it was enough to go outside with her baby and look up at the sky.

"Some nights," Cat said, and she thought of her son, a translucent pink curl spinning inside of her. "Some nights your daddy goes out on the surface where it smells like the Fourth of July and he looks at Earth. At us. When you're born I can show you pictures of what he sees. But really he's looking at the two of us, here on Earth, waiting for him to come home."

The moonlight reflected off her damp eyelashes. "Some nights," she said, "he's even forgiven me."

She knew they were all lies, but when she spoke she spoke the truth.

* * * *

Cat was pulling weeds in the garden when she heard the gate scraping open across the loose, dry soil. She leaned back on her heels and rested one hand on her stomach and brought the other hand up to shield her eyes from the sun. It was her father. "The garden," he said. "My God. It's just like when your mother was alive."

"Thanks." Cat smiled at him. "What's up?"

Her father shuffled forward across the narrow stone path, over to the black metal chair Cat had bought at one of the antiques stores in town and then set up next to the gush of wisteria. He sat down, his body hinging at the waist. Cat turned to face him. For a moment he just sat, his arm crossed over his knees, his eyes squinting at some point in the distance. Then he spoke.

"You visited Dr. Condon."

Cat didn't move. The grass prickled the backs of her legs. The sun warmed her skin. Distractedly, she laid her arms across her stomach.

"How did you know?"

"I called her." Her father shifted in the chair. "I saw you'd bought a charter plane ticket to Kansas. Thought I'd investigate." He paused. "I'm not angry."

Cat listened to the blood pounding in her ears.

"Granted," he said, "if you had asked me point-blank about it, about going up to visit her, I'd have . . . discouraged you. But to protect you more than anything else." He shrugged, looked over his shoulder. "I can't help but want to protect you. And that must have been . . . so painful."

"I'm an adult." *Even though I don't feel like it sometimes.*

"Oh, I know." Her father laughed a little to himself, then let his grin fade away into a frown. "I know."

"Daddy, I'm sorry I lied—"

"It's not that." He pushed his hands through his thinning white hair and looked at the sky. The plants in the garden rustled. "Cat, I'm sick."

For a long time, the only sound was the sound of the wind, rushing through the garden, rushing through the pine trees in the woods. Cat's first thought was that he had a cold. She would need to make him soup tonight. But as she looked at him—his gaunt face, the loose skin hanging off his arms—she began to understand.

"What?"

"I'm sick. I've been sick for a long time."

"What," she said. The heaviness of tears welled up behind her eyelids. She dug her hands into the soil. "What do you mean a long time?"

Her father bit his lower lip and looked away from her. "I mean," he said, "a long time."

"Why didn't you tell me?" *Why didn't I ask? Why didn't I notice?*

"I wanted to protect you. The first episode, Finn was able to help me, you know—"

"Finn!" Cat wanted to leap to her feet and pound her fists against the lemon tree but her pregnancy weighed her down like an anchor. "You knew since before Finn left! And you didn't tell me? Oh my God." She covered her face with her hands. Dirt streaked over her eyes, over her cheeks. It covered up her mouth.

"I'm sorry," he said. "You seemed so unhappy, I didn't want to burden you—"

"What is it?" She dropped her hands to the ground. "Tell me that at least. Is it . . . Are you dying?"

Her father sighed. He let his head drop. "We're all dying," he said softly. "We all die. But I have . . . a growth. In my brain. It was a little over two years ago when I found out. Maybe two and a half. Please . . ." He looked at her then, and already he looked like a ghost. "Please. I understand if you don't forgive me, but I ask—"

"Daddy," said Cat. She had begun to cry without realizing it. Tears streaked the dirt from her face and onto the top of her blouse. "How long do you have?"

"Years, probably," he said. "I don't know. They don't know. It's not . . . It was that one time, and I feel great most of the time. You know I'm still working. They gave me medication. I take it every day, I promise. Finn got me in the habit." His shoulders shook. "I'm fine," he said. "I'm fine."

Cat felt as though her entire body were disintegrating. The baby turned over inside of her. "Why didn't you tell me?" she asked.

"To protect you." He gave a short nod. "Yes, to protect you. You had so much sorrow in your life. I couldn't bear to add to it."

Cat took a deep breath. She wiped her muddy tears away. "I'm sorry," she said. "I'm sorry I didn't realize."

I'm selfish, she thought, and then she thought it over and over. *I'm selfish. I'm selfish.*

Her father stood up. Cat pulled herself to her feet, struggling the way she always did now. Her father clucked. "Don't apologize," he said. "I kept it a secret. I didn't want you to know."

"Why are you telling me now?" Cat walked across the garden so she was standing close enough to hug him. Her father laughed.

"You were brave enough to go see Dr. Condon," he said. "And she's insane. I figured you must be brave enough to deal with this." He spread his hands out in front of him. "I can't treat you like a child anymore," he said. "I'm sorry."

"Don't be." Cat leaned her head against his shoulder. "Don't be."

* * * *

For the next few weeks, Cat was on edge around her father. She expected him to collapse into her arms at any second. But he always stayed standing, and he didn't like when she reminded him to take his medication in the evenings. "You sound like Finn," he said. "Like a goddamn alarm clock." She had come down to the laboratory and stood in the doorway, leaning her weight against the frame. Her father waved an arm at her. "Don't you worry about me. Worry about that baby."

And eventually, as Cat realized her father was not about to die, as her belly grew heavier, she found herself almost reverting back to the way things had been before. A very faint miasma of dread hung over her actions, like the scent of expensive perfume. But it was so subtle and so slight that she was able to ignore it. Most of the time.

One day Cat was in the garden spraying the thick, fragrant jasmine with rationed water from the hose, watching as the droplets condensed in shimmering rainbows in the hot sunlight, when something wet and warm dripped down her leg. She dropped the hose and cried out and water sprayed across the front of her dress. She knew what she was supposed to do; she had gone over it at dinner with her father, whenever he changed the subject away from his illness. There had been a suitcase packed next to the front door for the last seven days. For an entire week, she kept missing items of clothing. Now it was time.

She stumbled into the house and shouted for her father. She found one of the intercom consoles and pressed the button. "Daddy," she said. "Daddy, it's time."

The house responded with its usual creaks and moans.

She pressed the intercom button again. "Daddy!"

"I'm here." His voice was just behind her and she turned, steadying herself against the wall. He wiped the back of his hand across his forehead. His chest heaved. "I ran up the stairs," he said. "Are you having contractions?"

"My water broke."

He nodded and took her by the hand. Cat barely had time to think. It didn't hurt yet. She touched her fingers to her belly button. *Baby, Baby*. She couldn't imagine the world with her baby anyplace but inside her.

They drove to the hospital two towns over. Fifteen minutes away something ripped Cat in half, a sharp burning pain that made her shriek and kick out her legs and bang her knees against the dashboard. Her father glanced at her. Sweat glistened on his brow.

"Hold on, Kitty-Cat," he said.

Cat leaned against the car seat. The pain dissipated, leaving behind an imprint, like a ghost. Sweat beaded up out of the pores on her back. Sunlight slanted through the car window, yellow and hot.

And then they were at the hospital, and Cat was flying down a corridor as bright as the inside of a fluorescent lightbulb. Another contraction and she arched her back against the wheelchair and screamed. Then she was in a room, in a bed, covered in papery sheets. The nurse-bot gave her one pill after another. Her father stood beside her in a gown the color of mint gum. When the contractions came she grabbed his hand and screamed. A robot arm whirred across the ceiling of the room, dropped down, slid something cool and metal into the base of her spine. After that the contractions didn't make her scream, though she could feel them still, she could feel her body stretching out numbly, her legs in two stirrups, the doctor's white hair bobbing up and down just in her line of vision. She felt the baby moving inside her. She forgot all the ways in which she was supposed to breathe. Even with her father standing beside her she forgot.

She was falling apart. She was the shell of a cicada. The baby was pushing its way out into the world and she was just its husk, the thing that carried it to life—

"I see the head," said the doctor, and Cat was overwhelmed with euphoria. *A head*. Like a real person, not a fetus but a person. She heard all the voices of the people in the room. She heard the robot whirring her pain away, its hand cradling the nerves of her spine.

"Almost there," said her father. "We're almost there, Kitty-Cat."

Cat tried to smile but her body was shaking and sweating and the muscles in her mouth refused to move. A starburst of intensity. She looked up at the bright ceiling.

Wailing. Wailing like the chime of bells. It sounded so far away.

"He's here," said someone female. One of the nurses. "Would you like to meet your son?"

Cat nodded because she was exhausted. For a moment she felt a rising sense of hysteria. They were bringing a wriggling bundle of blue cloth toward her. What if he looked like Richard? What if she looked into the face of her son and it was Richard's eyes that looked back at her, Richard's mouth twisted up in the anguish of being out in the world?

The nurse slid the baby into Cat's arms. He was heavier than she expected, and warmer. She wiped the red liquid away. His eyes were blue but they were dark, like river water rather than ice. His skin as pale as her own. A generic little baby nose, a generic little baby mouth. Cat wept. Her tears flowed over her cheeks and dropped down on his forehead. She wiped them away with the base of her thumb. The baby stopped crying and watched her.

Her father leaned over the side of the bed, his eyes bright and smiling above his paper mask.

Immediately, Cat knew the name she wanted. She looked down at her son, her beautiful son.

"Hello, Daniel," she said.

*　*　*　*

They brought Daniel home on a hot, sunny day, the first of many hot, sunny days to come. Her father drove. Cat sat in the backseat of the car, curled up next to the plastic baby seat, watching Daniel's tiny chest rise and fall. He had fallen asleep as soon as they got on the highway. She was overwhelmed by his smallness. She brushed the pale silk of his hair away from his forehead and he turned toward her, face scrunched up, his eyes a pair of wrinkles in the folds of his skin. Her father hummed tunelessly in the front seat.

Cat closed her eyes. She wanted to sleep.

*   *   *   *

It was difficult for her to get used to her new life with the baby. He woke up crying in the middle of the night and Cat had to trudge across the hallway to his nursery, formerly the room where Finn used to tutor her, to cradle him in her arms or change his diaper or feed him. She spent the next few months, which became quickly enough the next year, in a perpetual sleepless haze. Her mind never quite seemed to belong to her. Some days, during the brightest and hottest part of the afternoon, she felt as though she were dreaming even though she was still awake—voices seeped in and out of the white noise of the trees and plants and the house settling into its foundation. Sometimes she looked at Daniel and didn't recognize him. Those were the times she took him to her father's laboratory and left him lying in his inflatable playpen as her father worked on what he promised wasn't dangerous in the slightest, and she stumbled up to her bed (or sometimes Finn's bed) and slept.

But other times when she was with Daniel she was so overwhelmed with love that she would have to sit down to steady herself. Once she was bathing him in the kitchen sink, rubbing honey-colored soap into his fine hair—it had darkened since she brought him home, away from Richard's impossible blond and toward her own auburn—and the sunset spilling in through the window turned the kitchen a warm, luminous pink. Daniel laughed and splashed water across her face and then clapped his hands together. The room spun. Cat plucked him out of the water and held him close to her chest, laughing, feeling the warmth of his tiny fragile body. His fingers curled around the damp ends of her hair, and she understood in that moment why women choose to have children.

Time dripped by. Daniel grew into a toddler with huge, serious eyes. He liked to be outside. When Cat worked in the garden he explored the vast planes of their backyard, bringing her gifts of beetles and earthworms. Cat's father made him an army of little robotic toys in the shapes of insects and snakes, and Daniel would chase them through the dried-out grass, their motors grinding and squealing. When he caught one he lay on his back and held it over his head and squinted at it, turning it over in his hands. Cat watched him from the garden gate, one hand on her hip, sweat dripping down her spine. He held a metal centipede as long as his arm. Its little metal legs churned in the air. He flipped it over and let it crawl across his chest and laughed.

One day during the hot autumn, when Daniel was two years old, someone knocked on the front door. Cat was reading *The Wind in the Willows* aloud to Daniel on the couch. At the sound of the knock his head perked up, and he clambered over her lap and leaned across the couch to get a look at the door.

"Wait here," Cat told him. She stood up and walked into the foyer. Her heart thumped. They weren't expecting visitors.

When she opened the door, it was only the man who delivered packages, a slim white box tucked under his arm, nearly hidden by the drape of his sleeve. He scratched at the back of his calf with his foot.

"Caterina Novak? I have a package for you."

Cat nodded. She took the package from him and pressed her thumb against his computer tablet. He nodded and thanked her and walked back to the white and blue truck parked in the grass. The front door swung shut. The package was cool and slick against her palm. The return address was that of Richard's lawyers. She closed her eyes, sighed thankfully.

The papers. The final papers, the ones that would make her divorce official. Richard had stalled them for so long after that day he'd come out to the house that Cat had almost forgotten the divorce hadn't yet gone through. Months had gone by since she last thought of Richard in any concrete way, but for the first time in years she felt normal, the way she should feel. She ripped the package open, took out the narrow gray hard drive.

"Mama?" Daniel leaned over the side of the couch, staring at her with his big dark eyes. She smiled at him. He held out his arms for a hug, and she ran in and swooped him up and held him close to her. She kissed the top of his head.

"Come on, Daniel. Let's go into the kitchen." She set him on the floor, and he tottered off ahead of her. She pulled out a chair at the breakfast table and sat down and Daniel climbed up beside her, stood in his own chair and watched as she slid the hard drive into the kitchen computer. The papers flashed on-screen.

It was over. Richard was gone.

Cat glanced over at Daniel. He was looking at the screen along with her, as if he could read those rows of letters. He looked up at her and smiled and jumped off the chair. Cat scrolled down to the bottom of the document. She pressed her thumb against the screen, and then she went and dug through the junk drawer until she found a writing stylus. She signed the papers for her divorce in the kitchen of her childhood home, her son jumping from tile to tile behind her. The air conditioner rattled the walls of the house. The sun burned up the soil outside.

It took two seconds for her to sign her name. She thought, *Now I can start over*.

* * * *

That night, after Cat had slid the hard drive into a padded envelope and set up the shipping details on the computer, she lifted Daniel onto her shoulders and took him outside. The night air was cooler than she expected—the closest they ever came to a true autumn anymore, a faint chill in the night air like a vein of peppermint in a mug of hot chocolate. Daniel ran into the yard, and she wrapped a shawl around her shoulders and sat on the porch steps.

"Don't go so close to the woods," Cat said. The moon was out, sliced in half by the shadow of the Earth. Cat pulled out the pack of cigarettes she had slipped into her pocket before coming outside. She didn't smoke as much as she used to, but she still kept a pack tucked away in her vanity drawer, and sometimes, some nights, the back of her jaw would ache and she could taste the tobacco burning her throat. Behind her, the screen door slammed.

"I thought you gave that nasty habit up."

Her father stomped across the porch. He lowered himself down on the stairs beside her, carefully laying a canvas bag in the grass at his feet. Cat blew her smoke in the opposite direction.

"How you feeling?"

"Great." She squinted at the moon. "I feel great. It's official." She dragged on her cigarette. "How are you feeling?" She looked over at him. He was frowning, his brow furrowed, his eyes sad. Looking at her looking at the moon.

"I feel fine, as I always do."

"What? I worry about you." She pointed at him with her cigarette. "What's in the bag?"

"Oh, some more toys for Daniel. Here." He handed the bag to Cat. She set it in her lap. Daniel was still prowling in the shadows, ignoring them. In the moonlight his hair looked dark as ink. Cat reached into the bag and pulled out another robotic creature. This one was smaller than the others, the size of her palm, and made of tarnished metal. It was as smooth as a stone.

"It's a rock." She leaned back so she could see the contents of the bag in the porch light. "It's a bag of rocks."

"It's not a rock." Her father laughed. "These are my best ones yet. Let me show you." He took the thing-that-was-not-a-rock out of her hand and pressed down on it; immediately, the metal split open to reveal a faint luminescent glow. The robot whirred and lifted up off the palm of his hand and then zipped into the night, heading toward Daniel.

"Holy shit," said Cat.

Her father grinned. "I programmed them to recognize Daniel's DNA code. They'll stay close to him."

The little ball of pale light buzzed up close to Daniel's head. He jumped. Peered at it suspiciously. It darted away from him, then hovered in the air centimeters above him. He jumped up and caught it. The light slipped between his fingers.

"It's pretty cool, right?" Cat called out. Daniel nodded and walked toward them, his hand still cupped around the robot. He came to the edge of the yard and unfolded his fingers. His face was illuminated. The light caught the sheen of his eyes, and for a moment they almost seemed silver. Cat's heart clenched. It was the last thing she ever expected to see: eyes flashing silver.

She pulled out another cigarette.

"Here, buddy," said her father, setting the bag on the grass. He took the robot out of Daniel's hand and showed him how to activate and deactivate it. The robot buzzed into the air. Together they reached into the bag and activated the other robots, one at a time, while Cat smoked and leaned against the porch and tried not to cry.

Cat lived in a world in which it was no longer necessary to believe in magic, but as she watched her son lighting up one robot firefly after another, his dark hair falling across his eyes, his skin pearly in the moonlight, she wondered.

* * * *

Cat took Daniel into town to register him for the Montessori day school that had opened on the Farm-to-Market road, next to the art galleries. She had considered keeping him to teach herself but decided it would be best for him if he met other children, even if they were the offspring of the teenagers she had known in high school. Her father refused to offer his opinion on the matter.

"I raised one of you already," he said.

The day school was in an old farmhouse, surrounded by square herb and vegetable gardens, the pecan trees strung with twinkling homemade wind chimes. Daniel clutched Cat's hand as they walked up the stone pathway, his fist wrapped around her two middle fingers. He looked around the garden with alarm. This was why she had decided to enroll him in school, because he was nearly five and the wider world seemed to terrify him. She wrapped her arms around his shoulders—he was so small, a normal size for his age but so small in relation to Cat and all the people she had known in her life that it seemed Daniel's bones were hollow, like a bird's—and guided him up the porch steps, through the heavy wooden door, into the school's dim, cool corridor. Ms. Alvarez, the principal, stuck her head out of one of the rooms. She was young and pretty and wore her hair pulled back in a sleek black ponytail. She smiled at Daniel before she smiled at Cat. "We're so glad you could come down today."

"Daniel," said Cat. He burrowed in her hip. "Daniel, this is Ms. Alvarez." She smiled at the principal apologetically. She could feel Daniel's breath through her skirt.

Ms. Alvarez smiled and shook her head. She crouched down so she was at Daniel's level. "I see you have a dinosaur on your shirt."

Daniel peeked at her with one dark eye.

"Do you like dinosaurs?"

He loves them, Cat wanted to say, but she kept quiet. Daniel pulled away from her, just slightly. He nodded. He looked so solemn, so impassive. *Just like—*

"Would you like to see some dinosaurs?"

There were a few seconds of heavy silence. Then Daniel said, "They're extinct."

Ms. Alvarez laughed. "Of course they are! But I have a few holo-models you can play with."

Daniel nodded, and Ms. Alvarez led him across the hallway into a classroom. Cat trailed behind. She had never been that comfortable around children. Daniel was different, but he was her son.

Ms. Alvarez switched on the lights. The classroom was full of color and smelled of plastic and disinfectant. Cat had never stood in a kindergarten classroom before. Or an elementary schoolroom. It was like standing inside a kaleidoscope. The principal led Daniel past the cluster of computers to the holographic station tucked discreetly in the corner. It looked like a black glass cube. She tapped one of the station's sides, entered in a pass code, scrolled through a menu. Daniel followed the movements of her hands, and Cat felt a surge of love. It happened now and then, when she watched Daniel without his knowing. He needed a haircut—she was bad about keeping track of those.

A trio of apatosauruses appeared on the top of the holographic station, along with a strange, tropical-looking tree. Daniel gasped, turned and looked at Cat, his smile huge and bright. It was a much better holographic station than the one they had at home. One of the apatosauruses bit at the top of the tree, and tiny green leaves flaked into the air and disappeared.

Ms. Alvarez left Daniel to play with the holo-models. Her

demeanor had changed. She was more professional now, more serious. She led Cat out into the hallway.

"He seems very smart," she said. "Very precocious."

"He's shy. He's not . . . he's not used to people."

Ms. Alvarez smiled reassuringly. "That's not as uncommon as you think."

Cat wiped her hands across her skirt. Her palms were sweating. She was not used to being a mother in public. Ms. Alvarez glanced back into the room, and Cat did the same. Daniel had brought a *T. rex* into the scene, and the apatosauruses swung their tails in defense.

"I think he'll do well here," Ms. Alvarez said. "I can show the two of you around, if you'd like."

Cat nodded. "C'mon, Daniel," she said. Daniel looked up at her, frowning. For a moment she was afraid he would start wailing and thrashing on the floor and Ms. Alvarez wouldn't let him into the school, but then he stood up and trotted over to her. Cat pulled him up close to her knees, wound her fingers through his hair.

Ms. Alvarez smiled warmly. "It can be scary sending your child off to school for the first time."

Cat laughed. She found this oddly reassuring. "I never went to school. Not at his age."

"Homeschooled?"

"Basically." She hesitated. "I had a tutor, but . . . I pretty much just ran wild in the woods."

Ms. Alvarez smiled as she led them out into the hallway plastered with student paintings. "You think that method did well by you?"

"It did, actually. Got to figure things out for myself." The end of the hallway was flooded with sunlight. Light reflected off the tiles. "I want something similar for Daniel."

Ms. Alvarez nodded. "Well, I think our school will be an excellent choice. You've seen the gardens. Would you like to see the media lab?"

Cat nodded. She held on tight to Daniel's hand as they moved through the sunny hallway, Ms. Alvarez chatting casually about the Montessori method, about a child's instinctual drive to learn.

Cat was mesmerized by the school. She imagined Daniel rushing through the hallway with a backpack bouncing on his shoulders. She imagined him prowling in the garden. Eating lunch at the little round tables in the cafeteria. Making friends. Growing up.

Cat bent down, scooped Daniel up in her arms, and kissed him once on the forehead, because she was so swollen with love.

*   *   *   *

Cat asked Daniel what he thought of the school as they drove home.

"I liked the dinosaurs."

Cat laughed. She pulled into the driveway and parked behind her father's car. Daniel climbed out of the backseat and ran to the porch and pulled himself up on the swing, the way he always did when they came home. Cat wedged herself behind the screened-in door. Swiped her key in the lock. When she pushed her way into the foyer she knew immediately that something was wrong. She recognized the vibrating silence of the house from those months after her mother died. "Daddy," she said.

"Mama, what's wrong?" Daniel pulled on her hand, and she glanced down at his solemn dark eyes. He looked up at her inquiringly. She swooped him to her chest and held him close and then she rushed to one of the intercom panels. Held the button down and called for her father. Nothing. She slid Daniel to the floor.

"I want you to go get on the computer, okay? You can watch your shows."

Daniel didn't move, just stared at her. She pressed the intercom button again and heard nothing but the crackle of static. *Maybe he's just outside.* She guided Daniel into the living room, where he opened up his laptop. The light brightened his face, washed out the outline of his soft features. Cat left him sitting on the couch. Blood rushed in her ears. She took the stairs down to the laboratory two at a time and slammed the door open. It was empty. The computers hummed and blinked. The air seemed undisturbed. Cat dug her nails into her palm. She went to her father's bedroom. Dark and empty. Outside. He must be outside, despite the unusual heat. His car was in the driveway.

Cat ran out through the kitchen door. She ran out onto the airless screened-in porch; she ran out into the sweltering yard. Cicadas screeched like a broken-down machine. She couldn't breathe. The heat increased the world's gravity, and her lungs constricted inside her chest. It was too hot to run but she ran anyway, around the side of the house to the garden she had transformed in the years since Daniel was born, lush with flowering vines and rows of herbs.

"Daddy!" she shrieked.

He was sprawled out underneath the citrus tree. Her citrus tree. The branches were heavy with lemons she hadn't bothered to pick. In the dappled shade her father lay on his back, his arms splayed out at painful angles, his skin pale. She dropped to her knees beside him and felt for a pulse. She held her breath; she willed her own heart to stop beating, just long enough so she wouldn't confuse the two, so she wouldn't suffer that moment of false hope. But no. She felt something fluttering inside him. She put her hand on his chest. She didn't know how to do any of these things. She didn't know how to save a life.

Cat didn't want to leave him lying there in the garden but her comm slate was still tucked away in the bottom of her purse, inside. She ran back through the yard. She ignored Daniel when his eyes followed her across the living room, the music from his show tinny and grating. She could do only one thing right now. She pulled her slate out of her purse. It slipped against her palm. Her fingers shook. She connected with emergency services and ran back outside, out of the humming house and into the chattering brightness.

"He's passed out," she said to the operator. Her voice rose and fell with the motion of her steps. "I can feel a heartbeat. I found him like that." She rattled off the address without thinking and then wondered if she had given the wrong one. She was aware of Daniel following her. She heard only snatches of the operator's voice.

"Don't move him . . . be there shortly . . . calm . . . good."

In the garden, Cat switched off her comm slate and dropped it in the soft, dry soil. She took her father's hand, clammy and limp, in her own. Daniel stood beside her. She tried not to cry. Daniel didn't say anything for a long time, and then he said, "He isn't sleeping, is he?"

Cat took a deep, shuddery breath. She shook her head.

"Will he be okay?"

"I don't know." With her free hand she pulled Daniel in close to her. She kissed the top of his head, smelled the powdery scent of his shampoo.

"I don't want Grandpa to die." A trembling in his voice.

His eyes were wet.

"He hasn't died yet," said Cat, and that was when she heard sirens, from far away, caught on the wind.

EIGHTEEN

They took Cat's father to the hospital two towns over where Daniel had been born. Cat followed the ambulance in her car. The EMTs had asked her about the tumor in his brain: *Has he been taking his medication? Has he been exerting himself?* She had stuttered out answers, not knowing if they were true.

Now she set the car to auto-drive and leaned back in her seat, digging her nails into the skin of her arms. Daniel played with his portable holobox and made spaceship noises under his breath.

In the hospital, she sat in the waiting room and stared at the row of vending machines blinking across the way. She felt herself slipping back into that familiar, robotic numbness. She hadn't cried once. Every now and then she heard Daniel sniffling beside her and she wrapped her arms around him but it felt insincere. *Don't do this. Let yourself feel. Let yourself feel.*

When the doctor came out in her long white coat, Cat sat straight up. She took a deep breath. The doctor didn't smile. Daniel looked up from his holobox but didn't say anything.

"He's fine," said the doctor. "For now."

"For now?"

The doctor jerked her head toward the hallway. "I'd like to speak to you." She led Cat to a cluster of rooms at the end of the corridor. Cat sat down in the hard chair and rubbed her forehead: the yellowish fluorescent light gave her a headache. The doctor sat down behind her sleek metal desk and folded her hands and said, "You know he has a brain tumor."

Cat nodded.

"It's gotten worse. Much worse in the past few months, from what I can tell from the scans." The doctor looked down at her hands. "He was taking medication?"

"Yes."

"It's not working anymore." The doctor looked back up. "I'm sorry."

"I don't understand what you're saying." Cat shifted in her uncomfortable seat. The doctor pushed away a strand of hair that had fallen across her forehead. She sighed.

"He's dying, Ms. Novak. The scans give him only a few months."

Cat's heart collapsed inside her chest.

"Thank you," she said. The doctor's face twisted up as though she couldn't understand why Cat was thanking her. Cat couldn't understand it herself. She stood up, knocking the chair across the office floor. "Thank you," she said again. "May I see him?"

The doctor nodded. "But I should warn you. He may not be himself. We're working on getting him stabilized. We'll have some treatments for him—for pain, mostly." She smiled wanly. "But other than that . . ."

Cat nodded and pushed back out into the hospital corridor. There were too many people out there. The sight of them made her dizzy. She stumbled back to the waiting room. Daniel still sat in one of the chairs, playing with his holobox. She rushed forward, gathered him in her arms. "We're going to see Grandpa," she whispered into the mop of his hair.

She held Daniel's hand as they walked down the hallways to intensive care. The nurse at the desk told Cat that Daniel couldn't go any farther, that he was too young, and so Cat, numbly, blindly, left him sitting with the nurse before stepping across the boundary into the ICU. She followed the hallway down to the end, and then there he was, her father, laid out on a bed behind a heavy blue curtain. His eyes were shut, and his skin looked gray in the hospital light. She pulled a chair up next to his bed.

"Daddy," she said.

For an eternal minute he didn't move. Then his eyes slowly opened. His pupils contracted into two black dots. "Caterina," he said. "Caterina, you have to call Finn." Cat bit down on her tongue to keep herself from weeping. She grabbed his hand, held it loosely in her own. A thin wire snaked from his ring finger to the computer console on the wall. He opened his mouth, closed it. "Call Finn," he said again. "Let him know . . ." He closed his eyes. "I'm so tired. Like my mind can't keep up." He opened his eyes again. "Call him."

"Daddy, I can't." She choked on her own voice. "He belongs to STL now, remember?"

"Of course I remember!" All the color had leached out of her father. "But you can still call him! You remember! The program he wrote, years ago. You remember."

"No." Cat leaned forward over the bed and smoothed her father's hair across his forehead. "No, I don't remember. You told me there's no way—"

"I did no such thing. The code, Kitty-Cat! In my lab computer!"

"The code? What code?"

"The code! The program!" Cat became aware that the beeping of the heart monitor on the wall beside the bed had sped up. A nurse-bot buzzed into the room, stopped at the foot of the bed.

"The patient needs to rest. Please see the front desk for more information." The nurse-bots reminded Cat of the android that worked at the coffee shop in the city, the way they lit up when they spoke. But that was the only similarity.

Cat stared at it, still holding her father's hand, as he tossed his head back and forth on his pillow.

"Please, ma'am," said the nurse-bot. "This is intensive care."

Cat took a deep breath. She turned back to her father. Pressed her hand against his forehead until he lay still.

"Call him," he said. "Call Finn."

"Okay, Daddy," said Cat. "I'll call Finn."

* * * *

Cat came home from the hospital exhausted. She slumped on the couch in the living room, and Daniel crawled onto her lap. He curled up there like a kitten. She ran her hands over his hair, watching the ceiling fan fling shadows across the wall.

"Daniel, I need to do some things." Cat's voice sounded strange: parched dry, empty. "Do you think you can entertain yourself on the computer while I'm working?"

"Is it about Grandpa? The things you need to do?"

Cat nodded even though it wasn't about Grandpa, not really. Daniel slid off her lap and trotted into the dining room to retrieve his plastic laptop. She wondered if he understood what was happening. *He's not sleeping, is he?* Daniel seemed to have a better grasp of the world than she did sometimes.

Cat went downstairs to her father's laboratory. She switched on the intercom system so she could hear the beeping, chirping noises of Daniel's computer games upstairs. Then she sat down at the old computer on her father's desk. She opened it up and watched the screen flicker on. She closed her eyes. *Welcome back, Daniel*, the computer said. It had always been easy for her to stay calm, and she just had to do it for a little longer, a little longer . . .

She opened her eyes and brought up the files labeled with Finn's name, the same ones she had dug through before she flew out to the desert to meet Dr. Condon. She had scoured these files years ago and never found anything like what he described. *A code. A program.* Her father was delirious with sickness, had forgotten the implications of Finn's purchase by STL, but part of her didn't want to give up the hope that the code was real.

She flipped through the files, pushing them aside with the tips of her fingers: the same schematics, the same elaborate-looking mathematical equations. Then she found something new: a folder labeled "Finn Miscellany." It was not stored on the directory, which was why she hadn't seen it before. It was located only here, on her father's computer. She opened it.

Photographs. Photographs of the inside of Finn's torso. A video file of Finn looking straight into the camera, labeled with the year Cat turned six. She did not recognize the background. And at the sound of his voice, distorted through the computer speakers, she realized she could not watch for longer than a few seconds.

Cat found a file labeled "Emotion Project." She tapped it with the tip of her finger, watched as it blossomed across the screen. Page after page of incomprehensible code. This wasn't what she was looking for: this was what had sent him away, not what would bring him back.

She closed out the file. And then, after forty-five minutes of searching, she found it. It was a single file tucked away in a folder that had been tucked away in another folder, like Russian nesting dolls. It was labeled "Emergency." Cat opened it, expecting more schematics. Instead, she found a short program, simple enough that even she could understand it. High school level. When executed, it would send a blip to a portion of the circuitry in Finn's brain. The notes blocked out at the end of the program said: *May cause minor sparking. Nothing problematic. Receipt program already implemented.*

For a long time, Cat read the program code over and over, until she lost all sense of its meaning. She almost forgot to breathe. Her father had told her there was no way to contact Finn. That it was an impossibility. She should have known he was lying.

But there was still no way to send a message: no way to tell Finn why the computer in Cat's father's laboratory had connected, however momentarily, with the computer in Finn's brain. She wondered what the note meant by minor sparking. She thought of a tiny pistol going off inside Finn. A flare.

Cat brought the keyboard up on the touchpad. She typed in *exe*. She hit return. For a moment the computer paused, and then *attempt successful* appeared onscreen, the curser blinking and blinking and blinking. She felt like nothing had happened. She typed *exe* again, and again the program informed her that her attempt had been successful. This time, she shut the computer down and turned around in her chair and leaned her head against her hand.

She sat in the laboratory, lights winking around her. The computers sounded like they were sighing. On the worktable was a scatter of wires, pulled out of the abdomen of a new metal insect, a butterfly the length of her arm. The wings were made of some gossamer, plasticine material, so thin it felt like silk. The wires dangled like entrails. Cat held the butterfly up to the light and color refracted through the wings, orange and red and gold. Its stillness unnerved her, and she knew that it would remain still, that it would never have a chance to move, because her father was dying.

* * * *

Cat spent the next days in a fugue. In the mornings she did her routine chores—dropping Daniel off at school, sweeping the back porch, watering the garden—and in the afternoons she drove to the hospital to sit with her father while he slept in the white light of the hospital room, sleek robot nurses sliding across the gleaming floor. He had become much more coherent since the day the ambulance brought him to the hospital, and the doctors had moved him out of the ICU, into a private room. Cat slumped in the chair next to the bed and watched his chest rise and fall, listening to the steady beeping of the robots and the life-support machines. The air smelled of the pine cleaner they used on the floor. She could barely smell medicine; she could barely smell sickness.

"Did you send a message to Finn?" he asked one afternoon.

Cat straightened up and looked at him. His eyes were clear and bright. He smiled.

"You did," he said. "You found it. Good girl."

"You told me—"

"Oh, I know what I told you. Good thing I was half-mad after they revived me, huh?" He laughed, and his laughter turned to a cough. The nurse-bot unfolded itself in the corner but didn't say anything. "Finn actually made that little program. When I first found out I was sick."

Cat didn't say anything.

"He asked me to keep it a secret, which . . . That was when I first realized something was wrong with him. He said he didn't want anyone to know about it, but . . . It's so simple, isn't it? Elegant. The sort of work only a computer can do." He coughed again.

Cat smiled even though she didn't feel like it. Her father was so pale he blended in with the white sheets, with the walls, with the impossible light. She couldn't think about Finn right now.

"Have you heard from him?" he asked.

"No."

"Oh, send it again. It's just Finn being recalcitrant. We had that receiver buried so deep in there not even STL could muck it up."

"If I ever hear anything," said Cat, "I'll let you know."

That evening, Daniel asked her questions she couldn't answer.

"Has Grandpa's brain stopped working?" He sat at the aluminum table, the same one she had sat at as a child, kicking his feet against the chair legs, the way she used to do. Cat ran cold water over a bowl of pasta. She looked out the window.

"No," she said.

"But if it does, that means he'll die?"

"His brain isn't going to stop working." *Don't lie to children. Be upfront.* "He has a . . . growth, there, that affects the jobs his brain has to do." She carried the pasta across the kitchen and dumped it in the pot of marinara sauce bubbling on the stove.

"Do you believe in ghosts, Mama?"

Cat nearly dropped the pot of spaghetti across the kitchen floor. "Why do you ask?"

"Well, if you believe in ghosts, then it's not so scary for someone to die, because you can still see them. You know, they'll keep on being there."

Cat turned from the stove. Daniel stared at her. God, his hair was so dark. It was darker than hers now.

"Grandpa isn't going to die," Cat said sharply, because she was tired, and the steam from dinner was making her head spin. She drew the back of her hand across her forehead. Daniel blinked, recoiled a little, and then turned back to his laptop. Cat immediately regretted losing her temper and telling a lie. She pulled Daniel into a hug and the moist heat in the kitchen masked the tears on her cheeks.

* * * *

One afternoon, when her father had been in the hospital for nearly a month, with no change in his health, someone knocked on the front door.

Daniel was at school and Cat had been smoking a cigarette in the living room, watching through the windows as birds fought one another in the yard. When she heard the knock she dropped the cigarette on the chair's armrest, burning a small, neat hole into the fabric. Immediately, she thought, *Richard*, and as she walked into the foyer she picked up any detritus that might suggest a child lived in the house. She shoved all the toys she had gathered into the hall closet and then pulled the door open.

A young man with lovely dark eyes blinked at her. "I'm, ah, I'm looking for Dr. Novak," he said.

Cat dragged on her cigarette.

"Dr. Novak is in the hospital," she said. "I'm his daughter."

"Oh," said the young man. "Oh God, I'm sorry." He held out his hand, and Cat shook it. She stepped out onto the front porch and put out her cigarette in the ashtray.

"Can I help you?"

"Maybe." The young man smoothed his hair back away from his forehead. "My name is AJ. AJ Aziz. I'm a cyberneticist with Selene Technologies. You know, the lunar base."

"I know."

"I was hoping—" AJ hesitated. "I was hoping to talk to Dr. Novak about his android, George—"

"Finn," Cat snapped.

"Oh, right, of course, sorry, I forgot." AJ shuffled his feet against the porch. He seemed at a loss. Cat looked at his tiny bullet car parked in the drive, brand-new and shining in the sun. It looked out of place here in the woods.

"What do you want to know about Finn?" she asked.

AJ looked at her brightly. "Oh, are you in cybernetics, too? I hope so, because there's something really weird going on with him up there. Like a signal . . ."

There was an earnestness in his expression that she found appealing. Also, he called Finn *him*.

"Why don't you sit down," she said, nodding toward the swing. "I'll see what I can do."

"Oh, thank you!" AJ grinned. Cat pulled out another cigarette and lit it. AJ sat down on the swing but Cat stayed standing, leaning against the porch railing.

"Well?" she asked.

"Okay," said AJ. "Here's the deal. I work with Dr. Korchinsky—she's one of the scientists stationed up at the lunar base. A cyberneticist, like us." Cat didn't bother to correct his mistake. "Anyway, Dr. K does all the work on George—I mean, what's his name? Finn?"

Cat nodded.

"Well, she does all the work on Finn up there, and I do all the work down here. A few days ago there was this weird . . . anomaly, I guess, in his circuits. Sort of like his system rebooted. Happened twice. The second time he let off some sparks—from his teeth, I think. Anyway, Dr. K was totally baffled. Said Finn told her nothing had happened. He . . . He lied."

"Yes," said Cat. "He can lie." She pulled out another cigarette and lit it with her old one.

AJ didn't respond. He was too involved with his story, as though he had rehearsed it on the drive out to the house and couldn't be interrupted by his audience. "So Dr. K tracked the source of the anomaly. It took a while, but she eventually tracked it here." AJ spread his hands out wide. "Dr. Novak's residence. Which makes sense. Anyway, she wanted me to get in touch with Dr. Novak to ask about the anomaly. I mean, what is it?" AJ looked at her then.

"I don't know." Cat blew smoke into the air.

AJ frowned. "Really? I mean, it's weird that it was sourced from here, don't you think?"

"It is weird." Cat paused. Thoughts churned inside her head. She had no business trying to bullshit a cyberneticist. "It may be some old messaging system. My father may have sent something—from the hospital, I mean. Maybe."

"Huh. What kind of message?"

"I'm not sure." Cat smoked her cigarette all the way down to the filter and flicked it out into the yard. "Dr. Aziz, is there any way I could talk to Dr. Korchinsky? About Finn?"

AJ blinked. "About the anomaly, you mean? The message?"

Cat nodded.

"I suppose." AJ paused. "You'd have to come out to our offices. We've got the communication hookups and everything. Maybe next week sometime? That would give me a chance to get everything set up."

"I could do that." Cat paused. "It'll give me a chance to visit my father in the hospital. He knows more about it than I do."

"Oh, of course." AJ pushed back in the swing. "Is Dr. Novak doing . . . all right? I was sort of hoping to meet him. It's why I drove all the way out here." He smiled. "He's kind of my hero."

Cat sighed and pulled at her hair. She listened to the pine trees shaking in the wind.

"He's dying," she said.

AJ stared at her, his eyes wide. "Oh," he said. "I'm sorry. I didn't . . . I didn't know."

"It's okay." Cat nodded, trying to convince herself that what she said was true. *It's okay.*

"I'll call you. About coming to talk to Dr. Korchinsky."

AJ stood up and shook Cat's hand again. She forced herself to smile at him. She had no intention of divulging any secrets about the anomaly in Finn's system. She only thought if she could talk to Dr. Korchinsky, who was on the lunar station, who spoke to Finn every day, she could somehow convince Finn to come home, to see her father before he died.

* * * *

Cat set an appointment to drive to the STL offices in the city, to meet with Dr. Kristine Korchinsky. She called Maybelle from the pie shop and told her she needed to go into the city over the weekend. She didn't offer any details and Maybelle didn't ask, but that was because everyone in town knew about her father, and the nature of his illness—a wasting disease, the sort of thing you disintegrated from—was noble enough that the suffering of her family endeared them to the gossiping old ladies at the pie shop.

She drove to the hospital. Her father slept despite the brightness of the room. She sat and watched him and waited until one of the nurse-bots woke him up, sliding a thin silver needle into one of the veins of his arms. His eyes fluttered open, and he stayed still while the nurse-bot took a sample of his blood.

"Cat," he said when the bot had whirred away. He twisted his neck so that he was facing her. "When I was little boy they had actual nurses." He grinned, and the grin stretched his skin taut across the bones of his face. Cat barely recognized him. "Guess it is my fault, though? The bots? I don't really mind them."

"I'm going to STL this Friday," Cat said.

Her father's eyes widened, and he tried to sit up. Cat pressed her hand against his chest, and it was all she could do not to snatch it away—she felt the bones of his sternum through the flimsy fabric of his gown. "Don't strain yourself, Daddy."

"Why?" her father asked. "Did you hear from Finn?"

"No, not exactly." And then she related to him the visit from Dr. Aziz.

"So I'm going to talk to them," she said when she had finished. "About Finn."

Her father closed his eyes. "Thank you." She didn't think he was speaking to her. He had always been an atheist, but maybe in the hospital that didn't mean anything anymore. His eyes opened. "Maybe you can get him to come back."

Cat didn't say anything.

"If anyone could get him to come back, it would be you." He turned to her again. "You do know that?"

Cat didn't believe him. She didn't believe that Finn would come back for her. She wrapped her father's hand in her own.

"You should rest," she said.

Cat drove home and picked Daniel up at school. After dinner, she took him to the ice cream shop on the interstate. Daniel ate his ice cream cone and regarded her suspiciously. She never bought him ice cream.

"I'm going away for a few days," she said.

Daniel continued to lick at his ice cream. A tiny stream of it melted over his fingers.

"Why?"

"I'm going to talk to someone."

"Is it my dad?"

Cat froze. She had never told Daniel, once he was born, about his father. She had never told him about Finn. She had never explained why she spent so much time out under the moon.

"No," she said slowly, and she dreaded the inevitable flood of questions—*Who is my dad? Can I meet him?*—but they didn't come. Daniel looked down at his ice cream cone.

"It's someone I knew a long time ago," she said. "Someone Grandpa knew. You're going to stay with Maybelle. Is that all right? From the pie house?"

"Maybelle smells funny."

Cat almost laughed. It was true; Maybelle had that mothball smell she always associated with old women. But she only said, "Now, Daniel, that isn't kind."

He shrugged.

"She promised you can feed the llamas."

Daniel considered this proposition. He scrunched up his brow in concentration. The ice cream dripped onto the table. The llamas belonged to Maybelle's husband; he kept three of them on the land behind their house. Daniel liked to point them out whenever they drove past them on their way into town.

"Will they bite me?" he said. Cat had no idea whether llamas bit or not, but she smiled and said, "Of course not." And then she wiped up the melted ice cream with a handful of napkins.

Thursday morning she hugged Daniel longer than usual when she dropped him off at school, holding up the line of cars building up behind her. He wiggled out of her arms.

"Maybelle'll be at the usual spot," she said. "And you can call me if there are any problems. And I'll drop off your suitcase now so it'll be waiting for you—"

He nodded and slunk out of the car. She knew he wasn't happy about her leaving, and part of her wished she could take him with her—but no, he would have questions, and she was not prepared to give him the answers.

She drove away from the school, taking deep gulping breaths. She drove to Maybelle's house and rang the doorbell. Maybelle answered, clapped her hands in delight.

"I'm just dropping off his things," Cat said. "Thank you *so much*."

"Oh, honey, it's no problem. We miss having kids around here."

Cat nodded. Maybelle's house was new and full of light. It looked nothing at all like Cat's house; in fact, it reminded Cat of the glass house, though at least the walls were solid, and Maybelle favored frilly, old-fashioned furniture that was too heavy for all the open spaces and hidden skylights.

"You'll be back on Saturday?" Maybelle asked as she led Cat down the hallway to the guest room where Daniel would be staying. The sheets were already turned down. Cat tossed the suitcase on the bed.

"Absolutely," she said. "I'll call if anything changes. And you have my number—"

"Of course. Don't you worry about a thing." She smiled. Cat knew she was generating in her mind all the reasons why Cat would leave, suddenly, in the middle of the week. Cat also knew better than to give her any hints.

"Thanks again," Cat said. She walked out Maybelle's front door to her car. Her own suitcase lay on the backseat. Sunlight fell in shards through the leaves of the trees in Maybelle's front yard. Maybelle stood in the doorway, watching her.

And Cat drove away, her palms sweating, her heart racing.

* * * *

Friday afternoon came much more quickly than she expected. She stayed in a cheap motel near the STL offices. Everything about it was faded, as though it had been left in the sun too long. Even the complimentary breakfast looked worn out. Cat ate her beige toast and thin eggs and went up to her room to wait. She kept her computer turned on in case AJ needed to talk to her, but she never heard from him; she never heard from anyone.

An hour before it was time to go, she pulled out her gray Chanel suit—an artifact of her time with Richard, a luxury she had never brought herself to throw away—and dressed. She put on stockings despite the heat and wound her hair around the top of her head. Applied eyeliner and mascara and lipstick. Then she sat on the edge of the bathtub, sliding her stocking feet nervously against the tile, and sent a spoken message to Daniel's computer.

"I hope you're having fun at Maybelle's. Don't spend too much time on the Internet. Say hi to the llamas for me." Her voice echoed off the bathroom walls, and it sounded much more cheerful than she felt. Cat felt like she was going to throw up. She drove to the offices. She parked her car in the visitors' garage. She went into the lobby and told the receptionist she was there to meet AJ Aziz.

"You can go on up," the receptionist said, her eyes not once moving away from the screen of her computer. An enormous monitor was set into the wall behind her, flashing images of the lunar station. Cat lingered for a moment, half hoping to see Finn. She didn't.

The elevator was narrow and modern and made of glass, just like the STL offices. As the atrium fell away below her, Cat clutched her handbag a little too tightly. Air-conditioning blew down the back of her neck. The elevator chimed, stopped. The glass doors slid open. Cat stepped out into the empty hallway. Her tall heels clicked against the tiles. She could hear herself breathing. She was so light-headed she almost didn't think she would make it to AJ's office.

"Dr. Novak?"

His head appeared in one of the doorways. He held out his hand, and she shook it. "Did you get a chance to talk to your father?" he asked.

Cat nodded dumbly. *Dr. Novak.* The sound of it made her heart hurt.

He jerked his head toward the elevators. "Shall we? The conference room is all set up. Do you mind if I sit in?"

Cat shook her head, and they walked side by side back to the elevator. He pressed the up button. They didn't say anything to each other while they waited. Another chime. Up they went, so high Cat thought they might take the elevator to the lunar station itself. But then the doors slid open, and AJ led her through a hall identical to the one they had left. And then through a pair of swinging doors that opened into a cavernous dark room. A long, low table stretched from one end to the other, and a screen was lowered in the front of the room, the STL logo splashed across it, glowing faintly.

A half second after they entered, the lights flickered on. "Okay." AJ gestured toward the table. "You can sit right here. I'll need to test the camera."

Cat walked the length of the room. Her legs shook. She slid down in the chair, set her handbag beside her. Folded her hands on the table. AJ pushed a black camera the size of her fist so that it lined up directly with her face. She didn't move. He looked at the camera and then at his laptop sitting on the table and then at her. His eyes were the same color as Finn's. He adjusted the camera's arm.

"Perfect," he said. "I think that's it." He nodded to himself. "I'm just going to sit back there. I might type a few notes on the tablet. Is that all right?"

Cat nodded. She wondered what would happen when he learned that she had no interest in explaining the engineering behind the signal.

AJ tapped the computer. "We're dialing up now." He watched the screen. So did Cat. It went black and then went white and then suddenly she was staring at the face of the woman in the video she had watched that sweltering afternoon in the glass house. *Kristine Korchinsky*. The woman looked more serious now, her hair pulled back in a severe ponytail, the skin around her eyes pale from a lack of makeup.

"Is everything working?" she said. The movement of her lips didn't quite match up to the sound of her voice. Cat could see the white walls of the lunar station gleaming behind her. "I don't see you—oh, there." She smiled insincerely. "You're Cat Novak. AJ said you had some information about that anomaly."

Cat nodded. She looked at the camera. "Yes," she said. "Is there any way I can speak to Finn?"

"Who?" Dr. Korchinsky frowned. Cat opened her mouth to speak but then Dr. Korchinsky said, "Oh, you mean George, don't you? He did call himself Finn, before flying out here."

"You said him," said Cat. "Like AJ."

"What? Oh yes, well, you get used to him, you know . . ." Dr. Korchinsky touched one hand to her hairline and looked away from the camera. She sighed. "Dr. Novak, my time is precious. What's going on with that system reboot? Did you or your father send it from Earth?"

"Yes." Cat hesitated. "I mean, I did."

"Why? He's not your concern anymore."

Cat wished she could talk to Finn directly. She wished she could touch him.

"My father is dying," she said flatly.

Dr. Korchinsky's face softened.

"He wanted Finn to know. I didn't even think it was possible to contact Finn at all. I'm not a cyberneticist, by the way. I studied philosophy in school, and I used to roll cigarettes in a vice stand. Finn programmed that beacon, and he made it easy enough for me to use." The words came bubbling out, and Cat was afraid she would start crying. "So if you could send Finn my message. That's really why I came here today. I'm divorced, and my father is dying, and I'm sorry."

She had not meant to mention her divorce, hadn't even meant to say she was sorry. She had told herself over and over that this was not why she had driven into the city, not why she had lied her way into the STL conference room. But now that she was here, now that she sat at this conference table and saw the perimeters of the walls where Finn lived, she couldn't help herself. Cat heard a chair creak from the back of the room. AJ. She felt guilty, thinking about him sitting there, listening to her conversation, knowing she had lied to him.

"Your father," Dr. Korchinsky said. "Daniel Novak. Yes, I believe George—Finn—will want to hear that. As for the rest—"

"He's in the hospital," Cat said. "He has a brain tumor. If Finn could come home, and see him before he dies—"

Dr. Korchinsky held out one hand. "I want you to know that I'm sympathetic. I really am. But STL will not take too kindly to me sending property back down without cause."

"Property!" Cat's voice echoed off the conference room walls, leaving a faint reverberation. She covered her mouth with her hand. "What about the rights bill? He can't be seen as property anymore."

Dr. Korchinsky's face darkened. "Things may be more complicated than you realize."

Cat had no idea how to respond. For a moment she simply stared at the monitor. *More complicated? How?*

"Please," she finally said. "My father—he saved him. He took care of him."

Dr. Korchinsky frowned, and Cat saw in her eyes exhausted sadness. "I know," she said, very softly. "This is a very . . . unusual circumstance. And STL's legal department basically does nothing but find loopholes . . ." She glanced at something off camera.

Cat looked down at the table, gleaming beneath the overhead lights. Up on the screen, Dr. Korchinsky shifted her position. The sound of rustling paper.

"I would send him down this moment if I thought I could get away with it," she said. Cat looked up at her image. "I'll see what I can do."

Cat took a deep, sighing breath. "Can I see him?" she whispered. "Can I talk to him?"

Dr. Korchinsky looked so sad that for a moment Cat thought she was staring at her own reflection. "He's out on the surface," she said. "I'm sorry." There was a long pause, and the screen crackled with static. "For what it's worth, and this may not be much, but . . . he has spoken of you." She smiled. "You were . . . You were friends, right?" A slight hesitation on the word *friends*.

"Yes," Cat said.

Dr. Korchinsky smiled, tilting her head downward. "I'll tell him. I'll tell him everything. And fuck it, I'll tell STL this whole conversation was legit." She glanced up, away from the camera. "Okay with you, AJ?"

Cat held her breath. AJ coughed, clearing his throat. "Fine with me." Cat's cheeks burned.

Dr. Korchinsky lifted her hand like she was reaching for the camera, and then stopped. "Oh," she said. "By the way. Let me give you an e-mail address. George doesn't have one but if you want to send him anything you can send it to me." She paused. "I promise I won't read your message." Cat whispered a thank-you. She pulled out her comm slate and entered the address into the contact list as Dr. Korchinsky recited it.

Dr. Korchinsky said, "I know what it's like. To be separated from someone you love."

Cat froze. She looked at Dr. Korchinsky's features, blurred by the camera quality, and tried to find some trace of irony. But her expression was clear and calm as a tide pool.

"I need to sign off," she said. Cat nodded.

The screen went black.

Cat sat still. An electric current was moving through her body. She heard AJ shifting in his seat behind her but he didn't say anything. For a long time she stared at the black screen and wondered if Dr. Korchinsky had lied when she said she would tell Finn everything. She wondered if Finn would come home—if Finn wanted to come home, if he thought of her father's house as home at all.

* * * *

When Cat drove to Maybelle's that night, Daniel was sitting on the stoop hitting a stick against the white cement. She turned off her car and bounded across the yard, scooped him up into a great big whirling hug. He shrieked and laughed, pounded his tiny fists against her shoulders.

"Did you miss me?" she asked.

"Yes," he said. Cat dropped him into the grass. She'd had enough sorrow the last few days, driving down the flat highway, remembering Finn, every touch he'd ever given her. Daniel threw his stick out into the yard and said, "Maybelle and Jim let me feed the llamas. They have weird teeth. But their fur was really soft."

Cat rubbed the top of his head, looked at the dark hair poking up between her fingers. Maybelle came out on the porch and waved, said everything had gone well, asked, with an inquisitive tilt of her head, how Cat's trip had been. Cat declined to offer any detail beyond *It was fine*.

She drove Daniel to the Dairy King drive-in restaurant over by the high school stadium and bought them both cheeseburgers and malted milkshakes. Daniel bounced up and down in his seat. "Maybelle made me eat shard."

"I think you mean chard."

"It was green and gross."

Cat laughed. It was easy to laugh when Daniel was around. She rolled down the windows and the unseasonably cool breeze blew across the front seat. The girl at the counter called their number. Cat picked up the food and went back to the car and said, "Why don't we just eat here?" and Daniel nodded vigorously. He always wanted to eat in the car at the drive-in, and she always said no.

The air smelled of bubbling grease and the faint toxic whiff of truck exhaust. Cat balanced the cup of french fries on the dashboard and took a bite of her cheeseburger. The salt was exactly what she needed. She had cried too much on the long way home.

Afterward, Cat drove back to the house. It loomed against the pale orange sunset. Daniel raced ahead, leaving his plastic suitcase on the backseat. He dug the hidden key out from under the potted plants on the porch and let himself inside, but Cat stayed out in the cool twilight air, walking in zigzags across the front yard, smoking one cigarette after another until it was too dark to see.

NINETEEN

As the days went by, Cat's father grew worse. She went to the hospital after her trip to the city and told him how she had talked to Dr. Korchinsky.

"She gave me her e-mail address," said Cat. "And told me we could e-mail Finn that way."

"Well, have you?" her father asked in his cottony voice. His eyelids drooped.

Cat told him no. Now that she had nearly communicated with Finn she was not so sure he wanted to hear from her. Maybe he hadn't been out on the surface of the moon at all. Maybe he had stood just off camera, listening in.

No, she thought. *He's not that cruel. He's not that human.*

Her father lifted one hand off the bed and let it hang limply in the air. That one movement seemed an enormous accomplishment. The hand twisted like a periscope until his fingers were pointing at her.

"E-mail him. Or her. Whoever. This has gone on too long."

"What are you talking about?"

Her father closed his eyes completely. He dropped his hand. She watched him struggle with the weight of his eyelashes. His head turned toward her. His neck was so thin. "This whole thing is my fault," he said. "It was too much at once, that was the problem. I'm not a psychologist. I don't understand this shit. So I just want to make it right."

Cat sighed. She wound her fingers around her father's. The treatments made him lose more weight and he looked shriveled up in his bed, as if he had died already. She saw the outline of his bones. She saw the threads of his veins.

"She told me she'd try to send him back to Earth," Cat said. "So he could . . . visit. Visit you."

"And you, too, of course." His face cracked into a smile. Before Cat could respond, a nurse-bot wheeled into the room. Cat's father sighed. "Time for my treatments," he muttered, just as the nurse-bot chirped, "Time for your treatments, Dr. Novak." He turned to Cat. "Go on, you don't want to watch this."

Cat smiled sadly. An enormous metal apparatus lowered down from its hiding place in the ceiling and hovered over her father's supine body. He closed his eyes. The nurse-bot rolled up to Cat.

"You will need to leave the room."

"Of course." Cat said good-bye to her father, and he raised his hand in response. She went into the hallway and shut the door and watched through the tiny window as bursts of white light filled her father's room. The treatments did nothing to help his illness, as she understood it. They only diminished his pain.

She waited until the lights stopped flashing, and then she went out to the parking lot, her mind blank.

* * * *

"Mama, Mama! There's a car outside our house."

Cat sat on the back porch drinking a glass of homemade limeade spiked with tequila. Two weeks had passed since the conversation with her father, and nearly a month since she had spoken to Dr. Korchinsky. Daniel ran up to her and tugged on the hem of her skirt. The air was hazier than usual.

"Oh?" Cat's heart raced but she was able to keep her voice calm and steady. "What sort of car?" *Richard.*

"A yellow one."

Cat drank the rest of her limeade in one gulp. She set the glass down on the ground and told Daniel to go to his room and stay there.

"But why?" he asked, his voice dragging out into a whine.

"Because I said so." Any other time she might have twinged internally at saying something so ridiculous, but with each rapid pump of her heart she saw Richard's face, broad and tan, his sharp white teeth, his expression when he caught sight of Daniel and counted backward.

"Go," she said, as sharply as she could. A waver rose through her throat. She ushered Daniel inside, through the kitchen door, catching the last notes of the doorbell as it echoed through the house. She pushed him toward the stairs, and he scowled at her from underneath the railing.

"Your *room*, Daniel," she said. He disappeared into the shadows.

Cat walked into the foyer. The doorbell rang a second time. When she came to the door she stopped and put one hand on the knob and tried to steady her breathing. She couldn't. She pulled the door open.

It was Finn.

Cat nearly screamed. She stumbled backward, away from the door, away from Finn. He didn't move. The hot dry wind pushed his hair across his forehead. It had been over eight years since she had watched him walk out of the glass house. It had been over eight years since the last time she touched him. She was so dizzy her eyesight faltered and the shadows beneath the furniture swam in and out of her line of vision.

"You're here," she said.

"Yes."

"But I thought—"

"Dr. Korchinsky called HR and reminded them they had to give me a leave of absence like an employee. Because of the AI bill. She threatened to go to the press with some of the . . . some of the less-than-legal things the company has been doing. So they sent me back in one of the cargo runs." He paused. She had forgotten the sound of his voice. All these years her memories had produced a facsimile—a higher pitch, a less mechanical cadence. Finn stepped through the doorway and closed the door behind him. The hot outside air lingered in the foyer.

"Where is Dr. Novak?" he asked.

"At the hospital."

Finn frowned. His eyes seemed to dim. Cat had never been so aware of the expression of emotion on a man's face until this moment.

"So I'm not too late," he said. Cat shook her head.

They hadn't moved from the door. He didn't have any bags, and he wore a pair of ill-fitting black pants, a ratty old band shirt. Otherwise he looked the same.

Cat thought then about her own face, the web of lines erupting from the corners of her eyes, the soft swell of her stomach left over from when Daniel was born. She touched her hair, and Finn moved toward the living room without saying anything more. When he passed her, electricity seemed to arc between them.

"I'd like to see him as soon as possible," he said.

"Of course." Cat followed behind him, chewing on her lower lip. "How long do you have here? Before you have to go back?"

Finn looked over his shoulder at her. "Three weeks until the next shuttle launch."

"Three weeks."

Finn nodded. He turned away from her.

All the things Cat wanted to say to him, all the things she had rehearsed during bright moonlit nights, evaporated on the tip of her tongue. *Why did you sell yourself? I'm sorry I used you. I love you.*

Finn walked around the edge of the living room. He touched the top of the couch. He touched the wallpaper bubbling and peeling off the walls. He stopped in front of the dusty windows and looked out at the yard: the brown grass, the rustling woods. He put his hand on the glass and the sunlight shone through his skin.

A creak on the stairs.

They both turned simultaneously.

Daniel pushed his pale face against the banister. Finn stared at him, and he stared at Finn. Cat took a deep breath. She held out her arms.

"Come on out. I want you to meet someone."

"You told me to go to my room," said Daniel. Finn looked over at her sharply.

"That was before I knew who was here."

Daniel crept into the living room. He looked up at Finn through the fringe of his hair and ran to Cat. She put her hands on his shoulders and pulled him close against her knees.

"Daniel," she said. "This is Finn." She looked at Finn when she spoke. "Say hello."

"Hello." Daniel blinked up at Finn.

"It's very nice to meet you." Finn held out one hand. Cat nudged Daniel forward. He took Finn's hand. They shook, and then Daniel dropped back to Cat's side.

"Finn is an old friend," said Cat. "He's come to see Grandpa."

Daniel considered this. He squinted at Finn. "Are you a robot?" he asked.

Cat closed her eyes.

"No," said Finn. "I'm an android."

"Oh. We learned about androids at school. There's one on the lunar station. Do you know it?"

"Him," said Cat. "Do you know him."

"I am the android on the lunar station." Finn smiled, and the smile was so easy and bright that Cat nearly gasped. It wasn't the smile she remembered; it was better. It was what his smile had always aspired to before. "Well, I'm not on the lunar station *now*, of course."

Daniel's eyes widened. "Can you come to my school? For show and tell?"

"No," said Cat.

Finn ignored her. He crouched down so he was eye level with Daniel. "I would be happy to come to your school."

Daniel clapped his hands together and turned to Cat. "I'm going to tell Robbie!" And then he bounded out of the room, up the stairs.

"You don't have to go to his school," said Cat.

"I want to." Finn's black eyes were impervious to her guilt. "Is that your son?"

Cat nodded.

"He doesn't resemble Richard Feversham."

The way he said Richard's name made Cat's throat tighten. "No."

"Dr. Korchinsky told me about your divorce." Finn did not look her in the eye. "I'm sorry to hear that."

"Why?" said Cat. "Why would you be sorry?"

Finn studied the dust that had built up in the cracks between the wooden slats of the floor.

"Because," he said, "that's what I am supposed to say." He looked at her, and she couldn't read his expression. It wasn't like before, when you could look at the blankness of his features and believe he didn't feel anything. Now he seemed to wear a mask. "Will you be able to drive me to the hospital?"

She nodded. "Do you want to go right now?" Her voice trembled. "You just got here—"

"I don't need to rest," he said. "You know that."

"Of course."

"You weren't doing anything, were you? I apologize—"

"It's fine." Even after all this time, she was still being selfish. The thought made her feel guilty and embarrassed. She wanted to keep Finn to herself, now that he was here, now that she could see him illuminated by the dusty sunlight.

"Let me go get Daniel," she said.

The drive to the hospital took half an hour. Cat had driven down this particular stretch of freeway so many times she no longer saw it. But with Finn sitting in the passenger seat beside her, his face turned toward the window, she was suddenly aware of the rippling rows of stunted corn, growing in land that had once been a swampy forest in the years before the Disasters. Aware of the little white agri-engineering buildings that poked up against the washed-out sky. Finn drummed his fingers against the car door, and Cat kept her eyes on the road, her entire body crackling with the desire to look at him.

Daniel peppered the silence with questions about the lunar station and the moon's surface, and Finn answered them genially, his words like sound bites in a corporate-sponsored outreach video.

When they came to the hospital, and Cat heard the swish of the automatic glass doors and the beeps of the nurse-bots, she remembered her father. She remembered why Finn was here at all.

Cat and Finn walked side by side, unspeaking, to her father's room, and Daniel clutched Cat's hand with a surprising force. She hadn't brought him to the hospital often, choosing instead to let him talk to his grandfather over the computer, thinking the white hospital, its walls gleaming like the side of a lightbulb, would overwhelm him. She could feel his fingers shaking now, and she drew him close to her. She could feel Finn watching them both. "Here it is," she said when they came to the room. She eased open the door.

"Daddy?" He was a mound of white sheets on the bed. When she spoke, the mound shifted, a face appeared, everything white except for the dark sunken hollows of his eyes.

"Grandpa?" said Daniel shakily. He slid behind Cat's legs and wrapped his tiny hands around her knees.

"My favorite grandson," said Cat's father. He moved to sit up and Cat rushed across the room, held out her hands to stop him.

"Daddy," she said. "Daddy, Finn's here."

Her father's head lifted an inch off the pillows. Cat heard Finn's footsteps behind her, thudding against the tile. Her father's eyes widened.

"You came back," he said, and his head dropped.

Finn stood next to the bed. Cat drew away. She wrapped her arms around Daniel's shoulders.

"Dr. Novak," said Finn. There was a sound in his voice Cat didn't recognize, a crack of disbelief. He took her father's hand in his own. "Daniel."

"How's the moon this time of year?"

"Cold and hot."

Her father laughed. Cat pulled Daniel toward the door. She would wait in the lobby. This was not something for her to see.

As she slipped out the door her father's eyes shifted toward her and then back to Finn. Finn did not turn around.

She and Daniel walked to the waiting room. Daniel didn't say anything when she plopped him down on one of the uncomfortable, sterile-looking chairs, and he didn't say anything when she asked if he wanted a Coke from the vending machine—just shook his head solemnly.

"Well, I'm going to get a cup of coffee," she said. What she really wanted was a cigarette but she didn't want to take Daniel outside into the hot parking lot. She walked into the concession alcove, swiped her bank card, watched the cardboard cup fill with thin, watery coffee. When she went back into the waiting room, Daniel stared at her.

"Grandpa's a ghost," he said.

"No, he isn't." She sipped her coffee, and it burned the roof of her mouth.

"He will be soon, though."

Cat set the coffee on the arm of her chair and reached over and hugged Daniel closer to her. "Yes," she said, because she didn't know what else to say.

"Can I see him again? Before he becomes a ghost?"

Cat nodded. "When Finn's finished talking to him. They haven't seen each other in . . in a very long time. Not since before you were born."

"Finn's nice."

"Yes," said Cat. "Yes, I think so, too."

Finn stayed in the room with her father for almost two hours. Daniel fell asleep in his chair, curled up, his head resting on the crook of Cat's arm. She read through the newsfeeds on her slate, forgetting everything five minutes after she read it. The hospital sounds were muted and far away. Daniel's breath on her arm was warm and moist and comforting.

Finn appeared in the waiting room. He walked over to Cat.

"He's dying," he said.

"I know," said Cat.

"I knew it intellectually of course, but I hadn't . . . I hadn't realized . . ." He ran his hands through his dark and unchanged hair. "It hurts. It hurts to see him."

Cat slid her arm out from under Daniel's head. He didn't wake up. She stood up and she was closer to Finn than she had been for nearly eight years. She wrapped her arms around his shoulders. She didn't even think about it.

He put his hand on her waist and pulled her close and there was that clean electric scent of him and he pressed his face against her hair and they stayed like that, for a minute, for five minutes, and it was familiar and safe even as Cat's heart broke over and over again.

"Mama?"

Daniel's voice was slurred with sleep. Cat pulled herself out of Finn's arms and lifted Daniel off the chair. He buried his head in her shoulder. When she turned around, Finn seemed to be smiling.

"I want to take him to see Dad."

"Of course. Shall I wait out here?"

"You don't have to." She dropped Daniel to the floor and led him through the hallway. Finn trailed behind them. She went into her father's room. A nurse-bot whirred beside the bed.

"His exhaustion levels are increasing," said the nurse-bot's disembodied voice. "Visitation is not recommended at this time."

"Ignore it," her father said. "I'm fine."

"We just wanted to come say good-bye." Cat brought Daniel up to the side of the bed. "Did you have a nice talk with . . . with Finn?" He wasn't in the room. He must have been waiting in the hallway.

"Yes." Her father's voice faded in and out like an old radio. "It was good to see him. It was good . . ." He closed his eyes. "Don't let him go back. He doesn't want to be there."

"What? How do you know?"

Her father smiled weakly at her. "I can tell."

"He said he can stay for three weeks."

Her father shook his head. "Don't let him go back at all. There's nothing for him up there."

Cat sighed. She knelt down so she could whisper directly in Daniel's ear. "Do you have anything you want to say to Grandpa?"

"Daniel!" Her father held out one of his hands, and Daniel stared at it, fascinated, like it was a dead bug. Cat nudged him forward. "How are the firefly bots?"

"They're good."

"You should ask Finn to show you how to make some of your own." Her father coughed, a small quick cough that quickly multiplied until his entire body shook.

"I miss you, Grandpa," said Daniel.

"I miss you, too, Danny. Don't let your mother make you eat too many vegetables."

Daniel frowned. He shuffled away from the bed, back toward Cat. The nurse-bot beeped again.

"Visitation is not recommended at this time," it said.

"We should go," said Cat.

"Bah," said her father. But his eyes looked watery and weak, and his voice was so soft she could barely hear it.

"I'll bring Finn back tomorrow."

Her father nodded and closed his eyes.

"We love you," said Cat. The nurse-bot skittered across the floor. Her father nodded again, wiggled his fingers, and Cat took Daniel out into the hallway, where Finn was waiting.

* * * *

Cat led Finn up to his old bedroom. The sheets on his bed were turned down, crumpled from the last sleepless night she'd crept up here to doze in the muggy heat. He didn't comment on it, just walked to the closet and pulled out a change of clothes.

He didn't comment on the tapestry that lay folded in the center of his desk, though Cat saw his eyes swoop over it, a brief mechanical pause as they took it in and his programming determined that he did not recognize it. She didn't say anything, either.

"I'll be downstairs momentarily," he said, his back to her. She stood for a moment in the doorway, and when he didn't move to take off his clothes she went out into the stairwell. The door clicked shut behind her.

It was strange to share a home with him again. He spent more time outside than he used to. She watched through the window in the kitchen as he walked into the woods or wove through the garden. He went out during the hottest part of the day, the sun a pinpoint of white light radiating out of the cloudless sky. In the evenings he played computer games with Daniel, and he laughed more than she had ever heard him laugh.

She drove him to visit her father whenever he asked, which was most days. They went while Daniel was in school, just as she had before he came home. He started working in the laboratory. She didn't ask what he was doing, and he didn't tell her.

The silence between them was heavier than the heat. And then one day the house computer dinged with an incoming call. It was a Saturday. Daniel was at a friend's house, probably eating homemade ice cream on the porch, reading comic books on his friend's expensive reading tablet. Finn was outside, down by the river. The computer dinged, and Cat knew immediately that her father was dead.

"Ms. Novak?" There was no video, just the hospital's logo. The voice on the other end was female, as crisp as an apple. She had a calm and businesslike way of speaking, the sort of voice you use to train dogs. "Ms. Novak, I am very sorry, but Daniel Novak passed away this afternoon at two thirty-three p.m."

Cat sank down on the couch. She had been expecting this for so long that she didn't even think to cry. She had cried for her father already. She tightened her fingers around the slate and listened to the woman and the computer's static and she said, "Yes," and "Of course," to all the questions about insurance and surviving family members. When it was over she switched off the computer and sat very still, the room full of dust, the fan stirring up the air-conditioned air.

He's dead he's dead oh God he's dead.

She walked outside. It was so hot she began to sweat immediately. She wasn't wearing any shoes but she walked to the woods anyway. Broken sticks and sharp hot rocks stabbed the soles of her feet. The sound of cicadas bored straight into her. The world was burning up. A heaviness waited behind her eyes. She weighed a thousand pounds. It was a struggle to make it to the river to find Finn standing shirtless in the green waist-deep water, the sun reflecting off the tops of his shoulders. She walked down to the river's edge, and then she stepped into the water. The sudden coldness shocked her; it sent reverberations up and down her spine. Finn turned. She pushed through the lazy, freezing current. Her dress clung to her thighs, wrapped around her legs, binding them together. The slimy rocks slid out from under her feet, but she did not fall.

"Your timing was impeccable," she said.

"What do you mean?"

"He's dead."

Sunlight bounced off the water and into her eyes. It caught on the tips of her eyelashes, blinding her.

"He's dead," she said again, and then she was crying. She pitched forward in the water, and Finn caught her. Her entire body shook. She was angry. She was crying because she was angry, because it wasn't fair for him to die so young, while all the fathers of her friends kept on living. It wasn't fair that both her parents were gone. It wasn't fair that the cells of his brain, the most brilliant part of him, had betrayed him so irrevocably. She slid down until she was sitting in the water, and Finn held her close and rocked her back and forth and when she looked at him through the web of her tears his face was wracked with sadness.

"He saved me," Finn said, his voice disbelieving. "A long time ago."

"I know." Cat cried harder. She leaned her head against Finn's chest. Water lapped at their bodies. His hands were in her hair. They did not kiss; they did not speak.

Everything had unraveled.

*   *   *   *

There was a wake. Cat filled the house with loud music and liquor and invited everyone in town and all the scientists who used to come to dinner parties when she was a child. Her father's coffin was set up in the middle of the living room, the monitor set into the wall playing a video of him: the day of his wedding, standing next to a version of her mother even younger than Cat was now, on a beach down along the Gulf Coast. Accepting an award from the woman who had been president when Cat was seven years old. Food and flowers and liquor everywhere. Cat could barely stand any of it. She'd had a few bottles of beer, and her grief was magnified: magnetic, even, drawing all the others toward her to share in their sorrow. She went outside and lit a cigarette in the dark garden, away from the music and the lights and the sound of people laughing— supposedly they were reminiscing but she didn't believe it. She sat down beneath the citrus tree, and she could smell the faint scent of lemons through the acrid smoke of her cigarette. The worst thing about it was that he had been alone in the moment he died. Maybe a nurse-bot had been there, gliding across the floors, whirring plaintively as the beeping of his heart slowed and slowed and then finally stopped.

Cat ground her cigarette into the dirt. She lit another one. Out in the unfathomable darkness, the gate creaked open. Cat wished she could curl up and disappear. Probably one of the ladies from town, coming out to check on her, to cluck over her, to make a fuss about her cigarette and her unwashed hair—

It was Finn. He sat down beside her.

"I don't want to go back in there," Cat said.

"I won't make you."

"Good." Cat dragged on her cigarette. Finn didn't say anything. Out of habit, she reached over and pushed his hair away from his eyes, tucked it behind his ear. He glanced over at her. Frowned.

"It's not the way it used to be," Finn said.

Cat closed her eyes. She leaned against the trunk of the tree. She was already so sad that this new sadness didn't even compare.

"I probably shouldn't have left," Finn said. "I understand that now. I should not have left him alone."

"Why did you leave?" The question shimmered in the air, a chasm of light between them. Cat wanted to hear him speak his answer.

In the darkness Finn was all shadows.

"I was angry." Then: "I don't want to talk about this."

"Why not?"

"It's not appropriate. Not now." He stood up.

"Why did you come out if you didn't want to talk to me?" For a moment, Finn didn't move. She felt him staring at her. Someone turned on the porch light, and the light reflected off his eyes so that they became two silver disks regarding her in the darkness.

"Well?" she said.

"I don't want to talk to you about that particular subject. I was . . . concerned . . . for you, however."

"Concerned."

He nodded.

"But you don't actually want to talk to me."

"I told you, I don't want to discuss—"

"Jesus, did you miss me at all?"

She hadn't meant to ask him that, but grief had left her weak. His silence threatened to overwhelm her. Her cigarette had burned down to the filter and the warmth of it singed the tips of her fingers.

"Yes," he said.

Then he strode out of the garden before Cat had a chance to reply.

* * * *

At her father's burial, Cat wore a black dress she had not worn since she lived with Richard in the glass house. It was the only black dress she owned. She held Daniel in her lap despite the heat, and he watched the proceedings with large, curious eyes: the priest reading passages from the Bible in spite of her father's atheism, the old women with their bouquets of flower-shop flowers, the crackling, dried-out grapevines hanging from the trees in the cemetery. When she began to cry, Daniel kissed her cheek and whispered in her ear, "Don't worry, Mama, I can still see him." And he pointed to a spot next to the sprawling old oak tree, and for a moment Cat thought she saw a shimmer in the air, like an oil slick or a heat mirage.

She was expected to say a few words. That was how Maybelle put it: *You'll need to say a few words.* She had not prepared anything, and when the time came, she walked shaking up to the podium. Her high heels sank into the loose soil. She looked out over all those solemn faces. She looked at the coffin covered in white lilies.

"I loved him," she said. "He was my father."

She stopped. She had no idea what to say. She looked at Finn. His expression was unreadable.

"I know he seemed like a mad scientist," she said. "Locked up in his laboratory all the time. But . . . he was a good father. A good grandfather. And I wish you all could have known him better."

Her cheeks were wet. The wind blew dust and dirt over the funeral, and Cat walked back to her seat. Daniel hugged her. Finn glanced at her and they stared at each other for a moment and then he stood up and walked to the podium. His suit was new, she realized. It was not the suit he had worn to her wedding. He put his hands on the podium and looked at a point on the horizon. "I'm sure most of you don't think I should be here," he said. "That I am merely a machine." He paused, and the wind ruffled his hair. Everyone seemed to have stopped breathing. "You are, of course, correct. I am a machine. However. I am . . . alive . . . in a sense, and I'm aware of this fact, unlike, for example, the robots that spray for mosquitoes in the middle of the night. And Dr. Novak—Daniel—realized this about me when he found me many years ago and brought me to live with him and his family.

"Daniel raised me as a son. He tried to protect me from all the horrors of the world. He failed, of course, but I am grateful for that." Finn smiled a little. "I have never endeavored to be human, a fact Daniel had difficulty accepting at first. However, he never looked down on me for it. And he made his mistakes. But ultimately he loved me—for who I am, for what I am. He loved me, not some version of me that will never exist. And for that I am grateful. It is a mark of true humanity."

When Finn stopped speaking, he dipped his head and stepped down from the podium. No one moved, not even Cat. He walked back to his chair. Eventually someone took his place, one of the engineers or scientists Cat's father had known before he married. The string of platitudes dissipated on the hot wind. Cat was crying again, a slow, silent sort of crying that was nearly imperceptible save for the moisture on her face. She watched Finn, who did not look at her from across the flower-covered coffin.

Afterward, when the service had ended, when Cat had walked Daniel to the gravestone so he could lay a single white rose in the grass, she found Finn loitering at the cemetery gates, watching as everyone piled into their cars to drive away. Her father's coffin was still set up next to the grave, locked into some mechanism that would lower it into the ground once the mourners had left. Daniel crouched down in the grass, watching the grasshoppers leap above the tangled mat of weeds. Cat lit a cigarette.

"I liked your speech," she said.

"Thank you," Finn said.

Cat smoked and leaned against the fence. The grainy wood poked the small of her back. "He told me the whole story," she said. "About how he found you."

Finn didn't say anything. Cat's hands shook. Daniel ran along the edge of the fence. The cicadas buzzed, and it reminded Cat of the day the hospital called to tell her that her father was dead. She snuffed out her cigarette on the fence and dropped her head on Finn's shoulder. He didn't move: not to pull her close, not to push her away. The sky was an oppressive shade of blue. Over near her mother's grave (her father's grave), the caretaker was turning on the lowering mechanism. A loud, mechanical lurch and then a slow and steady grinding, metal on metal. Cat closed her eyes. The cicadas. Machinery. Daniel shrieking and laughing as though the funeral had not just happened.

"Why won't you talk to me?" she whispered.

"I don't know what to say," said Finn.

TWENTY

On a bright, crisp morning, Cat's father's lawyer came to the house. He had called a few days after the funeral about the will, and Cat had asked him to drive to meet her, because she had a young child and it was difficult for her to get away. In truth, she was too exhausted to drive into the city.

After he arrived, Cat set him up at the dining room table. She lit a cigarette without asking if it was okay.

"Ms. Novak, I'm sorry for your loss." The lawyer was small and wiry with bland, beige features. He addressed her cigarette. Cat blew smoke toward the ceiling. "However, before we can get started, we're going to need . . ." The lawyer glanced down at his tablet. "Finn? The, ah, the android? I'm going to need him." The lawyer pursed his lips.

"Oh," Cat said. "Of course." She was surprised—not that her father wrote Finn into his will, but that he was allowed to do so at all. Times were changing. Times had changed.

Cat stood up and walked to the intercom. Finn was down in the lab. He was always down in the lab, when he wasn't out in the woods.

"Yes?" he said, his voice caught in the intercom's static.

"You need to come upstairs," Cat said. "For the will."

There was a long pause. "I'm on my way."

Cat slid back into her seat. She smoked, and the lawyer tapped against his reading tablet. The dining room doors slid open, and Finn stepped inside. He sat down, a chair between him and Cat. To Cat, it felt like a gap of miles.

The lawyer stared at Finn for a moment, eyes wide. Finn gazed back levelly. Then the lawyer blinked, and said, "Very good. Let's get started."

Cat lit another cigarette.

"I'm just going to read this out loud," he said. "Dr. Novak didn't go in for anything elaborate, no videos or what have you. Made it simple." He cleared his throat, leaned back in his chair.

"To my daughter," he began, and the sound of his voice—thin, high-pitched, not at all like her father's—jarred Cat out of her haze. She closed her eyes. "To my daughter, Caterina Novak, formerly Caterina Feversham, I bequeath all my possessions, including the house at 487 FM 5001 in Angelina County and the laboratory contained therein. In addition I grant her the total sum of my earnings at the time of my death." She could almost hear her father's voice, overlaid with the lawyer's. "To my grandson, Daniel Novak, I bequeath a trust fund to be held by his mother until he reaches the age of eighteen, at which point all funds will default to his person."

The lawyer paused. Cat had expected all of this. She looked at Finn out of the corner of her eye. He stared straight ahead.

"To Finn Novak, formerly Finn Condon, despite his status as an android, I bequeath three billion dollars, the total sum of money paid to me by Selene Technologies, Limited, upon his purchase for the Lunar Exploration and Settlement Project, and any interest accrued."

All the breath left Cat's body. She swiveled her head toward Finn. His eyes looked dark and liquidy. He looked as though he might start crying.

Cat reached out, across the chasm of that one chair, and put her hand on his upper arm. He glanced over at her, and then froze in place. For a moment it was as though they were alone.

"Do you have any questions?" The lawyer shifted awkwardly in his seat.

"No," said Cat, still looking at Finn. Finn shook his head, still looking at Cat.

"Very well. I'll just need your electronic signatures here." He slid the tablet across the table. Cat dropped her cigarette in the ashtray, pressed her thumb against the screen. The lawyer pushed the tablet toward Finn.

"Does he have . . . fingerprints?" he asked.

"Yes," said Finn. He did the same as Cat and then shoved the tablet back at the lawyer. He stood up and stalked out of the dining room. The lawyer watched him.

"Is he all right? He does . . . understand, right?"

"He's fine," said Cat. "Thank you for coming out here. I know we're in the middle of nowhere."

"Of course." The lawyer nodded. "I'll be contacting you shortly with more details about the financial transfers and so forth."

He gathered up his things, and Cat led him out the front door. The tires of his car spun out against the gravel driveway, and he drove too fast on the road into town. Cat took a deep breath. She leaned against the porch banister.

Her father's death was final now that all his things no longer belonged to him. A sudden surge of sadness welled up in the space behind Cat's eyes, but she didn't cry. Maybe she had cried too much. Instead, she went inside, into the kitchen, and pulled out one of the pies someone had brought over for the funeral. She sat down at the aluminum table and ate it straight out of the tin. It was key lime, drenched in green, sour syrup.

The screen door slammed. Finn appeared in the kitchen, haloed by the sunlight streaming in through the windows.

"Hey," said Cat. "Do you want to talk about it? The will?"

"No." But he came and sat down across the table from her. Cat took another bite of pie. He was watching her eat. He'd watched her eat before, but never with this intensity.

"Are you okay?" she asked.

"I tasted that one," he said. "It was rich."

"You taste things now." Not a question.

Finn looked away, toward the old refrigerator rattling and moaning next to the kitchen counter. "I always could. I just had no interest in it. Now . . . things are different." He paused. Cat took another bite of pie, slowly dragging the fork out of her mouth.

"However, I can still only have a taste. If I ate too much, the results would be disastrous." He shrugged. Cat scooped up some of the syrup from the bottom of the tin. The sadness was still there, weighing her down like water.

"I missed you," she said. "I missed you so much—" But Finn held up his hand.

"Please. Don't."

"Why not?" Cat threw the fork into the half-eaten pie and pushed it away. "What the fuck is wrong with you? You won't tell me anything. You won't talk to me."

"Your father just died."

"Is that what this is about, really?" She pulled at her hair. "Finn, he's been dying for *years*. Which you knew about, by the way. And didn't feel the need to tell me. So don't act like this was unexpected."

Finn's mouth pressed itself into a thin line. "It was still unexpected."

"Because you *ran away*. If you had been here, if you'd stayed behind—"

"I couldn't stay," Finn snapped. "Not after what happened. He told you what he did, I'm assuming? You haven't seemed particularly fazed by my new manner since I got back."

Cat didn't say anything. Finn was angry, and that had heretofore been unimaginable to her.

"Well?"

"He allowed you to feel," Cat said weakly.

"He shut me off," said Finn. "He removed programs from my system without my permission. And when he turned me back on, I felt *everything*. Everything I ever experienced. The person who created me abandoned me. As you know. I was abandoned and then betrayed."

"Betrayed?" whispered Cat. "He was trying to help you—"

"I wasn't talking about him." Finn's eyes bored straight into her.

Cat choked. Richard's face flashed unbidden in her mind. She gasped and then she began to weep.

"I'm sorry," she whispered. "I'm so sorry. I didn't—" She shook her head. "No. There's no excuse for what I did. I'm sure you hate me. But I'm sorry."

"I don't hate you." He leaned away from the table. Cat wiped her hand across her eyes. Snot dripped from her nose. She waited for Finn to leave the room but he didn't. She waited for him to speak but he didn't say anything.

"Do you know why Daddy did it?" she asked. "In the first place?"

"Of course I do," said Finn. "He told me afterward."

"It was a good reason, right?"

"It was a stupid reason. What use do I have for love? I'm a fucking robot."

Cat was crying so hard she couldn't respond.

"I'm a robot that is supposed to be human. That's why she made me in the first place. That was my purpose. My specialization. Not to assemble cars or rebuild civilization or even help run an outpost on the moon. Just to bestow meaningless affection upon her." Finn spat out the words. "And *that's* why I went away. To show her, to show your father, to show you—I'm just a machine. And I wanted to be owned like one." He paused. When he spoke again, his voice vibrated. "I refuse to be something I'm not."

Cat looked up at him then, through the net of her tears. She wiped at her nose. "I love you," she said, with a thrill of masochism.

"I know." But he seemed to falter.

"I don't care what you are," said Cat. "I used to, even though I didn't realize it. But I don't care now." She hesitated. "I saw the inside of you. It was beautiful."

"The inside of me?"

Cat nodded. She pushed her chair away from the table and walked over to where he was sitting and knelt down beside him. She put her hand on his chest. All her tears had evaporated, condensed into steam in the warm kitchen air. He didn't push her away.

"I want to show you something," Cat said.

"You're not opening me up," he said. "I don't care how beautiful you thought it was."

But she didn't open him up. She touched him. She touched the left side of his neck, his sternum, his forehead. When she had seen the pattern at Dr. Condon's house, she had memorized it immediately, without even realizing until now. "What are you doing?" Finn asked, watching her with suspicion.

Cat didn't answer. She grazed the back of her hand along his right cheekbone and pressed her palm against his left shoulder. Then she stood up and walked behind him and lifted his hair away from the back of his neck. She saw the switch, glinting in the lights. Finn jerked away.

"I'm not turning you off," Cat said. "Trust me, okay? For five seconds, will you just trust me?"

A moment's hesitation, and then Finn leaned back in the chair, falling into her touch. His hair was silky in her fingers, too soft for human hair. She used one hand to hold it out of the way and with the other she pressed the switch. She held her breath: but when she touched him he shook beneath her. The chair rattled against the kitchen tile. He grabbed at her hand tangled in his hair and held it tight. Tighter than was comfortable. The bones in her fingers pressed together, but she didn't stop touching that place on the back of his neck.

Finn cried out. Then he fell forward, his limbs twitching, his eyes flashing black and silver, and for a moment Cat stared at him in horror, afraid that it had been a trick, that she had done irrevocable damage. But no. It passed. His eyes faded to normal. He sank down against the table. He stared at Cat.

The air hummed.

He didn't stop staring at her. She was burning up. Her skin flushed. Her clothes felt thin and transparent. He looked straight through her.

He sat up, his movements shaky. Then he stood up and he took a hold of her hips and pulled him to her. They kissed. Cat was dizzy with the force of that kiss. He ran his hand up the line of her thigh, pushing her skirt up around her waist. She was already gasping. His touch was so sudden after so long without it that she could barely register the world around her: the familiar kitchen, the beams of pale sunlight. He hoisted her up; she wrapped her legs around his hips.

There, in the kitchen, Cat screamed to the empty house. She had forgotten the swell of desire until now. Eight years, five months, and forty-four days: that was how long she had gone without him.

* * * *

Afterward, they lay together on the couch, letting the day's sunny minutes drip by. For a long time they didn't speak, just let the frenzied air settle over their bodies. Then Finn shifted, turning onto his side. He touched her very lightly on the side of her face.

"You know I'll be leaving soon," he said. Cat closed her eyes.

"You don't have to," she said. "You meet the requirements now. They have to let you go if you want."

Finn didn't respond. The scent of him was everywhere. She listened to the mechanical whir of the gears inside his chest. When he finally spoke, she felt the whispery movement of his mouth against the side of her neck.

"For so long," he said. "I could only understand desire."

"What do you mean?" She would have twisted her face to look at him but when he spoke it felt as though he were kissing her.

"Desire is simple," he said. "Desire is something even a machine can understand." There was a stillness in the air that mirrored the stillness of his body. "But when I desired you I began to love you. You were the first being I ever loved. I didn't know it, of course. I had no idea what it meant, no idea what I was feeling. Love was never something I was supposed to experience. I don't think I was supposed to know desire, either, but she never expected me to meet you." He laughed against Cat's skin. "Later, after your father . . . when he took out those restrictions, I was finally able to understand the complexities of love. Even if I didn't want to. At first."

Cat stared at the ceiling and reminded herself to breathe. The sun filtered through the leaves of the trees outside the window, and the shadows flashing through the room reminded Cat of static and white noise. She realized she had known what he just told her all along.

Cat rolled over so that she could kiss Finn, and she kissed him again and again, until it was time for her to go into town to pick Daniel up from school. Even then she didn't want to disentangle her limbs from his. It was painful to stand up alone. She smiled down at Finn and he smiled at her and Cat let herself luxuriate for a few moments in the flickering shadows of the living room before she dragged herself out into the world, an action as harsh on her system as waking up from a dream.

* * * *

Later that evening, Cat cooked a dinner of grilled fish and macaroni salad, and she and Daniel ate it at the dining room table while Finn joined them, his hands folded in his lap, making conversation as they ate. Daniel didn't seem to notice anything different between Cat and Finn: he just ate his food in huge gulping bites before jumping up from the table and announcing that he was going outside to play with his fireflies.

"Put your dishes in the dishwasher," Cat said automatically.

"Mom!" But Daniel still carted his plate into the kitchen. Cat tilted her head to the side, listening to the clinking of silverware as it was thrown into the dishwasher. The screen door slammed. "He's been playing with those fireflies every night since Dad—" Cat stopped. "He made them for him. They're little robots."

"Yes, I found the schematics in the laboratory."

"He never made me stuff like that when I was a kid. I'm glad he did it for Daniel." Cat took another bite of her fish, and then set her fork down. She didn't have much of an appetite. Her body was too wound up with love.

"He would have," said Finn. "Made you toys. He was always drawing up plans. But he got distracted. We were very busy."

"I know." Cat carried her plate into the kitchen and dropped it in the sink. Finn followed her. Through the window Cat could see the electronic fireflies flashing in the darkness. Every now and then Daniel's laughter trickled inside.

For a moment Cat allowed herself to be content. Because her son was happy, and Finn was home, and they had all eaten dinner together.

"I'm going to go outside." She turned away from the window

without rinsing off her dish. She opened the door and held it open for Finn, and then she stepped out onto the porch. She could barely make out Daniel's shadow in the yard. The fireflies flitted and bobbed. Cat sat down on the porch steps, and Finn sat beside her. The balmy night air shimmered in the moonlight. Cat lit a cigarette.

"You shouldn't do that," said Finn.

Cat laughed, but she didn't put her cigarette out. "I quit when I was pregnant."

"Yes, I assumed so." He paused, tilted his head as he looked out over the yard. "I hoped so."

They sat in silence while Daniel chased his firefly bots. There were no real fireflies this time of year.

"I wanted to thank you," said Finn. "For the tapestry in my room. I presumed that you made it."

Cat didn't move. She felt his presence beside her. When she finally turned her face to him, he was looking back at her with his silver eyes.

"You're welcome," she said. "It took me a long time."

"It's very lovely."

Cat smiled. Tears formed in the corners of her eyes. She remembered how she wove their hairs into the fibers. She remembered the way her fingers ached after working on it.

"I wanted to make something for you," she said. She dragged on her cigarette. "It took me so long to finish. You'd already left. I'd already left Richard."

Finn nodded. Out in the yard, the firefly bots twirled up into a circle.

"I think that I may not go back to the lunar station," Finn said.

The cigarette smoke swirled lazily between them, but her blood began racing in and out of her heart. It was too much to hope for. She almost didn't believe he had said it. "Are you sure?" She looked over at the silhouette of his face. He nodded.

"I'd stay here, of course." He turned to her. "Would that be acceptable?"

"Yes." Cat trembled. The burning ember of her cigarette wobbled in the darkness.

"Why are you shaking?"

"Too much nicotine."

Finn reached over, plucked the cigarette out of her hand, and ground it out against the porch railing.

"It could be dangerous," he said. "They'll probably challenge my decision. They might find a loophole."

"We have a lawyer."

Finn smiled. "So you would help me," he said. "If I needed it?"

"Of course."

Cat saw the blink of the fireflies in the distance and the movement of Daniel as he trotted through the yard. She placed one hand on Finn's face. Her entire body was fevered: with love, with the possibility for happiness. And in that moment, she thought of her father, lying in a hospital bed, the light white and clean as death. *If anyone could make him come back, it's you.*

A single tear dropped down the side of Cat's face, and she wiped it away just as Daniel called out for her to watch the fireflies dancing in the darkness.

*   *   *   *

A few days later, Cat mailed off a completed tapestry to an energy company in California. It was her third commission since returning to the house in the woods, and she still felt a professional satisfaction in handing the package over to the deliveryman there on her front porch, something she thought she'd lost. As she watched the delivery truck trundle down the driveway, she imagined herself sharing the house with Finn, raising Daniel, earning a living with her artwork. It was a real life. It was *her* life.

Afterward, she rode her bicycle to the cemetery alone. The air was cool and damp with an imminent rain and there was a silence in the world, the silence that precedes storms. Cat thought she could hear the plants going into hibernation for the winter: the trees scraping off their old leaves, the grasses curling up in the dirt. She propped her bike against the fence and walked over to the plot of land where her parents lay buried.

It was the first time she had been to the cemetery since the funeral.

Loose soil was still piled over her father's grave. Cat sat down and tucked her chin onto her knees. She looked at the matching gravestones. She looked at the dates of her parents' deaths and calculated their ages: her mother dead at forty-seven, her father dead at sixty. People lived longer and longer these days. The dates on the gravestones were an anachronism.

"Finn's going to stay," she said, her voice ringing out over the silent graveyard like a gunshot. "I know! I can hardly believe it myself." She paused. "But you did leave him the money. Surely that had something to do with it." But Cat wasn't in the mood to talk to ghosts. She stood up and stretched and walked to the cemetery's edge, where there was just an empty field: no grave markers, just one-foot-tall golden grasses rippling in the breeze. Cat lay down flat on her back and looked up at the gray sky. The ground was hard and cold beneath her. She had always suspected that this part of the cemetery was crowded with unmarked graves, although she could never really say why: it was a feeling she got whenever she cut across the field, that there were people beneath her feet.

Cat thought about Finn.

She thought about the picture she had taken of him when she was in high school, the one she found years later in the glass house Richard bought for her. She thought about how she woke up in his bed this morning, right as the sun was sending out rays of pink light between the gray clouds: how his face this morning was the same exact face as the one in the photograph.

Cat wondered how old she would be when she died.

Forty-seven? Sixty? One hundred twenty?

Finn would never die. He would never leave her as her parents did, but one day, she would leave him.

She'd not considered it before, mostly because she never thought she could be with Finn. But now. Now he had decided not to climb back aboard the cargo shuttle, not to fly through the dark atmosphere to the moon. And Cat imagined herself in fifty years, in a hundred years, an old woman, painful to look at. She imagined the moment when she would die, her soul slipping away like a narrow beam of starlight. And she decided, lying there in the grass, still young, still alive, that she would not allow herself to stay buried in the ground. She would come back as a ghost, a mirage in the shadows of the laboratory. He would sense her, now and then, a shadow of light in a place where he wasn't looking, and believe that one of his circuits had shorted out, that an electron had misfired somewhere, that he was breaking down.

Or maybe she would live on the old-fashioned way. Maybe Daniel would have a child and that child would have a child and on and on, and every time Finn looked at her progeny, now an enormous sprawling family, the sort that rents hotels for reunions, he would see Cat, mirrored over and over again, in the eyes and mouths and limbs of strangers.

Cat sat up, suddenly cold from the chill in the air. She looked down at her hands: flesh and blood, still alive. It was pointless to concern herself with unknowable futures. She stood up and dusted the dirt off her dress. The air was heavier. She could smell the rain on the horizon. So she ran back to her bike, blowing a kiss at her parents' graves as she went past, and she flew down the shoulder of the highway toward home.

* * * *

On the morning the shuttle soared back up to the lunar station, carrying crates of freeze-dried food and clean clothing and microchips, Cat woke early. She dressed in the gauzy light, the hardwood floors cold beneath her feet, and then she crept downstairs, ears straining against the thrumming silence of the house, because part of her was afraid he would be gone, that he had changed his mind, that he decided the possibility of repercussions from STL was not worth the trouble.

Daniel was up already, watching cartoons on the monitor in the living room.

"Mama?" He squinted his eyes at her, like he didn't recognize her so early in the day.

She smiled at him and ruffled his hair and kissed his cheek. The cartoons flashed and trilled on-screen. She went into the kitchen and poured a cup of coffee. Her heart pounded but she was trying to pretend that everything was normal, that she trusted Finn not to sneak out in the middle of the night while the rest of the world slept.

Cat walked onto the porch. Steam curled out of her mug. The air was crisp and clean and smelled of pine and sweetly decaying leaves. She could see her breath. She balanced the coffee on the porch banister and then she lit a cigarette to calm her nerves. The world was utterly still, and she was aware of the movement of the inside of her body: the expansion of her lungs and the fluttery pumps of her heart, pushing blood out into her extremities. Her heart, broken a million times over.

The screen door slammed. Daniel shot out into the shivering yard. He dropped something in the grass, something sleek and metallic: the mechanical butterfly from her father's lab. He knelt down beside it, leaned over close, and then the butterfly soared into the air. The scales of its wings caught the morning sunlight and glittered.

The door slammed again, and this time Cat heard heavy footsteps on the wood of the porch. She dropped her cigarette to her side. Finn came and stood beside her.

"I found that in the laboratory," he said. "It was incomplete. I finished it."

Cat smiled. "So that's what you were doing down there all this time."

"Partially."

Cat shifted her body toward him. He stared out at the yard. There were a million problems with this relationship. Of course Cat knew this. She lay awake at night dreading the call from STL. She considered all the ways she could die before her time.

But she didn't think about any of these many problems, not in this moment, with the cool autumn air, the pale sunlight gilding the dying grass and the rotting wood of the porch, her son laughing in the yard with a butterfly the size of his torso. Cat put one hand on Finn's arm, promising herself that she would not hurt him again. He turned toward her and smiled.

Cat stubbed her half-finished cigarette onto the banister and flicked it into the yard. She wound her arm around his.

And then they stayed like that, Cat and Finn, unmoving, unspeaking, while the world changed around them.

ACKNOWLEDGMENTS

This book has been a long time coming, its creation spanning three years, two cities, and one small town. Foremost I would like to thank Ross Andrews, for supporting me as I wrote it, revised it, and submitted it—and also for showing me *Bicentennial Man* when I was almost done with the first draft.

Many others were instrumental in this book's creation as well, and I would like to take the time to thank them individually:

My parents, for their love and support as I pursued a writing career.

The book's two beta readers, Amanda Cole and Bobby Mathews, because their comments were instrumental as I prepared to release the book on the world.

Amanda Rutter, for plucking the book out of Angry Robot's Open Door Month submission pile, and Lee Harris and Marc Gascoigne, for giving me my first book deal.

My agent, Stacia Decker, whose comments and suggestions for revisions blew my mind and helped elevate the book beyond what I could ever have imagined when I opened that initial Word document in a UT engineering department office four years ago and wrote the first sentence.